BOOKS BY BEVERLY COYLE

Novels

The Kneeling Bus
In Troubled Waters
Taken In

On Wallace Stevens

A Thought to Be Rehearsed
Secretaries of the Moon (with Alan Filreis)

TAKEN

TAKEN IN

Beverly Coyle

VIKING

VIKING
Published by the Penguin Group
Penguin Putnam Inc., 375 Hudson Street,
New York, New York 10014, U.S.A.
Penguin Books Ltd, 27 Wrights Lane,
London W8 5TZ, England
Penguin Books Australia Ltd, Ringwood,
Victoria, Australia
Penguin Books Canada Ltd, 10 Alcorn Avenue,
Toronto, Ontario, Canada M4V 3B2
Penguin Books (N.Z.) Ltd, 182–190 Wairau Road,
Auckland 10, New Zealand

Penguin Books Ltd, Registered Offices:
Harmondsworth, Middlesex, England

First published in 1998 by Viking Penguin,
a member of Penguin Putnam Inc.

10 9 8 7 6 5 4 3 2 1

PUBLISHER'S NOTE
This is a work of fiction. Names, characters, places,
and incidents either are the product of the author's
imagination or are used fictitiously, and any
resemblance to actual persons, living or dead, events,
or locales is entirely coincidental.

LIBRARY OF CONGRESS CATALOGING-IN-PUBLICATION DATA
Coyle, Beverly.
Taken in / Beverly Coyle.
p.   cm.
ISBN 0-670-86398-X (alk. paper)
I. Title.
PS3553.0947T3   1998   98-2804
813'.54—dc21

This book is printed on acid-free paper. ∞

Printed in the United States of America
Set in Minion
Designed by Helene Berinsky

for
   John Louis Jones

ACKNOWLEDGMENTS

To Pamela and Alexander, that we may continue to grow in love and song, and to dear Henry, no matter how small the apartment! Many thanks to the terrific Virginia Barber Agency; to Jane von Mehren, formerly my brilliant student, now my brilliant editor; and to Vassar College. I thank family and friends always, and want to mention all manner of reading and assistance, including offers of hearth and home, from Mary Beth Caschetta, Nancy Ford, Peter Franklin, Charles and Katharine Henderson, Ronnie and John Herman, Julia Johnson, Laura Jones, Ann Imbrie, Heather Lyn MacDonald, Judi Meyers and Joe DeBalsio, Lois and Jary Nixon, Ann Peyton, Martha Rosas and Ralph Sassone. There are others. And to Polly Holliday, I owe a special debt of thanks for gentle petitions in the name of clarity; and to Max Case, Peggy Ellsberg, Julia Hoffman, and the ever bold WLG, thanks for various inspirations. For ongoing help, genius, hospitality, laughter, and conversation, I thank Archie Gresham, in whom few doubters have had a more believing friend.

CONTENTS

TAKEN IN

1

MALCOLM'S SON

SHORTLY BEFORE CHRISTMAS, IN A CROWDED ORLANDO SHOPping district, Malcolm grabbed at his teenaged children on either side of him and turned sharply into the street. He did it hurriedly, parentally, the way one does, without much thought—jaywalking himself, Matt, and Gretchen straight over to the hotel. Suddenly Malcolm was late for a plenary session in the Gold Room.

For his son, Matt, however, the whole thing carried terrible meaning. "Dad, stop! You're passing by on the other side! You're passing by on the other side!" He must have seen a homeless man down on the sidewalk. Malcolm couldn't see because of all the people, but he recognized the Scripture quoted, and he knew instantly that that's what was going to make him mad, that he *was* mad. "Come on, now!" he said, tightening his grip. Good Samaritan was a part young Matt would like to play in life, if half allowed!

Malcolm just kept on going into the street, deciding instantly to play out *his* poor part in the story of able-bodied pious men, squeamish at best, all running to the other side of the road at the sight of someone in need. *Passing by* was, indeed, the biblical phrase for it.

"Cut it out," Malcolm shouted when Matt began pulling away

from him. It was all fairly stupid—a struggle more impulsive than real. But, the next thing Malcolm knew, he was a father about to get them all killed. Cars were barreling toward them from both directions. His daughter, Gretchen, gave a shriek and ran on to the opposite curb, sensible girl. That gave Malcolm a free hand. In a burst of strength that one only reads about, he yanked at Matt with all his might, feeling the kid's shoulder pop from the effort. A red convertible came whooshing past, its horn wailing, its driver screaming his head off, which is exactly what Malcolm ended up doing. All told, it could not have been a more comic rite—a last wielding of authority over a tall, lanky senior in high school with whom one's patience is shot.

Inside the hotel, lobby attendants and guests streamed around them as they all caught their breaths. A slower anger, fueled by adrenaline, seized Malcolm. He felt boiled down to his own self-righteousness. Years of grieving were there too, he would say. He'd grieved for the closeness he'd had with Matt in the first ten years of the boy's life. Seven biblical years without it now. Malcolm was not over the loss.

"Listen," he said, "I'm sorry, I truly am. It was *my* decision." He really had not seen anyone in their path, but he pretended otherwise. "Give me a few more days," he went on, letting a little bitterness creep in, but mostly sadness, the truer feeling. "A few more days and I'll turn all decisions over to you, you understand?" He was a father holding out hope, and he wanted the hurt of loss to come through, or else the idea that he and Susan, the boy's mother, were feeling inadequate, if not unloved, and could Matt not sense that, even help them out a little? He caught his daughter winking at him; she was fifteen going on twenty, and she understood why he'd exploded.

He was sorry about this damn conference now. Gretchen by herself would have been terrific; she'd tagged along because she'd wanted to shop at the new Orlando Saks. Matt had said okay only after his mother's special pleas; Susan hadn't wanted him lonely in the big house while she too was out of town. Meanwhile the poor kid was turning to look out the large hotel windows. A set of revolving glass doors was admitting loud people and Christmas excitement into the lobby, and beyond that Malcolm and Gretchen could now see the fallen man, of course—one of those guys from the shelter, or else a struggling escapee from an underfunded facility, and who knew if he was better off here or there. Suddenly, as if given his cue, the old boy sat up with great energy. They could see him shaking a fist and giving everyone hell: Last time he was conscious, this had been a nice quiet street!

Smug? No, Malcolm did not feel at all smug; he felt terrible, most especially for his old hiking buddy. Matt could almost seem not the same person, that was the thing. Where was the kid who'd tramped through the Florida lowlands with Malcolm? Together these two had helped blaze a few wonderful trails which were now recommended in the better guidebooks.

Malcolm went to the boy and put an arm on his shoulder. If he'd gotten a sprain from that hard yank, Matt wasn't letting on. "Let's go over and give the man something," Malcolm murmured. Then he added, with some risk of seeming to needle, "I think he could use a snort. I know *I* could!"

"And what did he say?" Susan asked in their telephone exchange. Malcolm was taking a break from his Orlando meetings and dialing her at hers in Jacksonville.

"Oh, he smiled at me," Malcolm said cheerily. "You know that sweet way he has when he sees we're worried about it. Whatever 'it' is." Malcolm had been profoundly relieved to see his son smile.

Recently he and Susan had almost stopped trading stories. The trades hadn't been doing any good, because each was beginning to accuse the other of having the wrong responses. Malcolm Robb was not just a concerned parent but also (and no one was more aware of the amusing irony) admissions director at a small Florida college. All this fall, he'd felt quite the shoemaker with barefoot children what with his complaints and jokes to Susan that his own son had not even started, much less finished, his college application forms. Now Matt's eight forms to eight different places were just about due, and it was no joke, although Malcolm, in his nervousness, was still full of levity: Maybe it was Freudian that sons of admissions directors balked on their forms. Before the deadline, Malcolm had wanted to help out with the personal essay part, and was that so bad? What was all Malcolm's experience for, if not for that?

Susan was worried too, she said. But she didn't like his jokes about who all he was going to call to get Matt over the first hump, how the first hump was another Malcolm, sorting kids into piles of yes, no, and probably no. She didn't like his predicting a lot of "no's," even in fun.

He accused her, on the other hand, of clinging to the boy's flashes of brilliance. Secretly, Malcolm still believed in them too, but he argued aloud that to an admissions officer (not the boy's own father), Matt's essay, unedited, might seem a bit too simplistic, too spiritual in theme and content.

Well, Susan said, was that so bad? Was there no room for God in the essay—?

It was a difficult thing to answer.

—or for simplicity? Their son was not simplistic, by the way!

He knew she was right. It was his own profession that might be the problem, although one didn't say that aloud either. He had the advantage of seeing things from both sides. In person, his son was not simplistic (while on paper any kid might be), and from day to day, the boy did not seem a fundamentalist, unless he was one in the making or only when he put pen to paper. All Malcolm wanted to do was help. All parents helped with the essay, he explained to Susan. No kid would get in otherwise. They'd *all* sound nuts, not just Matt!

They were allies, Malcolm and Susan. Normally, they didn't dwell.

All this past year, in complementary ways, they had been settling on a half-dozen places—all state institutions they could afford. Susan then noted that it was they who'd done all the excited choosing. When pressed, Matt, as if to be polite, added one school to their list. He suggested State U, down in Danford, just forty miles south of where they lived in the north Florida town of Wyman. Malcolm had joked to Susan that he'd settle for anything now, short of Oral Roberts. Hey, even that; what did *he* know? He knew education, and that it was not a sin to pray for it.

But today Susan's tones made him back off even from the rest of the story about the fallen man—that hilarious yet heartbreaking part about the old guy waking up hopping mad. After Malcolm hung up he moved with his coffee to the Flamingo Room, thinking, she and I can't let this happen, this lack of trust in swapping stories. We're what matters, finally! A speaker was behind the podium testing the microphone, and already Malcolm was far away in his mind, revisiting an early moment—a time when perhaps he'd most believed in his son's brilliance. At ten, he'd up and said, "Dad, it says in the Bible that if a man has two coats he ought to give one away." Easy, easy, Malcolm had thought at the time. He had come into Matt's room thinking the boy was having a nightmare. He'd reach out to put a little lamplight on the subject, always comforted, maybe too much, by his children's good looks. They had Susan's fine facial features and unswerving brown eyes, Malcolm's thick dirty-blond hair and skin that took the sun well, straight and slender frames. "You learned that passage this week in Mr. Smith's Bible study class? About giving the second coat away?"

"Dad, do you know how many coats *I* have?"

They were subtropical people; off the job, shorts and snake boots were about all they wore. But they did have plenty of cold-weather gear, it turned out; they'd camped all over the place to test themselves. So, whereas Jesus had proclaimed two coats to be excessive, their son, just a little kid in Sunday school, had begun to count and count until his fingers fell off: beat-up windbreakers, ponchos, squalls, bombers, toggles, and parkas. Thinsulates, power-downs, water-repellent shells, newbucks, drawstrings, and Arctics—such a huge, worrying heap, the loaves and fishes of Lands' End outerwear. Years later, sitting in the Flamingo Room, Malcolm still smiled at the thought that, indeed, there'd been enough extra coats in that single Protestant household to have clothed the five thousand.

"Well," he'd said, "maybe tomorrow we can do something about this." He'd looked at Susan, come into the room to help out. Both then and now she was his oldest lover, practically his only one; the good sport, the best friend, the still sexy girl off whom Malcolm couldn't keep his paws. He smiled at an imaginary her, seated beside him here in Orlando. "Nobody's out there freezing exactly," he said, winking. Seven years ago this had caused the small boy to throw himself at his mother and sob aloud that he was going around with so many more than two—"way, way, way more than two!"

A fellow conferee tapped Malcolm's shoulder, excusing himself in the squeeze between Malcolm's knees and the seat ahead of him. A veteran of the aisle, Malcolm stared blankly at expensive threads passing his nose and continued musing, this time on the differences between his two children. Gretchen's confidence made her better suited than Malcolm was to a room full of power brokers, as today's ADs liked to think of themselves. He'd always assumed that the quieter child, Matt, would become a teacher—a good one like his mother was, not the haggard type Malcolm himself had been before Admissions. Granted, he and Susan had had to work hard with the boy. He'd been completely sweet as a child, but a loner—the one on local camping trips giving good-night hugs to the adults when the neighbors' boys were up to normal nonsense—giggles, scuffles, and plans not to sleep. The plans had never included Matt.

Malcolm's shoulder was tapped again. A young woman's high hemline, normally of at least some interest to him, was passing at a level of only mild awareness; such a big change in the profession, was all that a bare leg made him think. Sixteen years ago, at a barbecue, he'd been standing with his infant son nestled inside a faded Snuggly purchased at a yard sale, when out of the blue he was offered a change—a kindly rescue from public education. Roy Davies, then president of Webster College, was saying that he needed an admissions director, but it had been at a time when some presidents were still thinking of the position as a desk job. To Davies, just having a youthful spirit and loyalty was key, never dreaming of a time when ADs would hold conferences on image-making and demographics. It was amusing to recall old man Davies wanting to know if, given the job, would Malcolm be willing to drive a school bus of basketball players to some of the away games? "You'll be able to take your son!" Davies had cheered, and had raised a glass to all Division III's and maybe a championship for Webster some century.

Yes, indeed, and not just to ball games, it turned out. Malcolm had hiked and swashbuckled his dreamy child over every rock in the national park system, down every trail Malcolm felt it was going to take to keep the boy's feet on the ground. Somewhere along a perfectly glorious mountain pass or stream—as glorious a thing as God might offer in the next world—Matt had seemed to go his own scary way.

Well, Susan argued, only now and again scary. Malcolm felt it was a defensive position on Susan's part still to be insisting that quite a bit of time went by between the crisis of the too-many coats and the next encounter with Matt's take on things. Hard to say for sure; Malcolm remembered that from that time on the boy gave all his money away whenever he could; at age eleven he got more mail than Malcolm and Susan. But he also kept his own counsel. He smiled and brushed off his acts of giving. And when it's a small allowance, parents don't see it as such a big deal. Susan was correct in remembering that Matt was fully fifteen before he began wearing the one biblical coat allotted him—two years ago now, about the same time he began politely turning down requests to come hiking with Mac.

And when it first started happening, they'd still been able to joke with each other: The weather being so hot, their resourceful son had translated the one-coat idea into one pair of jeans and one T-shirt for himself. "Didn't you have all that on yesterday?" was how it began. None of the four Robbs cared much about clothes; on a hectic school morning any one of them might come to the table looking like yesterday. At school the boy had no doubt appeared little more than unimaginative punk.

He had made no show of his devotion, or whatever it was. He was secretly washing out at night—the one pair of socks and jockeys—until finally it was the humidity that did him in. They first noticed something was truly going on after the kid had started smelling moldy. "P-ewe!" Gretchen had said, sniffing in her brother's direction and making a face. Malcolm had sniffed too and searched for a tactful explanation. "You may like this outfit, Matt, but it's starting to sour on you. Better go in there and find something dry."

"It's okay, Dad. I'm late. See you tonight." And it may have been that that night he slipped his things into the dryer to elude detection. "It's just an experiment" was all he would say about it once they were on to him. "A school experiment?" Susan had said, a little too innocently. Her voice had trembled. She'd had tears in her eyes. The next morning they'd gone into Matt's room and had a guilty look around, with Susan confessing how relieved she was to find no boxed-up clothes ready to UPS to the needy. Then sensing Malcolm's discomfort she announced, a little dramatically perhaps, that she believed Matt to be the real thing.

Did she mean the real thing, religiously? Malcolm had flopped down on the kid's bed. He kept it friendly. "I'm a simpleton, religiously. If he's the real thing is that good or bad?" And Susan had laughed; because, finally, she'd never lacked a sense of humor about the situation. "Good for him, bad for us!" she'd said.

Living on one side of the Robbs were Gail and John Richards, both good friends, who agreed to ask their son, Johnny, what he made of Matt's self-denial. On the other side were Ted and Beth Harwood. They agreed to ask their twin boys, Wade and Wayne. Turned out all the boys had shouted angrily that Matt was neat and what did it matter if he dressed in the same clothes? John and Ted had told Malcolm, each confiding separately, that it was difficult to glean information from Johnny, Wade, and Wayne. Both sets of marriages were in a shambles; the boys would say anything in order to blow off steam about *that*.

So the mystery of Matt caused Susan to schedule meetings with counselors and teachers at the beginning of each year and several times during. Would everyone please keep an eye out? Everyone always said that they would; they sympathized and continued to be encouraging about what good parents the Robbs were. Last year Matt had seemed to give up the one-outfit idea and had started wearing changes again—at least one or two—enough to keep himself beyond scrutiny. About the other—about the stripping down to nothing—he politely dismissed it the many times Malcolm brought it up. Each time Malcolm let him know that it would be so good to talk about it, good for Malcolm himself, who *felt* he felt the mind-boggling gulf that separated rich and poor people of a nation and of a world. "I was being extreme," Matt said, "and it's not what I want." Malcolm had a distinct sense of the boy's understanding of himself, and also of his vow to stay silent about it, which was not a fundamentalist's way.

But was it a willful and withholding temperament? He seemed to dread his father's questions as much as Malcolm dreaded asking them. Talking about sex was a breeze by comparison. Several times he and Susan went to Paula, their minister, to talk over with her an almost curious liberalism on the part of their son—a fanatical silence about God? they wondered. They missed Paula now that she'd left Wyman to take a larger church. They'd all three had several good talks, and said they should have been doing it all along, Matt or otherwise. Paula had been very moody at Matt's age, she said, and all through college; she'd finally relaxed in graduate school. Paula gave them hope that if they could just get their son past this fervent phase—

Fervent. Yes, Malcolm had liked that. The boy was fervently

silent. Just a few hours ago, he'd blurted out that Good Samaritan quotation, but after that, he was almost not able to speak of it. And so okay, what about this: if the rest of the world watches television, who can fault a boy for going dumb? Could it be Gretchen? Malcolm wondered. Given the chance, Gretchen would watch TV movies night and day. However (and here was a very important point Susan had mistaken as a joke from Malcolm), Gretchen's heroine was, of all people, Elaine May! Malcolm had said to Susan just last week that any child's brilliant if peculiar admiration of Elaine May was a mystery he could enjoy.

"I know. Me too," Susan had said. "You and I have to talk."

They would, he was sure.

Malcolm squirmed in his seat at an incident he'd not yet mentioned to Susan and should have by now. Two days ago something else had happened. Malcolm had gotten a call about Matt from Oren Abel, a reclusive widower and their lawyer neighbor from across the street. He apologized for disturbing Malcolm at the college, but thought it best to tell him Matt was home from school; the boy might be sick and too proud to let his parents know. Malcolm jogged the few blocks home from his office to find Matt reading at the kitchen table at eleven in the morning. Indeed, it hadn't looked good.

"This book," the boy had said, holding out a large new Bible and letting its pages fall on either side of his hands with the weight of a cleavered piece of meat. "Maybe this is the only book I should be reading."

Malcolm had eased into one of the nearby chairs, listening to the way the house ticked when it was just the two of them during an odd part of the day. He found himself wishing Oren Abel had minded his own business. "Some books you'll study all your life," he'd said finally, "and that's certainly one of them." He wasn't yet certain that this was really happening—that his worst fear was being confirmed in this way.

"What do the other people study?" Matt said.

"The other people? Oh, I see. The others." Malcolm remembered his own actions as in a dream—remembered getting up to pull cold milk out of the fridge. "There's the Koran," he'd begun. "The Koran is in my library, any time you want to have a look. And the Bhagavad Gita. And—" He stopped.

"There isn't time, is there?" Matt was saying.

Out of Malcolm's mouth had come the hard truth. "No. No, I'm sorry to say there really isn't." He could hear his tone—man to man, a little too hefty in its effort to avoid seeming to say, Snap out of it! as if Malcolm were talking to John or Ted, both raising boys in houses to either side of him on the same drinking water. "Do you enjoy reading the Bible?" he'd said, not meaning to sound alarmed. Only meaning to convey the natural worry a father might have about a fanatic's deep end into which a well-meaning son might accidentally leap.

And how had Malcolm sounded today, upon hearing the Good Samaritan text? Not alarmed. Furious was how he'd sounded.

When he was tapped on the shoulder once more, he finally arose and made his lumbering way back to the lobby's fancifully large ottoman. Sprouting from its center were many elephant-ear plants and a lit fountain. He was exhausted, he supposed—from Matt worry and now from all this vanity. An alarmed or furious father is not altogether incapable of seeing that vanity is a very good thing for a son to avoid. This hard side of the college game was all about price-to-earnings projections and shrewd parents demanding value for their money. When pressed, Malcolm dreaded almost any kid's essay arriving on the steely desks of today's admissions types. What fragile idea—youthful and yet full of awareness—would do anything but sail over the heads of everyone in this three-hundred-dollar-a night hotel?

"Mac!" someone yelled. He pretended not to hear as he got up in his sudden determination to get in a workout by taking an aerobic walk from one end of Orlando to the other. "Malcolm!"

Malcolm smiled and waved as he picked up a white courtesy

phone near the registration desk and dialed his daughter in the room. He lied to her for some reason; said he guessed he'd better attend the closing banquet after all. Politics! Would she mind being alone? Earlier Matt had said he would find an empty conference room in which to do some homework.

"Good!" Gretchen said. "I can watch Barbara Stanwyck in *Double Indemnity.*" She rattled off other movie ideas from the hotel TV guide. She was all set for the evening, no problem.

With Gretchen there was never any problem. Never with Susan either. But the Bible-as-the-only-book episode and now the fallen man were bordering on secrets. He blamed panic for his newest reticence; panic and the fact that Matt had blushed when Malcolm asked if he *liked* reading the Bible. "Never mind, Dad," he'd answered in a soft way that suggested he was letting Malcolm off as gently as he could. He was forgiving Malcolm. "It's okay, really. I came home to think, that's all." Matt had even laughed, suddenly so very mature. "It's hard to think at school."

Malcolm had begun to almost sputter. "Listen, a few minutes ago it was dumb of me to say you don't have time. You have loads of time. You have your whole life! You know what I think? I think you're a scholar at heart. You know? A scholar stuck in a tiny town with dull parents. Why don't we ask Oren Abel to teach you some Greek?" On his son's face there had been a look of sympathy for him that had caused Malcolm's heart to pound. "You're bright, you could do it! And you have loads of time. How could I have possibly said you don't have time? It was the dumbest thing I've ever said. I want you to take it easy and not worry quite so much."

Outside the hotel, Malcolm stood looking at a gorgeous night. Orlando's taller buildings shone pink from a sunset he couldn't see. Alpine glow, of sorts. Out here was such a wonderful lull, all activity forcibly paused, except for what was still inside his own spinning head. It's going to turn out to be about sex, isn't it? Doesn't it all just turn out to be about sex, and then a person is on his way, at college or at whatever in the world he wants?

Well, almost whatever. Malcolm believed that he was not a father lacking all imagination. Certainly, if his son asked for bread, he would at least not give him a stone! Malcolm, laughing, crying, began quoting the Scriptures, which he could do as well as the next guy. "And if a son ask a fish, will he that is a father give him a serpent?"

Across the street was the spot where the homeless man had sat—a huge area, now empty and fallen into shadow. He wished he'd spotted the man. More purely, he wished he could take back that speech about Matt making all his own decisions from now on. It had come born out of fury. And out of fear too, building up and building up. He made a quick decision to walk west. He didn't want to stand in front of the hotel and recall how good it had felt to yank a beloved arm out of its socket. He would do it again, he assumed. That was sad and sobering, now wasn't it?—to want to do it again, knowing that he couldn't move himself an inch closer to what the whole thing was really about, and that it was somehow his own fault that he couldn't. Because the simple truth is we do have too much. We have way, way, way too much.

2

MATT AND ANGELA

THESE WERE LONG DECEMBER DAYS. MATT FELT INVISIBLE IN the school corridors filled with loud life. At three o'clock, the buildings began to spill. Other students parted and moved around him like fish, some passing through him as if he were the buoying water, and that made them light and free in where they had to go.

Water *is* body, a living support, if hard to see. He wondered if that's what he might write about in that essay he had to do, the not-doing of which was a big worry to his father—a father with a son not swimming toward a freshman year at a major institution. A mother smiling too painfully.

For most application essays, he must introduce himself by discussing a book or movie he'd been affected by. The task was making him giddy, implausible to himself, although it was not an unfamiliar feeling in his gut—the feeling that if he talks about the Book of books he's a dead duck, and while that is not a problem for him, it would be such a problem for Malcolm and Susan—their son not getting in anywhere. He'd been told even as a small boy how important college would be to him for the rest of his life, how wonderful a thing it was to anticipate ahead of time.

He didn't mean to be shoving his ambivalent position in their faces by not writing the essay. And besides, what he wanted to write was too private a thing. All that he read went into him like food to remake him inside. All that might come out of him in words seemed impossible to attempt.

But he'd at least been kicking around the thread of an idea. He could perhaps start with the Blue Danube Waltz in that famous movie. Recently he watched it again with Susan, who agreed with him, finally, that the waltz might perhaps be thought of as, yes, holding up the floating spacecraft in its weightless slow spin.

"I'm more like that," he heard himself say.

"You are?" she said softly. "How? Explain it to me."

"What if I just wrote about what we can't see?"

"Well, sweetheart, you can give it a try. They want you to start with what's on your mind, I think."

"I mean, it's in everything. There's an artist who says that the negative shapes on the canvas are as much painted as the positive shapes. I know that all the time."

"Would you like to study art?" Her voice gave her away. It quavered. "They want to know something about your plans, I think. You don't want to be too abstract."

"I know."

She smiled as he left to go upstairs to his desk to write it, to shape the thought for his essay, himself knowing full well that he couldn't say what he meant and be considered a sane candidate. His own professional father would be forced to put such an application into a pile with all the other apparently troubled hopefuls.

That didn't bother him.

What bothered him was Malcolm wanting to see the essay before he sent it out. There was such a fine line between freedom and failure, and Malcolm, too close to the situation, didn't walk that line very well.

Matt called George Murray, whom he'd never met. He'd been planning for months to put into one of his letters a query about taking a job at Murray's camp for troubled boys. Maybe it was not so out of the blue, or else there was luck in the timing of the phone call. It seemed the man was going to be in Danford in the week after Christmas. Did Matt want to meet him to discuss it? There was a Rhonda's Diner downtown convenient for him. Could Matt get there from Wyman? Did he have a car?

"I've always wondered how you found out about me in the first place," Murray said. "How long have you and I been writing? A couple of years? How old were you then?"

Matt could tell that the man was both friendly and naturally a bit wary. In Rhonda's Diner, Murray listened carefully, asked Matt a few questions about his family, and kept putting a finger down on his paper napkin and moving it around when he tried to answer thoughtfully the question Matt asked him; how had he chosen to leave a medical practice and found a camp? Matt had read about the place in some literature distributed by the United Way.

"Yes, well, as I think I wrote you one time, I have only a few boys on scholarship. I hope that will change. A lot of the families of my campers are quite wealthy."

As for going into this line of work? He'd never planned to until his early forties. One day he and his wife were playing ball with their own son, and they had a shared vision of a place. On a comic level he'd felt this must be what inventors or poets experience—a sudden seeing. Religious? No, not particularly. They'd just been talking together, and both seemed to hit on it at the same time—a place where they could work with a certain kind of kid.

"My kind," Matt said.

The man smiled and shrugged, reminding Matt of his own father in a mellow mode.

"Yeah, okay, your kind. I can handle another one of you, if that's how you want to think about it. You're not looking for a shrink, are you? We need high school counselors, not patients."

Then George sighed and looked at him with direct eyes. "Why did you ask if I'm religious? *You're* the one, is that it?"

Inside Matt the words formed, but he could only shake his head. He didn't think there were words for what he was. He knew better than to say he felt invisible.

George leaned in from across the table. "Young people your age are faced with a lot of confusion about what direction their lives should take. It's not a bad thing. And life does get less odd, Matt. You *will* find direction. I can see you're a committed person, and if you'll agree to let me meet your parents, then I think we can work something out."

After sitting quietly a while, George Murray pulled up a book from the padded diner seat and smoothed his hand over it the way a person does before he's about to relinquish something he still needs. The need caused George to delay the gift, caused him to turn to pages he'd marked. " 'I am a poet; I am always hungry.' " He looked up. "That's the urgent feeling, right? Plenty of hunger everywhere, and you can't quite get at it? Do you ever read poetry? You should. Here, listen to this: 'There isn't time for good manners.' " He smiled, letting it hang there. "These are some sayings of Theodore Roethke. You might like him. Some people can only express themselves in poetry." He leaned back, rested, then turned his head to the window, the outside world. "But how is one going to live on pure poetry and God? Huh? Does a person eat locusts? Hmm? You won't be effective out there in the street, Matt. Someday you might be, but in order to help others you need to grow cleats on your shoes. Otherwise, you'll start to—"

"—to lift off," Matt said.

George nodded. He held up the poetry book, then handed it over. "You do have to make time to read. Read widely." He was getting out of the booth, looking at his watch; past time for him to be on his way. He almost collided with other patrons, just then brushing past and plunking down across the aisle in the opposite booth. A man and girl. They were arguing.

George didn't notice, putting out his hand to shake Matt's. "Let's try you for a couple of weeks in January," he said, standing now,

stretching his back. "I'll have twenty boys for a couple of weeks before the second term of school starts up." He pointed at the book
he was lending Matt. "Someday I want it back. It will grow cold on
you anyway. Temperatures soar up and down. Do you know that
about life? Hot's always getting cold? Even God's hot gets cold. You
need some fat on your bones for when She withdraws for a time and
you're standing around freezing to death. You don't know what cold
is, Florida boy!"

He was leaving, but calling over his shoulder, "And be sure to get
that damn essay done. Just good manners this one last time? You
owe it to your folks."

He had been eclipsing the couple with his large body, and when
he stepped away and headed for the cash register, the man and the
girl came into view. The one was bent low, doing a line of cocaine
on the linoleum tabletop. He brought the straw up, breathed deeply,
and shook his head. Then he spotted Matt and grinned. "Hey," he
said sleepily. His eyebrows went up and down a few times. "Sorry,"
he said, "you caught me." He pushed the baggie slowly to the edge of
the table in Matt's direction, and it was the girl who shoved it back
at the man. She slid out of her side of the booth.

"People can leave you, Cooper," she said as she got in beside
Matt. "I can sit over here and be with this boy. I don't belong to
you." By now she was holding Matt's hand, her head flopping
against the high, padded seat. She was holding his hand hard, as if
she were about to lose her balance on a beam.

The man Cooper gave the two of them a stare and then grinned.
"That's nice. Somebody your own age. Maybe he'll take you home."

"I'll ask him," she said.

If he could explain it he would. That non-visible thing hovering
closer from time to time, and especially in these kinds of moments
when he understands how the world is: We are all displaced. But
not so much so that our individual pain is all we can feel, as in the
case of this girl, who is too exhausted by it. Hasn't eaten, can't. She

is permanently displaced. Her hand feels icy. How to get home is what she might ask if she knew to ask. Dared to. Never been there, it would seem.

"Are you Joe?" she said, eyes closed. "You Joe College?" Through rice-paper eyelids she seemed to see the book George had given him. She squeezed his hand, as if to say, I'm only going to sit here for a minute and rest, I'm not going to give you a hard time.

"Okay, Angela," the man was saying. It was a low simmer. He wasn't looking over at the booth now. "You stay there while I eat. It will be a goddamn relief."

"I have to go to work," she confided to Matt. "I work for this jackass. You wouldn't believe what a—"

"Keep it up, Angela," the man muttered. The waitress brought him two sandwiches, and he motioned for her to put one of the plates down in the opposite booth. "Eat, slut," Cooper called.

"Sir," the waitress said, "my boss don't allow vulgar talk in here."

"Okay," Cooper said. He winked at Matt. "We'll be good."

The waitress placed the sandwich plate and a hot tea in front of Angela. Cooper called out, "When I'm done, we're leaving, so eat, goddammit."

Matt saw she wasn't going to do anything but sit there holding his hand. She never opened her eyes. She was taking a little rest, she said. Matt wrapped up the sandwich for her in several paper napkins, and in a few moments Cooper stood up. He stretched. He put a finger in and cleaned the roof of his mouth. The girl simply groaned and got up, leaving the wrapped sandwich on the table. They were gone without further talk, Cooper with his hand on the back of her neck.

The waitress, curious yet knowing, came to Matt with a refill. "They've been in here before. It was the same then."

He looked up at her. The waitress was homely. In the safety of the diner and their shared knowledge of an underage girl being ordered about by a man she didn't like, she became sisterly and yet

flirtatious. ~~"I was good just then, wasn't I? Telling him to watch his~~
mouth?"

Matt smiled.

The waitress nodded, her gaze wandering out to the street. "But maybe I'd trade places with her," she said.

Matt shook his head.

"I would! She'll die young, but so what?" The waitress looked at the wrapped sandwich. "See, even *you* like her."

Then the young woman hardened her features and began clearing Matt's table. "You got twenty dollars?" she said.

"If you need it, sure."

"*He* needs it!" she said. "Take twenty over to Wendy's on the main drag. Give it to the guy. See what you get for it. I'm not kidding. You get her."

The waitress was angry yet pleased. He was interested. "I can always tell. Why wouldn't you be?"

If he could, he would tell her how he saw the girl's world as side-by-side with their regular one. But in hers he saw a hermetic seal. It allowed her to say things openly that people heard but did not respond to. Just now she'd been threatening to run away from the man, but the statement carried no weight at all. It had been like hearing a child in a bus station who is trying to pull away from a tight, mean grip. It could be a kidnapping, and no one would see it. George Murray was right: we can't walk streets and follow desperate people to their dead ends. Perhaps tonight; but what about tomorrow night, and the next? There was that text Matt loved from Saint Luke's, "Take no staves for your journey, take no shoes, take neither silver nor brass in your purse." He would read things like that and think how his parents had steered a course through marriage and love. They were blessed, and he didn't see himself as any better than that. That wasn't it. And if his parents ever got the wrong idea, he would have to face it and try to explain.

"Can I borrow your pen?" he asked the waitress.

"Oh, sure."

She stood for a moment, watching him spread out a paper napkin.

"One can think about a long war," he wrote, "or a long violent century, say, and in one passage of that century through the brain an entire span of time will carry less weight than the presence of an exploited girl. As if one's heart is torn out and bitten. On the other hand, all the battles and even the gas chambers of a century, thought about, can become quiet grassy meadows. In the past the movement of time seems stilled to pictures; here, alive, we flail up close to each other and right in front of each other and there seems nothing to do but to go to each other. Go and take no purse!"

Such stuff might get him in, taking out the exclamation mark or even the scriptural reference altogether, and then making it all a little simpler.

But how to say certain other things? What did it mean to get into college and leave people like Angela to their own devices? It seemed wrong.

Not sinful. He was not sure he knew or believed much, if anything, about sin. But wrong, yes. It made him twist in his bed at night. Maybe not everyone need twist. Maybe it wasn't wrong for those who are the visible fish to leave the Angelas behind. It was only so for those closer to the invisible. He knew he was real space after all, as real as a shadow on a canvas—a shadow requiring as much paint as a woman's arm; as real as the waltz holding up the spinning contraption, so beautiful, but so dependent on its sea of sound and beat. Everyone saw the spacecraft in the movie. What meant most to him, he wanted to write, was how the music held it up— the metaphor of himself, of how he saw himself. Or as if someone pulled out from him endless scarves, as magicians do. He liked the comic magicians—the ones who pretended to be surprised as the scarves kept coming, as if out of control—a torrential pouring forth of themselves, like lovely paper entrails.

That, and a ringing freedom in the emptying out of a school—

everyone flying this way and that, and himself seeing, almost as a ghostly shape, the end of this time of his life—the end of a named school, named street, town, and people whose children's long need of nurture has left a look of parental worry.

Write, he hears Malcolm plead. *Just write it!*

3

Oren Alive

For fifteen years Oren Abel had been a little in love with Susan Robb. No problem keeping it buttoned up in his vest each time she had him to the house, however. No, she'd arrived a young mother and had been busy from the start. She seemed to entertain almost for her mother's sake—a formal dinner party set with salt cellars whenever that impossible woman came to town.

He always sensed that he was liked for himself, even popular, despite Susan's occasional need for an extra gentleman at table. It was only that he and she never visited, just the two of them. It may never have occurred to her that he would even enjoy such a thing. She always sent Malcolm or one of the children over with some choice casserole or a sealed bag of holiday cookies. In all these years a wave from porch to porch was their biggest show of affection, and now everyone was older. Oren's passion was in check; invitations were less and less frequent. The world's schedule made crass demands on the most well-intended.

He would be the first to admit certain flaws in his character. He was not aggressive. He was even shy, although wise enough to know that "shy" is what others say; applied to oneself, one has no idea what it means. He knew this much: He was not the person his good neighbors would ever contact in an emergency. Rousing him required harder pounding on his door than most of them could manage.

But right around Christmas, it happened. One night Oren heard it—someone wanting him. On the third or fourth loud knock, he may have sensed that his life was no longer quite his own. His more reasonable, daily self groaned as he rose slowly out of his chair and turned off the set, certain this was only the prank of fleeing kids from another street.

And then his entire house seemed to tilt. There was his neighbor, Susan Robb, standing dripping wet on his porch. She'd thrown her jacket over Gretchen's head and nothing over her own. Just that made his heart quicken—that sensuous wet hair and a huge curtain of rain behind her, the color of gunmetal, beating out its rhythm in the nearby drops that pelted his steps as well as the street and rooftops several hundred feet away. It sounded like hail.

The daughter stood wide-eyed, glad for this little excitement. But Susan seemed to be impatient to be seeing him, finally. Her look said that he was not what she needed in this emergency, but now it was too late for her to change her mind.

Oren's pride was pricked immediately by that look. "You two get in here out of the weather!" he boomed, stepping onto his porch in a manly fashion and hurrying them into the hall. Hang it all, he would rise to this occasion before he'd have her doubts so quickly satisfied.

Susan began apologizing, explaining that she was alone and had just gotten a phone call from the Danford police.

"Danford!" he boomed again, not giving her a chance to continue. "My goodness, they're all thugs down there." He said this despite the fact that Susan had taught high school in that city for a long time now and probably knew it better than he did.

"A captain named Jensen called me," she said.

"Eddy Jensen!" Oren shouted. "He's our sheriff's brother-in-law, did you know that? Well, why would you know that?"

It was a lucky coincidence that Oren knew this fact. Knowing it aroused him in a more complicated fashion—first that annoyed glance of hers and then Eddy's name, an old reminder of his father's days. Oren tried not to stare at the wet T-shirt swelling out at him like a life preserver. He was so shaken she might as well have been explaining to him that Malcolm Robb was dead.

"He's all right," she was saying, almost choking up at the idea that he might *not* be.

"But he has to be in some kind of trouble!" Gretchen said, chiming in in a wicked way, as if she was the only one to see that Oren was in the middle of the rush of blood to his groin and still thinking they were talking about Malcolm.

"It's Matt," Susan explained. "He's—"

"Somebody probably thought he was shoplifting," Gretchen said. "He dresses like the homeless."

"Honestly," Susan said, "I wish you wouldn't interrupt me."

Gretchen gave Oren a grin from behind her mother's back, as Susan pressed on to explain that she'd merely come over to tell him she was driving to Danford to pick up Matt. Since Malcolm was gone, would Oren mind watching the house?

"Matt's going to need a lawyer," Gretchen said. "That's really why we're here."

Susan spun around and held a finger in front of the girl's face.

"Well, for God's sake, Mom, when have we ever asked Uncle Oren to watch the house?"

Indeed, they never had. Susan Robb appeared momentarily confused. Then she said to him, "Oren, I'm sorry. I don't know why I'm bothering you. Maybe Gretchen's right."

"Maybe not!" he said. "But at the very least you need someone to go with you in this rain!"

It was a few moments before he got on lights and herded the two down the long, sooty hall. Once in the kitchen, Oren felt giddy and much less embarrassed by the state of his despicable kitchen than he should be. He was a dapper man with dapper exteriors, from the expensive suits he wore to the care with which he kept up the outside of his house. Inside, he and the house were a shambles.

He found some old tea towels for drying off. He made Susan sit at the cluttered table while he called up Eddy Jensen, just picked up his ancient, steel-mounted wall phone as if it was nothing to be calling; as if Oren were part of the system. Oren well *could* have been, if he hadn't dropped out so early as to be quite humorous. They'd been in the same freshman class back before Eddy enforced the law. These rural counties liked to keep law in the family; liked to phone up to the next town and be informed of the right politicians, the right comers, the right winners and losers whose powers could be called into play at will. That was Hutchenson Abel, Oren's long-dead father. Oren wasn't ever a player; Hutch had seen to that. He dreaded hearing Eddy pretend otherwise.

"My God, it's Oren!" Eddy said immediately. "How long's it been, old buddy?" He was jovial. He was accommodating. "Hey, listen, I'll drive the kid up there for you myself. It would be a genuine honor."

"Why don't you tell me what's going on, Eddy?" Oren said. "What's the trouble?"

Eddy laughed and laughed. "This kid's a lucky bastard, that's all I can say. He keeps getting luckier by the minute." And it was at that point that Oren knew a great deal more than Susan Robb did. She was seated and he was standing, his hip just near enough to her upper arm to feel imagined warmth and no small amount of thrill in looking down on that T-shirt as he listened to Eddy tell him that they'd picked up her son for soliciting a prostitute.

"There has to be some mistake," was all he said. The T-shirt was olive green and new—the softest, newest olive green T-shirt he'd ever seen in his life.

Eddy explained that it was an operation they'd been trying to break up since the beginning of the holidays. Some bum in a Santa Claus suit was pimping for a sixteen-year-old he was keeping in the back of a car.

"I see," Oren said. He thought about putting his hand on her neck just where her damp hair curled. Then he seemed to catch the daughter squinting at him, doubting him, as Eddy continued with a few details about the kind of opportunity this lowlife, coked-out piece of scum had been offering the junior high boys in Danford. He wasn't even a pimp, Eddy explained; he was a college-boy junkie of some kind and she white trash. Their operation was to work Lester Street between the university bookstore and Wendy's. Mere schoolkids somehow knew that if you gave twenty dollars to the Lester Street Santa in front of Wendy's he'd take you around the block to his car. It had curtains on the back windows. You were allowed to climb in with Mrs. Claus for three minutes.

"I see," Oren said. Again he bravely returned the daughter's stare. He feared she'd seen his fingers twitching. He'd always been something of a twitcher, he'd have her know; it meant nothing.

Eddy continued to brag that he'd gotten the guy on film. Several of the kids had helped set him up for the sting. Eddy knew all those kids, practically; Matt was the only one he didn't know. "He was inside the car, though." Eddy laughed. "I'm afraid we got *him* on film. How old is he? He's older than junior high, right?"

"A high school senior, Eddy," Oren said. "An honor student and the son of a very good friend of mine."

"Honor student," the daughter whispered to Susan, "that's a good touch."

"You keep an eye on him until we get there, Eddy. We're starting out from Wyman now."

"Oh, I want to see you, Oren," Eddy said. "I surely do. It's been far too long."

When he got off the phone he was full of improvisations. "It's nothing," he said, which only caused Gretchen to fold her arms.

"Now, now," Oren insisted, "they've confused Matt with someone else." He had no clear plan in mind, but he was buzzing with excitement and cool command. In this mood he led them back into the hall, where he pulled his coat and a large umbrella out of a closet. "It's a silly mix-up," he was saying, herding them to his front door again. "Someone's going to have to answer to us about this." Outside on the porch, he wondered aloud if Gretchen might not prefer to stay with the Richardses or the Harwoods while he and Susan made the trip to pick up Matt.

"Nope," the girl said, "sorry."

He saw for himself that the Richardses' and the Harwoods' Christmas lights were not turned on. That's when he realized that he ought not to flatter himself. Lawyer or no lawyer, Susan had come to him first because no one else was home.

He locked up his house, hurried them across the street, and made Susan turn off her lights and get a blanket for Gretchen to wrap up in in the car. Just waiting on the Robb porch intensified the night—the girl's mother dashing in to get the blanket and car keys. He stood anticipating the highway and sitting beside her in darkness as they drove. Beside him right now the daughter made small talk as they stared out at the heavy black rain. "This month Gail finally left John," the girl offered.

"No!"

She nodded. "John's a mess."

"My word!" Oren said, thinking, There you are, you never know when. But the daughter simply grinned up at him as if to warn him she could read his thoughts with nothing more than streetlights to help her.

In the car Susan kept quiet; it seemed to make her stiff-necked, as if having to drive in ignorance about her son was irritating, although not something for which she blamed him. Oren saw it almost as a kindness that he undo his seat belt and execute a quiet shift to center. "It's nothing," he breathed into her ear. He hadn't breathed into an ear in he didn't know how long, a pleasure now so strong it was as if he were suddenly going to once and for all kill Eddy Jensen, join a health club, firm up a bit, and seduce his neighbor's wife.

"When we get there I'll go in and sign a release," he breathed. "You and Gretchen wait in the car. Don't worry, we'll talk about all this later. It's a mix-up" His whispers made the daughter dive into the backseat blanket and the mother sink into thought. Or maybe it was the downpour of rain and her determination to get them there and back without a silly accident. Just beyond the speeding car, Florida was doing her big weather show. Strobe lightning flashed the fields of winter rye in and out of view.

He'd never intended to get to the point of such eccentricity as to be thrown by a moment of neighborly business. True, he was Wyman's most famous shameface—a show for the old families his father had carefully fleeced. Was that what this moment was—a freaky sense that tonight, or sometime soon, he might be permitted to put those old days far behind? Had he been hanging on to them, perhaps, for sheer convenience? He wasn't sure. His only task right now was to keep a few things going beyond her son's misstep. This was a most unlikely car ride. It would not be offered to him again any time soon.

As he sat beside her, the fire seeped out of him just enough for him to reflect that there'd been many times over the years when he might have acted on strong feelings but had known better than to do so. He was no flirt. What's more, it would hardly have been in his best interest to have been rejected and then to have missed out on her altogether—her French sauces in the seventies, her curries in the eighties. The out-of-town mother was a trial, but Susan was not. Once in a while she'd asked him the right questions about himself— what he read, what he thought concerning this or that issue. Oren was not without his lively points of view at table.

Granted, the strain of the nineties had cramped his style. No parties. Everett Street couples now collaborated on one or two sensible cookouts a year—grilled chicken with chilled wine and a salad.

Mostly salad. These days every man and woman in the country tossed their red leaf and endive inside bowls as big as hubcaps.

But who knew what the salads might mean in terms of their happiness? A man such as himself could not determine (and had not cared, frankly) which couple did or did not get along any more—in life or in bed or in theory. Maybe now they had all more or less caught up to him. Life for one and all can eventually become a little too comfortable to let you snap at things. He himself had lasted a remarkably long time with energy enough for an anonymous Danford woman and a restaurant once in a while. At some point he remembered the slow shift from taking the woman and skipping the restaurant to taking the restaurant and skipping the woman.

He'd not intended it. It had slipped up on him like a friendly sludge, an oil spill that kills the quacking ducks inside you a few at a time. A small-town widower with a hired car. Well, hell, he had cultivated the comedy and the seclusion because he had some money in the end, and Wyman had had to swallow that. Fortunately, there'd never been resentment on the part of Susan's bunch, the outsiders. They were all too fulfilled for envy. Nor had they ever known his father and shared in even the last smoldering resentments, now pretty much ashes.

"The officers apparently picked up my poor kid not far from here," she was saying in whispers, looking around as she pulled to the curb and stopped. The daughter was asleep, or pretending to be. Susan leaned toward him. "Matt is a peculiar person, Oren. Very religious, did you know that? He compensates." Her eyes darted about. "He's not completely unsophisticated."

The two sat quietly. Oren studied her profile as she talked and stared out at the dimly lit police station. He could barely recall the boy's face, had never taken the least interest in her children.

"I don't know what this is all about," she said, "and truthfully I don't care. As you said, this is just some mistake. But on the whole I'm worried. Matt can look like a religious fanatic"—she began to laugh despite the pain—"and I don't think the other fanatics deserve him."

Had Oren not been so smitten, he might have told her that maybe her son was not such a fanatic as to miss out on a semiprofessional hand job.

"He's sweetly touched, Oren," she said. Instead of pointing to her head she pointed to her heart. "He's going to wander inside a spiritual life."

He repeated the phrase to himself in the same rhythm. It was dark. "Someone said not all wanderers are lost," he offered.

"Thank you," she said. "That's true."

She paused, and it was as if she still wanted to talk for a moment before letting him go into the station. For his part, he wouldn't have minded talking several days. Who was he kidding? Talk was what he needed, esprit de corps was all. The last time he'd tried anything physical, he'd been impotent, and the woman had gotten so hysterical about it (about *herself*) that none of it had seemed worth it to him anymore, especially now that there was cable.

"Sometimes I see my son having to shade his eyes all his life," Susan said. "Headlights coming at him, stunning him. It's never sweet daylight for him, you know? Gretchen gets up in the morning humming her little tune, practical as all get-out. I am too, for that matter. So's Malcolm. Our son won't own a car. A bicycle." She looked at him and then had to laugh. "He hitches rides. He's worked a little modern technology out in his mind, I'm happy to say."

Oren waited. She sighed. What went through his mind was how that week Florida was suffering the aftermath of a killing outside a Planned Parenthood. Some crusader had sprayed a blue van with bullets and left a young doctor trapped and dying inside.

But surely that wasn't the path she was dreading. "I'll be back in a moment," Oren said. "None of this will be so very strange by tomorrow."

"You're right. This kind of thing is *not* what's strange."

"Soon we must talk more." And that's when Oren had begun to lie. "I was rather like Matt once."

"Honestly? I'm surprised."

It was a terrible lie, but there was nothing to do now but compound it. "Yes! Born again several times over. I got through it, Susan." He paused and then added: "So will your boy," which was really all he'd meant to say.

The police station was about empty by the time Oren entered to look for Matt and confront Eddy, who had not bothered waiting to see him after all. Oren was relieved enough to feel a little faint.

He found Matt sitting on a bench, reading a magazine. It was a *Watch Tower* publication, and the sight of such literature always made Oren testy. "Who on earth gave you that?" he said.

The boy threw the magazine on the bench. Apparently that was where he'd found it. He turned to give Oren the surprisingly steady gaze of someone for whom it doesn't really matter who comes to the rescue. That was Oren's very first impression of him. An encounter at last summer's cookout hadn't made much of a mark. He and all the Everett Street children had, by now, begun to ignore each other as the young and old do when parents stop intervening.

"Listen to me, Matt. Your mother thinks you were picked up on some vagrancy charge. Do you know what that is?"

"Loitering, you mean."

"Whichever you prefer."

"There's a distinction."

"You like quibbling, son? You just about got yourself thrown in the slammer!"

Yes, he remembered then; at the last cookout, the boy had sat apart from everyone, too handsome to appear sullen. Both the Robb children were blue-eyed, gorgeous children, but Oren did not recall this purely Tibetan gaze from the boy. Very effective, very effective. He would try to ignore it.

"I think you and I should keep to a story of loitering," Oren said.

He could see the boy's Adam's apple move in his throat, big as a yo-yo. But he showed no boyish hint of fear, no normal relief that his mother hadn't been told.

"We'll say that you hitched a ride and that when you got here you lost your wallet."

The boy closed his eyes in a kind of weariness of spirit, or as if none of this would ever be his idea of a solution. When he raised no objection, Oren pressed on. "The problem began when a store manager mistook you for some kid who's been shoplifting. It was all a misunderstanding, except for the fact that you had no business being without money and no way to get home. Got that? The cops were trying to teach you a lesson. No one really gets arrested for loitering."

Matt kept his eyes closed. "But they do."

"From what I can tell," Oren continued, "a few parents have been promised something. No arrests, no newspaper reports. And as for your mother finding out, Eddy Jensen owes me one."

For the first time in the exchange, Matt seemed interested; or was it that finally Oren had said something that had nothing to do with him? Then the two of them almost laughed, as they might over some casual remark about it all coming down to Eddy owing. One couldn't help liking a kid interested in what was both larger and smaller than his own predicament. "What does he owe you?" the boy said.

"I looked the other way one time," Oren found himself confessing. The boy nodded. "I've done that."

It was hard to read anything there that wasn't likable in some fashion. Maybe it was the nicely competing flashes in him that made him likable—first high-flown and then friendly and down to earth like his parents. Religious or not, he seemed to have comic insight.

"I know you don't get out much," the boy said. He was smiling. "This was good of you, coming out with my mother like this."

It was perhaps the first time Oren had ever come close to wondering what it would be like to have a straightforward son like this;

one could be so candid with him. "What do you make of me not getting out?" he asked, his spontaneous desire to know surprising him and then making him feel a great wave of self-doubt. He really did need counsel, it would seem, and this was hardly the proper way to go about it.

The boy was hesitating. "Make of your not getting out?"

"Never mind," Oren murmured.

"Is it just that you could have more of the world?"

"Yes," Oren said. "Yes, exactly."

He was relieved to see the boy close his eyes, put his head back again, as if tired or else pretending to be tired so as to help Oren out of the spotlight. He was not a boy to press his advantage or pretend to be wiser than his years or butt in.

Once inside the car and seated beside Susan Robb again, Oren felt confused about his loyalties now. Suddenly he was immensely uninterested in sons; they could all go straight to hell. His mind buzzed. It began to hit him that he'd stupidly set up a secret between himself and the son when he should have set it up between himself and the mother. For God's sakes, he'd gotten it completely backward!

Later that night—perhaps as late as midnight, the hour of schemes and their finer tunings—he came outside to smoke a rare cigar. How can I shift the emphasis? he mused. First he would tell her the truth, that her son had had a rather innocent encounter with a prostitute. In the act of telling her, he'd also advise her on some small point or other, something very small. He might merely suggest, for example, that she let Matt tell Malcolm the incident in his own way and in his own time. It would be the most innocent of advice giving. If she took it, if she didn't rush to tell Malcolm about her night ride to Danford, then there'd be the most harmless of secrets between them. Maybe only briefly there. But that's intimacy enough, not inappropriate for such a woman. Make it neighborly enough, and no one pays it the least attention.

*　*　*

Neighborliness had always been his father's métier—a contemptible trait to Oren, recalling Hutch-like acts of kindness toward people from whom he was also stealing. He was an estate lawyer. He simply dipped. Oren was twelve when he was first told, and he knew absolutely it was true. The news that reached him early on concerned his father's purchase of a car for a wealthy widow. Hutch went out and bought a two-year-old Cadillac for Mrs. Stapleton as a thank-you for her trust in him and all of her referrals. Oren learned of it through a playground bully's half-hearted taunt. "My dad says your dad had that gift car paid for seven times over. He's a slick crook, is what my dad says."

In an unguarded moment Oren had shared with his young wife that playground scene—then the growing taunts at almost every social event he could remember attending after that. Had Hutchenson ever confirmed this? Mary asked him. It had seemed an almost ridiculous question to Oren, betraying his bride's average intelligence. What father confirms anything? What cowed son ever asks? Oren had witnessed only one thing in the end—Hutch's suicide. And this he never shared with anyone. It was never publicly announced. Eddy Jensen's father, county coroner, had been paid off ahead of time; he wrote the death certificate in Oren's presence—cause, heart attack. It had meant nothing more out of the ordinary than a closed-coffin funeral with the town attending and everyone glad to keep the clean slate when it came to men of rank avoiding indictment.

But his wife's intelligence was not truly at issue. Mary Tanner had been an inexperienced young woman with a trust fund; her people were landed but of the farming class. Oren had wooed and married her years after Hutch got away with it all. Miss Tanner's trustee, one of the good old boys back in 1959, had presented Oren as a proper match to the Tanner family, which at that point consisted of Mary's childless aunt and uncle.

Mary Tanner, pale and sweet. Not a girl who could grasp what men like his father had expected of Oren—that he be a step ahead of others at all times. People were fair game. "It never once occurred to my father than I might be horrified, even paralyzed, by his deceptions."

"But surely you're not going just on what you heard as a child from other children?"

"No, Mary. There's my mother, who in her own way ruined me too with her views of heaven and hell."

Mary died young in a car accident; Oren's mother lived forever. She'd turned away to her letters and tracts in the forties, however, thereby abandoning Oren in some essential way he'd had to spend time thinking about. Luckily he'd been smart as a child. He'd known it was all a little too simple—Hutch ensconced in one part of the house and dear Florence in another.

As he told these things to Mary, Oren had seen fear in her eyes. She had a grasp of basic psychology and must have realized—too late to turn back—that she'd married a man with even less experience than herself. Oren was virginal, reticent, passionate to the point of mortification. He'd had one primal scene in his life. It consisted of the time he'd found Hutch dead of a shotgun blast. In the week of their honeymoon he'd told Mary too much; the pair was in a state of shock anyway, never mind his account of Hutch's frauds and then his very head blown off in the middle of the night. His father had left a note. "Oren, do one thing right. Call Lewis Jensen. He's been paid to fix this."

He'd done several things right—kept his mother out of the room, put a pillowcase over the head, called Lewis Jensen. In the note his father said, "I never could have counted on you as things went on," as if it were somehow Oren's fault. When an investigation was in the wind, Hutchenson implied, he had understandably given up the fight—no one to fight for; Oren quite hopeless.

Take this silly thing with Susan Robb. It's half a century later, and at the oddest times Oren can hear the old man start to laugh. "Ha! typical. You can't engineer an affair with a middle-aged schoolteacher? You going to let the son do it for you?" Because, sure enough, it is Matt who crosses Oren's path the next morning and attempts to compound the secrets that, in the night, Oren schemed to start up with the mother.

"Matt!" Oren said, smiling, stepping out onto his front porch the next morning. He looked at his watch. It was barely seven. Still, he liked the boy; liked the open, honest face. Her face, in fact.

"It's my mother's style to send me over like this to thank you, so I've preempted her." Matt even looked a bit embarrassed at having chosen words slightly beyond his means. "Not that I don't want to thank you," he added, pulling out a white envelope that Oren took to be a fee payment. "I've been to the cash machine in town this morning."

Oren snapped, "Put that away! I was doing what anyone would do!"

The young man seemed to wait for his elder to calm down. "This is for the girl," he finally said. He stood waiting for Oren to remember that there *was* a girl. "She needs help."

"Help? I can't get this to her! I refuse."

"I promise I won't have anything more to do with her," Matt was saying next, but only by way of timing his exit to coincide with his mother backing the car out into the street. The very sight of her threw Oren's heart into his mouth. The boy was calling over his shoulder, explaining that his mother was taking him out for some breakfast. Did Oren want to come along?

"Wait," Oren called after the boy, "I take it you're not confiding in her?" He was having second thoughts himself about confiding in her. In apparent good spirits, she was tapping her horn and waving at him as her son came running. The energy of her made him start to buzz. A few moments from last night, a few parts of his religious conversion, began converting him all over again. He must have this, something of this. He didn't quite know if it was sex or family or the idea of taking one's child out for breakfast. It was all there in her substantial arm waving at him. Talk about intimacy. Perhaps there is always intimacy in a mother's look of gratitude, enough in this case to give Oren a terrific jolt.

He stood some moments on his porch after the car pulled off. Then the telephone began ringing inside his house, and, despite his discombobulation, he knew exactly who it was going to be. Eddy Jensen was just enough politically tied to Wyman through their own sheriff Randall and just enough tied to the past to make this follow-up call, fishing for thanks. It surprised Oren that Eddy thought him part of the circle. For a second he felt flattered until he remembered how much he hated the circles he'd been cut out of—or been spared through what he had told his wife was a merely a love of solitude. He didn't know which now.

"It was good of you, Eddy," he said, hearing his own father. "I won't forget," he added, feeling almost wonderful, almost in the swing of it for a moment. That Eddy was a swine didn't matter; it was part of the kick, he realized, talking to swine. "Right now, I happen to need more information about the girl." He felt a little tough, a little bit lawyerlike and hardnosed.

"You've seen her kind before," Eddy muttered, "believe me."

Oren felt flattered yet again. "She seems to have made an impression on Matt Robb," he said, taking a peek inside the envelope. He counted five hundred dollars. The amount surprised him. "Any chance my meeting her, Eddy? The parents are worried about disease."

"Cry-mo-knee!" Eddy said, irritated at parents generally. He had several Danford sets of parents on his case, too, as if their idiot sons hadn't broken the law.

Meanwhile, the amount in Matt's envelope was giving Oren ideas. At the point of saying to Susan that, conscience-stricken, he felt it best to tell her that Matt, regrettably, had had a little brush with a prostitute, he would do two things. First he would return this money (such nice proof of the incident, not to mention her child's sense of responsibility, which all mothers love), and then he would provide some passing information on the girl, the briefer the better. He would have her be a girl with a family willing to take her back; he would have it that Matt, in his need, had stumbled on an almost nice girl; he would have it turn out terribly sweet.

In and around everything else he was feeling this morning—his voice, his posture, his ability to maneuver in the world of good old boys—he felt himself on the brink of love. At his age, if it resulted in a simple friendship, it would be a minor miracle. That's all it is, he thought. I've had no friends, no joy of that kind.

"Is the girl on her own, Eddy?"

"Who, Angela?" Eddy laughed. "Until that boyfriend gets out in a few days, dear oh dear, I guess she *is*, poor thang."

"How can that be if she's underage? I wanted to report to the Robbs some kind of family here."

"Family?"

Oren started over. "Eddy, I need something firsthand about the girl. That's all I'm asking."

Eddy heard a pun and laughed again. "Oh, I can get you something firsthand," he said, and then, to cover his crudity, he went on to give Oren the address of a flophouse in Danford. Eddy didn't like to think of himself as completely without the kind of rank Oren got by birth—undeserved and unearned. In cooperating, Eddy saw an opportunity to get a little high-handed. "You know, Oren, I've heard you've been a peculiar recluse all these years, but I didn't know how true it was. You mind me giving you some advice?"

"I do mind," Oren said, reddening at Eddy's old ways, his old worm's wriggle under a person's flesh. "I do mind very much."

"It's my sincere hope," Eddy went on, "that this girl stays on her own until the wolf gets her. Beats the tar out of me why people think girls like her need my tax money to give her a home when her own people have had the good sense to kick her out. I have a cousin, the best thing he did with one of his own kids was to kick him out."

Oren was sorry to be down this road, Eddy Jensen lecturing to him over the phone. The man was off and running and very grateful for the chance. "Let me tell you something, Oren. We got more pieces of shit like her down here than we can scrape off our boots. I don't expect my taxes to house and feed shit that's going to be there for me to step in tomorrow. You? You go right ahead."

Oren became cheerfully loud. "Eddy! Sorry we didn't get to meet up last night!" It was how his father used to deal with men who got out of line. "Meanwhile, thanks so much for your help! I won't forget it, I really won't!"

"Okay, you bet," Eddy said, backing off, taking his cue. "Be seeing you, Oren. You take care now." But the man just couldn't stop himself from adding, "Remember when they were just called Trouble? These days, unlike yourself, I've just taken to calling them more what they are. Unlike yourself. You be careful where you put your foot down, you hear?"

So it was hard not to be a little bit in Angela's corner—this piece of muck on Eddy's boot.

At first Oren was sure she had a shaved head, but he was proved wrong. It was a boy cut of fuzzy-looking bleached straw and black-black roots, the color of dominoes. By contrast, everything else about her was a grab bag of cheap scarves that she seemed to have stitched together herself. She was in costume for some romp across a stage in a child's dance recital.

She could use a friend right now, she told Oren, and then immediately excused herself. He stood in the dirty hall and watched her fly into her cupboard of a bathroom and slam the door. Oren couldn't help overhearing.

"Are you ill?" he said when she emerged. Her face had paled, causing her makeup to age her into a floozy.

"I've got an ulcer in my gut," she explained. Weakly she motioned him inside. "I'm supposed to be under a doctor's care," she said, falling comically to her knees and then throwing her small frame onto her futon. "Who are you, anyway?" she moaned. "Somebody gave you the wrong idea if you think I'm for hire."

The outfit was layers and layers of her own ragged invention. A big wind would kite her from one block to the next. But he could see that she had a lot of angry strength, even if she was at the moment weak as a kitten.

"I'm not here for anything," he said.

She sighed. "I never know who's going to walk in—the cops, the law, maybe just one of Cooper's old friends stopping by. Cooper deals."

Under all the scarves, she wore a mottled bodysuit of some kind, revealing an undeveloped chest, like the raised section of an inverted picnic plate. She rested herself on one elbow while he explained who he was and that he was here to give her a little money if she'd promise to stay away from a certain friend of his. "One of those boys from last night is a friend of the family." He added, "from right here in Danford," to keep things simple. He addressed her kindly and offered her a hundred dollars. "You're to stay away from Jimmy. Is that real clear?"

She was kindly too. "You want to know the truth? I couldn't pick a single kid out in a lineup. My whole gig is like being blindfold on Halloween." She looked at the crisp twenty-dollar bills he'd handed her. "You want this back?"

"You keep it," he said. He would return Susan the full five hundred and let this smaller amount be his own affair—something that he might or might not allude to later in a neighbor's offhand way. Susan wasn't to think of paying him back; he'd let her buy him lunch sometime.

In his mind they were already at lunch, glasses tinkling, and him trying to describe this Angela's burgeoning sense of fashion; how her ears were so radically pierced it was as if someone had used a staple gun.

"They told me you were sixteen," he said. "You're a bit older than that, aren't you?" (A hoop for every year?)

"Take a guess," Angela said, raising herself on one elbow.

"Quite legal," he ventured. He thought about this. "Absolutely legal."

"Very good! But see, that's not what it says on my birth certificate." She got up in a flounce. Fluff and feathers followed in her trail. Soon she was retrieving a birth certificate from her purse and pointing out a date. "According to that I'm awful young, right?"

"So you're what? Twenty?" he said.

She grinned. "Next month."

He looked over the document before handing it back to her, a bit chagrined that he could no longer tell phony from real himself. "If they fell for this, how is it that you got sent back here and not to a facility for minors?"

"Good question." She sighed, world-weary. "Lucky I have this legacy, right? All mine for a few days. If I was smart I'd get the hell out of here while he's in lockup." She looked around at the bare, dark room, equipped with a futon and hotplate. "Hey, it's home."

In addition to a table and two chairs, there was a set of pasteboard boxes stacked in one corner with her name printed clearly on them as if this was all she owned in her own right. It may have been those boxes with their bits of bright cloth poking up at the top that inspired him. Why be the bad messenger? he was thinking; why tell on poor Matt when Susan would enjoy it so much more if he just told on himself, coming here like this, her night ride having gotten him so confused that he'd had to find an Angela to keep from making a pass at *her*. Already he could hear her laugh softly, sympathetic, and say how surely any number of available women would find him attractive.

That was the far better start—to tell on himself instead of her son. He'd return the gift money directly to Matt, and not to the bewildered mother. If the boy wanted to help Angela in some way, well, he needn't worry. Oren himself was on the case, and the boy was to redeposit his funds before his parents found out, for heaven's sake.

He wouldn't mind explaining to Susan that he only wanted back into the picture of life, so to speak—fully engaged, hopeful. He knew already that it was going to be impossible to commit an interesting sin with Angela just to get a story going. He felt not one weak stirring of desire. Angela was in the bathroom again. While he waited, he checked to see if there was any way to make them both a cup of broth or tea. I haven't been a person, he was thinking. I don't deserve Susan Robb, or anyone else.

Angela had a sewing machine, he would begin with Susan over lunch or over coffee out on his front porch in full view of Malcolm. The sewing machine was quite real. There it was—a pink portable on the floor between the pasteboard boxes. Angela was not a smoker, he would continue, describing the way she nevertheless *acted* like a smoker, someone about to light up—energetic, full of anticipation, full of hope herself. Among the lowest of the low, there's hope—as ordinary and elusive as that of the highest of the high perhaps—those sleek models in *Vogue* the girl clearly admired, for there on the floor was her stack of magazines. Tell me your hopes and dreams, my dear, he decided to begin with the girl herself, just to see where the story might lead before he gave up and got himself on out of there.

The story would be too predictable. There was nothing in the cupboard but packets of duck sauce and a lone tea bag with red Oriental calligraphy on its tag. Angela had been eating from cartons her whole life. He felt profoundly depressed until it hit him that he really could take her to a restaurant! Good God, she was probably anemic. Or, if he couldn't stand the thought of the two of them in public, at the very least he could telephone a supermarket and order a delivery of canned goods—some soup or cola she could keep down. Should he get her to a doctor? He felt moved by this idea and how easy it would be to do a few simple things—at the moment nothing more difficult than making tea and seeing what else was needed. If a woman such as Susan were here? Wouldn't she just wash out a couple of mugs to drink from?

He discovered that one of the mugs read "Boss." This would be

Cooper. Oren was getting a clear picture of the guy—a man jerking around by the chain a much less experienced young woman. Girl? She did seem young. Or had started out young, so disentanglement might not be so easy. Some start out captive and end up willing partners.

Over the tea he learned a lot. His not being a social worker seemed to open her up. She'd been on her own for ages, she confided to him with a little pride—some prostitution, most merely waitressing. Right now she was in a slump. Her car gig was her lowest. And that was the phrase she used—her lowest.

"Tell me about the car gig," Oren said, looking about him and finally picking the larger of the two chairs and pulling it around in front of the futon. Susan wouldn't have to know that Angela's car was anything *Matt* knew about. The car could just turn out to be Oren's—a car with curtains Angela made herself. Susan would love those curtains; *he* loved them.

"For starters," Angela said, "I wear a wig."

"Do you really!" he said, feeling something close to a stab of pain hitting him in his arms and legs. His tea leapt on its own, as if a small fish was inside the mug. "A wig! Is that because boys don't like your short hair?" He wasn't quite sure what fish had jumped. Whatever it was, it was gone.

"What do I care what they like? No, I just don't want them spotting me on the street in broad daylight. I also wear sunglasses, a big granny dress. None of my usual." She was holding out her arms to suggest these scarves were her own creation in case he didn't realize it. "Ta-da!"

"I see," Oren said. "That's very smart, Angela." She was young. He saw that now. Sixteen. Maybe younger? Lord.

"You like it?"

He had been referring to her cleverness in wearing a wig and sunglasses, but he wasn't going to withhold the small compliment she took it for. "Yes, I think you look quite fetching." He raised his tea mug in salute. "I had no idea young women still sew."

"I do it all by eye," she boasted. "I'm what's called a natural. I don't need a pattern."

"Remarkable." He thought about the well-meaning person who must have told her this—a caseworker perhaps.

As for his having a dalliance, a story with which to amuse Susan, with which to make himself vulnerable—well, he was going to have to make it all up, the pathetic encounter he'd had as a substitute for the real thing, for Susan. Angela (he'd put her much older), Angela, he would begin, was what they used to call the Baptist backslide. Susan would smile, disarmed, or at least polite, and in one smile of sympathy at the harmless comedy of his situation the two would move toward friendship; finally he'd have taken a risk. Vulnerability and risk were watchwords of mental health these days. He hadn't viewed a hundred thousand hours of daytime TV for nothing, some of it soap opera in which of late various young to mature women had amazing insights into older men.

After all their catching up, Susan just might reach over and take his hand one day, both of them getting up and heading into his house, in full view of innocent Malcolm out there waving and dragging a brown Christmas tree to the curb. If not this year's tree, then next year's. He would take it quite slowly.

"My hopes and dreams?" Angela was saying. "Isn't that what I'm supposed to be asking you?"

"No, listen," Oren said. He felt a wave of protectiveness toward the girl, whatever her real age. He made himself grasp both her hands with their short purple nails. "I'm happy to give you more money because it looks like you need it, but I have nothing else in mind for today. Drink your tea, and later we'll get something to eat. Meanwhile, you can tell me about yourself. I'd enjoy that. Your story, as it were. We all have one."

Once she'd almost attended a cosmetology school. Cosmetology school was a dream, she guessed. Did that count?

She was cute, the way she mused that maybe it ran in her family. Rayleen had claimed she'd been a beautician briefly. Rayleen was her crazy mother. She was always bragging to her boyfriends about her kids, especially about Angela and Corey, and Angela knew how that sounded. You wanted to kill Rayleen. She was so full of it—how some day soon she'd be coming to get you from this or that miserable place.

Angela didn't need coming to get. One day there was Desiree. Desiree and her girlfriend Trudy, two smart runaways who'd had their own place and only wanted one other girl roommate to pitch in fifty dollars rent money and keep a low profile. They all met at a laundromat at about the time Angela realized she was old enough to be on her own. Angela loved doing all the voices in her little story.

" 'You look mature,' Desiree said to me. 'You could pass.' "

"Pass?" Oren said. "For what?"

"Desiree didn't want anyone looking underage. We could all get busted and sent back."

"I see."

"Anywho—" It was the first of many *anywho*'s—her beautician's voice, for which she was a natural from the soaps; a bit part. "Anywho, Trudy talked a lot about a boy named Bert, so when I moved in I took Bert as my last name. Trudy thought it was this amazing coincidence. Trudy wasn't too bright, but oh God, Desiree loved that big dumb girl. Nobody ever loved me like that." She paused and turned her long-nosed, heart-shaped face right to him. "How about you? Anybody ever love you?"

"No. Not a terribly whole lot, no."

"Too bad for us, right?"

She'd had the name Angela in mind for a long time. Rayleen congratulated her when she finally caught up with her. " 'Angela's a nice enough name. And this is a nice place you girls have here. I should have brought you a plant.' " Angela's eyes watered, just to be thinking of her mother. "Even Trudy could see she was mean-streaked as hell."

In the lively telling, Oren found himself seeing the whole thing— Desiree pulling Angela out of the house to have a little chat; Desiree getting hopping mad, snatching at her arm and hissing about how that Rayleen in there was going to bring the cops down on them, anyone could see that. Desiree would be glad to kill her if it came to it.

Back inside, Desiree had let the woman sit there stoned on the couch for an hour. " 'Angela,' " Rayleen had repeated. She didn't think much of the name after an hour, and Desiree not offering even a beer and looking so butch. "Angela" was a common alias, Rayleen observed. It was like the Smith of whores.

"Your own mother said that?"

It got back to them in two weeks that she was laid out and just where Angela could show up for the funeral service. They didn't have a phone. Trudy found a note under the door one morning and got scared. Trudy said it was bad luck to have Rayleen taken by the devil after having words with her in Desiree's own house.

" 'Bullshit,' Desiree said."

That one time, stoned on their couch, Rayleen had looked at Trudy and sort of blocked everyone else out. " 'Don't forget I have Corey. She's my little girl. Angela's bright, but Corey is a child prodigy, and Angela here thinks she's going to get rich and buy a trailer and steal Corey from the system. Angela thinks she's a lot better than me.'

"You know what I told her, Oren? I told her I was. I told her I was a whole lot better than her."

"Good for you," Oren said.

Maybe. Angela wasn't sure. Trudy said it was very bad luck, words like that with your own mother.

"So you said some pretty direct things," Oren offered.

"Direct? You could say that. I've got a mouth. Anyway, Desiree might have needed my fifty bucks, but she didn't need me messing up their life. She wanted me out of there since I spooked Trudy. Trudy had an altar in the house. I never figured out what Trudy was into in the spirit world."

"What did you do next?"

"Nothing. Cooper was next—Rayleen's boyfriend, wanting to

take me under his wing. It's how I have this ulcer, from being under his stupid wing."

And then the girl cried—openly, inconsolably, her face collapsing, her nose flattening—but not for herself, it turned out. It was over her half-sister, Corey, who was five, who would hate Angela's guts all her life.

"Now," Oren admonished, "what a way to talk."

She'd told Corey more lies than shells on a beach. Hard-sand lies, though—hard enough so you could dig down to keep from getting dragged into the ocean. A trailer park and other stuff. She'd planned to make them happen. Stupid Rayleen was the opposite. She never had enough fight to keep from getting dragged in, blub, blub. Cooper had listened to Angela express this idea at the funeral and then used one of his fancy words. " 'You mean not enough *purchase!* Your mama sure did lack purchase.' " He was whispering because the body was no more than ten feet away. When you sat down you could only see the tip of Rayleen's nose sticking up. " 'You're lucky to have purchase. Let me tell you, it's a real mystery who's got it and who doesn't.' "

"There's some truth there," Oren said. "But don't cry." He moved the chair a bit closer, his stiff frame barely allowing him to lean over and pull up her chin. "You miss your mother?"

"No!" Angela said. She sat up straight and smiled with such an open and unexpected expression of goodwill toward him that he was truly taken aback. From time to time, she could seem as wholesome as a glass of fresh milk. She needed help. Why had no one helped this girl out of this?

Anywho, she said, old Cooper could talk like that; it didn't matter if he was high, low, or crazy. He was educated—the first person like that she'd met. At least he'd been able to grasp that she had this plan to better herself. She had written "purchase" down in a book of blank pages Cooper said could be like a diary without the dates. " 'Keep it for notes. I know girls like you. You write everything on the backs of your hands!' He meant me and Rayleen. He said he'd never met people so smart and so ignorant at the same time as us, as me and Rayleen."

So she kept a vocabulary section in the book and memorized his big words. "Want to see it?" she said to Oren, pulling it out from under the mattress.

"How long have you been with this—?" Oren stopped. Cooper might well be a man with protective qualities of the superficial kind. Junkie or not, he was bound to fill in as just about everything—mother, father, brother, and boss. Oren looked around. This was a pigsty like his own place, just small.

"You want to see it or not?" she was asking.

Soporific, Oren read from her book. *Ebullient. Arboreal. Strabismal.* "Strabismal?"

"Cross-eyed. See? I got this one eye that crosses when I'm tired." She widened her eyes at him. "Can you see it?"

"It's easily fixed," Oren said. "You need glasses."

"I know that," she said, a little defensively. "We're going to get around to it." She opened her mouth. "See that?" she said, pointing to a filling. "A good dentist did that. Coop's not cheap. And he's not stupid. He could teach in a college if he wanted."

"Indeed," Oren said. *Stamina. Fulcrum. Buttress.* "You have all this memorized? There must be several hundred words here."

She was going to do her high school equivalency one of these raining days. But in fact she was worried about her memory on tests. She had no memory. She had one single one of her childhood, and it was of Rayleen having a little bit of purchase. Did Oren want to know what it was?

"Of course," Oren said.

Okay, they are both inside a church without air-conditioning, her and Rayleen. She has her head in Rayleen's lap and is letting herself get fanned. She's maybe eight. There's a rush of cool air, and then the short wait for it again, as if someone's blowing on you lightly and you're just like these other people; you too live in a trailer roasting a chicken while you're at church.

"That's all the purchase you require?" Oren asked. "A trailer?" That was the fish jumping. Oren would buy it himself; Susan, wearing one of those new green T-shirts of hers, would help him pick it out!

After church Angela even sensed those people were trying to help Rayleen. Her best time was the time they went to that trailer after the sermon and there was a family gathered around food in baking dishes.

Cooper had laughed and laughed after hearing that memory. He said he'd been aware there really were people like her and Rayleen, but he'd had to get low down to meet them. Kid Row, he called her and Rayleen. " 'There are fifth graders out there who know more than your mother knew. But hell, you take me, I come from the upper class, and in my own way I can't be helped either.' "

"Upper class?" Oren said, feeling doubtful now. "You don't mean from around here?"

"California. He has a check every month on condition he stays away from them. They hate him. Didn't take me long to see why. But hey."

Hard drugs, pills, weed, and alcohol. That was Cooper. Every day, every week. Lately he'd been going through his money by the middle of each month. That's why they were doing the car gig. Flat out of money. "A whole trust fund, and it all goes in his arm or up his snout. Look at this place."

For a few days he'd go straight. Those weren't always good; or else maybe they would be. He was recently starting to be real paranoid and jealous, realizing that she could be with someone while he's unconscious. But sometimes he still seemed to take an interest and say how he needed to be checking her homework. "Ionized. Cooper wanted me to think of magnets as big as the two World Trade Centers. Addicts like Rayleen and him get within the field. They're metal filings no bigger than eyelashes."

There's a visibility to young intelligence sometimes. Like a flash of gold tooth. One part of Oren thought how easy, even stimulating, it would be to help her. The other part of him was thinking how well a good deed can sit with a woman like Susan. He would let Susan in on the whole project. Who can resist old fuddy-duddies nursing stray cats at the last minute? Such men go straight to heaven!

"Everybody has *some* purchase, right, Oren? Even Rayleen. She traded it in for smack, may she burn in hell."

"Now, now," Oren said.

There was one good thing she had managed, she boasted. She'd managed to keep Cooper a secret from the Sulloways, the foster parents to Corey. They didn't mind Angela coming around to see Corey. Corey was better behaved as a result. But they all took care; a social worker couldn't know about Angela coming to see the two kids, given the fact that Angela herself was still on the books, her whereabout unknown or not sought after at this point.

"Two kids?" Oren asked.

"Yeah. There's Ricky. I never said Rayleen was bright. Anyway, I figured as long as they never saw me with a man, they'd keep letting me come."

"So, you want to be the boss some day," Oren boasted on her behalf. He meant it sincerely. "Your own certified digs! That's very ambitious."

This provoked a flash of fire in the girl's eyes, as if to let him know he was suddenly out of line. "I'm used to guys making fun of me," she said, turning and retreating among the boxes, silent. Oren wasn't sure if he should turn in his chair and look at her over his shoulder.

Finally he decided not to. "I wasn't making fun," he called.

But she was pouting. How amazing! How amusing, in fact, to be sitting here in a ratty chair waiting for this Angela to get over a little huff, their first quarrel.

Funny, yes, but at the same time sad. When he craned around he could see the large personalized "Angela" boxes and only the girl's legs extending across the floor, the rest of her hidden, just one foot moving back and forth as when a cat twitches its tail. He decided she was worth the wait while she made up her mind about him.

He called out, "You need a friend right now, remember?" He kept his back to her and stared out the one dirty window above the futon. Soon he thought he heard her begin to scratch about, but his hearing was not acute these days; he didn't really know what she was up to. It sounded as if she might first be changing her clothes and then rattling around at the sink.

In another few moments she was back on his side of the room, coming around to the front of his chair and handing him her mug of tea with one hand while she reached for something she'd draped around her neck. "Here," she said in a new bouncy tone, "put these on. I want to see what you look like in these."

Oren found himself not quite free to pull back from her. He attempted to steady the brimming mug she'd thrust into his right hand. And quicker than he could think possible, she was working a black stocking over his left hand and snaking it up to his elbow. "Wait a minute," he was saying.

"See, I like the way men's hairs swirl under nylon." She was smoothing out the transparence. "See?" she was saying, "your arm looks tattooed. Wait," as he immediately got to his feet. "Wait!" She rushed to her stack of boxes, several of them tumbling in the distant corner as Oren dropped his gaze, looked at his arm, and felt a pre-electrical moment raising all the hairs on his head. Then it was more as if an actual lightning bolt cleft him in two like an old tree. "What's this now?" he was saying, but he did not look at his arm again or dare move as she came running back to him.

"We'll protect your nice suit with this," she said. A large silky tent dress came sailing over him, languid and loose like a slow-motion mushroom or parachute descending. When it landed over his eyes, Angela turned into a negative of herself, her vague outline leaning in. "Can you see me?" she laughed until he emerged out the top and she began removing the trembling mug from his grip, grabbing at his hands, shaking her head in pity at the shabby condition of his nails. "Later, I'll do these for you."

"I'm not into this sort of thing," he managed to gasp next, his eyes clamped, his clearer mind hearing her feet rushing away again.

"Not into what sort of thing?" she called. Then she scolded away, scolding him, scolding the boxes, muttering as she went through them. "Oh God, it's just because men your age are so straight. Into what? I'm a cosmetologist, I told you! I'm just going to give you a free treatment!"

He couldn't move. Two fingers moved, but only to feel the silky fabric where it hung. He opened his eyes and kept looking straight out, not wanting to look down for fear he would see his toes at the edge of a ledge and a drop of some several miles into a canyon.

"I don't want a treatment," he said hoarsely.

She was back, chattering away. "Would you believe a cosmetologist's set and a sewing machine are the only nice things Cooper's ever bought me? He did it to shut me up. I love fixing friends, that's all. Since I was little and lived in this place with twenty-five people. I've been doing it since I don't know how long. I play with stuff. Here, try this. This is something Cooper likes me to do to relax him."

All this time she was easing him back into the ratty chair and pushing his hair out of his eyes with a black velveteen headband. "Didn't you ever have a woman tweeze you? Coop loves to have me tweeze him. I call him Tweezer. Men don't get enough pampering. How do men unwind? Later you can let me shave you. That's real relaxing, when a guy gets a shave, right?"

The full treatment, she was calling it, positioning his head, getting a warm cloth to soften his face. She had tapped into an energy all her own. Released now, she was slamming her cosmetologist's kit firmly into the only other chair in the room, dragging it noisily over to him. She couldn't wait to get started, an artist at her canvas, she mused. "That's what Cooper says. It's his only compliment, ever. I really hate Coop, you know. I don't want you to think I'm going to waste my time with him for too long. God."

He was seated there with his back to the large stuffed boxes of fabric, and now he knew what was in them—his childhood in her thrift-store gleanings—the silk to protect a suit, something she'd brought to cut up later for a costume; the jerseys to go over the silks, suedes and boas to go over jerseys, maybe an old fox whose remembered beady eyes were still there in some half-vengeful bite or smile on the top shelf of his mother's cedar closet. A length or two of ribbon; a pair of soft kid gloves; the accessories he and his cousin Jerome would put on cautiously lest a bracelet drop to the wood floor and all the company below look up, a stern mother squinting at the ceiling and deciding that it was surely not Oren and Jerome up there handling things no one ever thought to forbid them. Jerome had killed himself at nineteen.

"You have to get used to this," Angela was explaining, her steady breathing close to his face. He closed his eyes, as if he sat in a dental chair, relinquishing himself to capable hands without the least difficulty; floated at the thought of that boxed fabric—the wholly slippery shape and surface of it. He allowed himself no thought of how he would interpret this later. He had enough basic information to know this had nothing to do with being homosexual, contrary to the common belief of members of his generation and class. He had a clothes fetish, pure and simple. Well, not simple. He'd read up on it. An old stocking snaking up one's arm, a silk dress, a piece of velveteen can be as much about fabric and one's mother as about much else. The only illness comes as a result of a ban on the wife indulging the husband. The image of his wife, or else someone paid not to run in horror from the room upon being asked. . . . Lord, for Oren the thought had always seemed far, far worse than going without.

But here he sat, smelling cedar and wondering how in all this time a satin-lined hat with a pearlized pin may have been waiting and keeping watch above his head. Its steadfastness reminded him of the patience of the lesser saints; they ask of the penitent so very little—a crumb, a crust, a smile of passing recognition.

Susan, he was suddenly thinking. That's what this was about. It was *she* he could tell—could, as it were, tell on himself. Just about this! His brain, independent of his practicality, had been trying to send him this message now for the last twelve hours. She would have heard of the cross-dressing phenomenon—rare in Wyman, perhaps, but not dangerous. Men liking the full treatment once in a while. Men in dresses. Susan was a baby boomer. She wouldn't go running from the room!

Suddenly the idea of her taking the news in a kind way struck Oren as something almost sacred—a mature woman not just kind, but interested, engaged, and confident enough to reach out and add her own knowledge to his. Conversation! Hell, it could all start and end with that. Just get me started talking, he'd finally plead. It's all that I need, and quite enough to ask of you.

In grief and pity for himself, Oren started to laugh.

"You okay under there?" Angela said, lifting the steaming towel.

Oren smiled. "Fine, my dear, just fine."

"Well," Angela said, disappearing from view again, "don't get too comfortable. You said you were going to buy me dinner."

"Ah yes, a nice dinner," Oren said. "Are you hungry then?"

"I'm starving!" Angela said. "Aren't you starving all of a sudden?"

Oren thought long about this. Finally he said, "Angela, I think I'm famished. I think I'm truly famished."

4

DEMONSTRATED BAITING

MALCOLM, ROUNDING A CORNER, HAPPENED TO HEAR SUSAN say to Gretchen in the kitchen, "So we're agreed? We won't tell Daddy at the moment, okay?"

"Mom, I bet I know what it is," Gretchen said. "I bet Matt's joined some sort of group."

"Group!" Malcolm said, striding in and causing the two women to jump in fright. He was scared too. "What group?"

Gretchen hesitated. "Well, there's the Campus Crusade, and there's—"

"Holy cow, the Campus Crusade? You mean for Christ?"

"Malcolm—"

"Susan, they're the ones getting kids to drop out of college and go serve!"

"He's not in college, Malcolm."

"Hey, so much the better for them!"

"Where, Dad? Where do kids serve when they drop out?"

"Russia is fashionable! Any place they know nothing about!"

"Just don't be baiting him, Malcolm, until we know more."

"Mom, is baiting like when you—?"

"I never bait him, Susan! What are you talking about?"

"You did it just yesterday, Mac."

"He did? Cool. So is it like—"

"You can't hear how you sound, honey."

"How I *sound?*"

"Is baiting when—?"

"You expect too much, that's all I mean. Calm down."

"No, you mean me, of all people!"

"See? Now you're baiting me!"

"He is? Help me out here, I'm trying to broaden."

5

ESPRIT DE CORPS

Oren's first good citizen's act later that afternoon was to secure another five hundred to return to Matt Robb. In the middle of downtown Wyman, he shoved his bank card into a small slot and got strength from repeating a phrase, turning meaning into pure rhythm. "Men in dresses," he practiced aloud. There was that jump for joy, as he interpreted it now. Susan Robb wouldn't bolt. She would know something, for heaven's sake. She would know more than he did.

He was clearheaded, fully clothed, and enough in his right mind to flag down Matt Robb returning to his house under cover of twilight. Oren more or less accosted the boy from behind shrubbery. "I want you to take a little walk with me," he said. He guided Matt to the other end of Everett, where two new families by the name of Greene and Scott lived with young children. No one was outside to overhear.

"Either you take this money back, or I'll tell your parents." Oren's envelope trembled visibly, but the boy would not put out his hand for it. "Listen to me," Oren continued, "I tracked the girl down. She's got resources. You don't need to worry." Then he felt some embarrassment for sounding so impatient. The boy's face was disturbingly kind. Oren added, "Your mother is worried about you, you know. Shouldn't she be? This is a lot of money!"

The boy fixed on him something of a steady gaze, although there was not anything defensive or self-preserving in his eyes. "Parents have to worry," he said softly.

Their two houses stood several hundred feet away. In the dusky light, opposing front porches on all the houses jutted out like weak scaffolding.

"Yes," Oren said. He felt such uncertainty. The boy's mother was a woman of responsibility toward work and family, and especially toward this decent and vulnerable young man. I must not trouble her, he thought. But later it wouldn't seem as if this sentiment captured what he experienced in the next awful seconds of his life. With a certain ordinary motion of his hand, he touched his own brow and caught a glimpse of the inevitable failure of effort in all human life. The vision came from neither the boy nor himself. It was as old as the grave and maybe all of human time—a failure of the universe to mean.

More immediate was the sensation that he and the boy were becoming unmoored. Someone at dockside was lifting, from its huge hook, a rope as big as a man's arm. Oren heard it land in tepid water, and soon he bobbed like a empty can, metallic brown. He saw himself turn the color of used pennies. He was an old barge containing a huddle of rats—each of them alert and fearless as they moved around inside his skull. One of the rats put its nose through an open eye socket. Oren heard an electronically generated shriek, as if someone had touched live microphones. A side seam in the barge split. He was taking in water, his suit soaking up a runoff from some spill. But then it seemed he had fallen down and that Matt was there to prevent his head from making contact with wet sod in front of the Greene and Scott houses.

"Help me up!" Oren groaned. "I'm wet. Lord, I've wet myself. This is the end."

"No, it's not," the boy said softly. It was an attempt to comfort. "You'll be all right." He was removing his jacket to make a pillow for Oren and then running away fast to get help, leaving Oren to lie where he was. He moved a few fingers over grass that felt like rubber. He prayed he would die like this. There was not enough time to catch up to the meaning of things. He'd waited far too long.

Then Susan was a white mist coming slowly toward him in the dark. She wore a gray sweatsuit and could be seen in outline the minute she put a foot beyond her own door and floated to him from up the street. The sight made the lining of his heart begin sloughing. It hurt him. Where there should be stabbing pain of stroke or of heart attack there was only the mind's deep hurt. He sucked on an old tooth as if to locate the ache there and yet not there.

"Oren, can you talk?"

It was Susan and Malcolm alone. Lean arms went around his shoulders as he was being lifted up. "Easy," Malcolm said. "Easy does it."

"I'm dead," Oren said. "Pray God I died." The two seemed to laugh in relief that the dead man could quip. Very soon Oren was all the way into his front parlor, insisting that he had no family doctor to call. He was vaguely aware that they ought not to be seeing the inside of his house this way, but all he could do was moan and wait.

The doctor finally contacted was a young man named Hegg, a friend of Malcolm's and so badly in need of a referral that he agreed to come to the house. It was Dr. Hegg who eventually helped Oren out of his clothes and into a silk bathrobe. The thing almost stopped Oren's heart—a fancy silk paisley robe his wife had given him years ago, never worn. The young doctor had to have plunged straight into the closet to a back hook, hung with old sweaters and other castoffs.

He helped Oren into the robe and then listened a second time to his heart. He listened for a long while. Was there no heart there?

"What made you faint like that?" he finally asked, a studied minimalist who wasn't going to let Oren get the upper hand.

"Fatigue," Oren said weakly. "I'm tired."

"Hmm, perhaps," the doctor said. He began checking everything else—blood pressure, temperature; he palpated Oren's neck and throat while Oren sat contemplating the irony of a long-rejected silk robe to cover him, to confuse him.

"I'm going to let you sleep here in your own bed tonight. Tomorrow you come in for a complete physical. Come at around ten."

Floating to his bedside was Susan, her green eyes taking his breath away. He could see her concern, and in his shaken state he began to assume, madly, that she could divine the comic nature of his crisis.

"I'm a grotesque," he blurted out, looking at his robe, half in indication of what he meant. What did he mean?

"Oren," she said, smiling, "you lie back." She began adjusting pillows.

This should have cleared his head, but he was swimming in the pity he felt for himself—so warm and soothing in an otherwise intolerable moment. "Don't let me disappear," he said. His heart swelled to full size for the small self he'd never attended to, never fed. Then he laughed; he was seeing himself as the Invisible Man of the old classic movie. He was thinking how the frightened villagers saw the man only in those times when he moved about in a hat or a scarf, everyone screaming at the sight of floating fabric.

"I mustn't be allowed to disappear yet," he said. "You won't let me, will you?"

"No, no," she said. "No one's going to let you. You rest now. I'll come over in the morning."

"It was starting to be easy," he moaned.

"Disappearing?"

"Yes!"

A light came on in the hall. Malcolm stood in the door to the darkened room. Susan called, "I'll be right there."

Malcolm stopped—a tall acolyte, ducking his head and backing out of the room. Oren put out his hand to the wife. "I'd almost done it," he said.

"Disappeared, you mean?" She was settling him on the pillows and moving the bed lamp closer to his reach.

"Yes," he said, feeling himself start to slip away and praying it was only Dr. Hegg's pill and not the same vision of self-neglect and death kicking in. It would be sad to die now—now that she'd promised to come see him in the morning!

She showed up at nine with a thermos of coffee and a refusal to take no for an answer. She was going to drive him herself to Hegg's office for the checkup.

Her black coffee made him experience his shrewd old self. Wasn't it she who was making an overture of some kind, capable in yet another new T-shirt, leaning first toward him and then away? Already she was reaching for cups in his cupboard, putting milk in their coffees and sitting down in a way that was almost forward, certainly frank. He was shocked.

"Oren," she began, "I have an ulterior motive in being here."

"Do you?"

"It has to do with something you said the other night on our way to pick up Matt. How you once went through a religious crisis when you were young. I thought perhaps—"

"Oh no, not that," Oren moaned. The surprise and disappointment shook him badly.

"You told me I could ask you about it," she continued, "but I won't if you've changed your mind."

Oren's head cleared. When he looked he saw her smiling with uncertainty lest she'd trod on private territory.

"I did have a little talk with him," Oren said. He felt sorry for that sad look of hers.

"Oren!" she said, reaching out and touching his arm involuntarily. "You're wonderful, Oren!"

"We spoke only very briefly, you understand." Now he had raised her hopes. He tried backing down, and then he recalled something he'd completely forgotten: Great God, he'd threatened the poor kid into taking back the money! "Matt seems to be struggling with the witnessing part of the program," he said. His old gentleman's matter-of-fact tone amazed him. "Do you know about that sort of thing?" he continued, "the witnessing part?"

"Vaguely," she said, leaning in, alert, interested.

This is schizophrenia, he thought. I'm two people at once.

"They're required, you see, to profess their faith to strangers on the street. They're asked to go up to people and witness to them on the spot. You can imagine the difficulty. It's something between a thrill and pure degradation."

Susan was nodding, her eyes brightening with courage. "I'm so happy he would talk to you about it," she said. Then she seemed to have to look out a window. "Go on," she said quietly, more somberly.

"Eventually you start to doubt that your leaders know what in the devil they're asking you to do! It's a pyramid situation you're suddenly into. There's no product."

Susan kept staring out at nothing.

"The leaders' goal is to make you earn your spot at the higher level. You want to be with them, you see, but they're keeping you in boot camp. That's where Matt is, I think. Boot camp. It's hard on the nerves."

He reached for her hand. He'd made her cry. He should be shot.

"But he's the real thing," she was saying quietly and firmly through her tears.

"Well, he called himself a fake, which is always a good sign." Oren could see that she'd give a lot for a good sign. So would he.

"Oh, but how could he think that! That's so sad. He's not a fake. Oren, that's so sad."

What have I done? he thought.

She got hold of herself. "Malcolm and I have feared from time to time that we could lose touch with him," she said. "When you kept talking about yourself disappearing, I was particularly moved." She smiled, turning her sympathy to him, not wanting to take center stage in this matter of Matt. "So, what did you mean last night about yourself, Oren?" She smiled sweetly at him. She even seemed to look at his robe as if, again, she was on the verge of divining his problem. And for himself now, he knew absolutely nothing. His sixty-five-year-old self had bamboozled him. Who the hell was he?

"Last night you asked for my help," she was saying.

"No, no, you're absolved, you're completely absolved," he said, laughing, straining not to sob. He made a big, sweeping sign of the cross in the empty air between them. She had brought on the dizzying whirl from last night. He put his head down. He spoke into his lap. "Susan, here's what it is."

But he couldn't go on, at least not in an entirely straightforward way.

"It's one of those last phases I've got to get through," he finally said, laughing. "I'm in boot camp myself."

She put another hand on his arm, and he turned his bent head to view her touch this time while she spoke. "Whatever it is, Oren, I say it's okay to step up to the plate and swing bravely."

"Well," Oren moaned, "in my case—"

"Be bold, that's all," she said. "It's one of my originals. 'Blessed are the bold!' " She laughed. "Let's see, I should do the whole beatitude: 'Blessed are the bold, for they shall be surprised? For they shall be *bowled* over!' Ha!" She was quite happy with this second fix. She grinned at Oren, as if he'd inspired it.

"Don't assume I follow your drift," he said, deeply ashamed of himself now and even more confused because he was feeling unaccountably better.

"No drift, Oren! I've recently been looking at how soon I'll be dead, that's all. What am I waiting for, I've been asking. I tell myself every day: Be bold, woman. Step up there and swing. Whatever fate is pitching, just swing at it. Your kids are grown, so what can it hurt?"

He looked at her; she was quite gorgeous. "In my case, I guess I could get killed," he hinted, smiling at her.

"So?" she said. "There's worse things."

"There's disappearing, you mean," he said, agreeing with her.

"Absolutely!" she said.

"Step up to the plate, eh?" Oren said. "Be really bold?"

"Yes! It's one of them beatitudes, Oren." She laughed.

Then she seemed to take up an imaginary bat and swing it right at his head.

The two of them were quiet on the drive to the doctor's. Had he, in fact, taken a first swing by wearing his new robe out in public like this, covered over by only a trench coat?

He went in and out of feeling completely sane and completely crazy. He sat trying to sort which. Already he was getting used to the sight of his legs—dry and scaly. Did that mean something? Once in a while he'd feel that he had it—some presence he was carrying, some closeness of self before death, a closeness to the ornamental world at hand. Renewal and bravery.

He longed to try once more to tell Susan, a mature woman, what it was that had both emboldened and weakened him, but he did not think now that it amounted to one thing. He would have to swing blindly instead of speaking it lest he go mad and rush into the streets like some prophet in the poem, come to tell them all that he was back from the dead. He would wear just a sign of it: a dress to hide him, a dress to expose him. No one would understand it. For a moment that seemed exactly the burden he must bear—to confound others as he awaited personal clarity. Bottom line, he had no choice. He must conspire to be visible or else be a permanent drop-from-sight. And an overdue drop it would be too!

Meanwhile she was digging into the pocket of her parka as she drove. He knew her hands now, even if he didn't always know quite what they had to offer. Out came yesterday's five-hundred-dollar bank envelope, too familiar for Oren to bear. Matt's money! He grinned like an idiot as she handed it to him, and she could only assume he was glad not to have lost it.

"Matt said it must have come out of your suit when you fell. He jogged right over it this morning!"

"What do you know!" Oren said, "I must call that sweet boy up and thank him."

She eyed Oren from across the seat of the car. "After your appointment with Dr. Hegg, I could send him over." She hesitated, perhaps not wanting to overstep her bounds. "You two connected, I think." He heard her sigh. "I can hope, at least." She was making no bones about the fact that she needed Oren.

"Send him over, send him over!" Oren boomed.

When she looked at him quizzically, he smiled. "It's just that I'm a little dizzy," he said.

"And I'm a nuisance. I won't send him over, Oren. You might not be feeling well later. You let me know."

Outside Dr. Hegg's office he convinced her that he'd call for his car after his checkup. Secretly, he wanted very much to be alone with a memory starting to flood him. It was during the month or so right after Mary's death, when he'd been a textbook case of wild sexual excitement. Passion often followed the death of a spouse, he knew that; but in his case it had taken an odd form that he'd never tried to analyze. One day he'd called for his car and had himself driven all the way over to Jacksonville, where he wasn't known. He'd ended up in an old dime store, telling a saleswoman that his wife had asked him to pick up dress shields for a formal gown. Did the saleswoman know where they kept the dress shields?

She had looked him up and down before finally nodding. "They're over there with the sewing notions," she announced rather loudly.

"Sewing notions?"

"That's right."

He hadn't known about sewing notions, exactly. But in time his ignorance was dispelled. He'd lingered for a long time in the needles and threads as he began to recall this old aisle from his childhood— the seam rippers, the pinkings, the colored sequins, the hooks and eyes, all the rick and all the rack.

At the checkout counter there had been a woman with a black

mustache. He still remembered the way she'd turned the dress shields packet over and over in an effort to find something printed on a small blue sticker. Half the sticker was missing, so the woman got on the intercom for a price check. Oren had stood and waited, the packet crinkling in the mustache lady's hands. His mind had gone to blazes, standing there thinking of his mother's dress shields. She used to sew them herself. They had elastic loops into which one slipped an arm. That day in the old dime store the sound of the packet was almost too much, too brittle, like the wrapping on a garter belt, all its lost dangle hitting lightly against the sensitive part of a woman's leg as she breathes through nostrils in an effort to get the thing exactly in place.

The accoutrements of women. He had fled the store in panic and deposited his purchase in the nearest trash. His poor wife. It was because her accoutrements had both attracted and repelled him that he'd not been able to really love her properly and that he was relieved that she was gone. Surely she had died dispirited and at best numbed. He had made her take a separate room in the house, perhaps so that in his mind he could seal the whole thing off. And days after her death he'd had someone come and box up her things. He must have sensed that otherwise he might have wanted to handle them, salvage them, give in to the fetish he'd sealed away in his mind. Poor girl. Had she died very much alone and destroyed, quite ready to go? Perhaps in some way she'd let that car slam into her, her arms full of packages all flying in different directions. That too he'd properly sealed away, that step into a busy street. A few simple years went by before, relieved, he one day realized that he no longer remembered her.

Once inside Dr. Hegg's small waiting area, he felt another shriek about to rise in his head. It was back. He had to put his head down. Again, he became first a floating barge, then more of a bobbing tin can. When the nurse came to call for him he was in an icy sweat.

She had to help get him from the waiting area into the examining room, where she also helped him out of his robe and into a blue paper gown. She said it was all right if he wanted to keep on his shoes and socks.

The doctor spent quite a bit of time with him, thumping this and that, drawing blood, asking questions and getting back the negative answers of a man in excellent health who took no prescription drugs, did not smoke or drink or have a history of high blood pressure or an interesting history of any kind. Dr. Hegg began suggesting that he might want to make absolutely sure of things by having an MRI done down in Danford. But from everything Oren had suggested, Dr. Hegg was going to guess, at worst, this was a case of Ménière's syndrome.

"It's a form of chronic vertigo," the doctor said. "There's not much I can do for you except tell you how to live with it. Do you know that movie?"

As new-man-in-town, Dr. Hegg, however professionally lugubrious at the moment, showed his disappointment a little too openly. He'd surely been hoping for someone prominent like Oren whom he could treat and possibly cure.

"As I say, it's chronic and a bit tedious," he said flatly. "You'll have to learn to recognize when a spell is coming on and look for a soft landing. A couch, a mattress." The young doctor smiled. "But not, of course, a swimming pool!"

"I think I'm having a vision of some kind," Oren said.

"A vision? Nonsense!"

The nurse was leaving the room to answer the telephone. "Were you too dizzy to dress this morning?" the doctor asked. "In future you'll have to sit down to put your pants on. Vertigo is more of a nuisance than anything else." The man was becoming bored, faking engagement. "You might get nauseated once in a while. Disoriented. Some people have a harder time adjusting to it than others."

It was in hearing the verdict, or Hegg's easy dismissal of life itself, that Oren began to have another attack. First he got the barge feeling, then the tin-can feeling, things bobbing and ducking. In the hold he heard the sniffs and scratch of rats living on nothing. He put his head in his hands. "I need you to recommend another doctor," he said. For a moment the bobbing stopped. The rats seemed to listen.

"Sure. I can recommend another doctor," Hegg said, sniffing. The gall! Here was a case of vertigo wanting a second opinion.

"In Danford," Oren added. He pulled his head up and saw that he wasn't going to faint. "I need a doctor for a friend who has an ulcer." He was thinking excitedly how men in dresses ... men in dresses help the poor. They help the sick and the lame.

"A friend?" the doctor said sarcastically; he even flushed.

"I have to step up to the plate bravely," Oren said. "I see that now. I don't think this is vertigo at all."

The doctor possessed admirable control. He sniffed again. "Step up to the plate, did you say?"

"It's a baseball metaphor."

"I'm aware of that, Mr. Abel. Lie back down again, please. I haven't finished here."

During the rest of the examination Oren kept silent. He lay perfectly still. Passing through his mind was the expression, "*Having one's head examined*," but he also heard an opposing idea. In deciding to be bold—and it was not something small he had in mind now—he was seeing Angela's dream-trailer and her potted geraniums, followed by her delayed reaction to getting her wish, her shock at being helped, being given what she asked for, her inevitable flight from it. Susan would be the first to tell him he must not delude himself or presume to know this girl's peanut heart. After years of deprivation, they don't know what to ask for. They ask for trips to Graceland and to Disney World. Say Paris, and they might not be able to tell you the country it's in.

But never mind all that. He was imagining the two chairs pulled together—his and Susan's. He would begin with just the fact of a disadvantaged Danford girl whom he meant to help. She had a horrible room, and he was a good mind to find her an apartment near the university campus. That was, in part, how the conversation would begin, with some offhand mention of Angela in a neighborly exchange over coffee. The only pleasure in doing a good deed was to do it by stealth and then nudge it out into the open.

"Put this back on, please," the doctor was saying, handing Oren his robe and leaving the examining room.

Alone, he tried rehearsing aloud. "I'm stepping to the plate," he began, still seated but only a little dizzy. "I'm wondering if maybe you, Susan, wouldn't mind being out there for me to hit to."

He sat for a long time before standing up carefully, tying the robe, feeling completely steady. He reached for his trench coat, which he put on one sleeve at a time. Instead of tying the coat to hide the robe, he left it open. His robe showed down the front and hung inches below the hem of the coat. Then there was a whole lot of white leg; then the ugly socks and shoes.

Outside several people in the waiting area had their noses in magazines. Someone whispered to him from behind, and he turned to see one of the librarians from Webster College.

"Mr. Abel, do you have your car out there to take you back home? I'm sorry you're not feeling well."

"I'm fine!" Oren boomed. Everyone looked up. There were a few efforts to take in the hairy legs. Noses returned to magazines. In this setting a robe was about illness and convalescence. Here was Oren needing to go on home and back to bed.

Out on the street it was a different matter. He'd not called for his car. Did he have the boldness to walk on home like this, shins exposed until the villager eye searched out the brown socks and the old man's funny shoes? But finally he did. He struck out, his body finding balance and gravity and his mind frothing like a dandelion gone to airy seed and silk. He was being borne into the air.

Yes, of course, there'd be the hectic first year, he began musing. (Musing bravely was vertigo's cure!) "I know, I know!" he began to explain to Susan in his mind. "If I get involved, I know I'm not to dream up some simple ending. She'll be in my life for good. What's left of my life is mercifully short. I can't lose now, can I? That's your whole point!"

A car full of loud teenagers drove past Oren, and he heard merry encouragements—an inmate, a psychiatric patient who has walked away from the rolling lawn of an institution. "Don't let them lock you back up, old man!"

He smiled and gave a friendly wave to the kids, making a mental note that this exposure might not be something he'd want to attempt at night. He imagined a bottle sailing out of just such a car and hitting him in the head.

There was her physical and spiritual welfare to attend to, he continued to muse. Who knew how young she was? All she'd had was boxes of fabric, abuse, and television. On that hopeless foundation he would have to give up the rugged baseball slug as a working metaphor. For Angela one might have to settle for, say, miniature golf. Not a stepping to the plate so much as giving a ball those many little whacks; the many misses and skids into penny ponds, the ball crashing into the paddles of a mechanical windmill or jumping down the mouth of the wrong plastic frog and rolling farther away from the hole than when you began.

"Love your outfit, Mr. Abel!"

One could venture to think of schooling for her, perhaps. That was reasonable. Her and her vocabulary lists. He could weep! There were night schools. During the day she'd catch up; do overtime with him and even with some of the other families on Everett Street. Math in one house, English in another. A block effort. A rally. Some small college would give her a chance one day. Hell, Malcolm Robb would give her a chance at Webster. They owed Oren, what with him insisting that time they not name a wing after him. The Oren Abel Wing.

Now he *was* a wing! he thought.

He turned into his old familiar street, the trees seeming to greet him in whispers of encouragement, as if to say that here he would always be safe. Who knew, he was thinking, but that he might live long enough to see it through to some remarkable, if ragged, finish. He had a shot at both long life and Malcolm's sudden death. With care he could get in twenty years, Susan Robb driving him to the many graduating ceremonies, having always meant herself to go out and get one of these waifs. All of middle America means to get one and then finds itself glad when waifs turn out to be harder to find than the concept suggests.

A footfall sounded on his porch later that evening as Oren sat in his dark house, having moved on in his daydreaming to a few renovations he and Susan were making; in his mind they were married now and she full of great ideas for giving this old place her own personal touch.

In fact the footfall matched Susan's, so he was surprised when he yanked the door open to find Harry Rawlins, his attorney, standing there wheezing. Oren's affairs were simple. Harry had drawn up a straightforward will years ago, and that had been about it. Now and then they ran into each other in Danford and caught up on things. It had been a while.

"Look at you, you tiresome old coot," Harry said, "you stopped getting dressed these days?"

"Harry, I am dressed!" Oren crowed. He felt terrific. He opened his arms to display the robe, thinking how he had to start sometime, and this old friend was safe as Susan Robb. "Harry," Oren boomed, "it's a long story. Come in, come in!"

Harry hadn't waited. He'd pushed on into the dark hall and was now closing the door tightly, as if he didn't want anyone to hear why he'd showed up like this. "First thing Margaret said to ask you, Oren, was how this girl got hold of our name. For God's sake, you keep our card in your wallet?"

"Yes."

"Well, she found it. We don't handle blackmail, you know."

Harry shoved Oren carefully aside and headed for the old kitchen.

"Margaret said to tell you hello from her, by the way, and to remind you we're only here out of the goodness of our hearts and that you're to make me decaf. I can only take it with skimmed milk."

"How is Margaret?"

"Alive. Not dead, at least. And still the smart one. She said to tell you she can't understand how you could get yourself into this much trouble given how little you've been up to lately. Boy, when you step out you do it good."

The man left behind him a sour-smelling trail, as if he was no longer bothering to bathe. He sat at the kitchen table and began rif-fling through papers but seemed unable to find exactly what he was looking for. His breathing was heavy. "Let's see here." He had one sheet held up and was looking at it through bifocals. "Let's see here. Full name, Angela Bert. I think it's an alias."

"Harry—"

"Shut up and pay attention. This man she's been hanging out with, he's way ahead of you, Oren."

"Cooper," Oren said. "See, I know everything. I'm going to help this girl get away from that dope fiend."

Harry raised an eyebrow and looked at Oren. "Dope fiend, Oren? People haven't used that expression in forty years! Good God!" Harry returned to his notes. "I thought his name was Warren. Wait a minute." Harry shuffled to new pages. "Warren C. Reece," he read, looking up. "Maybe the *C* is for Cooper, I have no idea. Haven't met the gentleman. It's the girl who came to me this morning. I can't de-cide if she's stupid or very bright."

"Bright," Oren said. "She has purchase."

Harry studied him a long moment. He laughed. "Margaret's go-ing to love this. You now speak in a foreign language!" But then he began looking over his papers again. Oren sat noting, irrationally, his old friend's crow's feet, deep as channels. This was what real work did to people. Harry had always loved real work. There was character in that face.

"She hardly has to blackmail me, Harry," Oren began again.

"Shut up. According to her, Cooper got himself to a lab a year ago and paid for a DNA test on himself. He did it in anticipation of her snagging someone like you." Harry stopped. "She says she'll demand your DNA results about the time she does an amniocentesis and nails you for bigger things than she's after right now."

Oren found himself somewhat moved. "She's pregnant! Of course!"

"No! It's a ploy! They all throw that one in! She's no more pregnant than I am. How can I make you pay attention and quit interrupting me?" Harry lowered his voice. "It's to do with photographs, Oren. I didn't even ask to see them. She's young. She says she loves you, and that she only wants your house."

"My house?" He laughed. "Lord, when I last spoke to her she had in mind a trailer."

Harry drew a long face. It was as long as he could get for effect. "You won't be serious for a minute?"

"Harry, it's been my plan to help her. I've had a vision you'd scarcely believe. If she wants this old house she can have it." He was so amazed, he had a sudden joyous thought. She'd need income! He'd rent a room here!

"Listen to me, Oren, do you have any idea how young she is?"

"Yes, I had begun to guess."

"It's her MO, Oren—showing that birth certificate and telling someone like you that it's phony. Especially someone like you."

For a moment Oren was stung. "There are plenty of people like me!"

"You're not listening, Oren. She's fifteen. She *wanted* you to think she was older. Do you realize you almost wouldn't have to touch a girl that young for her to have you up on a morals charge?"

The two men sat for a moment.

Then Harry said, "I lied before. I saw the Polaroids, so relax. I'm hardly shocked." He was nodding thoughtfully. "Oren, all I'm saying is that these days if the kid is fifteen it just don't matter what you're wearing."

* * *

Oren's joy was difficult to contain—the thought of Angela going for broke in this perverse way of hers. It made him recall, of all people, his great-aunt Meryl—the dreadful Easter Sunday she'd tried to arrange for him when he was a kid. Old maid Meryl! She'd badly wanted him to be the one among fifty Sunday school children to find the chocolate egg, to win the prize she'd bought and paid for herself. He'd been appalled at her for telling him ahead of time where he'd find it. The night before the hunt she'd pinned a blue note to his pillow instructing him to look in the crook of a certain tree. Poor old fool—he had thought even then—poor old Aunt Meryl, setting him up.

What he was thinking now was how he couldn't see much difference between that warped, lonely old lady, long dead, and this young, unloved, thrown-away girl. Meryl's mad lifelong efforts to get what she wanted; Angela's attempt to extract from Oren what he was so willing to give.

"How in the world did she take photographs?" he mused.

"From behind!" Harry shouted.

They were quiet for a time. Harry grew somber, reflective. "You know what she told me? This guy she's with is such a junkie he once tore up the apartment looking for his Polaroid camera. He almost killed her before she convinced him he'd pawned it the last time he was short."

"See, Harry?" Oren said. "I'm a godsend. Before I die I'm going to be someone's godsend."

Harry had come prepared to show Oren several clever ways he could handle this Angela, bright or otherwise. But when he discovered Oren was not going to heed a word of advice, he asked for a bourbon, and to hell with Margaret.

"For starters," Harry said, "the law won't let you deed property to a mere girl. Let's say you could! The state ain't about to give *you* custody of Angela Bert."

"I'll move out. She can be here with a governess."

"Lord, listen to you. Governess? This is America."

With very fresh eyes, Oren looked around. It was as if someone had already unbuckled a craggy tortoiseshell and lifted it straight up from his back.

"You were born in this house!" Harry protested.

"Harry, does it ever hit you how soon you'll be dead?"

Harry groaned. Oren already knew exactly where he could call and arrange a perfectly adequate place to stay. There were the furnished one-bedroom apartments over in Morningside Groves, half of them going begging now for the last year. They knew him at Morningside Groves; he could walk over right now and get a key to one, his toothbrush in a small bag, a coffeepot, a few books, as if winnowing right down to something like Cooper's place, only clean and with maybe a phone. But maybe not!

"What kind of friend would sit and let this girl walk in here and take you lock, stock, and barrel?"

"What does that expression mean? I've never understood lock, stock, and barrel."

"Oren, I've changed my mind. You face the morals charge and get yourself chained down for a few days."

Oren felt like strolling from kitchen to parlor just to be reminded of all the nonsense he no longer wanted.

"Can I ask you something?" Harry was saying. "Can I ask how you're going to keep this Cooper from moving in here? Let's say she really wants to get away from him. Do you realize that after about two days here all alone, the next thing you'll know she'll have called him up herself!"

"He doesn't have a phone."

"Oren, he's her man. She'll hitch a ride to town and tell him where she is! It's why prostitution works. Where've you been?"

"She's not a prostitute."

"Oh, brother," Harry said.

Oren poured Harry another shot of the treat Margaret regularly denied him. In a little while they were reviewing a few old times,

Harry confessing that his and Margaret's joint practice was boring him these days. She still had stamina for it, but he was tending to watch ball games. Oren's situation was certainly a diversion.

"How did you get so passionate about this?" Harry said. "The state you're in you could talk a hungry dog off a meat truck."

After a while it was clear Harry shouldn't drive home. Oren put on coffee and moved them out to the porch to sober up. Harry enjoyed the view. Ten years ago he and Margaret had moved to a farm below Danford. Harry mused that he missed a quiet little street of friends like this, not in the least realizing how it stabbed Oren. To think how he'd wasted this street of friends.

Well, he was going to change some of that.

"Oren, here's what I'm going to do for you," Harry said, "since you're hopeless. Tomorrow I'm going to put together some documents for her to sign. The very least we can do is make her sign an agreement that she's not to let Cooper or anyone else move in here. I'm going to have some fine print for her to read. If she's bright she's going to know there's such a thing as fine print. It will help. I'll advise her to sign. She's got to trust me. In the long run, we want her thinking I'm working for her."

"You are working for her, Harry!"

"I'm going to get her to agree on a fee for me—a percentage of the cash you're planning to give her. I'll have gotten her a stipend. She'll not be expecting that."

"Excellent," Oren said.

To Harry it was all a deal to placate a child. "She'll split soon enough, Oren, if she's got money."

Oren let it pass.

"Meanwhile, you will remember her age, won't you, from now on? You can't be having sex with her, boy."

How did one explain? He tried. "It's not about sex, Harry. It's a bold swing at something."

"Well," Harry mused, "I want you to stay away from her apartment until she's moved. And I want you to stay away from this house too for a few days. She's got to trust me and Margaret for a while. She's not predictable, Oren. She's a loose cannon. You know that, don't you?"

"You'll help her move her things and then really look in on her, make sure she's all right?"

Harry leaned back and put his feet up. "Margaret's been as bored as I have. This is a nice project. I guess we better get her moved right away before that guy gets out and is all over her."

"Tomorrow!" Oren said. "Do it tomorrow. I can be out of here in the morning."

"Is there much furniture?"

"Just junk. But it's important to her."

"Well, we got the horse trailer we can use."

As Harry became more and more purposeful to himself, he had more and more opinions. Oren had at least one or two things in his favor. Cooper's general lowlife position, to start with, Harry said. Cooper couldn't resist the smarter move of running off with some money if he ever found any in Angela's account.

Oren told Harry about all the trouble she'd gone to. It was quite remarkable.

They were quiet awhile before Harry finally cleared his throat. "So, is the dress thing a homosexual-type thing?" Harry had now adopted the low murmur he used whenever he was feeling superior to his old friend, which was most of the time. "I'm broader minded about this sort of thing than you are, for Pete's sake, so don't get bent out of shape with me asking."

"I don't mind. I think it's something to do with a vision of death I had. It doesn't now feel sexual in any way."

Harry cut him off short. Harry was clearly terrified of death. "Well, okay, I can get my head around that." There was a pause. Harry couldn't keep his eyes from wandering to the awful legs and visible shoes. He cleared his throat again. "What do we call you now?"

"You call me Oren, of course!"

"Okay, stay loose, don't blow your top at me."

Best not to speak of visions of any kind, Oren mused. Better to think about the cold and rainy winter this year.

"You think it's going to stay unseasonably cold like this, Harry?"

"Could be," Harry said, glad to switch to the weather.

Unbeknownst to Harry, of course, weather was truly important right now, not a matter of small talk. Oren wanted it cold for a long time. Hot weather was sure to follow—in Florida it dominated the scene—but if it would just stay cold as long as possible, Oren could wear the trench coat over the robe. He needed time to figure out how he was going to go around Wyman without the trench coat and somehow not get himself killed.

6

MALCOLM AND THE TENANTS

FOR THE ROBBS, THERE WAS ALWAYS THE JANUARY BREAK TO be at home with each other between terms, but today Malcolm was clocking time in his study, thinking. A religious group? Could that really be the reason Matt was withdrawn, more than usual? The idea wouldn't have crossed Malcolm's mind had Gretchen not put it there. Now her guess seemed right on the nail.

Tonight Susan was cooking her annual same-day birthday dinner for Malcolm and Matt. Tonight she would not just serve up a course of favorite foods; it would all be followed by cake and candles that he feared would strain him to some breaking point. Or if not the cake then the unwrapping of matching father-and-son gifts. Chip and block, he sat thinking. Pea and pod.

Oil and water.

For her sake he would be a good sport and put the whole group fear out of his mind for tonight. Also that other unknown—the something she'd asked Gretchen not to tell him about quite yet. Well, he didn't like waiting, particularly; didn't like pretending, no matter what the secret was, that Matt was on track with his college plans, with his life. Just as Malcolm would get to this point, he'd circle back to the idea of some group and the boy's early leap off the deep end.

After lunch he sat chopping walnuts for the cake and thinking more positively. This time next year things could be turned around, a different story. With any luck, the kid would be home from FSU or even UVA. Either place, both fine in their own ways. He'd be newly tracked and getting on with his life. Malcolm imagined the two of them chopping these same nuts together, Matt having met some girl (or maybe some boy—hey, you never knew), and sitting here with Malcolm a year from now, smiling, embarrassed to be in love. He'd have had his Intro to Philosophy course—something rigorous, yet enlivening and expansive. They'd each grab a beer and go out on the porch to have a terrific conversation. No, an utterly fantastic conversation.

He knew he was dreaming, but it pleased him, and so he was also pleased when he looked up from his knife and bowl and saw that Matt was quietly entering the house from the mud room. He paused in the kitchen doorway. Malcolm smiled at him, then knew immediately. It wasn't going to be good news.

"I thought I'd better tell you," Matt said, "I just got accepted into Bluxham Junior College, out in the Panhandle."

One warning look from Susan was enough to silence Malcolm until he regained composure. A junior college, while not as bad as a group, had never once come up in this house.

"Gosh," he began, "I had no idea you were interested in Bluxham. Did you have any idea, Susan?" Of course, this must be her secret, and how on earth could she not have told him? "When did you apply, Matt?" he continued. There was this insanely merry ring to his voice.

"I didn't," Matt said. "I mailed them my transcript. They don't make you wait."

They don't make you wait. Thunderstruck, Malcolm wondered how any admissions director could have a son capable of an observation quite this uninformed. "Yeah, well," he began quietly, "college isn't like joining the army, Matt. You have to wait, you know. And you usually don't decide until you hear from your other choices."

"I won't be hearing," the boy said.

"You will. After you apply, Matt. We gave you four hundred dollars in application fees. Remember? You'll hear from a few places."

"I'm going to have to pay you back the money, Dad."

"Pay me back? What are you talking about?"

"It's just—"

"Matt, if you spent the money, then okay, you owe us. But it's not like we don't have another chunk to give you. You have to make applications, son. This is crazy."

It was too late for anyone to say, by the way, happy birthday. Malcolm looked at Susan and tried not to let baiting creep into his voice. In fact he went way way calm, despite every reason to be upset: "Matt, you know about applying widely! And you know that not doing so is—" He refused to say crazy again because it so clearly was. "It's just really, really odd. Right? Susan?"

Susan cleared her throat. "It's not like you to keep us in the dark about something so important."

So she *didn't* know. The realization gave Malcolm his first unguarded moment. "Yes, it is," he said, getting up from the table. "It's exactly like him."

"I couldn't see wasting the money," Matt said. "I'll pay you back. It's my other news. I have a job."

"No," Malcolm said. "What job? Forget it! We're talking about college and ultimately your entire future."

Matt blinked. "It's a two-week job of counseling kids. They've got this year-round camp in Torreya. The director wants me there by tomorrow if possible."

"Not possible," Susan said quietly.

But Malcolm was shouting. "Wait a minute! There's a group you're not telling us about!"

He stopped. He actually began to laugh; couldn't remember his own father shouting as badly as he was getting in the habit of. He could only press mightily on with the funny, ha ha, story of coming home at Matt's age and announcing to Larry Robb that he and Susan were hitchhiking across country, Larry exploding right on cue.

Susan grinned. "He sure did, Matt. I've never seen your grand-father so mad."

"Matt," Malcolm began again. "For you to decide on a junior college without consulting us—for you to tear up your applications—"

"I didn't tear up anything," Matt said.

"But you haven't sent them in, have you? No. So I think I have to ask you what this Bluxham thing is really all about!"

"What do you mean?"

"It's not accidental, is it, that a camp in Torreya and the junior college in Bluxham are within five miles of each other."

Malcolm watched the boy walk to Susan. He was too cold, even as he reached out to take the sandwich she was offering him. "Dad's right." He stared at the plate and then put it down. "I want to work at this special place next year and attend college at the same time. It's what I want."

Susan leaned against the counter and breathed in deeply. Malcolm wanted to ask if Matt really thought Bluxham was a college at all.

"Here, I'll write down the number," Matt said. "George Murray. He's the camp director and wants to meet you. Could you call him? He's shorthanded this week. He needs to know if I'm coming."

"And we need to know what kind of director he is," Malcolm said.

"What kind?"

"Yes!"

Susan intervened. "And this is Murphy's number?"

"Murray."

She turned to Malcolm. "Well, Dad and I will just have to let you know later, Matt, after we talk to him. You haven't given us any time, so that's the best we can do." She turned and faced the sink. "Mean-while, I want us all home on time for dinner right at six, got that?"

Malcolm waited. Matt gave him a little shrug as if to say that he'd gladly spare him the evening if he only knew how. When Malcolm detected that Susan was crying, that she was choosing now to be emotional, every patient bone in his body began rebelling: Women fold, he thought, men confront. "Matt," he said, "it seems to us you've been looking for your own little world for a long time. Are you sure you're going to find it at a junior college and a Bible camp?"

That was the moment Gretchen, eavesdropping or quite by chance, chose to walk in on them. Just back from her drama workshop at the school, the girl had more bounce than was safe for the neighborhood building code. "Happy birthday!" she said, completely oblivious to the lit fuse in the room. She opened the refrigerator and stuck her head inside. "Did you guys know there's a U-Haul out in Uncle Oren's driveway? The old man's moving out or something!"

Matt had already slipped out the back and was gone again. When Gretchen pulled herself from the fridge, there was nothing in the room but two parents quiet enough to cause her to look first at one and then the other. "Who died?" she said.

Malcolm feared he wouldn't be able to keep from jumping down Susan's throat, or from grinding a spoon in the disposal, or from hugging both his women frantically. His lifelines. Whatever secret they had about Matt, they were merely trying to spare him from it— some new disappointment. It wouldn't top this one.

He left the kitchen, dreading the uphill climb they would have to make toward the annual hilarity of the matching underwear, pajamas, and slippers. All that was needed were a few groans of affection, he reasoned. Bluxham! It was a tiny town sitting ten miles south of the Apalachicola National Forest. Malcolm was hard pressed to recall a camp in that neck of the woods until he remembered with some bitterness how a third-rate camp could crop up anywhere when people get fired up. A house, a barn. One soggy pasture and these people would call it a camp.

He went into his darkened study and stood staring out a lifted single slat in his venetian blind. He lifted this slat a lot; merely a bad habit. Indeed, today there was, as Gretchen had been trying to tell them, some kind of U-Haul contraption sitting in plain view in Oren's driveway. It looked like a gizmo for a troupe of traveling performers—top-heavy, with the unmistakable length of a coffin. Someone had painted it with a kind of shiny black tar. Free tar from a road crew.

Malcolm dropped his slat. He then sat so he could lift one up a little lower down.

A flowered fabric—a dress or a kitchen curtain—hung halfway to the ground from the open trailer door, and junk of all kinds lay everywhere else. Oren must be dead, was Malcolm's first thought. His nephews, Nick and Frank, were already taking revenge, renting the wonderful old house to people who didn't know how to pack a trailer; they only knew how to stuff and unstuff it.

No less than Susan and Dr. Hegg together had been keeping an eye on Oren. The entire street would know if anything bad had happened to him. They'd have seen the ambulance; hell, they'd have had to call the ambulance themselves.

He left his study to go outside. He pushed out onto his front porch, where Susan sat in one of the big rockers as if waiting for him. She knew better than anyone how hopeful Malcolm had become last year, congratulating Johnny Richards, and Wade and Wayne Harwood on their many acceptance letters. Johnny was now at Georgia Tech, and Wade and Wayne were both at Wooster.

"Listen," Susan said, "assuming his applications are ready to go into the mail tomorrow, I think we better let him go to this camp. It's just for two weeks. I'll drive him tomorrow, meet the director."

"Hell," Malcolm said, plunking down, "one minute I care and the next minute I don't. I know you're caught between us, and besides, if

I don't let him go I'll only make matters worse. Just make sure it's not some firetrap dorm and that the people aren't nuts. And we have to know what group they are. Find out the damn group."

He saw his wife thinking, thinking. Was she thinking how to handle *him*? "You know," she finally said, "just now you were remarkably graceful with Matt. I was rooting for you. I was hoping you were going to go ahead and tell him the whole hitchhiking story, since you raised the topic."

"Odd, because I was thinking how I'd never be able to tell him that story."

He heard her sigh at his unwillingness to have the moment lightened up a bit as she brought up a favorite bit of their history—the two of them getting themselves arrested in the sleepy little town of Seward, Nebraska. A rookie cop had happened to shine his flashlight at a large Dutch elm near the courthouse and thought he was seeing antiwar protesters in the act of assembling a bomb inside a sleeping bag.

Susan pointed at Oren's house. "Do you suppose he could be in the hospital? I dialed the old number over there, and a recording said he's got a new one. Unlisted."

"Maybe that Frank character is moving in with him. He's the nephew who did time in a reform school."

Boys, he was thinking. Oren had Nick and scary Frank. Next door John Richards had promising Johnny. To Johnny you could say straight out what had been going on in the sleeping bag in Seward, Nebraska. He was the kind of kid very likely to be delighted.

"What was the name of that town?" Susan mused, in a last effort to take them back in sweet time. It was from behind the wide, clean bars of the tiny Seward jailhouse that he'd asked her to marry him. An elderly sheriff had found them a minister, his own brother-in-law, who was ordered to bring in banana bread for wedding cake. Sheriff, deputy, and minister were all in love with Susan by the time Malcolm got her out of there.

"I was sitting here thinking," she continued, "it's time I told Gretchen about getting married in custody. I've got those pictures we never showed around. The whole thing is going to tickle her to death."

"But not Matt, right?"

"I mean, the details are so marvelous, and the way your father talked to me. Remember?"

"I bet he didn't tell you we were going straight to hell," Malcolm said.

"He would never use that kind of language. What are you talking about?"

"I'm talking about our son, Susan! I'm talking about the kind of language our son would use."

She gave a sigh and got up. She didn't even have to say Malcolm was being perverse. He knew he was. He really had very little evidence of his son's language, or how he sounded.

She got up to go; errands to run. Meanwhile, did they want to call up this George Murray?

Yes, better do it this afternoon, Malcolm said. Have a chat.

Then they decided No. If they rejected the idea on the basis of a phone call, they would have less credibility. Her meeting Murray herself tomorrow and seeing the setup firsthand was the best plan. She was about to leave for her few errands when Malcolm grabbed her arm and pulled her to him. He asked why didn't they go get into some trouble; Seward always made him think of trouble.

She kissed his mouth. He was just feeling guilty, she reasoned. She'd go do a few things and be back later; she'd check to see if he was still interested.

It was an hour or so later before he came out to the porch to sort through his mail. He noticed that the U-Haul was gone. He was just settling into mostly junk-sorting when there was a loud slam over at Oren's. A cat ran off into low shrubbery to get out of the way, and someone began screaming from inside the old house that he was going to cut her lousy throat and then his own.

Malcolm froze as a small human form seemed to explode onto the porch, then leap into the yard and tear off around the back of the house. Malcolm saw after-streaks of streaming red-and-yellow scarves. He wasn't sure what he saw. Everything got quiet again.

Then from the back of Oren's house came a rusted-out white Chevy. It was nosing slowly into view. No motor sounded at all. It was as if the release of its hand brake had set the car rolling forward. Malcolm began to make out a bleached head of hair above the steering column. Her body sat too far down to allow her to see that a man had come onto the high porch. It clearly was not Frank Abel. Malcolm had never seen the man before—someone angry, quite furious. He began by shaking his fist and then vaulting Oren's porch railing and landing on top of the car. Everything lurched. No one moved. A kid on his bike skidded to a stop and waited to see what would happen. Even in the time it took Malcolm to duck into his house and peer out his front window, the tableau remained the same, the guy slowly slithering down onto the hood, clinging there like a live ornament, a flattened flying squirrel baring sharp little teeth at a frightened driver.

Malcolm eased into his office chair. He was prepared to dial 911. The guy began to move, first peeling himself up and off the car and then careening crazily around to the driver's side and snatching the wife or girlfriend into full view. She was small and dressed in an outfit that seemed half rags, half fancy. Maybe it was a costume, a kimono, a colorful throw-on. As she was being pulled across the yard and back up the porch steps, she seemed to crane her head around and give Malcolm a look. She seemed to know exactly where he was hiding.

Her stare was part of the method of two seasoned screamers, Malcolm thought, the kind that know in a single afternoon whether or not they have an audience. She saw that Malcolm had been sitting on his porch minding his own business, that he'd barely had time to get inside to give them their privacy, that he'd had no place else to go.

That he hated them already.

He found Gretchen making herself an omelet in the kitchen.

"Did you see what just happened?

"Yeah," Gretchen said. "It's a big, big world out there, Dad, so keep loose." She took a knife and halved her omelet. "Here, eat this. You're going to need your strength for later." Handing over big slabs of cut buttered bread, she took her own share on up to her room and left him alone.

Susan later found him in their back downstairs addition, now their new bed and study quarters and sun porch. For the rest of the quiet afternoon, the large house, full of books and old LPs, rang in separate little thunks and echoes that filled Malcolm with a sense of well-being. For a long time he read a book, sprawled out on the couch in his front study. Later, as he moved about the house, it was touching to overhear Gretchen upstairs rehearsing with remarkable urgency.

"*Uncle Vanya*," she explained when he padded into her room in his socks. "We're doing monologues. I have a speech at the end of the play about angels, but I know Mr. Mulert is going to hate how I do it. If you can't find the edge, he's upset."

Malcolm ended up helping her with her monologue, and soon it was early evening. They heard mother-son exchanges down in the kitchen. Matt was home early and helping with dinner. Susan would make sure of those applications and checks and all the rest—the packing for camp, the drive to Torreya tomorrow. She'd find the right moment to work in the importance of Matt keeping an open mind about college.

As he stood on the stair landing listening, Malcolm began to feel not just grateful. The idea of two weeks without Matt exhilarated him. They could pretend he was already gone to college—gone to Bluxham, to Mars. The three remaining onward Christian soldiers would get a chance to see what it was going to be like next year. He hadn't only imagined, had he, the guilt at how easy it was for three to get along? Now perhaps this old house would work the way it had always been meaning to but had never had the chance. Without a certain well-meaning boy living in it, could it be that this old house was finally going to rock and roll?

An odd thing happened just as they were about to sit down to the joint birthday dinner. It happened as Malcolm, still in his silent socks, pushed cheerfully in to ask Matt if he could stop packing and come down now; the table was set.

Matt's room was dark, and for a moment Malcolm thought he was taking a nap. In fact, the boy was crouched down in front of a window, and he more or less jumped out of his skin at suddenly being discovered by Malcolm, who had just had a Scotch and a smooching session with Susan and was feeling terrific. "What's up?" he said in a chummy voice, as if he were John Richards talking to Johnny. "Is somebody over there making love?"

As he bent down to look out the other window, one of Oren's old upstairs bedrooms came floating into view. "Holy cow!" he breathed. He was reminded of a cat with its hind leg sticking up above its head. Right now there were two in the air and an ample male ass moving around. With his son only ten feet away, it was a great relief when the couple fell apart so quickly that it was possible for Malcolm to pretend he hadn't seen anything. There came a clear sound of a child crying from one of the other bedrooms, so perhaps all Malcolm saw was the girl's bottom as she left the room and the guy getting up and beginning to yell. The precise wording of his curses was less clear than the rhythm—all too familiarly lame and self-absorbed. Malcolm was suddenly on the side of the girlfriend. Or was it mother?

New light came on in a different room, and the crying baby—a toddler in a blue romper—was lifted from one of Oren's large antique sleigh beds. Another older and very blond child was also in the bed—a five- or six-year-old girl in a nightgown.

"You guys sitting here in the dark?"

Gretchen's voice came from behind Malcolm. She was loud and close enough to give him a heart attack.

"Hey, we've been calling you!" she said, a little miffed. "The food's getting cold! What's the matter in here?"

Malcolm pounced at the light switch, and the screen outside went black. "We were just saying you were probably wondering what was keeping us, weren't we, Matt?"

"Yeah! We were!"

Gretchen's eyes narrowed. "So? What is it?"

"Nothing!" Malcolm said.

"We were having a chat," Matt said.

"A chat?" Gretchen looked back and forth between them. She grinned in mock innocence. "So stop chatting and come on right now." She let her voice trail after her as she turned back into the hall. "Okay?"

Left alone, they both performed twin acts of expelling air and then shoving hands in tight jeans pockets. "Birthday boy!" Malcolm finally found voice to say. He burst out laughing.

"Yeah," Matt said, looking down at his feet. "I wonder what matching gear Mom's going to get us this year?"

"Don't know," Malcolm said, feeling drunk now. "Something perfectly useless!" He was so elated to be in cahoots about almost anything that he couldn't stop now. "How does your mother do it?"

"Don't know," Matt said.

They both had their backs turned conspicuously away from the windows. And Malcolm's next thought was just as happy as his first, just as innocent. He honestly did not mean a thing by it. "Whatever it is," he chirped, "you can always give yours away, right?"

For a moment he prayed (shit!) that the arrow wouldn't hit the boy's literal heart. Malcolm wasn't alluding to anything biblical or personal; he'd only meant, of course, that since Matt was leaving tomorrow he could, without detection, get rid of whatever extraneous set of not-quite-right, nonreturnable gear it was going to turn out to be this year.

"Nah," Matt said. At first it seemed he was not the least stung by any reference to his old trauma. He was only embarrassed a little, shaking his head at the old man who couldn't stop baiting him. "I'll hang on to mine as a keepsake," he said, turning and heading into the hall, leaving Malcolm alone in his socks until he heard Matt say from the top of the stairs as he was descending, "because this is probably the last time we're ever going to do this."

7

O.O.C.

THE NEXT DAY GRETCHEN AND HER TEAMMATE URI WERE given ten minutes to work up a character study during their last half-hour of the drama workshop time. It was to be more improv than scripted. "Just a fast thumbnail sketch," Mr. Mulert said. They were to create someone angry and "O.O.C."

Out Of Control, he went on to explain; only they were supposed to use restraint too. Lots and lots of restraint.

Already Mr. Mulert was starting to pace. "You people have to realize that a superb actor can convey cold and hot at the same time."

He was a young man of not much restraint himself. They were starting to worry. Lately he was tending to turn on them, pained and pleading.

"Does anybody *know* why cold and hot can go together in a scene?"

One could hear one's classmates swallow. Mr. Mulert no longer liked it when they answered his questions. He wasn't as crazy about them as he'd been in the fall when he'd told them too much about himself, when he'd wanted them just to call him Chuck and to know—hey, why not?—that he'd been in some huge play last winter before his nervous breakdown, before his move back to Danford to be near friends.

"I'll tell you why!" he shouted. "Because language imposes false opposition! Try to hear me now." He was always asking them to try to hear him, which usually meant that they were supposed to write something down. "Language makes oppositions, people! Only art makes wholes! You got that?

"Holes?" Uri whispered. "What kind?"

A thumbnail moment was already forming in her head—the balletic movement from yesterday in which some O.O.C. guy over at Oren Abel's had sailed into the air and landed on a girl's car. Gretchen had watched him making everything tick in the driveway for five beats before he'd started sliding down. He wasn't shouting and cursing any more. He was just lying there pressing his mouth to the windshield and you had to picture what his scary restraint looked like from inside the car—his lips pressed to the glass, all slimed out and bloodless. Like snail bellies.

But of course it was Uri who would get to do that—that terrific whole bit with the mouth. Great material, she knew. In the end her idea turned the sketch into Uri's show, but that was just life. Gretchen was used to the supportive role of the girl gripping an imaginary steering wheel and thinking how someday, without quite pushing over the top, some angry but mostly restrained guy was just going to go ahead and kill her.

When it was over, Mr. Mulert seemed a little impressed, but no one clapped; even in your loyalty you might risk him thinking you were enthusiastic about work he must, for your own good, tear to shreds. Chuck the Ripper.

Besides, weeks ago his professional opinion on them had come in: they were all borderline hopeless, too immature or too emotional or too earnest (that was Gretchen), or dead lazy.

Mr. Mulert was suddenly shouting. "Hey, whose idea was this?" No one moved. He walked over to dead-lazy Uri and looked him up and down.

"Hers," Uri finally said.

"Really?"

Mr. Mulert paced a big circle around Gretchen. "That was good!" he shouted. "Did you people see that? She didn't go over the top! She let us meet the moment!"

Praise was as embarrassing as blame. Gretchen felt herself blushing. "That was actually terrifying!" Mr. Mulert said. For a brief instant he seemed to see her standing there. "How old are you?" he said softly. Too softly. His fierce eyes began sweeping over the whole sorry lot of them—all the Immatures and the Emotionals he had not yet reached. "How old are any of you people?" No one spoke. The man was like this all the time—first hopeful, then enraged.

Someone finally had to tell him, "We're fifteen."

The answer mortified them all. It seemed to cause the man to begin to sink to his knees and then to fall sideways, his head hitting the wall. "Okay, take a break," he said, shutting his eyes and lifting a hand with which to wave them off.

He didn't say anything more to Gretchen after that. Clearly she was a fluke.

A coincidence occurred that afternoon after she went in to let Malcolm know she was home and planning to walk to Wyman Drugs for shampoo. He asked her to get him a ream of paper from the copy shop next door, and she was only at the sidewalk when the girl over at Uncle Oren's called out to her, wanting to know if she ever did any baby-sitting.

Gretchen hadn't seen her and two little kids over there watching. As a group they were small. The girl, wearing the same odd serape she had on yesterday, looked today as if she might weigh ninety pounds.

Gretchen crossed the street, keeping one hand shoved in her

pocket and thinking how this was the person she'd just *done* in front of gaping fifteen-year-olds. She hoped it wouldn't be obvious.

At first the baby, seated in the girl's lap, smiled at Gretchen. He took fingers out of his mouth and pointed. The girl announced that this big three-and-a-half-year-old bruiser was Ricky, who had a cold and wasn't looking his best. "Are you, Ricky?" Her own name was Angela, she said, and this big blond glamour-puss here was Corey, age five.

The baby hid his face for the introductions, but the five-year-old ran right up and tapped Gretchen's elbow before folding pale, skinny arms across her chest and scowling as if she already knew Gretchen's whole story. "Is that your dad or what?" She was pointing to Malcolm's front study windows, where everyone could see him holding up a single slat in his venetian blind. "Cooper says he better stop spying on us or else you know what?"

"No," Gretchen said, "what?"

The child was flat out of ideas. She ran into the yard. "Watch! Watch me do something," she called, her cartwheels turning into various kinds of sweetly futile collapses into the grass.

"Maybe we're too weird to baby-sit for," Angela said. "I figure you heard us screaming like we were going to kill each other. Not that we would."

"I would," Corey called, a perfect sidekick. She knew it, too; she knew she was too quick for most adults and that the small peel-off tattoo on Angela's upper arm gave them an edge over Gretchen. She returned to sit beside Angela on one of the risers and began adjusting the Velcro straps on tiny pink falling-off sandals.

"Cooper does most of the screaming," Angela said. "Hope you won't bust us. I'm not supposed to get this house if I let Cooper move in." She got down eye-to-eye with Corey. "I'll be back on the street if I let boys in, right?" She made the child nod up and down to forcible pulls on her head. But Corey gave Gretchen a sidelong stare. "She's the one who'll tell, not me," Corey said as she wriggled free and ran off into the yard again.

"Cooper hasn't moved in here," Angela muttered in a low tone, "just in case anyone asks."

"You mean in case Oren Abel asks?" Gretchen said. "I wouldn't ever tell him anything."

"No?"

"No. Why would I?"

"Hey, maybe you have a crush on him. How should I know, I just got here."

You had to say something, so Gretchen said, "He has a crush on my mother," by way of getting some kind of leg up.

And for a moment it worked. The girl seemed ever so slightly bested. Gretchen picked up a little piece of twig and then tossed it in front of her. "My mom's this earnest type. She's my whole problem."

"And what kind of problem is he?" Angela indicated with her head that Malcolm was still over there behind his little slat, spying.

"He's harmless," Gretchen said. She liked the way the dialogue was proceeding. Angela was the real thing—a true improv in type and temperament.

"I'd say your dad's kind of hunky," she mused. "We've seen Mr. Hunky out in the yard a few times." She suddenly got up from where she was sitting and turned her back to Malcolm. "Let me feel your hair texture," she said. "It's nice. You ever put it up or you always let it go wild like this?"

Corey was immediately jealous. "She's a cosmetologist," Corey complained to Gretchen. Then she brightened. "I'm going to be a cosmetologist."

"You are?" Gretchen said. "When?"

The child put her hands on her hips. This was a triangle already. "You should go home," she said, first sticking out her tongue then swirling around in the yard as if to keep out of trouble with Angela. She dropped into position for a headstand. Her pink sandals kicked hard but refused to rise. Gretchen stepped to the child's side and held out one arm to allow legs to bump up and find the balancing point.

"Not bad," Gretchen said. "Don't close your eyes. Find a tree and keep looking at it." She turned to Angela. "Or is that for rowing a boat?"

Angela laughed. In Gretchen's experience most people didn't laugh unless it was at their own material. She caught another glimpse of Malcolm and, in a sudden rush of joy, almost waved at him so he'd catch on. He looked pretty silly from here.

But she didn't wave. Clearly Angela was too full of responsibility and kids to care one way or the other about Malcolm. "I just hope I can keep this all going," she mused. "My lawyer has this whole thing about me being on my own."

Gretchen didn't quite know how to pick up on "lawyer," for Pete's sake. Was she supposed to? No, she wasn't. Angela was looking around at the monstrous house looming from behind and threatening to swamp her. Then she stared at the whole neighborhood as if she were somehow expected to run that too. "Your parents probably think I'm out of my league." She was the kind of person who first paused and then pounced. "Right?" she said in a slightly threatening tone.

She reached for a soda can and took a long drink from it. "So can you do it for me? I guess you'll have to ask your parents. If your dad's bored you can bring him. Corey likes to be read to, don't you, kiddo?"

Corey said no, she could read on her own, she was a prodigy.

Angela lowered her voice. "It's no lie. You'll see. Don't forget your toothbrush. I might stay gone a few days."

"She's just joshing you," Corey explained, her headstand starting to wobble. "She has to get glasses. She's going blind."

"Not so blind I can't see your underpants. Even Gretchen's daddy can see your underpants." This idea made the child laugh and then lose her balance. Her curses were a bit shocking. Angela gave Gretchen a private look. Behind them the phone rang once and then stopped.

"That's Cooper," Corey taunted.

"Shut up. It is not."

"We saw this guy blowing out candles," Corey said. "Was that your boyfriend?"

"That was my brother," Gretchen said. "That was just Matt."

"Just Matt's a good name," Angela said. "Bring Just Matt with you later."

"Can't do that," Gretchen said. "Joined a cult. He's a boy missionary."

She could have done a riff on boys getting themselves mistaken for shoplifters, but it wouldn't have been as good as the zinger, the great thumbnail sketch. Boy missionary; that was good. Otherwise Matt was impossible to do—spacy and kind—hardly as easy to type cast as she'd just done. But good material is everything, Chuck claimed, and, in a moment of need, a real artist will sell her own mother for it.

"So, where you going right now?" Angela said. "You going to town or something?"

"The drugstore. You need anything?"

The girl reached out with a professional's hand again. "You've got great hair." She lifted a curly mangled cluster and then let it fall. "You need a trim, though. When you're ready, I'll do you. I can do full cuts, too. Yours is free."

Gretchen nodded. "Thanks," she said. Then she felt her first misstep coming. "So are you renting from Oren for a while?" It didn't fit the theme at all. Wrong, wrong, wrong.

Angela looked away and then back, squinting. "Hey, if I ever did decide to trim you, I'd make you bring a note from home. You know what I mean?" Suddenly she was up and yelling. "A little note from all the idiots on this whole stupid block!"

Corey didn't blink. She just looked at Gretchen and gave out the sweetest smile.

"Hey, all you home owners!" Angela continued to yell. "Hey, all you registered voters!" A dog started barking from somewhere. Across the street Gretchen saw Malcolm drop his slat. It was great.

"So, you don't need anything?" Gretchen said.

"Not from you, I don't!" Suddenly the girl was crying. "Maybe this is all some kind of trick."

"Yeah, but what kind?" Corey said in a fast pickup.

"Right," Gretchen said, "a good one or a bad one?"

Corey sat cross-legged in the grass and waited. She looked at Gretchen and kept smiling. Gretchen smiled back; she had no idea where they were now. It was heaven. All you could do was just keep the floor level. Try not to strain, Chuck would have advised. Underplay, underplay!

"Don't worry," Angela finally said. "I've got friends."

"No, she doesn't," Corey said quick as a flash.

"So, I'll see you later, Angela," Gretchen said. "What time you want me?"

"Forget it," the girl said, becoming a bad sport. "I've changed my mind."

He would have said don't push! Build! Build on small strokes.

"In that case I guess I'll get lost," she said. She waved fingers at Corey, who was clearly intrigued. Corey waved a finger back. Two against one, and very quiet about it.

"Hey!" Angela called, "I'm sorry, okay? Can you come at six? A couple of hours, max." She closed her eyes. "Please. I'm sorry."

"She really is," Corey said. "Don't be mad at her."

Gretchen turned and counted. One beat, two beats. "Who's mad? I'll see you around six." The child was following her, watching Gretchen slyly check to see if Malcolm had lifted up his little slat again.

He had. But waving wasn't what you did on this side of the planet. Over here even a five-year-old knew that if you waved you'd put an end to the yokels.

Gretchen winked instead. "Bye," Corey said, remaining so extremely economical for five. She was no fluke. She was a find, and so was Angela. She had never improved with three before. Three was practically impossible to do without years of experience, Chuck said.

When Gretchen got home she went right into Malcolm's study to give him his ream of paper. She was about to tell him of her funny conversation with Angela when he up and asked her instead if she'd had a glimpse of their new neighbors, as if he hadn't been standing there watching.

"Sure thing," Gretchen said. She flopped down into one of his reading chairs. This was not like him, and she found herself amused. "She's a single mom, I guess, not much older than me."

"Really?"

"Yep. Real smart. Asked me if nonstudents are ever allowed to use the Webster College library."

Blink, blink. Blink, blink, blink. It was what he did when you threw him off.

"Don't worry," Gretchen said. "I told her they aren't allowed." She now understood what baiting was. She dragged over his new hassock and put her feet up. "She also wanted to know if there's some kid who could do her yard."

She was inspired. (Hey, he had started it!) She watched him ease his bad back into the chair behind his desk. "Is Oren renting?" he asked.

"*Do* we know anyone who could do her yard?"

Recently the creaky dads around here had purchased a communal sit-down mower almost as big as a tractor. They took turns doing all the yards now—John, Ted, and him. He had to know what she was driving at. He made this surprised face. "Oh, no you don't," he said, shaking his head.

"I can mow it myself," she said. "I can do it tonight when I'm over there baby-sitting." It was her trump.

"*Baby*-sitting? Since when?"

Susan walked into the room just as Malcolm was lowering his voice into that reasonable tone, all kidding aside. "Seriously, Gretchen, I'm not sure it's a good idea for you to start in over there." He looked at Susan. "Right? We don't know who these people are."

"I've already said I would," Gretchen said. "You and Mom will be right here!"

She watched him return to the window and look out. She probably should have told him right then and there that they could see the lifted slat out there and that he was making them paranoid.

"For God's sake, Susan, who are these people?"

Gretchen looked at her mother. "When did he turn into this?"

"What's the matter, Malcolm?" Susan said. "Won't we be here if Gretchen needs us? Anyone going to ask me about my drive to Torreya?"

"How was it?" Malcolm murmured. He was still at the window, as if somehow this was only why he ever came to the window, just to figure out who they were.

"Angela and Corey and Ricky," Gretchen offered. She looked at her mother. "I'll be home by eight or nine."

"Okay, Mac?" Susan said, winking, then shaking her head to let Gretchen know she hadn't yet told Malcolm about Matt getting arrested in Danford. "Maybe Gretchen will find out where Oren is." Her mother lowered her voice. "Seriously. Think you can find out?"

"And what about that awful guy?" Malcolm said.

"What guy?" Gretchen said, shrugging at her mother and whispering she thought Oren must be renting or something. "I never saw any guy, Dad," she called.

"You most certainly did! You saw that fight as clearly as I did. We talked about it!"

"Oh, him," Gretchen said. "He's not there now."

"Really? Are you sure?"

"You two can slog this one out without me," Susan said. "Anything on the stove?"

It was Malcolm's week to cook.

"So, Dad," Gretchen said as she took up her own exit, "I'll make a deal. While I'm over there I'll get the scoop for you." She almost added, "They can see you, you know!" Good discipline, not saying it. At dinner she didn't tell about her improv sketch either. She felt mature, less earnest. How would you relate it anyway?—Chuck yelling out such amazing, amazing praise at how terrifying she'd sketched that guy.

When she got over there, Angela took off walking. She said she was going to go look at things. She hadn't had a chance to see the town yet. She was going to bring them back some ice cream, if they were good.

Corey turned out to be somewhat jealous of Ricky, who wanted to be held the whole time Gretchen was being shown everything interesting in the house. Corey led her through a path of clean laundry folded in almost every room, starting in the living room, where Gretchen was surprised to see Oren's ratty furniture still in place, his lamps, his rugs, all the same table junk—little silver ash trays with a paper clip or rubber bands in them. His books were all there, his unused piano piled with old sheet music, old magazines stacked in the corners. What was fresh was the clean laundry and the comforting sound of things still turning in the dryer off the kitchen. Angela was washing boxes and boxes of clothes.

In the kitchen the cupboards were loaded with canned goods. When Gretchen opened the refrigerator to get Corey a cold drink, she saw milk, hamburger meat, sodas, raw carrots, a jar of peanut butter. The freezer was full of steaks, and there was something about the stacked packages that suggested Oren had had all this stuff delivered. You could just tell; it was sort of over the top, the way someone would order for you if he had no idea what you really ate.

Corey came up to her. "Are you spying on us?"

Gretchen slammed the freezer door. "No!"

"Looks like you are."

"So, are you going read to me?" Gretchen said. "I don't know any girls your age who read."

Corey ran out of kitchen and came back with an ancient *National Geographic* from the living room.

"What, from this?" Gretchen asked. "How old are you?"

"Just point somewhere," Corey said. Gretchen's doubt only added to the fun, it would appear. And so finally Gretchen turned a few pages before pointing, whereupon Corey's eyebrows went up into her head as if a reading of "The Three Bears" was about to begin: "The lore of this strange custom speaks to its ability to sustain the power of the elder tribal members through various bouts of modernization and inevitable contact with the outer world." She smiled up at Gretchen. "Point again," she said.

"Gee," Gretchen said.

"You want to see my room?" Corey snatched the magazine from her hands. "Come on," she said, pulling everyone out of the kitchen and down the hall.

"Gee," Gretchen said again, tripping after her, the baby riding on a hip like potatoes. "So is Angela going to start you in school soon?"

"She can't! She's not my mom!"

"Oh," Gretchen said. They were headed up the stairs now. "So where's your mom?"

"With God or the devil," Corey called back over her shoulder. "Take your pick."

"Then who's Angela?" Gretchen called.

Corey stopped at the top, putting hands on her hips and looking down. "She's just *Angela*. She's not anything. Hurry up!"

"Who's Cooper? Is he your daddy?"

Corey had had enough questions. "Nope, nope, nope, you're a dope, dope, dope."

She headed off into one of the upstairs rooms. Just then they both heard the sound of Malcolm's innocent tractor mower. Its roar grew loud and then louder as the mower came into the yard, causing Corey to run right past Gretchen and down the stairs again. "A helicopter!" Gretchen followed in the general excitement. The warm weight of the placid little boy in her arms felt strangely sweet by the time she got to the porch. Out here the sight of her father waving from the mower was healing. He was smiling as if he were living up to some agreement they'd made—or making amends he didn't even have to make. This was the kind of thing that made her love him, brag about him to her friends sometimes. Right now it was the way he'd decided to make himself famous with Corey by wearing a bandanna tied into a kerchief. He looked like a peasant lady, seated high on that mower with a knot under his chin and a bonnet peak at the top of his head. Corey took one look and let out an elfin squeal as Malcolm waved and then disappeared around the east side of the house and roared on to the back. Just the way he'd let his face go suddenly sober was a clue that when he came round on the west side Corey could expect something equally amusing from him. She tore off along the porch to wait. Yes, there he was again. This time he'd tied the bandanna over his nose and mouth as if he were going to hold up a bank.

Corey called and called as he passed slowly along the whole front width of the house again. Malcolm refused to acknowledge new attempts at getting his attention. Once more he disappeared and reappeared, this time the bandanna over his eyes.

Corey had a fit, of course. He was an old dummy! He was going to have a wreck! But he missed all the front yard trees, and the trick undid Corey, made her run off the porch and beg for a ride. Malcolm finally stopped, lifted his blindfold, and jumped at the sight of her before allowing her to climb into his lap for the remaining turns around the house.

By that time, Gretchen felt calmed down. But she didn't know what to do yet—what to make of these little kids, whether to tell her parents about their not being Angela's. Slowly she began to rock Ricky to sleep on the old porch swing. A toddler, at a moment like this, was a solid bit of sane world. She was able to ease into the house and make a pallet in the living room for him out of several couch cushions. For a long time she sat patting him on his square back, hearing her father and Corey from the front windows.

"Is that an octopus?" she heard Corey ask.

She saw her father lift his head to consider this question as if it had never been asked by his own children; to look for the billionth time at the street's most famous live oak, named Octopus Oak by Gretchen herself, the one that spread in a scary tangle over most of these houses from the Richardses' yard.

"Sure looks like it, doesn't it?" she heard Malcolm muse as he waited while the child counted all the tree's creepy arms. "An octopus oak," Malcolm finally agreed.

Don't let them be Cooper's kids, Gretchen thought.

Angela showed up at the time she promised, but she showed up in a car. With Cooper. Perhaps she had walked to where the guy worked. But it had to have been all a lie about him not moving in with them. Gretchen watched him open the car trunk, look in, then slam it as hard as he could. She didn't ask any questions. She just stood on the porch and waited as he came walking toward the house with Angela. It was hard to tell his age, but this was no boy. He could be thirty or forty.

Corey bolted at the first sight of him, pounding her feet up the stairs. Cooper made it to the porch in time to hear her banging the door to her upstairs room.

The first thing out of his mouth was stupidly foul, its direction unclear, as if he were merely cursing the ground they all walked on. Angela halfheartedly attempted to introduce Gretchen, but he managed to shove past and disappear. He too stomped up the stairs, slamming doors; Corey would know she didn't have a thing on him when it came to being unenthusiastic about seeing someone.

"Yeah well," Angela said, then repeated all of Cooper's curses in a falsetto voice that made her laugh. "You want to have a cold drink with me on the steps? I forgot the ice cream."

It seemed her only offer at the moment. It would be rude to say no.

For several minutes they sipped diet sodas on the risers and smelled the cut grass without comment. Gretchen noticed that she and Angela had the same size feet.

Gretchen leaned back and tried to relax, which was hard to do. It was as if she was wasting the girl's time, even if Angela herself had made the suggestion that they hang out.

She relaxed by considering the light streaming from the windows opposite. Malcolm was seated openly at his desk, his window shades raised to suggest that not only was he there now in plain view, he was not leaving his post until she got home.

John Richards was moving around alone in his big old house, turning lamps on and off in various rooms. They'd felt bad for lonely John all this year, but from over here she saw how he appeared to move in and out of peaceful chambers. He was bathed in amber light.

"He gives me a pain in the gut," Angela said, but she was talking about Cooper. "Corey absolutely hates him, but one time he saved my life, so I owe him."

"You don't owe him!" Gretchen said almost immediately, although she had not known she was going to say anything. She lowered her voice. "You don't owe him! It's the first rule of life."

"I'll write it down," Angela said.

Across the street they watched the family car pull in. Susan had done one of her late dashes to the 7-Eleven, Gretchen bet. Susan pulled to the back and entered the house through the mud room, where she had a light on. Both parents seemed determined not to appear to be checking on things over at Oren's house, but clearly they were.

"Your mother, I take it," Angela said. "Her I've yet to see in the light of day."

Gretchen shrugged. "You'll like her."

"She teach you that first rule of life?" Angela had one of those chronically disrespectful voices she almost couldn't help. Meanwhile she was pointing at Malcolm. "And will I like him?" The girl seemed agitated all of a sudden. She whispered several long sentences, as if talking to herself would prevent her striking out at Gretchen.

"Want me to go?" Gretchen said.

"This is just all such a joke," the girl said. "He screws up everything in my life."

Then dump him, Gretchen wanted to say. She could get away with it in the dark, a stolen line—one girl telling another girl just to dump him. Just dump him. It was fun to practice. Just dump him.

She couldn't interpret Angela's jitters, exactly—the way she began clawing into the black pocketbook she'd brought outside with her. She looked as if she were digging for smack, but she ended up pulling out a pair of new glasses in a new case, first turning away to get the glasses on and then turning back and vamping. "Ta-da!"

Dump him. Just dump him.

Angela was taking out a mirror and looking at herself. "These cost a ton, but you know what we did? We got them at the college!"

"The college? You mean Webster?"

"I didn't know what he was trying to pull at first. Right away he's asking the woman at the switchboard if they have a lost-and-found, explaining how I was just there for an interview and stuff and left my glasses. She's going, 'Really?' like she knows he's a maniac, which he is by the way."

"I saw."

"But wait, then she goes, 'Well honey, let's just see if your glasses are here!' Turns out she's got nineteen shoe boxes full of them, and I'm going, 'Gee, it's so hard to tell, they were new and I can't hardly remember—' And Cooper's going, 'Hey, these look like the ones! Put these on, Ange!' Meanwhile he's gone right for the Pierre Cardins. The old lady's going 'Hmm,' and he's going, 'It's them, Ange! They look terrific.' And then we just start thanking her to death and walking on out of there with these, like, four-hundred-dollar frames. Eye Wear charged thirty bucks for the lenses."

Angela handed the glasses to Gretchen, but then came the serious mood shift. "I have plenty of money," she was suddenly saying. "I know I look disadvantaged or something. It's because I haven't done anything with my talents."

Gretchen started to speak, but then didn't. The girl was growing furious again. She took back the glasses and then suddenly pulled out way too much baby-sitting money from her wallet. When Gretchen drew back, the girl acted like she'd like to snatch her bald. "Hey, give it to charity!" she yelled, grabbing at Gretchen's shirt front and managing to cram down several twenty-dollar bills. Right before she flounced into the house and slammed the door, she paused for one last remark. She didn't appreciate people coming over and just mowing her yard like this without even asking her.

8

CELL PHONE

THE CALL CAME AT TWO IN THE MORNING, JUST AS HE WAS slipping off into something deeper than the sleep of prayerful men. Of funny men.

"You awake, Oren? Harry says I'm not supposed to bother you, but I couldn't help it."

"Are you bored over there, Angela? You'll remember that's my biggest concern." Oren drew aside heavy drapes and let light fall in from the parking lot. Outside, five complexes, all identical to his own, were making their protective circle around the expensive cars in the lot. Wagon train.

"You're never going to let me into your family, are you?"

"My family?"

"You're always going to be ashamed of me, aren't you?"

"My nephews will know about you, Angela. Nick and Frank will know. I'm not going to keep you a secret."

"Yeah, but they'll never welcome me in, will they?"

"They don't welcome *me*, Angela!"

"I'll never meet Nick and Frank's cute *wives*, right?"

He couldn't get off the train. It kept going. "Frank is unmarried, my dear."

"Still, you'd hate it if I ever met him, right?"

"I haven't said that. I'm going to have to sort out what we'll do along those lines."

"*Along those lines.* Boy, is that just like you!"

He wasn't sure where this was coming from. He suspected Harry had helped to make the girl a bit paranoid, what with his fine print and keeping Oren unavailable. Oren himself felt that he was abandoning her in some way. It was exactly the panicked edge in the girl's voice.

"What did you do this evening, Angela? We have to make sure you have enough to do."

"I'm giving you until Lincoln's birthday, Oren. I'm looking at this datebook you gave me. I think by Lincoln's birthday you ought to introduce me."

He sat with his new cellular phone, listening while she turned pages in a daily planner. He'd asked Harry to give it to her as a symbol of what had happened to her. She had a house; she had a life.

But he could hear the resentment. She riffled the pages loudly as if shocked to be running up on all these holidays no one had ever bothered to tell her about, big and little, American and Canadian. She began rattling them off as she flipped the pages in a kind of fury—Memorial Day, Armed Forces Day, Victoria Day, *Flag* Day!

"I'm writing it down in the *book*, Oren!"

"There are many holiday occasions, Angela," Oren said, "and I'm sure we'll rise to a whole lot of them in time."

"Name another one. Name one we'll rise to."

"You go to sleep now, Angela. Think you can? Don't want to lose the day tomorrow."

"What's that supposed to mean? Just now you said you wanted to know what I've been doing, not that it's any of your business."

He could hear her breathing. He should call for his car and go over there and calm her down. The shock was too great. She didn't know where she was or where she was going. The irony struck him. He was finally home, and she was completely dislodged.

"I got my glasses, Oren."

Now he could hear a childlike crow that belied her belligerence just moments before. "That's wonderful, Angela!" he sang. "Getting things done! That's the whole idea!"

He held his breath.

"I got those people from across the street to mow the lawn too," she said. She was back to an almost threatening tone once again. Harry had made her agree that she wouldn't be asking the neighbors to be over there helping her from day one. He'd explained to her Oren's plan to take her around to say hello. Oren saw that the wait had been hard on her nerves, that the neighbors would seem like monsters to her now.

"Well," he said, "and how did it go?"

"You're so full of it, Oren."

"A few days, Angela. Remember? That was all Harry was suggesting you wait."

Old friends on Everett Street; so much for them, he thought, lying awake in their beds right this moment listening to her screaming exactly where Oren could go soak his head.

"You have patience, Angela. I know you do. It was only a simple agreement."

His, not hers! She would see him in a month, she screamed. Did he understand? He could forget the end of the week as planned. If he came *near* this house before Lincoln's birthday, she'd have him arrested, and that went for the idiot man across the street, who, she suggested, Oren better tell to quit spying on her before she went over there herself and tore his eyes out of his face.

9

CASH

EARLY THE NEXT MORNING MALCOLM WATCHED FROM HIS front porch as Susan and Gretchen pulled off to meeting and workshop respectively. He had been up for a good part of the night and was now planning to go back to bed and get some sleep. A Webster freshman over on the campus had threatened to jump from a modest height and had scared Malcolm pretty badly. It made him pray for his own and count his blessings. His own strange Matt was safely ensconced at a sudden camp. He should smell the coffee.

Susan hadn't yet told him much about Matt's camp. She wanted Malcolm to drive with her on Saturday to see it for himself. He was going to be pleasantly surprised, she said.

Right at this moment he would be quite glad to be surprised, pleasantly or unpleasantly. At least his son had a direction and a passion he could grow out of. Loners like poor Lloyd Reniere could only come up with the idea of jumping off a low ledge.

Malcolm had kept an eye on Lloyd, as he had with all incoming freshmen, and had been pained to see the boy going around all fall with a baseball cap pulled rakishly to one side as if he thought its brim hid the hearing device behind his ear. Not so long ago

Webster College had been a friendlier place for such boys; today the processes of natural selection were crueler. Maybe Lloyd would have been better advised to pick a larger school and not let admissions directors like Malcolm pounce on his high test scores and inadvertently promise a welcoming atmosphere at a small setting. He thought of his own son, of course—perhaps better off at a junior college of his choice; a camp; a group; an identity.

To make amends for Lloyd's misery and that of a few others, Malcolm's determination this morning was to cancel a planned three-day hiking trip into Georgia, much as he felt he needed it. Malcolm was determined to be present and accounted for when the question was again raised about keeping a dorm open during the winter break. It was a policy dear to old President Davies's heart. The new president was said to hate it. Used to be that the foreign students needed that dorm left open during their winter breaks because they couldn't get home. Not anymore, the new president was arguing. These days the foreign students were all frequent flyers.

Malcolm sat down in one of his porch rockers and began to work on his counterargument. It was the regular kids now who needed a dorm left open; their families were in disarray, and they had no place to go. Did they visit their fathers off in the Virgin Islands with a girlfriend or their mothers honeymooning somewhere else with a new husband? Whether Webster liked it or not, a significant portion of their regular students were virtually homeless.

The counter to Malcolm's counterargument went something along the lines of the following: No, no. Wrong, wrong. These days kids just didn't want to make the effort to get home! They used the open dorm as a base for trips to and from various watering holes, and they left behind seriously depressed and dejected classmates— the Lloyd Renieres. Remember when faculty used to bring a student home for dinner during the break? It didn't take much to figure out why the tradition had died. Back then the guest, nine times out of ten, was a polite, well-spoken, interesting, and *grateful* foreign student.

In his mind Malcolm was just about to rise to expand on a few other points in *his* argument. He was tipping back his rocker and beginning to think it out when he heard a scream from Oren's front porch.

"Why don't you take a picture, it'll last longer!"

Malcolm brought his chair forward and squinted.

"We're getting sick of you, you know that?"

It was the young mother or girlfriend! If she had a name, Malcolm forgot what Gretchen said it was. But she was pointing at him, all right. She was moving right down Oren's front steps, the toddler straddling her left hip. Malcolm stood up and began to come down his own steps to greet her. He was fascinated to see that even in her fury, she actually paused at the curb to look both ways before crossing Everett Street. Her smallness became painfully evident as she approached.

"I'm Malcolm," he began, still hoping there was some mistake. "You met my daughter just yesterday. Gretchen's the one who babysat for you."

The baby's fat legs were gripping her hard, and its head got bigger and bigger as she came closer and then finally stopped on his walkway and looked up at him. She had a fringe of hair, a fringe of metal on both small ears. Her face was a map of welts, as if she'd been crying. The baby, apparently used to crying, noticed only Malcolm, at whom he pointed with joyous recognition, recalling last night's friendly waves from porch to lawn mower.

"Daddy!" the baby squealed.

In other circumstances it would have been sweet.

"I ought to call the cops," the girl said, but at this point Malcolm was aware that she had merely crossed the street to get a better look at him. She was not really angry. She was confused, frustrated. He felt a mix of fear and sorrow for her, even as he reminded himself that he was completely worn out from his all-night ordeal with Lloyd.

"Malcolm Robb," he repeated. "You met Gretchen."

"Yeah," she said, "I did."

She sounded defeated now. Bouncing into view over on Oren's porch was the boyfriend or whatever he was—the furious character who Gretchen had said was no longer around. There he most certainly was.

He was wearing black boots and boxers—a man with a pasty white face, who might be approaching middle age and who seemed amused at Malcolm being snagged as a third in an argument that had been going on inside Oren's house. She'd better get back there, the guy yelled, or he'd come settle her hash.

"Now I'm *really* going to get it," she said.

This Malcolm had not expected, even if he should have. "Are you afraid?" he said.

"Sure," the girl said, but she was actually grinning at him. Then she stuck her tongue out—an act that made Malcolm feel further out of his depth than he'd felt in years. No gesture from either of these two people allowed him to imagine a future in which they could all live in peace. A tornado trailed after them wherever they went. They needed someone as funny as Malcolm to witness it. They needed someone like Malcolm out on his porch or in his yard to look forward to whenever their blowups landed one or the other of them in plain view.

Malcolm took the high road nevertheless. "If you're afraid," he ventured, "you don't have to go back over there just now."

"Who are you," she said, "the crisis person?"

Last night Lloyd had yelled a host of obscenities—none of them as hurtful as this all-too-apt phrase. In an unfamiliar wave of weary resentment at his college role, slowly sucking life out of him, he found himself smugly reminding himself, But this one is not one of yours, Malcolm. Quite thankfully, not one of yours. Last night Lloyd had first cursed and then leaped right on top of him, leaving a visible dark hole in the pride-of-the-college azalea bushes growing close around Comstock Hall.

This morning he did not turn away, however. Later he would remember with some bitterness how he invited her into the house a second time, and how it was she who turned to gaze at the man with whom she had become enmeshed. One sensed she had no idea how to reverse this or any other moment in her life.

How does a person like this go into reverse, he thought as he watched her hike the baby up higher on her hip and stand for a moment before beginning her return trip. In the time it took her to cross the street, a small plane flew overhead, ripping the quiet morning into rags as one tears an old shirt.

"Who's your friend, Angela?" he heard the guy laugh as she got back to her own yard. "You got yourself a little friend?"

She was not one of his own. Thank God!

Nevertheless Malcolm stayed at the front of the house instead of returning to the back bedroom to sleep. He lay on the couch in his study and listened to more muffled shouts from Oren's house. Was this when one called the cops? Did one wait for something worse? Last night when the switchboard operator heard Lloyd scream-ing, she had called Malcolm first and a campus security officer sec-ond. Malcolm was a known father figure, and a jogger who could arrive from his house barely panting. Still, he was outdated. The switchboard operator too, calling him up the way people used to call up firemen to rescue kittens out of trees.

He fell asleep on his couch. An hour later he heard faint, repeated slammings of car doors. Angela and the booted boyfriend twice her age seemed to be packing the car for some excursion. He heard the guy yell—where was the damn volleyball? Malcolm sat up finally and went to his window to lift the slat in his blind.

A volleyball was already sailing out the front of Oren's house and bounding in Malcolm's direction. He saw the little girl Corey, who ran after the ball and then stood and seemed to stare at his house.

"Get in this damn car right now," he heard the guy say, as if the kid were his own. It seemed more likely that the man would have a child this age than would Angela. Either way the sight of Corey, seeming to look for lawn-mower Malcolm, made him feel sick at heart.

A folding chair got piled into the trunk, and stacks of towels put into the backseat along with Corey and the baby. When the boyfriend disappeared into the house, the whole front of Oren's place stood rock still. Finally Angela sauntered out and glanced Malcolm's way, as if to let him know that she hadn't gotten it after all. Just fooling.

He waited until they were gone and then headed out for a sprawl in the front porch glider. He took his cordless phone in case anyone wanted him, but now he was feeling quite sure that he should just go ahead and take off tomorrow for his planned three days. Who needed him, really? He should disappear as planned, all by his blissful self. He envisioned several of his birthday presents dangling off the back of his pack—the new hummingbird feeder, the new binoculars. Home on Monday; no one would know he'd been gone.

Alone in the glider, he napped quite soundly until Gretchen rang at one-thirty to remind him she was staying the afternoon and night at Uri Jurinko's house in the country. They had their workshop parts to rehearse. The fabulous sessions with Mr. Mulert were almost over, and she was bummed. Regular school was starting up on Monday.

"I could do this full time," she sighed into his ear.

"Uri's parents *are* going to be home tonight, I take it?"

"Dad, come on—"

"And you really do sleep in Uri's sister's old room?"

"Daddy!"

"Want to know how many Webster students it takes to put in a lightbulb?"

"Don't try to weasel out of what you just asked. Me and Uri? We're from kindergarten, remember? Not to mention he's got this thing for Chuck and about ten other guys at the moment."

"Uri?"

"Bye-bye, I love you, worship and adore you. See you tomorrow after class. The Jurinkos are picking up. Remind Mom."

It may have been then that he had a premonition. He blurted out to her, "Hey, I don't want you over at Oren's doing any more baby-sitting. Okay? I have bad vibes about those people. Who the hell are they?"

"The world's on its head, Dad. Think of art! It's the only flame. And back to that earlier topic. Even if I was with some guy, which I'm not, you should just count your blessings, you know. And I even have this theory about Matt, did I tell you? I think you should stop worrying."

"You're right! I should definitely stop. I'm stopping right now!"

He heard them both laughing together even as a strange weight of dread, heavy as a watermelon, sat on his chest. They said their chipper good-byes—take care, have fun, see you, love you—then he slumped back into the padded glider. Maybe it was only the tired-ness, lack of a full night's sleep. One suicidal Webster kid, and you're suddenly feeling your age; one cranky new neighbor, and you're sud-denly an old man.

He jumped slightly. Several wobbly sprinklers came on over in Ted and Beth Harwood's yard. To his left, John Richards's new auto-matic system began its softer start-up, a low, high-tech hissing. Mal-colm arose finally and made it to the steps to sit on the riser and watch a friendly car pull up. John got out and waved off James Hick-son, the Economics Department chair, who could sometimes make his black Cutlass ease down the road like a limo.

"That was James!" John called and then headed up his walk and steps. "Susan's invited me for dinner," he called from his porch.

"What, again?" Malcolm said.

"Yeah, you want me to bring the salad?"

"That would be helpful, you bum."

Neighbor phones began ringing. Malcolm was able to hear John's as soon as he got his door open. "See you later," John called.

To his right, he was able hear Beth and Ted's phones, muffled but multiple. They seemed to trigger his own. The thing went off in his hand, first surprising him, then reminding him that this could be his first telemarketing call. He'd read somewhere that they start in at this time, trying to catch part-time workers, mostly women, as they get home. Then he remembered it would be his parents. In the past month it was becoming his father's strategy to call Malcolm during the day as he often came home from the campus for his lunch. Capable Susan had always threatened the role of ultra-capable Larry.

"Dad!"

"Wait," his father said, "here's Mim picking up."

Larry Robb was in a wheelchair. Three strokes in the last year. The situation made younger Mim tend to fight with Malcolm as if he'd just stepped into their apartment.

"You remember that crowded hall closet we have, right?"

"Small," Malcolm said, "very small!"

"Small?" Mim complained.

"Son, when are you going to let us know about August?"

"It's the size of a phone booth!"

"You were supposed to decide about August last week."

"It's all his war junk!"

"It would be nice to know, Malcolm."

"I'm pitching everything out of there. Maybe I'll just pitch him out!"

That was when Malcolm heard the guy's low tailpipe scraping the smooth surface of Everett Street. They were back. Some outing had been clearly aborted.

"Pitch *me* out?"

He didn't like to be found sitting there, seeming to be waiting for them as they eased by in their car before making the turn into Oren's drive. But that's exactly what happened. The pleasure of it caused the boyfriend to flatten his hand on the horn. Malcolm brought his knees together and continued to sit with the phone to his ear, thinking *shit, shit, shit.*

The tailpipe scraped on Oren's slope at the start of the drive.

Malcolm couldn't tell if the girlfriend was giving him a mock wave or merely letting her pale arm trail briefly out the passenger side as the car eased slowly to the back of the house. Everything seemed to go ominously dead.

"Malcolm?"

"What?"

"We thought you hung up on us!"

At around three that afternoon he took a walk into town. To purchase what, exactly, he couldn't remember later. That part was a blank. Close friends would say that the afternoon resulted in tragedy. But technically that could not be the case. Our lives are not tragic unless we are people with a potential for great good who end up doing evil. Malcolm only came out of the drugstore with a little package in his hand—the shock later wiping out for him a memory of what he'd bought.

There was the girl, Angela, with Corey hanging on her legs. The baby was sitting on her hip. They were using the pay telephone on the corner. All three were hysterical.

It was the baby's crying that frightened Malcolm the most. He would not have been alarmed had he not known the child's sweet disposition. In the presence of all things bloodcurdling, the baby had seemed good-natured, having heard and seen everything there was to hear and see. But right then he was flailing his arms, hitting the frame of the phone booth, too upset to know that he'd smacked his hand. The mouth came open impossibly wide, locked in a pathetic red trembling of spittle and tender tongue. The desperation in that wail made a few people stop and consider the scene. Small arms waved in spasms. A vein stood out on a purple head. Malcolm hurried forward as he might have hurried to grab a child choking on food.

At first there was no acknowledgment that someone was lifting her baby in the air. She began screaming into the telephone that her boyfriend had ripped a phone out of the wall at her house. It wasn't a regular phone. It came right out of the wall and didn't plug back in.

"Tell them there's no jack," Malcolm said, leaning into the booth. That made the five-year-old cry and then raise her arms toward Malcolm, who scooped her up too, amazed that her spindly weight seemed less than the baby's.

"There's no jack!" Angela screamed into the phone. Her jaw was set. There was only the mildest look of recognition in her eyes as she stood and waited while someone put her on hold.

Malcolm called her by name and told her his own. "Can I help you?" he said. "You were upset with me this morning, so if I can help you in any way—"

This made her face contort to keep from breaking down. "He's got a fever," she finally said. The baby's fever was the last straw. She'd walked to town to call the phone company, she said, and get baby aspirin. Right now her whole life was a complete wreck.

"It'll be all right," Malcolm said. "I'm sorry about that old phone at Oren's. I don't think he's had a change over there in forty years." The weight of the children felt almost comforting, as if a healing balm was held out to his own floating anxiety. "Hey, Corey, don't cry. You guys don't cry now."

The little girl's eyes swam in steely blue. "Okay," she sobbed.

Angela was slumped against the glass, but then she stood up to listen; someone was back on the line, obviously giving her a break. A truck could be at her house later in the day.

"What time?" She looked at Malcolm. Then she listened and couldn't remain civil. "I can't pay you in cash. He's got my purse, he's got my new bank card!" She looked at Malcolm again. This was how hard the world came down on some people. "This isn't my fault!" she screamed into the phone.

"I can get you cash," Malcolm said, and she nodded and promised the person that she'd have it, then listened a long time and finally had to promise again, had to listen again to the fact that the repairman would be instructed to ask for cash.

So there was Malcolm holding the two kids and steering Angela across Main Street to the automatic teller, the guy Cooper sitting in his car the entire time at some distance down a much smaller side street, Tibbit Street, which was full of shady and terrible cool. Had he seen Cooper's car, Malcolm liked to think later, he wouldn't have been alarmed, only better prepared.

Cooper had apparently watched him put down the older child in order to get his bank card out of his limp wallet. After that stop at the automatic teller, Malcolm had taken everyone into the drugstore to get baby aspirin and then brought them all out and walked them home. The little girl did all the talking, and nothing much was said between himself and Angela that was not also said to Corey, cavorting ahead of them, turning around to look at them. At around four Malcolm observed the phone van arrive. After that he went to the kitchen to start some dinner.

"Honey, did you say something?" Susan called to him when she got home a half-hour later.

"Yes!" he called back, "I want you to come in here and have a look at this grater!" He was standing in the kitchen, waiting with some impatience as she put down her packages in the hall. There was something sweet about the way she entered to find him holding the grater over the sink. Susan always found affectionate possibilities in what otherwise tripped Malcolm up. Or perhaps it was that she thought she heard love instead of irritation in his voice as she ducked under his elbow and hugged him before he could prevent her.

"What's the matter?" she said, "what did I do?" She breathed out a minty cloud. Her nose touched his hand as she peered earnestly at the spot where he pointed.

"There!" Malcolm said. "See it?"

The grater had not been properly cleaned. A curling tendril of cheese clung to the inside wall—the common side, where the cutting edges were crescent shaped. He held the opening very still so he wouldn't lose the evidence. If it were carrot pulp on the diamond side, would he have been a better sport? One needed a toothpick in those impossible openings.

But she would not have heard in his complaint either bad sportsmanship or tiresome pettiness. Always domestic conflict offered up to her its smooth side. She was blessed. She flattened her head on his chest while he talked so that his deeper tones set up, she said, all the delicate bell bones in her ear. "Hmm," she said, listening to his ribs as she reached inside the opening of the grater to put the curl of cheese in her mouth. She made a big swallow by way of admitting all her shortcomings.

"I'm going to lie down," she said. She ducked lightly back under his arm as if she were ducking a turnstile. "I'm not going to last until dinnertime if I don't get my feet up for a minute."

He had forgotten she'd been at the dentist all afternoon. Absentminded herself, she was not one to care about his forgetting her whereabouts during the day, forgetting any anticipated dental work. There was only lightness in her voice, no tone of even having to rise to the moment. She undressed and called out details from the back bedroom—a few X rays and one deep filling was about all Carl had done to her. In his kindness, he'd given her a lot of painkiller. She felt as if she had a furry animal where her tongue used to be. He called back a few answers to her as she sighed and flopped into the bed before growing quiet. His brain may have, right then, planted the silent seed of mortification and shame in one of his frontal lobes. Him and his grater. Surely he hadn't been irritated over a bit of dried cheese just moments before the horrific pounding started up at the front of the house!

They had one of those old-fashioned door knockers. Someone banged it many long seconds, over and over. Susan came flying out of the back bedroom to tell Malcolm that it must be an emergency at the very instant Malcolm spotted the guy through the smoked glass at the front of the hall. It seemed crazy that he was about to try to make him stop that noise when already he had a prescience that he was a goner, that they'd been arguing over there, and that in her fury about his leaving her without a phone or a car she'd said some-thing suggestive about the money.

Malcolm pulled open the door, and money was precisely the issue. When was he going to learn to mind his own business? How did he think Angela was going to pay him back? In trade? They were both broke, he must have gathered, and they happened not to be able to pay anyone anything at the moment. He didn't know what Malcolm had in mind, but he was over here to tell him he'd smash his lousy face if he so much as showed it at the window. He was a lousy, stupid son of a bitch—spying on them since Sunday.

It was never a matter of having to explain anything to Susan. She came to Malcolm's side in the hall, lifted his elbow, and asked the man what this was all about. She rested lightly under Malcolm's armpit. He felt a sexy arm go around his back as she eased him through the door and onto the porch, forcing the guy to step back a foot or two. She waited for the door to close and then asked the guy his name.

He didn't answer. Perhaps he reacted badly to her attempt to teach him courtesy or else to her seeming not to want him inside her house. Maybe he detected a calm firmness. Something had made him wilder. His screaming caused John on one side and Beth on the other to come out on their porches. That wasn't good. The guy's eyes darted around as if he felt surrounded. Ted was down in his yard resetting a few sprinklers. "Malcolm, is there anything you want me to do?"

That wasn't good either—perhaps the very thing to light new fuses, because suddenly there was a visible gun. Two porch-level and one yard-level witnesses would see the guy threatening them with a firearm as Angela appeared out of nowhere. She seemed to swoop into the yard from across the street as if she'd seen everything from her own porch and come running. She was carrying the baby and screaming up at Cooper: Was he crazy? was he nuts? no one had done anything except give her a little cash from the machine!

And he may have waved the gun only to scare her back across the street. Later John and Beth concurred that the shooting happened in the few brief seconds it took Susan to run down the steps to take the baby from Angela, whose yells were clearly making matters much worse. Déjà vu for Malcolm, who'd reached for the same baby in town. This time he was thrown off balance by something, so he didn't see Susan reaching, exactly. John, Ted, and Beth all did. And even to them the guy, still beside Malcolm on the porch, hadn't seemed to fire as directly as he must have. The cops couldn't find the bullet later. He'd fired so directly that the bullet hit and kept on going. Even before an ambulance team was permitted to remove Susan's body, the cops had begun looking; for an open-and-shut case against the guy they were better off finding it while the body was still there as a guide. But it was almost impossible, this particular bullet being so small and so hell-bent on avoiding any more of harm's way.

That was the other amazing thing. The baby was not hit. He had been fast in her arms as she went down. She'd seemed to cover him and stop his screams. How a bullet somehow passes through one individual but misses another, the sheriff said, was one of the many miracles of life and chance. And he'd seen plenty of those before, if not quite this one.

10

MATT

A FEW EMOTIONALLY DISTURBED WOLVES ARRIVE, AND IT IS Matt's job to give each Wolf a map of the campgrounds. He is their leader.

Bears, Panthers, and Lions all have different leaders. All arrive by noon, and throughout the blackening pine there is slow progress—duffel bags dragging and no one talking as each finds his assigned hut, a one-room cabin big enough for several double bunks and a leader's cot. They have instructions to drop their duffels on a bunk and come outside immediately. Empty-handed, the boys appear somewhat gloomier than they did at the central dining hall. They are young and don't know how to buddy up yet.

George Murray finally moves in with his clipboard and begins to dispatch Lions to the latrine and Panthers to the kitchen. All Wolves and Bears must clear brambles off the nature trail, George explains. He bends down to eye level with a complaining Bear. "Use your map! Use your head! Get going!"

Later, after dinner and vespers, Matt's four charges—Robert, Jason, Todd, and Kevin—follow him and his moving flashlight back to the Wolf Den. They all wait for him to introduce himself. There's no place to unpack, Matt explains. No drawers, no closets. Their duffels will stay zippered closed and lined up side by side against the south wall. They can use the empty lower bunks to arrange their clothes in neat piles. Two lower bunks next to Robert are free. "Extra shoes go under your duffel," Matt said, "jackets and hats go on these pegs. Pick a peg and use it. Neatness counts."

"For what?"

It's the biggest kid, Kevin.

Matt can read in the other three faces a strong urge to run out again, to flee the beginning pangs of homesickness. It starts with a welling up of ache. These are boys who feel something like this all the time—displaced in the world at large. None of them had any appetite at dinner. Now it's dark, and their stomachs are growling. Camp is hell.

Each one attempts to make up his bunk according to Matt's instructions, first tugging at the starched sheets and then circling around to little purpose. They get in each other's way. The bedding refuses to go smooth. The ancient pillows feel like flat rocks.

Matt inspects their efforts. "Around here we do the Florida tuck," he says. He gives a hard shove with his hand. "Thusly, thusly, thusly, and thusly." Only Robert is amused by this.

"You from some foreign country?" Kevin says.

"No more foreign than yours," Matt says.

They're sure they won't sleep, that they might even cry themselves to sleep. None of them can take in the idea of living with Robert in the same den. Robert has Down's syndrome, but to them he has the slack mouth of an idiot, the wet smile of someone too eager. Robert repeats his name over and over and is given looks he can't interpret. The rest are livid—almost ready to push him away, smash his face. When he speaks, he sucks in air. He has the eerie voice of a machine. "Raahbert. My name is Raahbert," he says in tones of renewable hope. And it is the hope that makes him the only one among them who is unafraid.

"Robert, you can pass out these sandwiches."

Matt has opened his backpack, and in various parts of the room he knows the three other boys are trying not to appear grateful for food they can eat.

"Sandwiches," Kevin mutters.

"Peanut butter and jelly," Matt says, handing them off to Robert, and I got you guys some chips."

Outside Wolf Den, he's arranged two facing logs for them to sit on. He troops them out to the logs to eat and asks them if they know about the man who got his golden arm stolen. The boy named Todd doesn't seem to have too much trouble taking the sandwiches proffered by Robert. But Kevin and the one named Jason both refuse. They wait for the potato chip bag to come around. They eye each other to see if this means they can gang up. Neither is certain. Neither wants to gang up wrong.

At lights-out, Kevin and Jason begin to undress and to eye each other, in the flesh this time. They both have the same contours. They look to see which of them is better equipped, relieved that it's pretty much a draw. At ten and eleven years old, they are the same small size. They have huge feet instead. They wear incredible weapons for shoes. Barefoot now, Kevin climbing up, not watching what he's doing, kicks Robert in the head. Robert is seventeen, almost a grown man everywhere, although he has the face of a baby. This paradox infuriates the younger boys.

There is so much wailing from Robert that Matt puts an arm around his shoulders and looks at what is now a small gang. Todd, Kevin, and Jason appear to exchange looks of general disgust as a first bonding emotion. Eyes lower. Matt tells Robert it was an accident; he's okay, and he can stop crying now. Poor Robert has acne. When emotional like this, he can look like a raspberry muffin.

Matt remembers himself with big feet and nothing else. Big clubs for feet. At a Y camp with Johnny Richards years ago, his flat sole-slabs had seemed to crash-land as he shot baskets on a badly varnished court. His feet kept on growing all the next year. For a long time nothing else on him seemed to budge an inch. Not a hair. His stand-at-attentions were never bigger than an ordinary big toe. Boys care more about that sort of thing than breath itself. The first night at camp they try to break the walls down with their lack of size—a loosely federated gang trying to kick at doors and windows, at real retards and imaginary girls.

Now, in the enclosure of their upper bunks, they have no power. Camp makes them powerless. Here, with lights finally shouted out, they seem to float. The three small bodies show a little sag on the underside of the mattresses, but they are only what a sack of potatoes might weigh.

Matt remembers the college-boy counselor of his own day, just as he too was about to shout out the lights. Other accidental kicks at other heads. No formal trial, because the counselor had been too exhausted back then to sort it out. He'd pushed everyone into bunks. Lights out, a dead, blinking dark. A few bursts of laughter hung here and there before he shoved the one or two persistent loudmouths into their pillows. Perry Como's "Lord's Prayer," sung like an anthem, had nightly flowed over the lake from speakers high in the live oaks they'd been told were unusually rife with owls.

"What had I dreamed back then," he wrote, "as the hymn came to its climax—a masculine and enviable voice?"

In his memory it is Perry Como. *The king-dom and the pow-er,* Mr. Como still croons in his memory on some nights as he strains to recall how he felt. He and those owls, the hootings of the same alive place. To be less an individual—behind, before, above, between. His identity had not been important, or only as a yearning part of what had somehow already taken place.

"And just to be in this bright breathing right now. It is night. Night wants no more of my twisting of sheets. I have wasted too much time feeling stripped to a burning love I have known about ever since I was this age—ten or eleven. Over the years I have learned that love asks no more of you than you have to give. It is enough to return to these places and push your heavy duffel in with the Wolves, vigorously, as if you are throwing an ordinary shoulder to the plow."

In a few moments all his boys fall out of character and become gray lumps, a blue glazing of sheets in the moonlight and in the mattress sags of bunks where even he doesn't weigh very much. They begin to slip off, to unravel. T-shirt sleeves. The bright patches of jockey shorts. Matt raises his head for a final check. Small butts rise up like prairie dog mounds. Out his window he watches a smudge of light swinging over the ground, a swinging flashlight making its way from hut to hut, a jumping circle on the ground. It disappears and then reappears. It is the first security checker, Hamilton, a junior from Mercer College. He told everyone at the first staff meeting that he thought it would help if they all shared their stories. How had they all come to God?

George vetoed the idea. "There's plenty of time for our personal stories," George had said.

Sitting in that circle, Matt detected which among them was comfortable or uncomfortable with the suggestion. Hamilton didn't any longer know how not to sound the way he sounded about his religious fervor. Talk and brave practice had made handsome Ham a retard-for-God, pausing now and then like a bum taking swigs straight from a bottle as he tried to share what few of them wanted shared, quite. But they were all troubled about it. Most kids their age are, at least from time to time. The college essay is meant to help get them over it a bit.

My God, Matt was tempted to say to Ham. He was tempted to tell Ham how little Ham believed in God. How much closer if he could find in the pointless, quiet, occasional hootings of the natural owl, the wise and invisible skinnings of the self, the lift of something useless away, like the cut and winding twirl of rind.

"To peel oneself from top to bottom," he wrote, "beneath which there is freedom—that I believe in. But I have never tried to tell this to anyone. I can't make it mean for others; only for myself. And even to me there is sometimes an insane and echoey feeling, as if I'm falling into mist and am not meant to be on the roll as a name."

The confusions follow the certainties and the other way around. When the confusions return, they invariably rise like gorge, and he can feel as if he might lose direction. Only the first time was exhilarating—when it first happened, at a camp like this. He had been about ten, sitting out on a dock at lakefront while the others swam around his feet in the water. He sensed the odd vapor of insight. A mist spread out from himself to the green tree line, where he remained a while in his mind, his imagined fingers seeping into the distant bulge, the hardness of an opposing, distant bank of trees. Nothing felt solid. He was inside those pine trunks, part of the tree line and the mist. Above it, between it. Behind. Before.

In order to recover, he had dived into the water—if only to get back some heft, some feel of lungs drawing in and of arms pulling the so-called identity of Matt back to what people called living with others. The on-duty counselors had come striding into the water to snatch him out, to drag him to the sidelines, where he was plunked down on a log. He was severely reprimanded. Diving off the dock was expressly prohibited. *Expressly.* After the shouts, Matt had felt he was neatly pieced together again—the now identified breaker of rules, Matt Robb. But who he was, by blood and spirit, was permanently other. Type O, the universal donor.

"Body and soul can fly apart like that again at any time. This was comforting to me at the time, as if I'd discovered that I was more liquid and spirit than bone and sinew. I was someone prone to air just as some are prone to mass. I tried to tell this to a girl at the camp that year. She was a bronze medalist on the balance beam, and on talent night she performed her mat show for us on an improvised padded floor. Afterward I explained how to me her body was lifted into the spirit. I told her how the watching eye followed her movement to see the fluid whole and not the individual."

He had hurt her feelings.

* * *

"Don't you have a girlfriend? Don't you even have a picture?"

Jason has eased over onto Matt's side of the cabin. He fingers a few of Matt's possessions—a piece of mica rock resting on the crate beside his bed, which is not a bunk like theirs but a cot with a quilt and an Ansel Adams on the wall and another crate covered with a weave Malcolm brought him from New Mexico. An enormous flashlight sits on the floor. Susan got it for his birthday. She might have purchased it for a son hired to move two-ton barges in and out of locks.

"Don't let him drool on that," Jason warns.

Robert has picked up the flashlight and is handing it to Matt.

"He drools on everything," comes another warning from Kevin, who this morning wants to be called Hulk.

Later as they shower in the open bathhouse, they eye Matt naked, pretending not to. Matt is hung. In the quickest glimpses of him, the boys swallow down jealous lumps in their throats. He's a man; they are boys.

Once inside the dining hall, he senses the sickness of kids trying to eat breakfast. They're still too numb, too full of nerves for the scrambled eggs. No appetite. Part of that is due to the medication most have to take. They go for the starch—corn bread and biscuits.

The trick is to get them shaken out of themselves. It's an act of faith. Heading down a trail around nine o'clock, they start finding nature very close-cropped, loamy and green, snaily and a little poisonous, a little villainous, a little scandalous. City boys, some of them. Kevin is from an Atlanta family and has been sent to more places than most boys have heard of. His parents have spared no cost. Wolf denning is a last resort. But Todd is from a farm. He's had plenty of outdoors to keep him from going crazy, but he did anyway. Took scissors to small cousins once; he is here in a camp for special kids only perhaps because the cousins did not die.

"Here is an interesting variety of beetle," Matt says, squatting to pick up a large specimen the size of a buckeye. "This is a beetle that has to hibernate in colder climates." He looks to see who doesn't know this word, *hibernate*. Only Robert.

Jason is suddenly very active. The starch is turning to sugar.

"There's this African beetle. He can play dead a long time. He lets himself be dragged off by ants and everything. Like he's dead. Once the ants finally get him inside their house—" Jason stops. Except for Robert, he has everyone's unswerving attention. Robert is sitting down with his feet out and his back to them. Todd and Kevin have moved in closer without knowing it. They breathe and seem to wait for Jason to undo what he's about to tell them. Surely it can't be true.

"What happens?" Kevin wants to know.

"What do you think happens, Charlie?" Jason says.

"Does the beetle wake up?"

"You got it, Charlie. He wakes up and begins to slaughter everybody in sight. Stuffs himself. It's pandemonium down there! Blood and guts all over the place."

"Smart move," Kevin says finally. He looks green. Todd is completely white. A whole week at camp still looms ahead, a horrifying stretch of time they've never suffered.

But Jason has called Kevin "Charlie," and Kevin will perhaps wish to live up to it. Each wants a nickname for himself and has never known how to get one. It's a start.

They hear loud yells, then high, piercing screams; something gone wrong in the heated pool, where the day's first free swim is taking place. Robert jumps up to take Matt's hand. Robert can't move fast. He has the gait of a wounded crab. Matt drops his hand and breaks into a run. He calls to his group to follow behind. In the distance, the pool shouts seem to have grown more organized. Something's gone wrong, but George is giving orders. The shouts of the campers are turning to silence.

There has never been a swimming incident at this camp. They learned this fact last night, the glowing first evening they spent together as strangers of trust. Water safety was the top briefing after the boys' various parents departed, after the hasty retreat of a few court-appointed guardians who had accompanied some of them on buses. Never a swimming incident because the routine is practically foolproof—a buddy system, a schedule of ten-minute checks, certified training, a twenty-boy limit, an A-level insurance inspection, not to mention whistles, bullhorns, diving rules, and the immediate suspension of swim privileges to any boy getting the least bit out of line.

Still, the worst may have occurred. Counselors from all parts of the camp come running. Their various small boys trail behind like ducklings. For a moment Matt sees a kid's big feet. George has fallen to his knees. His mouth-to-mouth is meticulously slow. The careful rhythm of it has begun to hypnotize the nearby watchers, grown quiet as another lifeguard, Leo, circles around George and the boy. Leo causes the circle of watchers to open up and close down, like a shutter.

"It's that kid Loren," someone near Matt says, one of the Panthers. The Panther is trying to get close to Kevin and Jason, who have already joined forces against Todd and the retard. They've been divided but not conquered in their first day. Today they will form a twosome for protection. The Panther might win over Jason. Kevin will be pushed out, to settle either for Todd or for no one.

The boys encircling George and the near-drowned boy are shivering in the sun. Rattling from excitement more than from cold. Towels drape over a few, a few hands tuck under chins, a few opposite shoulders are gripped hard. Bony elbows point down, skeletal.

"Is he dead?" someone whispers.

The cook and the one secretary run out of the dining hall that doubles for headquarters. A few boys are reprimanded for crowding in, but soon everyone is forgotten in the transfixing sight of George's rhythms, his pauses between one transfer of air and the next. Whoever brings the blanket goes unnoticed. On the ground, man and boy seem to begin the determined give-and-take—the one breathing for the other. And that seems enough, Matt thinks that night in bed. Prayer falls into the moments like thought. We always believe we are breathing on our own, but we are not. Something breathes for us always.

He raises up and sees that the flashlight bouncing along outside is drawing closer to his cabin. Someone is bringing a message. Matt gets up to find out what the matter is. He pushes open the screen and steps outside to meet George, continuing to think with great pleasure how today he was permitted to see it—the something visible, breathing into the boy.

"Had the boy lain there feeling the momentary loosening of himself to join with it?" Matt reads with his flashlight the paragraph he has just composed, wishing it made sense. "Invisible resuscitation is really the truth of a matter which we are not permitted to see except in flashes. I, with everyone else, looked in to see the boy cough and sit up and begin to breathe on his own. Perhaps only to me did it seem as if that which breathes into us daily had merely withdrawn from sight once more, leaving us to cheer the individual creature, who was, in fact, so much less a single being than he appeared."

11

SAFE HOUSE

WITNESSED BY THE VARIOUS MEMBERS OF THE OLD GANG—John Richards, Ted and Beth Harwood—was that slow rise of Susan's arms, coming up and out to the baby. Most memorable was the blast of sound, however, followed by cries and shouts, everyone ducking—except for Gail Richards, who was, oddly enough, supposed to have been there.

Gail had made specific arrangements with John. She and her new boyfriend were to have come by at five to pick up an antique sewing machine—a Singer treadle that, right then, John had been hauling to the front porch. His reasoning was that it would be half on its way when Gail arrived; she wouldn't have to come inside, a situation John was tiring of since his own awkwardness made him appear petty and mean.

A blast of gunfire, and everyone (except for Gail, who was late) began hitting the decks, crouching behind whatever was near at hand. John used the noncontested treadle. Several seconds passed before any of them sensed that the guy was running; that he was dragging the girl with him back across the street.

Malcolm's right eardrum was punctured. He felt as if he'd been given a blow to his head, and for several moments he, alone of all the gang, believed that Susan was still at his side as they both fell, tripping over something on the porch and landing sideways, Malcolm's arms automatically flying up to cradle her or to roll on top of her before touching the right of his face, where everything felt numb from the blow with a blunt instrument that would turn out to have been only the report of the gun.

He was deafened, and all his other senses drew in to save themselves—vision, touch, taste. He tucked a moment or two, didn't hear the voices or see John run from his position. Briefly, it appeared to the others that Susan and the baby were a unit—a heap in the yard. John reached them first, rolling Susan on her back and lifting up the baby, whose crying had been beyond Malcolm's hearing anyway, as had been all the shouts and noises after the gun went off.

Ted Harwood told the police and the sheriff later how he'd remained crouched for longer than he liked to admit. But it did mean that he watched as the guy streaked across Everett. No, they were not holding hands; the girl was being dragged, screaming. She was thrown into the car. Ted had no idea who they were, or that Oren Abel was no longer around. When did that happen? Anyway, they then seemed to pile into the car, the guy dropping his gun in the grass just to the side of the driveway, which not even Ted saw at the time. He remained crouched while the guy, failing to align his wheels, tore backward and almost hit a tree in the Robbs' yard just this side of the curb. Ted remembered seeing John fall to his knees and hold the baby, John's back turned as if half anticipating a crash. Both the curb and the brakes prevented that, and the guy seemed to gain enough control to speed down Everett, making a right turn onto Diamond Avenue. Why Ted hadn't had enough sense to get a partial plate number, he couldn't say.

It was early evening. Professor families on Diamond Avenue were inside, preparing meals. Activity at the college itself was low because of the winter break. There would turn out to be one witness at the corner of Diamond and Johnson. A white early-model Chevy made a loud left turn. The witness was just then coming out of the same drugstore that Malcolm had earlier visited across from the ATM, and the left turn would have taken the car past the phone booths as it headed north. Cooper was within minutes of Interstate 10 at that point. The police learned his name from the child Corey, speaking in that chilling flat voice of hers. None of them soon forgot that voice.

Corey Rangle. She was not Angela's child; she was a half-sister. And Ricky Rangle was a half-brother. Her mother was deceased, she said, but Corey clammed up after that and would not say anything about Cooper or how all of them had come to be in the house at this time. She seemed not to know Cooper's last name, but later led police to his room, where they found steroids in a prescription bottle filled out in the name of Warren C. Reese. They found nothing on Angela; her primary ID must have been in a purse that was in the car at the time of the crime. For a while they thought they were looking for an Angela Rangle.

From Interstate 10, Cooper had a choice—east to Jacksonville or west to Tallahassee. And if he picked west, then he'd be given another choice within twenty minutes—Interstate 75—where he could travel up into Georgia or down to Danford and points farther into some of Florida's most remote farm country. He could take all back roads, of course, and avoid the superhighways.

He had no police record.

Right after the shooting it was Beth Harwood who, over shouts—Find a phone!—first saw Malcolm as she stood up out of her crouch. From her distance she assumed that he was hit. She ran down her steps, aware that everyone saw Susan but not Malcolm. It was Beth who attempted to speak to him before running into his house.

Find a phone? None were at their stations inside Malcolm and Susan's house. Beth ran around searching, too frantic to think to hit a page button. Instead she hurried back out, stepping right past Malcolm, in order to get home to make the call.

That was about the time Malcolm began to sit up. His position did not allow him to see over his shrubs and into the yard but rather brought him up high enough merely to see Beth reappearing on her porch as she rushed inside, her door slamming silently because he was so deaf.

At that moment Malcolm realized that he was fully alone, that he'd lost his hearing, that he'd hurt his back falling, that he ought to stand up but could not do so. Instead he managed to get on all fours and crawl to the steps, where there was a open view between his high shrubs. But the view was odd. It contained Susan and the baby, with Ted and John attending. Malcolm began to fall again, this time head-first down the steps just as John, still holding the baby, failed in his lunge to prevent Malcolm from hitting the flagstone. At that point John and Ted both assumed, as Beth had, that Malcolm was wounded.

People piled out of their houses—the Scotts and the Greenes from the far end of Everett. Roweena Joyce, the retired insurance actuary whom they almost never saw, who lived on Jackson Street, happened to be out for a late-afternoon walk. Choosing Everett Street would seem providential to her, as it would for several Wyman cars that happened to be on Everett just then. Someone used a car phone at or about the same time Beth was running around.

Beth's sister Gloria, visiting for the weekend, was awakened from a nap in an upstairs room. She rushed the baby into the house while Ted and John stayed at Susan's side. They felt for a pulse once more. They closed her eyes. It was at that point that they happened to see the child in Oren's front yard, bending down and picking up a gun out of the grass.

John yelled and pointed at her wildly, and Ted ran to see if the little girl was all right. Ted didn't see the gun, didn't hear clearly what John was yelling about. John himself got up from where he'd been kneeling. Coolheaded, he caught up with Ted, motioned him off to one side, and approached Corey alone. He reached for a baby stroller in the yard, pushed it in front of him, and suggested she put the gun inside the stroller.

Others kept back. The five-year-old then placed the .35 exactly where John wanted it. She told him her name was Corey. Ted rushed in at that point, pushed the stroller all the way back to his own house, and asked Gloria and Beth to guard it. In a cool moment, Gloria snapped a picture of the gun in the stroller.

John picked up the child and held her. He sat with her on Oren's steps. Almost the first thing Corey said was how she'd heard Cooper say he was going to kill that guy if he didn't stop spying on them. Corey was immediately affectionate with John, wrapping her arms around his middle and resting her head. At one point she looked up at him and said, "He killed the wrong person, didn't he? He was supposed to shoot the man who mowed the lawn. He was funny. He was so funny when he mowed."

This was later passed around—a child's matter-of-fact explanation for what she'd overheard in her house. Geez, Malcolm spying? It was later spoken of again and again, but not in the hearing of anyone beyond the old set. They assumed Corey would, for better or worse, repeat it herself once she was taken into custody. It didn't bear repeating from them. They gave it no credence. Malcolm was no Peeping Tom, for God's sake. The guy was obviously some paranoid psychopath. Everyone in the old set told the sheriff that the man seemed to be on something. Angel dust? The way he'd jumped around screaming like that.

The simultaneous arrivals of police and ambulance caused sirens to echo on Diamond Avenue and on the campus beyond. In the next hour, a few winter-break students, staff, and surrounding faculty residents assembled behind a police barricade. It was a shocking crime scene by that time. The baby was not there, but rumored to have been there, now abandoned by its mother who'd been kidnapped, the gathered crowd heard; she was staying at Oren Abel's; but was that really Susan Robb's body over there mostly covered with a blanket? Malcolm sat with her head visible in his lap. Malcolm! So it had to be Susan! People cried. People couldn't believe what they were seeing.

Malcolm was conscious of his hearing returning in the time it took several medics to find Susan's carotid artery. He watched as a final but quite futile and completely official stethoscope inched between the top buttons of her blouse. Malcolm cradled her head to his chest, kissing her temple; he was allowed to sit undisturbed for quite a while. He was examined briefly. Someone gently lifted his chin and asked him politely to relax. He felt his lid being raised and his right eye examined with a pin light; then the left. He was thanked and addressed by his first name, asked the day of the week and the name of the president of the United States. He'd known these policemen for years and years. They named his two children and asked if either were expected to be returning to the house; was there a way to prevent such a thing so that the children might be given better preparation to learn what had happened?

This question briefly gave some reality to the moment. No, Malcolm answered, both children were away. Than he panicked. "John!" he yelled. It was his first real sound.

"Malcolm," Ted said. "John's over at Oren's. I'm right here."

Then everyone would see Ted put his ear to Malcolm's mouth while Malcolm whispered for a long time, Ted nodding. It was a long paragraph on how Ted must get word to the Jurinko family, Uri's folks. It seemed so small but so important a blessing that they lived out of town, on rural Route 41. Ted must get to a phone and tell them to turn off all radio and television, tell no one that Gretchen was there, not let her or Uri answer the telephone. And as for Matt, there was some camp phone number or other in the house, Malcolm didn't know where. Susan would have put the number of a George Murray on the refrigerator or on her desk off the back bedroom.

"They're sealing up the house, Malcolm."

"My God, Ted, get the sheriff to take me in there first to get that number." He looked down at her. Wasn't she just asleep? In a moment she would open her eyes and tell him exactly where to find the number.

"Susan," he said. "Wake up, honey."

Ted ran off to get help. Someone approached to give Malcolm a shot of Demerol. It made Malcolm start yelling for John again, who was suddenly at his side.

"Hey there, old buddy, quiet down, quiet down. I'm not going to let them give you that. I'm sorry." John began whispering, rubbing Malcolm's back as you do a child's. And then Malcolm didn't know anything for a while, gone into some altered state, comforted by his friend, by the still warm head of his wife in his lap, by the natural drug perhaps released in the tantrum. No one tried to give him an injection after that.

They let him sit with her as long as possible before asking if he would stand, please. He surprised himself in not panicking as someone carefully removed her head from his lap and covered her with the rest of the blanket, someone else putting hands under both his arms and lifting him to his feet. They'd given him the right amount of time. He could stand. But the late afternoon was just then starting to twilight down over his head. It was a noose, a black cloth with no slits. "This is my fault," he said to himself, waiting for the trap to open somewhere below his knees.

They let him stand for a while longer. Ted seemed a blur, guided some distance away by burly but soft-spoken Sheriff Creel, known to all by his first name, Randall. He ordered his men around without ever raising his voice. John was next to be guided away and then Malcolm.

"I'm going to be asking a few questions when you all are ready. We got a bulletin out on the car now, and we're trying to find Oren."

Someone strung yellow police tape around several trees. The porch was being secured by the same method, since the gunman had been standing up there. An officer was directed over to Oren's house to get Corey from the neighbor, Mrs. Greene, who had briefly subbed in John's place when John had to comfort Malcolm. Corey was taken into custody along with the baby boy. And then John, Ted, and Beth were asked to gather in one place. The Harwood house was chosen; they would all be questioned individually in the slow time to follow.

Malcolm, unwilling to let Susan out of his sight, refused to go anywhere indoors. A kitchen chair was brought from somewhere and put in the side area between the Robb and Harwood houses, where a jungle of high shrubs allowed him both to see Susan and to stay hidden from the crowd that was still growing behind the barricades as the search for the missing bullet dragged on. There he was again questioned in soft, kind tones about where exactly Cooper was standing when he fired.

The delay meant the unavoidable but surprisingly quiet arrival of the local press. One man and a car. Soon there was no quiet of that kind: a van from Jacksonville pulled to the corner of Everett and Diamond. More barricades went up. The sounds were loud— shortwaves and various squawk boxes. Officers walked the trajectory route many times—from Susan to the street, from Susan into the Richardses' yard, from Susan over to Octopus Oak. They eventually tried these different routes in front of a few rolling cameras as Malcolm sat watching. John whispered into his ear that the Jurinkos had been contacted; Gretchen would not be told until Malcolm could get there. Also a phone number for Matt had not yet been found, but when it was the camp would be asked to drive Matt home in the morning. Malcolm was not to worry.

Quickly news seeped back to the barricades, to the hushed crowd on Everett. Speed meant that people heard the publicized terms of Susan's death even as she lay there, even as police seemed to be hearing, so that later several would recall how odd it was to be at the scene and to feel several frames behind a world that does not pause for anyone.

❧

Harry Rawlins heard the reports and sped to Wyman. He pictured Oren, larval and alone in his new apartment, sitting without radio or TV. He was afraid to break the news to Oren over the phone.

By the time Harry got there he knew, from updates coming in every few minutes, that Angela Bert was either kidnapped or a fugitive, that Susan Robb was gone.

Awful for Harry to see Oren begin to shake his head in a way that made him almost unrecognizable. His face took on dark lines—the awareness of personal responsibility. Harry tried tones of comfort and sadness. "You knew those folks real well, Oren," he began to say softly. He didn't like their good deeds toward Angela refigured as death on Oren's face. "Ms. Robb was a teacher, I recall," Harry said. "Lord, how old was she?"

Oren, dressed in his robe, began heading out the front door of his apartment, already wringing hands and looking around for Harry's car. Then, in the middle of the wide parking lot, Harry imagined the worst for his friend—that he might well be on the verge of a stroke, the fast untimely exit, male variety, poor Oren clutching at his swelling chest and expiring under fluffy clouds, circling above in animal shapes. It was Harry's own nightmare; he wasn't going to take chances, he told his wife when she accused him later of simply wanting to get Oren out of town.

Wyman had a new twenty-bed clinic. In his wisdom, Harry sped with Oren all the way back to Danford, to one of the best facilities in the state. "No," Margaret would say. "You were keeping him from being questioned right then. You did the right thing."

"It was a judgment call, Maggie. May you never have to make such a call with an old friend. It looked like stroke to me."

"I'm saying you did good! Calm down. When *will* they question him?"

"I'll let Randall know where he is first thing in the morning. As soon as they find that girl, you or I one have to get to her. Who knows what she's going to say about Oren?"

"You think they're going to find her alive? I'm picturing the guy throwing her out of a moving car."

"Lord, Maggie!"

"Well," Maggie said, "it's just likely, that's all."

Oren would remember the trip to the hospital as a failure to get back some phrase eluding him out in the coarse and distant landscape. Something entire and important was being sucked up under the roaring car as Harry gripped the wheel. They were a little boat skipping across a bigger boat's mean wake.

Oren kept thinking that if he could remember, he'd be able to survive. Then in a white room full of shiny surfaces, of nurses with needles, he remembered—*Blessed are the bold*—while lying flat on his back. Be bold, he wanted to say aloud. He heard soft-soled shoes on the linoleum, everyone going into action without much sound, Harry explaining that Oren had had a shock.

—for they shall be shocked.

A nurse leaned in. "Mr. Abel? What happened? Can you tell us what happened? What are you feeling, honey?"

He took on the action of the crime scene with his own body— the paralytic slow-motion moment in which Susan fell and Angela was dragged by her clothing and thrown into a car. Once Oren was stripped and blanketed and hooked up to a few monitors, two ER doctors began a battery of tests—probing, recording, talking among themselves as a starter rocket dropped away and Oren traveled on, leaving the rest behind and looking up.

"Mr. Abel, honey?"

How could he have abandoned Susan and Angela like this? let the one come trailing her troubles, and the other exposed? His old house must have become a tinderbox in one night, a lighted match tossed in. First a fight; perhaps even a small fight. He saw Cooper passed out for a while, Angela making a last phone call—*You're never going to let me into your family, are you?* He could detect the guilt in her voice now, baiting Oren because Cooper was back in her life, and her unable to admit the part she must have played in Cooper finding her so fast. So, bless her, she'd rung up Oren and acted ugly.

Cooper would have woken up again, still laughing at her little setup, her efforts, her bid for independence, her thinking she could go somewhere without him, until finally she raised her voice at him, told him to get lost or worse. Would their loud fighting have drawn Malcolm and Susan over, helpful people, to see what was wrong? He could see the Robbs, introducing themselves ahead of Oren's little introduction schedule.

"Honey?"

Any decent person might have been drawn over to an old neighbor's house at some sign of trouble, a young girl who appears to be playing with fire. So they would have gone over to say hello, welcome, as if it were all neighborly, which it would have been. They would not want to seem to be prying.

"Mr. Abel, sir? Can you tell us what happened to you?"

At camp, George Murray and Matt sat on the logs beyond the sleeping cabin, and Matt thought of how long-prepared he'd been. An abstraction until now. Now it was here, immediate. Most of the world knows death all the time. Death is like breathing to most of the world. They grieve but do not melt with misery.

No, that was not what he meant.

"I'd like to get paper and try to write something down," he said, getting up.

"I'll sit here with you, if that's all right."

Inside the cabin, the weightless boys were some of misery's many forms. As many forms as there were boys, and stretching out from them?—a howling host.

Someone stirred, and Matt waited to see if the child would wake up. A head rose and then flopped back to the pillow; a sigh followed, large as any adult's. In unison, two other boys changed position in a rustle of cloth. All was motionless again. All but Robert had had trouble falling asleep because of the early bedtime, the raucous noise of cricket and frog. Sleep came to them as exhaustion's friend. Now night, or whatever, oversaw young bones, raw nerves. Night

knitted at them with an old woman's silent needles. She started with
the socks.

"To grieve, not to melt with misery," he wrote. A seed of the
idea.

George went off to gather a little kindling. A low fire wouldn't be
such a bad thing. Just enough to stare at, he said.

"To grieve. Not to melt with misery.

"We don't have the power to change places and suffer for Angela, say—suffer in her place, melt into her, become her. The
waitress said she'd gladly change places. Spare us such errors of
thought, even in jest. Errors I've been guilty of myself in the past.
Trading places, standing in for someone else, is not what's asked
of us.

"But something mysterious is asked, nevertheless. Insight.
Sometimes I think I have it: we are not merely created; we join in
creation. Very difficult to grasp, because we feel so made, so individual. We can see where we seem to end and others begin. Misery and us, death and us. But each is of equal status, in equal
companionship to the other. The Angelas are from Misery and
the Robbs from Comfort, and in a miracle I think we meet to
create something.

"The how of it flashes on and off, gets up close to me at times,
smiles, and then slips away and eludes me completely. Blindness is
the plight of Comfort's citizens. Cut to a Comfort boy in fifth
grade (not me, but someone like me) raising his hand and asking
the teacher why for Pete's sake the starving people don't just come
here, where the food is! Why do they stay where there's *no* food?

"The boy hears the amused reply of the teacher and slowly
pulls his hand from the air. He looks at his hand, hates it, wants
to bite it off; how could he be so stupid? He may not ever ask a
question approaching this again.

"It was a very good question—only a turn away from the idea of my mother, from Comfort, doing what Misery cannot. Comfort can, as it were, go across the street at least. Go where the miserable live if they cannot come to us. That should have been the answer to the boy's question.

"Turn a question around, and a door sometimes opens. There is one direction possible in the boy's otherwise silly idea—us coming to Misery, who cannot herself travel. Mohammeds and mountains. Surely one of them can move. Otherwise, the Miseries are a world, the Comforts only little bells without sound. The brass, the tinkling, but no sound! So, in this line of reasoning, I've always known the answer to the question, If a tree falls in a forest—the answer is, Of course not! I know that better than I know whether or not there is a God. The meeting place between groups is the only sound. If this is too religious, then make it an aesthetic thing. In making sound, we make something come into existence. The coming into being of the whole. Just that. Wholeness is not born; it is created. Comfort goes out to where Death and Misery are, to a place—to the interface. To the interplace. The tree of love grows there and nowhere else. In my sorrow—"

"Matt," George is saying. "Why not stop for a while?"

"—what a rare thing I am looking at now. Misery, who usually cannot travel, has found a way to come to us. She is in a speeding car, but that is an illusion. I pity Cooper, now so painfully linked to us and the interplace of created goodness. He must be choking on it. It must be a scream in his head at what he's done. May he not hurt her—"

"Matt," George said. He was lifting the pen from Matt's hand and slowly reaching in to take the notebook too. "Why don't we take a walk around camp? I woke up Greg. He's going to drive you in the morning. Right now he's coming to spend the rest of the night in your cabin in case someone needs something. Let's you and I walk around a bit. I want to get you some food, too. Later we can call your house and you can speak with your father."

"Should I call now? No one else was hurt, you said."

"No. Matt, this is impossible for us to imagine. It's a crime scene at the moment. The police— We're to call much later."

"Dad—" Matt finally said, because he could imagine it all. The small fire seemed to disappear into the night. Swallowed up. And George was there, a firm arm on his shoulder, pulling him up and leading him on up to the main house.

❄

As Malcolm sat among the shrubs he could hear it still, the door knocker being pounded, then her arms curling around him and her nudging them both to the porch to talk to the guy. Why had he allowed it? And then allowed her to slip from under his arm like that, knowing what he knew already about these people, knowing as he opened the door that the guy was a walking bomb. Sometimes he'd fantasize about seeing a suspicious package propped up outside his office at Webster and knowing enough to turn right around and call the authorities.

While they looked for the bullet, Randall whispered some questions related to what, in Malcolm's opinion, might be Cooper's state of mind or motive; about Cooper's relationship to Angela—a relationship about which Randall would know within the next half-hour. His source was Eddy Jensen, the brother-in-law who called the Robb household to get a private line with Randall. From the Danford office's point of view this was going to be bad press; Eddy didn't need it at the moment, he and his office having had Cooper in custody, having released him to shoot a local schoolteacher. Criminy, Eddy said. He appealed to Randall's need, at the very least, to proceed with caution. For heaven's sake, it wasn't just Eddy's office whose rep was at stake here. What about the dead woman's family? Her own son had been arrested along with the shooter only days ago. So see? It was worse for Matt Robb than for anyone else Eddy could think of, including Eddy!

Randall's own men all heard him groan right there in the Robb kitchen.

Back outside, the husband looked pretty ignorant. He repeated an account of the shooter and his girlfriend seeming to harass him a bit; nothing about his son and the girl being tied up together. So Randall kept his mouth shut. It was Oren who was connected to the girl. Eddy had stupidly given out her address to old man Oren himself, an inexperienced recluse, so-called. The husband's account, poor bastard, was that he had tried to help his new neighbor get her phone repaired, and then her jealous boyfriend had come to his house in a rage.

"So Oren Abel is friends with these people, you think?" Randall asked very cautiously.

The man had no idea. In Randall's opinion, Malcolm's pure bafflement could not have been faked.

"And what would you say the girl is now, Malcolm?" Randall ventured. "Is she more of an accomplice or a hostage right now?"

Malcolm's neighbors were saying hostage. Malcolm himself was having to admit that he'd seen very little, which in itself was hard for him to admit to, that he'd fainted or maybe just froze, as men sometimes do under fire.

His dear old friends. His friends had worked as a team after the blast—a team! running to Susan like that, lifting the baby, and retrieving the gun from the older child. Gail had eventually arrived alone; not allowed past the barricade, she had borrowed a cell phone and attempted to reach John to find out the circumstances being shared, secondhand, among several weeping people in the crowd, some of whom had radios and were picking up more reports as they continued to stand watching.

A police unit from Jacksonville arrived on the scene to assist in looking for the slug and to help with other forensics. Not just

Malcolm's front porch and house and yard needed searching and sealing, but Oren's too. While these procedures were duly carried out, the gang remained together inside the Harwood house, and Malcolm continued to sit alone in his kitchen chair in the side area. The yard was lit up with spots. He could hear his phone ringing. He was consoled once more that the Jurinko's phone might be ringing, too, but all was secure over there. Malcolm could arrive for Gretchen any time, even in the middle of the night if he wished. Or he was free until morning; meanwhile, they'd protect her. And evidently Matt knew about Susan now. As John had promised, someone was to get him to Wyman by tomorrow morning.

At about eight P.M. the slug was found lodged in a rear left tire of John's parked car at the curb. Randall, so professional with both his men and the added out-of-town unit, now came to Malcolm. He was sorry this had taken so long; he was ordering an autopsy at the coroner's office in Danford, not that Malcolm was unprepared. Together they'd gone over the necessity of this. Still, Randall seemed extremely somber to Malcolm, as if the full weight of it all was now more firmly on his shoulders. He had fugitives on his mind, and that was a first.

"Just for overnight, Malcolm. I'm really sorry we have to move her all the way down there."

"No, I understand," Malcolm said, "it's only that, like I said before, I have to ride in the ambulance."

"Yes, it's all arranged."

And then he was overwhelmed. As soon as he moved from this chair, there would be so much more of the world. People, relatives, parents, not to mention Gretchen and Matt. Her department head, her entire school of teachers and students, her fellow choir members, and her reading group. The circles sprang open so quickly in his mind he felt a sudden fear that he would fall over. How would he ever be part of what used to be and was supposed to continue to be just the same but without her?

"About Oren." Randall was whispering in his ear again.

"You found him?" Malcolm said.

"No," Randall said. "Could he have moved out of town? That phone number over there is new and no longer listed in his name. We're not turning up one for him at all."

Malcolm gave out the doctor's name. "Oren came down with something a few days ago. We got him Dr. Hegg. We got him David Hegg."

"And that was right before these folks moved in on Sunday?"

"I first noticed them on Sunday. Then on Monday it was just her alone there with the kids. He wasn't there." Malcolm was about to mention Gretchen baby-sitting, but did not.

"And this man? All he said to you this evening was that he didn't like you getting that money for the girl?"

They were lifting Susan's body onto a stretcher.

"You said I could be with her."

"Give us another minute. They're going to make room for you inside the ambulance."

And so he waited. It was dark now as he sat in the chair and heard his friends come out onto the Harwood porch and stand there holding each other. Beth sobbed as the body was moved. They seemed to have no idea he was seated in the strip between the two houses. They would assume he was inside his own place. It was not that they said anything he shouldn't overhear. He learned that Gail had gotten through by phone and that it was she who was asked to telephone the Jurinko house to protect Gretchen. He felt better. He trusted in Gail's authority. She had more of it than Beth, than almost any of them except for Susan. Gail would be stronger than John, although harder hit.

He heard Ted comforting Beth. Then he saw that Randall was motioning to him from the ambulance, and he started out into view.

"Lord," he heard someone say. It was Beth's sister Gloria pointing him out to the old gang, who hadn't yet noticed him.

"Malcolm!" John called. He ran into the yard.

"What should I do, John?" Malcolm said. "I can't be in two places at once. I'm worried about Gretchen." He began emitting a noise that was deep, frightening. The sounds made him choke.

"Stay with Susan," John said. "I'll drive you back. Malcolm, can you hear me?"

"He shot into your tire."

John held out keys. "I'm driving yours. These are keys you gave me last summer."

He knew he was staring blankly at those keys, not really able to respond.

"Malcolm, you understand what's happening now? She's just going to be in Danford overnight, and then they bring her back in the morning."

"Where?"

"Crosby's? Jackson's?"

"Oh, I thought you meant back here to the house."

"Is Crosby's okay? I can make the call for you."

"Okay." For some reason Malcolm turned and waved to Ted and Beth. He saw Beth wave and then hide her face.

"Okay, so I'll be in your car," John explained. "I'll be right behind you."

"I have to do this, John," he said. "Just talk to her, I think."

"I know, I know. Go! I'll follow right behind and drive you back."

"But what about Gretchen?"

"Gail's going over to the Jurinkos'. She's going to sit in her car, and if the press comes, she'll deal. You want to talk to Gail?" John held out his cellular phone.

"You think I'm being silly? Should I go right now and get Gretchen?"

"No! Later it's going to be very important to her that you rode with Susan."

But by now he was already at the back of the ambulance. An attendant reached out, pulling him inside before jumping down himself, closing the doors after Malcolm, and going around to ride with the driver. The attendant seemed quite used to this arrangement.

The round seat provided for him was like the pull-down seats in an old Checker cab. Beside her, Malcolm's long legs extended in the same direction as Susan's. He removed the blanket and looked at her. He took up her left hand, the one nearest him, already a bit swollen but not badly. He warmed her hand.

"Susan," he began.

He touched her hair and was immediately glad. Her face seemed more at ease when he did that, and then he remembered that there had been nothing really out of the ordinary in her expression in the moment he had let her slip down the stairs in her instinct to take the baby from the girl. What had been wrong with *his* instinct? His arm should have clamped her in a vise.

"Susan," he said, his hand ending up near her ear, where he felt the earring she was wearing. It gave him something to do, removing both earrings for Gretchen's sake. He removed the bit of gold around her neck, a fine chain her mother had given her. She almost never took it off, nor the wedding ring that he was determined now to have. He removed oil from the back of his neck. The ring came off easily, and for a long time he folded it in both their hands. He almost put it back on her.

He began again. "I was going to tell you when you came in, but you had all that Novocain." Not even an imagined response, but he talked on. "I was going to tell you how they both got angry at me. Earlier in the day they both got furious at me."

In life she would have laughed: At you?

Yes, at him. He had that kind of face! They had happily seized on him, just their kind of sitting duck. "They accused me of spying on them."

You? How funny.

The ambulance stopped at red lights on its way out of town.

There was no siren, no flashing red emergency, just a slow creep and then on to route 40, and then I-75, her regular road to Danford. They were going to the morgue. Why name it otherwise? From the back of the ambulance he could see John's headlights. He was glad. John was right. There would be no reason to stay long.

"I'll go get Gretchen just as soon as we get you there. Matt's on his way in the morning. I'd let Gretchen go on to bed and sleep until morning, but I don't know—isn't she too old for that? You wouldn't let her sleep the night, would you, if the tables were turned? If it was me?"

No. Get to her as soon as you can.

"Right."

They both knew exactly how long this ride would take, and to-morrow after her autopsy there would be her ride back. He explained it to her. He smoothed her brow and talked to her. Simple things, as if the lights were out and they were chatting in bed at the end of a regular day. She had a low throaty voice, so it never sounded like advice. She'd just start to muse if he happened to say, "So, how would you tell Gretchen, if it was me you had to tell about? How would you do it?"

All I'd do is take her into a room somewhere at the Jurinkos' and close the door and hold her. Just sit and hold her. I wouldn't try to think up what to say.

"That's good. That sounds right."

She'll know that something's happened to me. She'll know. And don't you two try to analyze it. Absolutely anything moving in front of that man would have caused a snap like that. He was just ready to blow somebody away. Couldn't you tell? He was going to shoot somebody no matter what.

"It was my fault."

Stop it. That sounds just like you. Do me a favor. I'm dead—

He could hear her starting to laugh at her morbid turn.

—so, for once in your life can you try not to be so very much like you? You know, just as a little favor to me?

* * *

John found him in one of the far hallways, standing alone. No one else in sight. "Malcolm," John said.

Malcolm turned to look at him. "I'm ready to go. Just get me to the car."

"Malcolm, I want you to sit down here and let me tell you something. Malcolm, they have her mother on the phone."

"What?"

He would never be sure who called Susan's mother and let her know that the body was where it was, in Danford. But the woman had gotten through. She had spoken to John, who apparently walked past the deck just as the attendant took the call, mistaking John for Malcolm.

So Susan's mother had taken the news from John but then asked to hear Malcolm's voice. Evidently she was praying it was some evil prank—one of Susan's disgruntled or deranged students, perhaps. Of course, she knew and trusted John completely, but there was bitter hope that even John could be faked by a student or some evil person.

"It's me," Malcolm said into the receiver. "It's me, Malcolm."

He stood listening to the poor woman's outburst of first grief as she heard the very worst confirmed. In her sobbing he heard her ask him if he knew that she'd always had a foreboding, a premonition about him. Malcolm was too crazy to give any answer. There was no syntax he'd been able to put together since the gun went off except for that little bit in the ambulance when he talked with Susan.

"Malcolm, put John back on. Get him back. Put him back on." There was a pause. "Will you do that, please, Malcolm?"

He remembered how Susan had telephoned this woman after they were married, way back when it was all just a tiny Evansville apartment not far from the Northwestern campus. Small party noises had sounded in the background, and Big Susan had taken offense that they were calling during a party to say they'd gotten married, which she was not expecting. She directed her bitterness at her new son-in-law, whom she'd not yet met: "For a Malcolm you have an unusually soft voice," she'd said. "Your voice actually chirps, my dear, I can barely hear you."

From then on her tactic had been to note some funny birdlike quality about him—his seedy jackets, his feathered flying hair, his duck walk, and that chirp in his voice. "When I recover, I'll congratulate you," his new mother-in-law had said all those years ago. Now she was saying, "Will you put John back on? Will you do that for me, please, Malcolm?"

But John was talking to a man who said he was Harry Rawlins, Oren Abel's friend. He was there to explain his role in helping Oren set up a safe house for Angela Bert.

Malcolm broke in on their conversation, and Mr. Rawlins began again after whispered condolences. A safe house, he continued. Angela was a battered teen—the daughter of a mutual friend of Oren's and Mr. Rawlins. A friend from— Well, it didn't matter. It had been Mr. Abel's intent to get her away from a bad environment for a period of time. He and Mr. Abel had no idea that she would be discovered by Warren Reece, a stalker of sorts who was supposed to have been out of the picture. He followed Angela. There was a gap in the monitoring of her situation at Oren's house.

"I wouldn't have known to call it that," Malcolm said, "a gap."

He saw the man nod slowly and start to repeat how horrible this all was, how Oren was in shock over what had happened to Susanne Robb.

"Susan," Malcolm corrected him. "My wife's name is Susan."

John began to use his own body to shield Malcolm from the man. "There's nothing more the family needs to hear from Oren at the moment," John said. "It's Sheriff Creel you should be contacting."

Mr. Rawlins had the good grace to close his eyes and agree. Whispering again to John, he added that if there was anything, anything at all . . . He handed over his card.

Malcolm sat down.

"John," he finally said when they were alone. "Susan's mother wants to talk to you."

He was forced to reconstruct later all the hard telephoning John must have done that night. Since someone had taken it upon himself or herself to call Susan's mother, John feared that others would hear through badly placed calls. He began faxing and e-mailing friends and colleagues who may or may not have already heard on TV, who may or may not have gotten calls or else could think up ways to help him place calls and faxes themselves. He called Malcolm's own two sad but self-absorbed parents in their Massachusetts nursing home. "Assisted living" was what Larry Robb called it. That morning he had been turned down for a larger unit. Later, much later, when the pain was starting to be contained, Malcolm heard from John how his father had blathered on, even after learning that his daughter-in-law had been shot, about getting turned down.

John had thought out a great deal in the middle of this emergency. From his house he'd grabbed a clean shirt for Malcolm before following the ambulance in Malcolm's car. He'd come up with a plan for their return into Wyman: Malcolm would drop him off a block from the Webster campus so that he could make his way back to Everett Street and meet whatever reporters were there, hoping to get a photograph of family members. And then, as Malcolm drove on out to the Jurinkos' farmhouse, John would telephone Malcolm on his cellular and apprise him of the situation. That way Malcolm would know if he and Gretchen should stay out in the country with the Jurinkos for the night.

Malcolm was confused about the clean shirt until he realized he had just one small smear of blood on him. It was probably his own. He'd hit his head. At some point, someone had put a patch on his forehead. Malcolm looked into a mirror—his visor mirror—for the first time. Where had he gotten this patch on his head? His daughter would see it. He didn't know what he thought about that—was it some proof of his being right at her mother's side? He shouldn't even be worried about such a thing. He wasn't worried. And yet it went through his mind. How was it that anything like that could go through his mind?

"You'll be all right?" John was outside the car, bending in to look at him. "When I get home I'm calling you on that phone there, okay?" The cellular sat like a closed clam in the passenger seat.

At the Jurinko home the living room lights were on, but the rest of the house was dark. Gail's Toyota was parked in the drive, but she, in step with the plan, had not gone inside. She was alone. She was keeping track of things through John and now waiting for Malcolm, so glad to be able to tell him that she had not had to fend off the press. There was that much to be thankful for.

"This was good of you," he said. He kissed Gail on the forehead as they stood hugging.

"Malcolm, it's the saddest moment of our lives."

Malcolm held her from him and looked at her until her eyes filled.

"I'm going to stay with John tonight," she finally said. Then she shrugged at the irrelevance of that and of just about everything unconnected to Susan.

"John has been a rock, you know," Malcolm said.

A new light came on. Lev Jurinko had seen that Malcolm was now here. He began to emerge from the house in a slow, deliberate way.

Malcolm wasn't ready, he realized. He looked into the trees and remembered those grim fantasies that he used to assume all men have from time to time when they wince at the thought of a wife ever stepping into the path of something. Such thoughts of an abyss are normal. They just never include the children, since having to share an abyss with children is not what an abyss is.

12

REHEARSING

GRETCHEN AND URI HAD BEEN REHEARSING WHEN MR. JU-
rinko came home that afternoon in an exuberant mood. He'd just
then run into Susan Robb as he left Tom's Video, he explained, grabbing Gretchen in a one-armed hug, side to side.

"How I'm supposed to know you are coming here to study?" he
boomed, grinning down at her. He'd always made her love the trailing *k*'s of his Russian English. "Your mother's telling me you are
here working! 'Oh, really,' I'm saying. Meanwhile I'm hiding video
up my coattails!"

Mr. Jurinko's mood made Mrs. Jurinko irritable, as if she were
tired of turning down his volume. Instead she attacked his judgment. It was unforgivable of him to bring home a movie and tempt
the children away from their work!

Things seem to explode a little later—a shorter, louder exchange
that seeped under the door of the den just as Gretchen was about to
start her lines again from the top. Mr. Jurinko shouted that he didn't
like being told he'd done something unforgivable. A door slammed.
"Don't be sensitive," Mrs. Jurinko shouted back, "I don't mean it
literally!"

"Yes, she does," Uri said.

Within an hour they heard more fighting—an excited, muffled conversation. Gretchen and Uri had no idea that Mrs. Jurinko had just taken the telephone call from Gail. To them the sounds of crying had to mean that the earlier spat was escalating into something fiercer. "It's a matter of time," Uri said. "By March they'll be sitting in different parts of the auditorium." He look so miserable, Gretchen put her hand on his arm and said she was really sorry.

"You watch," he said, moving away from her.

Later she would realize that Mr. and Mrs. Jurinko had no choice. What could they do but continue to let the kids rehearse? Mrs. Jurinko brought them frozen yogurt at around nine, telling them that they ought to go on to bed. Gretchen felt sorry for her. Her eyes were still red from the fight. "We all sleep now, eh?" she said. "We're needing rest for tomorrow."

For a long time Gretchen lay in the older sister's bed and looked at the kind of magazines she tended to devour at beauty parlors, not that she ever went for anything more daring than a trim. Later, over the next several days, she would remember thinking, incredibly, about Cooper, about the excitement of Angela and of her very short hair; about the girl's strong sense of herself. It was time, Gretchen would remember thinking; time she cut her own big pointless mop, which basically she was just too whatever to style. What was she, shallow? Sitting in her classes, she'd sometimes known she was hiding behind hair, ogling the nongorgeous girls who had the courage to reveal the whole face, every crooked line, every defect. Susan, who looked great in a wedge, had recently said, "Your every defect? I *love* your every defect!"

She would remember hearing the phone ring repeatedly, the Jurinkos continuing to talk softly, intensely, behind closed doors. But she drifted off finally to a near-melody of murmurs in the background, and by the time her father arrived, his clothing full of John's cigarette smoke, she was deeply out. He had to call her name and shake her as if she were a child.

Back home, they held on for the rest of the night. They didn't leave a room without trailing after each other. From den to kitchen they padded back and forth, keeping vigil with a cable station out of Danford that repeated a paragraph on an alleged shooter at Wyman and a high school teacher gunned down in her front yard. It took few ingredients for things to become newsworthy, Malcolm whispered. "I've been told it was a safe house over there," he said, "for Angela." He wasn't angry; he was weak. They had better prepare themselves, he said—that kind of thing was a near sensation; and Oren Abel too, simply because of his father's old fame.

Maybe it was true that it was some kind of shelter, Gretchen said. Angela had claimed she had a deal about no boys over there. Gretchen had lied when she told Malcolm that Cooper wasn't staying at the house. Why had she done that? This was her fault. She should never have gone over there in the first place.

He rocked her, mouth in her hair, saying why had he opened the front door?

For several hours the cable station gave only Susan's name and profession; then they had Cooper's full name—Warren Reece. Toward dawn a police sketch of him made them both jump until they realized a sketch didn't mean he'd been found. There followed a make and model of the car and then another composite drawing, this one of Angela, to whom someone had given the impossibly symmetrical eyes of a raccoon.

"They're making her an accomplice," Gretchen said.

If she'd waved! Why hadn't she waved? This she could not share aloud—the two images, one of herself holding up Corey's feet and the other of Malcolm with his slat raised. He would not survive that idea of their seeing him watching them—and appearing large and snoopish, which he wasn't. She'd never once thought of him in that way. But she'd known that they did. She'd just let them.

You could tell something of his pain if you knew his voice from before. It was a thin reed now; but some men had reedy voices, so you would have to have known him from before to realize the scenes he was playing back: getting Angela the money, walking her and the children home, getting dinner ready, greeting Susan, opening the front door to Cooper. Which he shouldn't have done.

Before daybreak she went up to her room and sat. But being alone was nightmarish. It gave her Angela's tired whine, so appealing on a first hearing—*He saved my life, I owe him.* Gretchen had played the quick crony—*You don't owe him!* It had been too easy. Gretchen, the easy touch to a new girl saying she'll cut your hair if you bring a note from home. Suddenly you're good; you're on; you're quicker than usual. And so you sit there and let it drain off the loyalty you have. You don't even wave.

Once in the night she took the phone to her room and called John Richards's house.

"Who's this?" she whispered.

"Darling, it's Gail. Did you want to speak to John? Here he is."

"Gretchen? Honey, it's John." There was a pause. "Gretchen?"

"Where are the kids?" she finally said. "Did he take them, too?" She knew she was sounding insane. Still, it gave her something, calling up, trying to keep from really going insane. She didn't know where she was, looking around at old curtains she'd nagged about. She'd even *done* her old curtains, in fact—crossing her eyes and striking a pose of a daisy and making Susan laugh and agree it was time to buy or make new ones.

"They're foster children," John was explaining. He was on a natural high, she could tell. You had to keep going, because when you stopped—

"They have a place, at least. I got the name of the foster parents. Ed and Somebody Sulloway."

She floated high. She could see both of them talking on the phone—herself and John—and from that point on darkness spread out to a few dim lights, a world tucked in and at rest.

"Gretchen, you still there? Do you want to come over?"

"Just keep going," she said.

He'd learned a good deal. Ed Sulloway had confided in him, since John wasn't a social worker. The Sulloways were in trouble for having let Angela take the children even for a short while. Ed Sulloway had broken down on the telephone, John said. Nothing like this had ever happened to him; he loved those kids.

Corey had gotten to people's hearts in some way. How not? Gretchen could picture it, especially with John—the heroics of his recovering the gun, the little girl in his care for a while. He was needy, John was, but not in a hopeless way.

"What did she say?" Gretchen suddenly wanted to know.

"Who, honey? Corey?"

"No, my mother," she said. "What did my mother say?"

Matt arrived at about eight in the morning. When she heard a car pull up, she started to shake as if cold. Matt was fresh sorrow coming in. Her own and Malcolm's were a little bit tasted; Matt's was not at all. It was unimaginable, in fact.

"Don't be afraid," Malcolm said, pulling her to him. "It's the horror of the situation. It's not him. He's still Matt."

Was anything still anything?

They'd been told he was being driven here this morning, but they were not prepared for a young boy named Greg, younger looking than Matt, who pulled his car to the rear of the house. It cushioned the moment—Matt in tears but introducing Greg, the two boys looking paler than flowers because surely as they pulled in the sight of the tape and the house added something wild to any preparations.

So this was partly how it was going to be, she thought. You would be sitting in a room for a while and some sharpest cutting edge would begin to abate; but let anything happen—the phone ringing or Dr. Hegg stopping by an hour ago to ask if Malcolm needed him—and the edge moved inside the viscera. That word, *viscera*, she thought.

So it wasn't Matt. Malcolm was right. It was the look of Susan's being gone in someone's face that you hadn't yet seen. Malcolm stepped forward to pull Matt to him as he'd done Gretchen. Matt's duffel bag crashed to the floor. "Shhh," she heard her father saying.

She walked alone into the front hall to keep from thinking the oddest of thoughts—how they weren't going to work as a family now. Without Susan she wasn't sure they even went together. And yet the yellow tape around the trees out there! As if someone had cordoned off an area for a yard sale later in the day, and soon Susan would walk through the door and put an end to this joke.

When she reentered the kitchen, she found Greg and Malcolm alone. Matt had gone up the old servant stairs to his room. Ah, she thought, strangers were easier. Easier than family. "I've never been asked to do this," Greg was explaining to Malcolm.

Malcolm spoke kindly. "Do what?"

"Matt wants me to stay through and then drive him back to Torreya." The boy gave Gretchen a quick glance. "On Monday."

"Monday?" Malcolm said. "What's today, Friday? Monday is only three days from now!"

Right out of her mouth the words came in a hoarse whisper. "How can he stay longer? How can any of us?" she said.

Malcolm stared at the floor.

"George figured the funeral would be Sunday," Greg said, staring at her chest as he spoke. It was a habit few boys could avoid, whether your mother is dead or alive. "He said to tell you if it's a problem having me in your home that long, I can leave and come back."

"I was due to meet this George," Malcolm said. "What's today, Friday? We were going to drive over tomorrow to meet him."

"He would have brought Matt home himself, but we had an emergency with one of the kids."

So that was how she learned the day of the funeral. Sunday. Sunday seemed right, now that it had been given out by this gangly stranger. She must be prepared to receive all information in this fashion for a while—as a relief or as an assault. Nothing in between.

Malcolm made Greg a peanut butter sandwich and the three of

them stood in the kitchen for a time not talking. Finally he said, "I'll call George." Malcolm smiled. "Thanks for driving Matt."

"We just met," Greg said. "I'm the one that took him and his mom on a tour of the high school"—Greg caught himself—"since he's thinking about switching for the rest of this year."

Malcolm stared. "I didn't know," he said. "I guess we were all going to discuss it—" His laugh or sob came out as a bark.

Gretchen watched Greg give his half sandwich a forlorn look. "It's so he can keep his job at the camp on weekends."

"Hey, you didn't know. It's okay," Malcolm said. He motioned to Greg, and the boy picked up his duffel and followed into the hall to be led up the stairs in the entrance foyer. Gretchen, following, saw Malcolm and Greg come to a halt; Matt was in the foyer, looking out the large front door. He turned, smiled, reached for Greg's bag.

Malcolm said, "I'll take him up."

Could she be alone with her brother like this?

"You should eat something," Gretchen said. Her heart was pounding because she knew she should hug him, touch him. She could almost hear her mother saying it was so ridiculous to be scared, scared of grief. "For God's sake!" her mother said.

As she approached, Matt reached out and pulled her, the way Malcolm was so good at. It didn't even surprise her; it saddened her to think that, yes, closeness is what death can do for some people—either closeness or distance. She was glad of the former, but felt embarrassed that they'd not managed it before now.

They stood looking out at Oren's house and the yard and the street and John's car, still parked at the curb with its back wheel removed. Someone had gotten cinder blocks and made a prop for that rear part of the car. Matt smelled of clean soap. He'd been up there washing his face to start over with the pain. She'd tried this several times. It worked for a while.

"I can't remember what she was wearing," she said. She had started crying. "I just thought of something. We'll need to pick out an outfit."

His head above her head. She could feel him nod agreements. They stood there. She began to hear Malcolm returning from upstairs. They stood there hugging as he came down and stopped and attempted to take in how they formed yesterday's configuration of Malcolm and Susan at the door—about to open the door to see what that guy wanted, calm him down.

Malcolm had to sit on the stairs. His fresh crying was animal and private. The strain to hold it back sent him into a fit of coughing. She saw Greg hurry to the top of the stairs for a moment and then turn away, seeing that she and Matt were there to help.

They let Malcolm sit there a long while.

"I'm okay," he finally said.

They had to stand him up, one on each side.

"Take me up to the other spare room," he said. They turned him around and aimed him. "It will be better if I stay up here for a while," he said. "Maybe, Matt, you could get me some clothes moved up here."

"Sure."

They took him upstairs. They put him to bed.

Oren lay trying to analyze a certain low hum flowing through him. The many risible elements in his situation went in as dissonance but came out as small symphonies. And at first he did not know what this meant.

There was the nurse who felt sorry for him and the nurse who was amused by him and his scandal. Whenever they came within his range, he could hear that the two belonged in the same orchestral measure. All visitors and members of the hospital staff were various musical instruments. Sometimes he heard only the thin hum of the building's air-conditioning system and sounds of dripping faucets. Other times he heard actual strings, forgiving yet unsettling; or else it was a single high flute sound—audible to savants and dogs.

He affected a serene expression. While he lay listening, the rest of his body was another matter. He was like a clock that a ten-year-old child had taken apart and not been able to reassemble. Vital pieces of him were strewn about. If he stared at his left arm, he would see it inch, disconcertingly, in his direction. If he closed his eyes and listened to the music—on occasion a soprano descant of either Susan or Angela—the arm would sometimes jump and then crash to his chest.

Out in the hospital corridor, doctors talked in monotone murmurs to Harry. They were attempting a difficult explanation, in so far as it was troublesomely simple: the tests showed that there was nothing physically wrong with the patient.

He would not have known his case was being discussed had not Harry raised his voice in his loss of the upper hand—"Damn it, Mr. Abel is not a hysteric, if that's what you're implying!"

Oren heard more murmurs. Then,

"No! I want you to get in there and do something, is what I want. If Hegg had been on the ball last week, Oren wouldn't be half dead and laid up here like this."

Harry had his hands full, what with the doctors and with the need to pull in a chair close to the bed to confer with his client in private. In Harry's opinion, the hysteria business was tolerable, because it meant he himself would be fielding the questions from Randall Creel. "Oren, damn it, you might have had the good sense to tell me there was an entanglement between Matt Robb and Angela Bert that involved the police!"

Oren closed his eyes, amazed to hear how Harry's anger seemed logical. What was beyond logic (and besides, Oren couldn't yet speak anyway) was the way Susan had pulled out of him a notion of stepping to the plate for Cooper's throwaway girl. Or had she? When *had* the idea begun? When he'd found the girl had nothing in her cupboard but duck sauce? He'd ordered groceries, taken her to a restaurant. It had been easy, just to start somewhere. It had felt like a gift, even if he was excited about his new prospects. It had been as much about the excitement just to find himself so alive that day.

The story in Friday's paper was short, Harry informed him. So far (be thankful for small favors) a connection had not been made between Susan Robb and her son's earlier dealings with Angela. "Eddy Jensen is making the rounds for his own motives, of course," Harry said. "He's getting hold of the families of the other boys implicated to see if they can still keep quiet. It's in everyone's interest to do so, but leaks are bound to spring open. I just want to see the poor woman buried first."

Oren began waving one broken wing of sorts and was trying to cover his face with it.

Harry leaned in. "Oren, don't fall apart on me!"

But the unbearable loss of Susan and its sneak attack was happening, its meaning lost on Harry, who saw only a spasm of some kind having to do with guilt, with getting a neighbor lady killed. To Harry any neighbor's death would be equally sad and awful.

"Didn't I warn you Angela was the type to call up that dope fiend?" Then Harry said he didn't like the look of Oren's mad flailing. "Hang on, hang on, I'm going to ring for help."

Doctors were called and a sedative demanded. Oren did not resist. He knew he had to regroup and do it from places that were not the same as they used to be—places where faith might feature as something more than religious shenanigans. He'd always hated his mother's prayers. Oren had staked a claim in crueler and stony ground at twelve, right after his father blew himself to smithereens. For Oren the world's fathers had been shown for what they were: little men stuffed with straw. Oren had not known this at the time. He'd trusted his father the way one does before knowing to even name it as trust—as basic decency. Hutch had *smelled* trustworthy, like the smell of golf greens. His colognes, his clean collars and pressed suits. He would come to Oren's room with gifts of books and records, back home from a school board meeting or some function at the church. Then it came out. As a cynical teenager, Oren used to shock his mother with his frankness. Women and boys, he used to tell her. They're awfully good at making up fathers, whether it was God the Father or Hutchenson O. Abel.

"I can't have you confusing his mind more than it is," Harry was saying. "As you see, Oren's had himself a little ole stroke."

When he opened his eyes, he could still hear the high-pitched hum. Its attendant pale light was now bathing the room. Here were men pulling levers, and they would be glad to make him one. Oren, in this state, was easily dispatched with. Always had been, in any state.

"I didn't come here to confuse his mind," Randall said, very slowly.

Randall stood at bedside, moving the brim of his hat in circles. Oren watched and then said, "Hand me my dress. I'm getting out of here."

Harry cleared his throat. "You see how it is, Randall?"

"Yes," Randall said. "It's kind of like this Warren Reece has fell into a big convenient sinkhole, and Oren's going to do the same."

Authority figures practiced a certain grace of reply in these parts, and these two were getting warmed up to it beautifully. Harry was nearly cooing. "Things are like that sometimes," he said.

"My dress," Oren again tried to say.

Round and round went the hat. "I hear Matt Robb is a religious boy," Randall said. "See, Eddy and I don't want any more than you all do to have that boy exposed."

Both men sighed, and then Harry explained that Oren was asked for help by Matt Robb. "Went all the way to Danford on his behalf."

"Did the mother know, do you think, and she just never got around to telling the boy's father about the arrest? He's in the dark here!"

"The boy was never charged, Randall."

"No," Randall conceded. "No, he wasn't, you're right." They looked down on prone Oren. They looked him over, head to toe. Randall began to nod sadly; in his opinion, Oren's paralysis had a cause no one but themselves would grasp. "It's the mortification of it all, Harry." Then he cupped his mouth and whispered, "Was he saying something about a dress?"

"His dressing gown," Harry explained. Harry turned and called out as if Oren was ninety. "Oren! You cold, boy? I'm going to find you a blanket!"

"Oren!" Rawlins shouted, even louder than Harry had. "You lay right here and get better, you hear me? Eddy says for me to tell you the same thing. He don't want you worried. He's going to pay you a call, soon as he gets the chance." Rawlins bent down low to an ear. "You don't aim to be safe-housing your Angela types anymore, do you, Oren?"

Harry became animated, explaining how he himself was going to represent Angela when and if she was found. Harry and Margaret were going to find some good home for her. They were working with the system. It was going to be just fine. If they couldn't find a place for Angela, they were going to take her in themselves.

"It's good when people pull together like this," Randall said. "It's people that help people. The law can't only do so much."

"The girl and Cooper were never charged either, Randall," Harry ventured, ever so cautiously.

They were acting like Scout leaders now—Harry with his hand on Randall's shoulder, escorting him into the hall, and Randall asking whether he thought Malcolm Robb ought to be told, since sooner or later someone would tell, if not right away; the woman wasn't buried yet, so Malcolm ought to be spared; and besides, didn't Harry think the whole Matt and Angela thing was starting to seem beside the point?

Eddy Jensen never came close to a similar point of chummy agreement with Oren. Eddy tried, but he didn't have his brother-in-law's patience and understatment. He slipped into Oren's room at three in the morning to avoid Harry and Randall; he came talking a blue streak, saying he didn't mind the inconvenience of a house call, especially with Oren right here in Danford; what could be handier?

"And you're standing up!" Eddy said. "Are you talking too, by any chance?"

"A little," Oren said. "Right now I need your help."

"I know it, I know it! That's why I'm here. And I got you good news and bad."

"Eddy, I want you to help me get into my dress. I'm cold."

"Oh. Sure thing! Where is it?"

"I think it may be over there in that closet, if you'd be so good as to check in there for me." Oren felt as if he were directing the man to put his foot in a trap. He'd not ever felt such a sudden strength of will. When Eddy found the gown he shook it as if he were a matador ready for a charge. He grinned, never detecting a matched power coming at him.

"Warren Reece is stone dead, Oren," he said, guiding Oren's arms into sleeves. "That's the good news. We found them both in a Fernandina Beach motel. Reece makes a nice-looking stiff. Has a smile on his face. The bad news is that he didn't take the girl out with him."

Oren lifted his head to the hum. He waited. Just be Hutch, he thought as he tightened the sash at his waist and turned to look at Eddy. Just be stone. "She's not hurt," he said flatly.

"Hell no! Some people don't know when to do the world a favor, do they? But listen, I don't want you upset over it." He handed Oren a tissue right out of its generic hospital box. Eddy was shaking the tissue at Oren the way he'd shaken the dress. "You're crying, Oren. Here, take this! Mop up, for pity's sakes! We're going to figure something out, you and me."

Oren walked to the window and stared out.

Eddy excused himself and went into Oren's cubical toilet. He left the door cracked and gave out the sighs of men who drink beer all night. "This Reece!" he called. "Man alive, he put enough heroin in his arm to kill several. I don't know how it happened the girl wasn't in on it. Maybe it was the guy's revenge—leaving her alive and all the trouble she could get me into, not to mention you, Oren, not to mention the kid of the woman killed. Lord Almighty, if you think about it two seconds, that Matt Robb is the one got his own mama killed."

While Eddy tried out other scenarios, Oren looked at his reflection in the windowpane. He was on his feet, he was confident. It was Eddy who was scared.

Eddy, back in the room, began looking around for a chair. He was here, he said, to talk over how they were going to keep that girl from shooting off her big mouth. Maybe Oren and Harry had it all figured out.

He was just about to sit down when a nurse walked into the room; what in the world did he think he was doing here at this hour? Eddy smiled at the nurse and then winked at Oren. Touché. Oren had pushed the nurse button on him.

Well, well, Eddy said.

"Sir, I'm not leaving this room until you clear out," the nurse said, eyeing his badge, his gun, his pushed-back hat. "And I don't care who you are."

When Oren opened his eyes, Eddy was gone and the nurse, the one whose ping on his screen had been sympathetic, was standing there apologizing and saying wasn't it terrific that he'd come out of his trance like this. "You needed a good sleep!"

"I'm fine," Oren said. "My feet are cold. Did I come here in my shoes and socks, do you recall?"

"I'll see if I can find them for you," the nurse said. "Right now you're probably cold because you're hungry. I'll get you something."

"The kitchen's not closed?"

"We got a microwave for people coming out of trances in the middle of the night."

Food was a cup of boiling water into which Oren poured a packet of soup powder. The nurse had also provided peanut butter crackers and a carton of milk.

He telephoned Harry and Margaret, but they'd already heard through Randall about Angela and were planning to be at her hearing in Fernandina. It was set for ten in the morning. Harry was betting on a conventional hearing, no surprises. Then she would be released to them. Oren wasn't to worry. Harry would call him later.

Outside his room, two red Exit signs hummed softly at far ends of the empty hospital corridor. The only thing for Oren to do was confide to the woman at the nurse's station about needing some exercise. A little walk down to the lobby to wait for the morning paper? he suggested; dawn was almost here, and the paper would follow.

The one who liked him, Freda, nodded her head reluctantly— Well, all right, she guessed it was okay if he went down to the lobby. Then she changed her mind and said she better go with him. They could look at the new lobby renovations together. Two million dollars, she was told it cost, although she couldn't imagine why.

The nurse who didn't like him paid no attention to all this chatter. She took a clipboard and went off to make a few rounds.

Was he really hysterical, or had he been in here faking it all this time? Freda asked once they were alone in the elevator. She was flirting now, and Oren tried to think of some other terms for it. The college librarians always simulated awe at his ability to remember when, say, a next eclipse was going to be, so he pointed to the nurse's watch and told her that while they were down in the lobby he'd like to stand just inside the big doors and observe a little solar event due at 6:40 A.M.

She smiled and smiled. An interest in that sort of thing can start any time, couldn't it? It was never too late, was it? Was he one of the ones out there every evening last year looking at that comet?

Outside the hospital Freda became quiet and took him for a little turn under the trees. A soft wind took all her silliness away, and with it came the lovely movement of branches flailing over a deeply reddening sky. The nurse sighed. Oren, on the other hand, felt dizzy but in no danger of falling down in his gratefulness to Angela for being alive and to Harry and Margaret for being alive and to Susan's survivors and to this stranger.

So what was this solar event he'd promised? she wanted to know. Just that, he explained, pointing to the sun coming up in the east. Oh, she said, very funny, he was such a riot.

Who knew if he could be much help to people? he was thinking. But surely in the hums he'd been hearing all day and in the whisper of these old branches above the hospital, there was a message of some power, now available to him. He'd been hearing it all day that sorrow's joy was a blessed and brimming grief.

13

FRIENDS AND RELATIVES

EARLY SATURDAY MORNING JOHN RICHARDS BROUGHT OVER Johnny, who'd flown in late the previous night from Atlanta. He'd been touring for the winter break with his college debate team. Beth and Ted Harwood came early too, flanked by Wade and Wayne, who had been with girlfriends at the family's second home on Lake Jessup.

Johnny, Wade, and Wayne entered the house fresh from showers. They had their good looks and their dewy brown eyes and great haircuts and pressed shirts. They'd been debriefed and emptied of all their tearful and angry first questions about the shooting to which their parents had been witnesses. They knew more than Gretchen did, and she felt the subtle and kind way they handled this. They were all grown up now, college freshmen, but not awkward in front of her. None of them were referring to her mother as Ms. Robb any longer. They all called her Susan.

"Dad said to tell you he's already spoken to one of the children again this morning. Corey? He said he'd tell you about it later."

Her antenna was out a mile for any ploys—the longing on Johnny's part to hear what she knew about any of this. This mess. Oren's safe house.

When she stared instead of talking, she saw the color in Johnny's neck go red in big blotches—huge red continents with craggy shore-lines on his white, white neck. She knew she was right. He'd been probing.

"I'll make some coffee," Wade said, clearing his throat. Wade and Wayne both were in on it—Johnny's sly effort to draw Gretchen out.

Soon it was discovered that the house only had a standard coffee brand in the cupboard. Also there was no heavy cream. She over-heard Wade putting heavy cream on Wayne's shopping list and telling him to get the espresso machine from the house while he was at it. He murmured, "We might as well do this right."

Their shared job was to manage the crowds of mourners who were going to stop by today. That would begin later. For now they could hold Gretchen's hand as they took turns easing down beside her on the couch in the living room. Gretchen went as limp as a rag doll and did not resist their attention. One of the boys stayed by her side at all times, and she was not allowed to gaze out a window with-out Johnny putting an arm around her. She needed no drug to feel drugged. Their colognes drew her to them. They were all bigger than their fathers now. The muscles in Johnny's arms were hard. Tanned, honeyed skin with no hair.

The four parents, in various combinations, went up and down the stairs to be with Malcolm. All she understood for a while was that easing-down sensation—sometimes a boy on either side. In sipping their coffees and in the taking up of her hand there was a reality they could share. This was family, and it was their parents and no one else's who ran up and down, talking quietly to Malcolm in the spare room, helping him with decisions. The boys were to an-swer the ringing phone and filter through only Randall's calls. They were to jot down all other messages and receive visitors at the back of the house. A man was due to arrive to take down the tape at any moment, and no one wanted that loud knocker sounded at the front door.

Matt greeted the gang of three. "It's good of you all to come back home like this. How are you guys?"

"Matt," Johnny said. "I'm so sorry about Susan."

Gretchen watched her brother let himself to be hugged in manly tradition. He'd done such things his entire life, as long as Gretchen could remember—tried to be enough within the realm of expectation as to escape the notice that freaks usually get. For his whole life he had reminded them all of a deeply religious person who has to work at seeming ordinary.

Johnny fixed her a rich coffee with lots of cream and sugar, the first thing she was able to swallow that morning. The sweet bitterness momentarily revived her, that and his wrapping a free arm around her, letting her head fall on his shirt front. "Shirley Temple coffee," he said and kissed her hair the way all the fathers did. There was nothing she wanted to do about this.

Because with them she could cry differently this morning—with a steady gaze and no sound. The gang's most graceful gesture was to leave it unnoted except in the various kinds of touching and holding that contained the pain. It did. The quiet college-boy talk, the deft management of the first people to begin arriving—all of it kept her company while Malcolm remained upstairs and the senior Richardses and Harwoods went off to pick up the senior parents—Mim and Larry Robb and then Big Susan—from various airports. The Robbs were managing a flight into Danford, and Big Susan into Jacksonville. These things took time, and in the interval the house began to be flooded—not merely with food, but with flowers and cards, handwritten notes inside.

She went to the bathroom upstairs and looked at her eyes—unreal, swollen. She'd have no credibility with deformed child's features—a child who can't take it. She returned to the kitchen immediately and asked Wayne to empty a tray of ice for her. Upstairs she filled the bathroom sink with ice and water and submerged her face for as long as she could stand.

Someone was suddenly saying, An old actor's trick?

"Mom?" She stood up and looked around. "God," she whispered, "where are you?"

Later Malcolm sent for her, and she knew then that there was finally news.

"Hey," he said softly. "Come sit. I want to tell you now what I've just told Matt. Are you feeling strong? Sheriff Randall says it's all over with regard to Cooper. They've found him in a motel. He's dead, Gretchen. He took an overdose. It could be a suicide, it could be an accident."

They were alone in the upstairs spare room. He had made up the bed. It looked like an ironing board. He was using the old high-backed chair they kept up there, and the contrast between the neatness of that unused room and her disheveled father was startling.

"And Angela?"

"She's okay. She's not hurt. I don't know any details about her because—"

He broke down. She waited.

"Randall isn't giving me details," he began again. "He's not completely sure of me, you see—What in God's name was my relationship with those people, what with Cooper getting so worked up over me? Can you understand?"

She thought she'd be ill. There would be this fraction too much for her. It could come now or a year from now, and she didn't yet know what it would be—some part of this she wouldn't be able to hold up under. Malcolm had his head in his hands. Whatever else was going to happen was going to happen, he said; it couldn't be worse than Susan being gone.

He meant what Angela might lie about—the weird twists that a crazy person can put on things, depending on her state of mind.

"I feel bad, you down there with Johnny and the twins," he was saying, trying to change the subject, give her some attention he must feel she needed. "I don't quite know how to send everyone away." Then he started to laugh. This frightened her more than his crying ever could. "Listen to me saying I don't know how to send them away," he said, laughing. "I can do that much!" He rose to make his blind way out of this room and down the stairs.

"Hey, don't," she said. "Johnny's taking a million calls for us. You should just eat something. Some carbs." She both wanted to be with him and did not. "They're looking for Oren, you know," she finally said.

"They found him. He's at Danford General. He's had a stroke of some kind."

For a moment the house and neighborhood felt as quiet as any normal afternoon lull.

"Randall says it's psychological. The old man's full of shame."

"You mean because he was involved with her?"

Malcolm refused to answer. "There's something more important for us to talk about. I want to tell you something else. I've talked to that George." Malcolm was still bent forward into his hands. "He's okay. Not at all what I thought." Malcolm raised his head and looked at her. "He's a psychiatrist! Matt's found himself a sure enough shrink. It was why your mother was so pleased. She knew I would be, see, because I've been nothing but worried."

She nodded at him, smiling at him through tears. How was he going to stand all this? She must harden up for him, be adult for him. "Dad, it's going to be all right."

"I know. I think so, anyway. You won't think I'd be taking the easy way out, letting him leave? Just leave, for God's sake?" He bent forward again, rocking slightly.

When she turned her head she saw Matt in the door.

"You'll worry less, Dad," she said. "Matt being at this place he likes so much."

"But what kind of thought has he given it?" Malcolm didn't realize Matt was in the room. "Did Susan—" Malcolm couldn't finish the sentence, the thought.

"Mom and I talked about it," Matt said.

Malcolm looked up. He smiled in relief. He sobbed. "Really? Come here, Matt. Sit down and tell us. You have a plan?"

Matt came forward and sat beside Gretchen on the side of the bed. "It's a country high school," he said, "but I was hoping you wouldn't mind."

"Mind that it's a country school?" Malcolm said. "Of course not."

"And me at the camp for the rest of school."

"I'm open to the idea, but Greg was talking Monday. That's too soon."

She could see Matt blush. "I know."

"You're not really needed there, Matt. I mean, of course, we're all *needed*. But you're a fill-in counselor. Let's keep a perspective."

Gretchen looked at where her fingers were cutting into her palms. "What's that to us now, Dad? What's perspective now? Why can't we be wherever we want to be? Can it make much difference?" She didn't want to attack him. She began to cry again. They weren't going to make it, she thought. No decisions from here on would make a bit more sense than any other decisions, why couldn't he just see that?

But she got up finally and stood over them. She put her hand on his back, Susan's hand. "It's okay, it'll be all right."

"Did Mom tell you about the camp?" Matt said.

"She didn't have time," Malcolm said into his hands. "Is it because the man's a psychiatrist?"

"At least she got to see it," Gretchen said.

"Partly," Matt said.

"He sounds like a good man," Malcolm was saying. "But I don't know. Maybe we all need to be together. To mourn together. Don't we?"

No one answered him. Matt had his head in his hands now just as Malcolm looked up. Gretchen could see that he was staring at Matt's bent head. "It'll be okay," she said. "Mom won't mind. She doesn't mind."

There began to be one visit upon the next, one upon the next. People arrived and refused to leave—Susan's high school colleagues from Danford, a few students and parents, women from her reading group, church members, Malcolm's Webster colleagues, including the new president, Gretchen's ancient piano teacher, the principal of her school. There was a Saturday-afternoon din in the house and a big demand for the gang to meet and greet. With kind whispers John, Gail, Ted, and Beth had to help keep people moving on home. People lost track of the time; many wandered into the backyard and just stayed there, talking quietly—busy people who didn't get to linger with each other like this.

One telephone caller wanted to know if tomorrow there was to be any speaking from the audience. "Good question," Gretchen heard Johnny say. "There's this new minister. When he gets here, we'll let him ask Malcolm, and then someone will probably phone you." Johnny was allowing himself an impatient, funny roll of his eyes skyward. There was a laugh in the kitchen, irrepressible, but a first. Gretchen felt Wayne squeeze her hand over it. She smiled.

"Who is the new minister?" Wayne whispered.

She shrugged. She and Malcolm had stopped going two years ago when Paula Gayley finally left. The church had tried out several people in that time.

The gang kept that notepad going—logged in all questions right along with dishes and the visitors and decisions they were, by late Saturday afternoon, quite adept at making without having to ask Malcolm or anyone else. And, since Gretchen was there, they could consult her. Didn't such-and-such seem like the best idea? What if they just called up so-and-so and let her decide, since so-and-so would know what Susan would want? Was that okay?

She didn't mean to end up eavesdropping from her parents' room, where sounds traveled way too easily from one of the old heating ducts. It's just that they didn't know she was back there, off limits, even to Malcolm.

"Here, take this sandwich plate to Matt," she heard Wayne tell Greg flatly.

"I've never been asked to do this," Greg was saying.

"Well, let me help you out: take this and go!"

Several beats went by in which she assumed Greg left. Then Wade said to Johnny, "Have you taken a good look at Matt? He knows something about Malcolm, right? I think it's why he's getting the hell out of here Monday."

She got up to wash her face. It was not possible to think about what she'd just heard. Later there would be so much time to do that.

Big Susan was wearing the only perfume she'd ever used. Maybe it was her face powder. Comforting, familiar. She came to Gretchen immediately upon entering, and obviously relieved that Malcolm was upstairs or else gone to see his own parents at the motel. She lifted up Gretchen's chin and kissed her, looked around, and pulled herself up straight. She insisted that she watch what was coming out over the television. There was no TV at the B&B. She went into the den alone and closed the door. "You," she said, pointing at one of the twins when she emerged, "I can't remember which one you are."

"I'm Wayne."

"Take me back, Wayne." She turned to Gretchen. "I'll see you to-morrow. All you have to do is telephone your grandmother Mim." She looked away. "Forget it. I'll call. You don't have to call. Why should you? Larry and Mim never congratulated Susan on anything, did you know that? Not one achievement."

That's when Big Susan finally cried. No one could bear it. The boys found places to go. Only Gretchen sat there with her, holding one of her hands, playing with one of her bracelets, feeling the older woman's sense of uselessness in the world. Her flamboyance had come to so little, and she was nothing now that her only child was not around to enjoy her, as Susan so obviously had. Susan had taught Gretchen how to enjoy it. "Think of her as a diva who never did quite hit the C above C. I feel sorry for my mother. I reaped everything she sowed."

"Where was your father?" Big Susan was saying as she sobbed. "Standing right there and letting that man shoot? Just take aim and shoot like that?"

The phone rang and rang; there were whispers Gretchen stayed out of. Finally she took the Valium Big Susan had given her and went to bed and did not wake up until Sunday morning, to learn from Malcolm that Angela was being given restrictions with regard to Wyman and the Robb family.

"Restrictions?" Gretchen said.

Malcolm sat on the edge of her bed pressing tissue to his upper lip, where he'd cut himself trying to shave. The funeral was in three hours. Randall had telephoned to say that they hadn't been able to hold Angela because she'd committed no crime. Her lawyer was clear on that point. The best Randall would be able to do right now was slap on a restraining order. He'd told Malcolm that in his opinion Angela was crazy enough to try to come to Susan's services.

A restraining order sounded odd to her. It didn't sound fair, but she couldn't explain this at the moment. She knew what such an order was. She could practically see what one was. She was seeing one every second and would for the rest of her life. They were for boyfriends. Not for girls who came screaming into your yard trying to lure the guy away, trying to keep the guy from shooting you.

Nothing better suggested the complexity of it than the very different legitimate newspaper accounts. Wyman's weekly, the *Star*, was so small that Susan took up almost the entire issue. There was some reporting on the crime itself, of course. But mostly the text was a narrative of her life, the now profoundly poignant facts of where Susan Bennet Robb had been born and educated, where she'd met Malcolm, under what circumstances the two had moved to Wyman and "made it their home."

For two days the gang had kept the regularly delivered Jacksonville paper from being thrown into the yard. They didn't seem to credit Gretchen with getting to the bank of dispensers on the campus. Just the first-sentence requirements of what, where, who, and when could take one's breath away—how late Thursday afternoon, a Danford high school teacher was alleged to have been killed by a neighbor in an apparent dispute over money.

As for the gang, she knew that they read too and talked together before coming over to take up their posts for the final morning. It occurred to her that it was only natural. And after the funeral she imagined more as they cleaned the house of guests and they all got ready to go—imagined how frustrating it had been for them to be with her. Touching Gretchen, holding her hand, was the closest they could get beyond the teasing phrase, "in a dispute over money." She had said nothing, had not let one innocent-seeming question lead to anything else. In her mind she could hear them begin to whine to one another. *Judas Priest, if they only moved in on Sunday, how could there have been a dispute about anything? Who were they?* She could hear in those whines the sub-whine: *One semester away, and the whole neighborhood goes to pot! Tenants. When did we ever have tenants on this street?*

That evening she took warmed-up coffee and slipped out the back door in order to stand where she'd been standing undetected for guilty years now, listening with a kind of excitement in her groin to a marriage whose wreckage Ted and Beth kept secret from people. There was a window in the Harwood den facing out on the Robb side that had been cracked a lot of the time, innocently leaking out a lot of stuff no one was supposed to overhear concerning a not-so-great marriage. Everyone knew it; Ted and Beth just didn't know it.

"What do you mean?" a familiar woman's voice was just then exclaiming.

She heard Beth repeat her question with a little more hurt, a little more outrage. "What do you mean? Why don't you say it more plainly?"

And it was Wayne who answered. "Okay, Mom: a man doesn't come over to your house with a gun and start yelling at you without some provocation, is what I'm saying. By and large, he has to be provoked."

She wasn't sure who groaned. It was a male groan, intended to be dismissive. Johnny became the world-weary owner. "I don't think Malcolm Robb could provoke a mad boar."

College-boy laughter, while Beth, still angry, tried shouting above it. "Just tell me something, Wayne. How would Malcolm have had time to have anything to do with that girl? She moved in on Sunday. *Sunday!*"

More laughter. Not mean, just exasperated by a mother's one-dimensional take on things.

"And by Thursday, the man shoots someone," Beth continued. "I think he might just as well have come to our house and shot me."

No one spoke. She had silenced them with a bit of self-pity. Beth was noted for it.

"We're sorry, Mom," one of the twins said. "Calm down."

"You boys can make me so mad." Beth was crying now, and it was hard to hear what she said. Something like, "Just go!"

Soon the gang came quietly out the back of the house. Someone had car keys. It was over for them; time to drive to Danford and *do* something, for God's sake, just the three of them. Probably nothing more out of the way than a last meal together, home from college. They could spend time talking heatedly, free of the parents. They could go over it and over it—reintroducing all the options, including Malcolm having maybe tried something. *Do you think? God, Malcolm? Ranger Malcolm?*

Howls. What a relief. Thank God for Danford all these years.

And they would wear out eventually and start to talk about their old teachers, their parents' marital unwindings, Gail and her new boyfriend. *Come on, Johnny, let's have the details. You owe us.*

It was over. They would think of Susan perhaps a lot at first, and then only now and again, or when they came back to this street on obligatory visits to whatever parent stayed around. They would know by now the touching story of how Mr. Jurinko, in his naturally exuberant way, might have spontaneously said to Susan when he ran into her and was almost the last outsider to speak with her, "Hey, why don't you come on home with me? Call up Malcolm! I got a movie we can watch with the kids." Susan might have said "Why not?" because she was not a person to tell him they'd be tempting children away from their work. Especially not Gretchen, whose great passion in life was getting ready to do parts for that class. She would have called up Malcolm to meet her there, to pick up a bottle of wine on the way.

Susan had been killing two birds with one stone on Thursday, having her dental appointment and her car inspected at the same time. She'd driven her car to Andy's garage to leave it overnight; she'd walked to the dentist from there, and now she was walking on home at the moment Mr. Jurinko stupidly hid the video as they talked about Uri and Gretchen's enthusiasms. He had let her go, let her walk on home, refusing a ride because she liked that particular stroll. It was the shortcut from the west side of town through the small campus quad where Gretchen, Matt, and the gang had learned to ride bikes as small children and knew which tree roots pushed up which portions of the concrete on jaunty hind ends when they moved on to skateboards. It was part of their childhoods, the Webster quad. It wouldn't change now. The quad ruffled forever with that little bit of lifted skirt as she continued on under the canopy of trees, smiling at something, one of her arms swinging free and the other holding her briefcase, while the sun sank to the tops of the branches.

In town, only an hour earlier, Malcolm would have been holding the baby and shoving his card into a slot and talking about whatever he and Angela talked about, their lips moving and Gretchen able to translate the innocent conversation but not having the time for it, what with her mother still moving steadily forward, refusing to detour left, refusing to stop by Malcolm's office to see if he were there. Anything. Say if she'd detoured! She could have run into Gail Richards, who was delayed at her office in the Financial Aid suite next to Admissions. Susan would have poked her head in and persuaded Gail to go for an iced coffee and a little private catching-up. They might well have telephoned Malcolm to meet them somewhere later. They often ate in town whenever Gretchen stayed over at a friend's house and wouldn't need them for her dinner and homework. With the volume turned down, Gretchen could watch her mother chatting with Gail over coffee, the two of them deciding that Malcolm should meet them at Tea for Three or at the new brick-oven pizza place. *No way, I've got dinner half ready.* But she could have talked Malcolm into putting it back in the fridge. She could talk Malcolm into anything.

But she hadn't detoured. She hadn't veered one step. She'd just kept on coming, strolling in silence, Gretchen looming above her now like a big low blimp above the town, able to see down on trees and houses, the streetlights turning on, her own glowing house seeming to draw Susan willfully on. The old Abel place was like a doll's house without its roof. Gretchen floated above it. She could see Cooper arguing with Angela, pointing at her nose, shouting out the windows, working himself up, so that even if Gretchen had waved to Malcolm on Monday—

Why hadn't she? Nothing meant to embarrass him or anything, but just to seem to acknowledge him at his window, where he didn't think he could be seen—a good man, well-meaning, loyal, incapable of provoking a mad boar.

14

PACKING

MALCOLM DECIDED THAT HE WOULD GO TO BED FOR THE FIRST few days, but that he wouldn't do it from a vulnerable position. He made a list of things he needed to check on and attend to, the first of which was to call up that Harry Rawlins character, Oren's lawyer. By the time he heard the older man's soothing voice, Malcolm was pretty pumped up.

"I want you to understand something," he began. "It's going to be me and my daughter here at the house. I just want to make sure you people are not going to get careless and let Angela show up unannounced. She was over in Oren's house just long enough to make her mark and have screaming run-ins with me and my daughter. I've had visions of her coming here to scream some more, to accuse us. Maybe to apologize. Who knows? Just see that she doesn't."

Oren Abel was second on his list. "You tell him for me that he's not to come to us either," Malcolm continued. "When I want his story, I'll give him a call."

He knew his sudden overwhelming anger was only a clue to just how much had changed for him, just how on-the-surface the suffering had been so far. Now things would really start for himself,

Gretchen, and Matt, and he must at least acknowledge to himself that the ragged issues that had nothing essentially to do with his immediate family would have to go their own chaotic and independent way.

Matt's departure on Monday morning took place under the supervision of Gretchen, who pointed out that Matt was at least returning to where he'd last been with Susan and would not be far away; they would go see him often. It was Gretchen who packed him off with more clothes and books she thought he ought to have. Malcolm got into the spirit, of course, and lots of encouragements were exchanged before they let Matt get into Greg's car. There was a last-minute dash into the house to wrap up some food for the ride. Then Gretchen broke down, and so did Malcolm and finally Matt. There had been so many breakdowns; what was one more? The only thing now was that every day the deluge keep meaning slightly different things.

Matt should call, Gretchen said, her reddened hands on the open car window. "In a little while we'll come to see your new place." She went ahead and emphasized "new place." She said it bravely and with big smiles.

"Dad," she said, as the car pulled away, "are you going to be able to stand me being here?" She was joking in her mother's funny way. "I'm not sure I'm going to be able to stand you being here." Then they hugged. It wasn't hugging in any regular sense. It was more what one did to keep breathing, to keep finding air. Alone, she confessed to him that it was something like being held under. But not always. Sometimes being with another person was unbearable. And so it would go. Better two attempting it than three?

Malcolm found himself agreeing and feeling the numb amazement of his daughter's talk. She'd keep quiet until she found words. Then she'd nail it.

When they both turned to look at the house, a clatter of birds and normal sounds started up, normal dew on the grass, Susan's flowers needing a watering. Gretchen trudged off to turn on the hose, allowing Malcolm his private event: reentering the house all by himself for the first time free of the people who had been in and out all weekend.

People who had eclipsed something. Susan's library book lay on top of the piano, her checkbook on the mantel, a cup with its trace of her lipstick still on the desk on the back sunporch off the new room. The gang had cleared the house of all evidence of the many mourners eating, talking, leaving napkins around. *Her* things, they had not cleared. Cautiously he placed his thumb on the lip print. But he couldn't do it. He put the cup back where he found it. Life had to start from somewhere, but it didn't necessarily have to start from there.

The spare room upstairs would answer, the way motel rooms can sometimes answer. The kitchen was about the only other room he would need—a place for a glass of milk before going back up. He dreamed of Angela almost immediately upon putting his head on the pillow for his first real sleep. Not a long dream, just a blip of her cruising the house with yet another boyfriend at the wheel, the guy's blind pink tongue feeling the air as he grinned and looked Malcolm over. The dream car seemed to pass him by very slowly, dragging all its private parts along Everett Street and then on out of town.

Gretchen went to bed that day too. The phones were disconnected. No one stopped by. Everyone knew to stay away without being asked. The gang had worked out complicated runs to airports with Johnny, Wade, and Wayne. Malcolm heard various cars pulling off. His own parents had flown home last night, and Big Susan had a friend scheduled to pick her up and drive her somewhere today— Palm Beach or Fort Lauderdale, he couldn't recall which. He had a loud ring in his ears, as if recently he'd suffered a blow to his head. Then he remembered that he'd fallen down several times—the porch, the flagstone. The ringing hadn't been apparent until now, in all this quiet.

When he woke up, it was gone. Rest was what he'd needed, at least for that minor ailment. He could hear Gretchen padding around as quietly as a mouse. And being so sensible, he could hardly believe it. When he entered the kitchen, there she was, looking at the phone book.

He felt startled. "You aren't about to telephone someone, are you?" he said.

"Just the phone company," she said. "Someone is dialing us and hanging up. Have you heard him? I think we need an unlisted number now."

This news kicked Malcolm into action, at least for an hour or so. The person at the business office recognized his name when Malcolm called. She explained the process of making the change in his service and then volunteered that she was personally going to be sure that he wasn't charged.

Gretchen phoned Matt with the new number and put Malcolm on for a brief exchange. On being asked, Matt described the camp setup, but even upon listening to it for the second time, Malcolm could only get hold of the barest details. He couldn't concentrate. He understood that between now and summer the camp would have a few boys on the weekends. During the week Matt would attend school, and right now he, George, and Greg were building a cabin and he was learning a little about basic construction.

Later, after the second of these short conversations, Malcolm found himself flopping back against his pillow, thinking, I'm letting him go. And he had no will to do otherwise, almost no sense of what was happening. Maybe nothing was happening. He'd talked to George Murray again to thank him for whatever it was he was doing for his son. The man had paused and then said, "We'll meet soon." He had then restated his condolences and they had rung off in a completely conventional fashion—each was looking forward to meeting the other; Malcolm would get there right away to see the place as soon as he could and to talk more about the arrangements. That was fine, the man replied, continuing to make it clear that Matt was earning his keep, that Malcolm wasn't to worry about that. "He's my best counselor," the man offered in what was turning out to be a fatherly tone. It went a long way. In Malcolm's pain and grief, it was a relief. Hey, if she were alive, they'd be letting Matt do this anyway!

He sat up in bed. "Right?" he said.

Right! Susan said.

Malcolm wouldn't learn of certain town-and-gown ramifications until Wednesday. Webster's new president, on the other hand, had been taking incensed calls for three days about an inflammatory article published in the Sunday *Jacksonville Examiner*. Sunday, the day of the funeral itself; so Malcolm missed seeing it.

The article was purported to be about campus violence generally, but at second glance one saw that that wasn't the real topic. Webster College was the topic. There was a half-page color photograph of their quiet quad—the one through which Warren Reece had strolled in search of a pair of lost designer glasses. Reece had a college background; he'd attended an Oregon version of Webster, all set among shade trees too. The article went on to point out how Reece's recent visit to the Webster campus happened on the same night a look-alike student, Lloyd Reniere, tried to jump from the second floor of the large building shown looming in the background of the photograph—Comstock Hall. Thus were both Malcolm and Lloyd Reniere linked to Cooper. That students could be murderers gave Susan's death the hook the reporter needed, so that it was particularly awful for Malcolm to read, in the same context, of his own apparent acts of kindness toward both Lloyd and Angela (ergo Cooper by association) a few hours before the killing.

Naturally Angela and Susan were eclipsed by this better angle, which the reporter had gone to some trouble to develop. Both Reece and Reniere were rich, spoiled, and troubled, the writer implied. Pictured below Comstock Hall, in an inset of its own, was Malcolm's front yard, further evidence of the relationship between the shooting and the jump. Admissions Director Robb had been present at all scenes—dorm, cash machine, his wife's side as she was drawn into an argument having nothing to do with her.

Over the phone, President Norris approached gently the question of Malcolm taking a paid leave. Then the man walked over to the house, as if in final nod to old President Davies and his familial style. It was a delicate matter, Norris explained; it was entirely Malcolm's choice, but he wanted to be frank: as president, he had the students in mind, their parents, this year's *prospective* parents; alums, trustees, distinguished guests. Time would do a great deal in giving everyone, Malcolm included, some space.

It was interesting to Malcolm to hear himself agree, to watch himself behave so reasonably, as if, just like that, it all tasted leathery. Had he ever had a job, period? He remembered it, of course, but he couldn't remember it ever having been of much interest, and he guessed this must be how it felt to be seriously ill.

He enjoyed seeming his almost-regular self to the president—reliable Malcolm, low-keyed, candid, a man with whom one can be candid right back.

"How are your children?" Norris said. "I didn't meet your son when I stopped by the house."

"Matt," Malcolm said. "He's going ahead with a plan to change schools, as a matter of fact. He's going to be working at a boys' camp and finishing high school in Torreya."

"And he's taking this as well as can be expected, I suppose." Clearly there was talk going about of peculiar Matt; enough talk to reach the ears of a man with little time. Something of Matt had stuck with Norris, despite the boy's irrelevance to things at hand.

"My son is fine, I think," Malcolm said. "I'm making sure of both children, of course. My being available now is critical, so I want to thank you for coming to talk about this."

"You and I will stay in touch, Malcolm." Norris may not have intended to say this; it was Malcolm's capitulation that was drawing him out. "I'm talking only a leave here, you understand."

"Of course," Malcolm said. "We'll keep in touch. Thanks again for coming over like this."

It had been in the way the journalist had mentioned the designer glasses, a detail behind which Gretchen, by miserable, miserable chance, knew the real story and would never forget as long as she lived. But at least she was spared the journalist knowing about that. To the journalist, the Robbs represented the old days—the journalist's own old days, in fact—when an adult presence on campus meant something. When neighborliness resulted in something less than lethal. Common decency was the victim here. Malcolm, much to his credit, was behind the times, a throwback, the article implied. He had helped his neighbor.

Malcolm and Gretchen stopped using the front door. In two days the house shrank to narrow paths. Beth ordered them Meals on Wheels for a month. The delivery people were instructed to come into the mud room and leave everything on a worktable. Malcolm kept the doors, front and back, firmly bolted.

He let Ted, Beth, and Gail down gently from their responsibilities by explaining to them and scores of others that he didn't want visitors. "Don't call me, I'll call you," he chirped to them, laughing or crying. Either way his emotions tore them apart, and while they appeared awed by his strength, they were also relieved to be asked to stay away. He would be too.

This was Gretchen's trick as well, possibly Matt's, although he knew he couldn't rush to decisions. He must be strong for them; be around, let them have their feelings with him close by to talk, or not to talk, to be the one person they knew who loved Susan as they did.

He noticed John's lights on at all hours, and one afternoon he knocked on the back door to see if he could be of any help getting John off. He was overdue at Agnes Scott College for a stint as visiting economics professor for the semester.

He found his old friend sitting on his living room floor with boxes of books gaping open. File folders lay everywhere on the floor—John's tax records that he hadn't gotten to his accountant and so now was going to have to lug with him to Macon; his unpaid bills;

his lecture notes. All week he'd been moving these files around, looking into them, closing them back up.

"Depression," Malcolm said. He squatted down and looked around him at the papers slipping out of their nests. He could grant no kinder favor to people than to seem psychologically robust; or perform a kinder act than that of quelling fears busy people might have for him. His friends were very much busy people. In a twinkling, one can be so not busy, so not like others.

"Yes, it's odd," John said.

"Nonsense. You've been depressed for over a year now about Gail."

"Yes," John said. "Can I confess something awful? Susan's death had the effect of distracting me from it for three days."

"That's nothing to apologize for," Malcolm said. "John, you were wonderful. We couldn't have gotten through this without you." He meant it too—all of John's levelheaded moves, all his foresight, his take-charge instincts.

"Here's another confession, Mac. I loved feeling like Johnny was closer to me than to Gail during this time. I thrived for the entire time on how he trusted my opinions more than hers. It cleared my head right up."

Malcolm examined a spine of a book. Let him have it, he thought; it's only out of sheer habit one holds back the urge to speak truthfully. "You've always competed with Gail for Johnny, you know that," he finally said.

"Have I?"

"Now that he's managing so well without either one of you, I think he figures you can both go to hell."

It felt terrific. It was less to do with speaking, in fact; more to do with the simple realization that Malcolm wasn't going to have neighbors for a while. John would be away; Ted and Beth would be off trying, yet again, to salvage whatever they had left of their pathetic situation. In fact, long planned was a project to add a room to Ted and Beth's house on Lake Jessup. Even before Susan's death, it had galled Malcolm—their copycat idea of adding a room, as if they had any idea about the real stuff of love Malcolm and Susan had available, as if it was just a matter of saving up the cash. When he thought of what the bedroom and sun porch meant in terms of depth, he realize how irritating Ted and Beth were to him now.

John was nodding. He'd seemed to take his attack well. He continued staring at his planted feet as if waiting to see if Malcolm had anything else on his mind.

"Sorry," Malcolm said grimly. "I'm feeling freer than usual."

"Me too," John said. "I'm feeling freer too." There was a warning in his voice now.

"Hey, then go for it," Malcolm said. "Life is so short."

"You mean it?"

"I mean it."

"Malcolm, in your bighearted liberal way, you can't understand how I got Johnny for a son instead of you."

Malcolm thought about this. "You're right, I can't," he finally said. "He was a neat boy, too—just like the kind I always imagined having myself. Mind you, he's an obnoxious bastard now, but there was a time when he was a really good kid."

"Obnoxious bastard?"

"Yes, but let's not dwell on that. What I really can't understand, in my bighearted way, is how the one couple who had a good marriage on this block gets blown away while on either side of them are people doing it to themselves. I know I'm just being sentimental here, but geez, you would have thought that the one house that was working could have been spared God's wrath."

Ted phoned up later. Malcolm had a quiet talk with him, confiding in Ted how it was that he and Gretchen would probably not be able to stay in the house.

"You'd move, you mean?"

"Right now Gretchen and I are both talking to her," Malcolm confessed. "That will stop. Later it will seem more right to get us out. When I look in the yard, it's always going to be there."

"What neighborhood were you thinking about?" Ted said.

"What town, you mean," Malcolm said, "what state, what hemisphere." He realized, when the conversation was over, how again he was glad that Ted was too upset to focus, to be interested. Malcolm didn't want people interested. The isolation felt healing.

In a couple of days John was gone, his house all rigged with timed lights. Each night Malcolm and Gretchen had trouble sleeping, as a result of which they passed out like dead people in the afternoons. One afternoon Malcolm didn't hear a thing, and neither did Gretchen, until a loud pounding on the front door sent Malcolm flying down the stairs, wondering why he was living here now without a shotgun. He opened up to a young policeman just wanting him to know there really wasn't much to worry about, but he was sorry to have to report that Oren's house had been vandalized by some punks.

Only a few windows were broken, a back door pried open, a drawer of silverware tipped into the kitchen sink. They couldn't tell if it was locals or out-of-town curiosity seekers—idiots who had tracked the carpeting with muddy footprints and built a neat log cabin of human feces at the top of the stairs. Whoever it was hadn't seemed to have much in mind beyond a show of anger. "A shooting pumps people up in a whole lot of different ways," the young officer said. "There's this crime and then this whole letdown afterward. People need something to keep going sometimes."

"Yes," Malcolm said.

But the result was that his and Gretchen's needed isolation proved utterly complete. From things the young policeman let slip, it would seem that Oren, in all likelihood, was a mental case of some kind, living in his small apartment and never going out. That was something at least.

"How about I put all these up in the attic for now?" Gretchen said later that afternoon.

"What's that, honey?"

"Eighty-seven sympathy cards."

Malcolm nodded soberly. "I'll go through them. Put them up in my room."

"Well, okay. But I'm not reading any more of them."

Something was up, he could tell. "Why not?"

"Okay if I start back to school on Monday?"

"Of course. But answer me. What happened?"

It was a while before Malcolm got it out of her that some kook had sent a card containing a scrawled request for a nude photograph of him. Alarmed, he phoned Randall's secretary and blew his top at her when she answered him in lackadaisical tones. "Call the post office!" he shouted. "Call the college. I want these things rerouted to Randall."

"Sir—"

"No, you put Randall on! Why am I even talking to you?" When he hung up, Gretchen was there again in the kitchen. She didn't want to appear rattled by Malcolm's fury.

"What's that?" she said, coming to his side and fingering a pile of paper pieces. Malcolm had made confetti of Harry Rawlins's calling card.

"Nothing," he said, raking the paper into the palm of his hand. "I was wondering if you wanted to visit the grave. We haven't discussed what kind of people actually visit graves, but I don't know, I just thought I'd try it. It doesn't have to be a routine."

Gretchen considered this suggestion. "Let's take some kitchen bags so we can gather up the dead flowers."

"Okay. What else?"

Gretchen laughed. "A flashlight! It's getting dark! We should have done this an hour ago!"

"I couldn't an hour ago," Malcolm groaned.

"Yeah, I know what you mean."

And she really did. He saw that. To be with her was to be with someone getting it right, down to the subtlest feeling and gesture—even to the strange moments of curious exhilaration, very hard to understand, that then would leave them flat on their backs.

"Here," he said, tossing her the keys. "You drive."

15

GETTING GRETCHEN
OVER WITH

ON MONDAY GRETCHEN RETURNED TO SCHOOL AND FOUND
out that she'd have to decide about people. How not to hate them.

It had been the town's first near manhunt. Kids had been allowed
to stand before TV monitors in the language lab whenever they had
the time. At home they'd been yelled at, "Here! Get *in* here!" because
to get even a flash of Susan's photograph or Cooper's police drawing
you'd had to be fast. You'd had to really scoot.

Teachers' eyes filled up when they saw Gretchen. Chuck, the drama
coach, had almost certainly told about that O.O.C. guy Gretchen
had had Uri do—the one sailing off Oren Abel's porch just days before he killed her mother. Nothing of this sort had happened to any
student in the school, and it was pained inexperience she saw in
those teachers' eyes—relief that she was back, that they were getting
her over with.

But the kids didn't know how to be getting her over with. Her father had made someone's boyfriend mad. They'd heard of fathers
like that; they had fathers like that. From points way down the hall
kids turned and headed for exits as Gretchen passed on her first day.

They scurried into bathrooms, stairwells, and hall huddles. Uri said it was like seeing the Red Sea part.

There were attendant side glances and her friends' confusion and embarrassment in homeroom, although it helped that the teacher was right there to give her a long hug as she crossed the threshold. Everyone drank in that wordless embrace. By first-period math, hugging was the method of choice in getting Gretchen over with.

She tried to remember what can happen. In your absence, a whole school can reinvent you a little bit beautiful and thin. They must have been feeling high for days, and now she was back and not glamorous. She was a letdown. Finally, a manhunt needs a man. It needs the man to turn up alive.

Short of that, kids were going to the town diner to check on crazy Oren Abel. Uri let this fact slip on day two of her return. Oren was wearing a bathrobe and a trench coat, Uri explained. He was driving a car now and out of his mind, which was hardly surprising, given what he did.

With belated fellow feeling, she was suddenly sad for Oren. Kids were such goons. "What do they think he did?"

"Did! Gretchen, you can't go move some girl into your house! Oren should have known!"

"Known what?"

Uri lowered his voice and his guard. "That no self-respecting pimp is going to let you set up his woman at your house."

She was getting a sample of her friends' casual conversation. She put strength in her voice: "I bet they talk about my dad as well, don't they? You can tell me, it's okay."

His answer was too quick. "Not that I know of."

"Really?" she said. "So what does Oren do over at the diner?"

"He talks to one of the waitresses all day. She's somebody's aunt, some ninth-grade kid's aunt, apparently."

"Apparently? Why do you say that?"

"It's what I've been told. And that he has a car now."

She sat slumped on an outdoor bench suddenly in wonder at what possible difference Oren's having a car made.

"Here," Uri said. He put his arm around her and handed her a handkerchief. She hardly knew she was crying, it was so constant a state. The handkerchief was folded and pressed, something Uri's father had to have given him for the predicament of her.

By day three it got back to them that the drama workshop kids were jealous. Gretchen was as much theirs as she was Uri's.

"Sharon says I'm hogging you," Uri explained. Sharon was not a close friend but a workshop enthusiast who had helped talk Chuck Mulert into his winter break minicourse.

"Hogging me?" Gretchen said. "Now there's a phrase," she said, her mother speaking up out of nowhere.

"Sharon says she'd hang out with us if it looked like we wanted her to," Uri said.

Gretchen nodded. "A grief clique."

Uri had sort of glommed on to her. He was warming to it. He began to tell her she was doing great. Every time she showed emotion, he was all over her—"You're doing great, you're doing great"—as if in hiking she'd sprained an ankle and he had only to coax her, half-crazed and frozen, out of a mountain pass.

By Friday she wondered which was better, to have Uri hang out with her or the others not hang out with her. To have the spoken part be about poor Oren or about herself or Malcolm. Kids were frightened of her, she knew that much. They feared some power a real death had given her.

At Friday noon she finally said, "How do you mean *great*, Uri?" Emergency laziness had set in at school. Scandal was easier. Titillation the easiest.

"You know," Uri said, blushing, "you're really strong. I've been telling everyone how strong you are."

"You mean strong like this?"

She took her fist and hit him on his upper arm as hard as she could. People, side-glancing out of their various hall huddles, saw. They averted their eyes and, more embarrassed than ever, turned on her that chronically bad posture grown-ups mistake for slouching sullenness. Here was a new event at least—crazy Gretchen, the girl you wished you could ask a million questions, decking Uri Jurinko. They would surmise that that's what had happened: Uri had tried to ask her one measly question, and bang, she'd decked him.

Come Saturday she slept a whole day again. Malcolm was supposed to have driven to Torreya but had ended up talking to Matt on the phone. Again. She suspected he'd slept all week.

The rest did her some good, and on Sunday she felt she had a small breakthrough. She was standing in the kitchen cutting out an article from *Sound and Stage* that she thought Sharon would enjoy passing along to Chuck because it featured a contemporary playwright Chuck had said was worth knowing. In deciding to try outreach with Sharon, she let her mother's huge shears slice at the slick pages of the magazine article, and the scissors, old and heavy, were suddenly something she knew she could take to the hardware store to be sharpened and put back in repair, one of her mother's good habits.

The scissors drawer was standing open, and she glanced in to stare at the junk they'd kept in here for years. This kind of disorder put her under no obligation; she saw so much of it around her. Susan's clothes needed sorting, and her office at the back of the house was full of mail. In the kitchen there was a plastic bag of faculty mail from Susan's school mailroom and some arts notices from State U that she read closely every month. The bag represented the clock-stopping moment; it contained those items Susan had meant to sort or was in the very act of sorting when Cooper began pounding.

Gretchen peeked inside the bag. Meetings and notices, just as she'd known they would be. Glance inside that bag, and Susan jumped into the kitchen—almost the whole of her, the efficient movement of her hands, the deft sorting before putting aside the classic movie calendar so Gretchen might choose a few good ones by circling her picks with a red pencil they kept in that same narrow drawer. But always disappearing, too, that pencil, and her mother always calling out—half exasperated, half bemused—*Come on now, who took the red pencil?*

She searched the drawer. The pencil was miraculously there. Her eyes swam miserably as she got it out, sat down with the movie choices, and circled two Barbara Stanwycks and a Ronald Colman. She put the calendar under the magnets on the fridge and hoped to God it wouldn't jolt Malcolm to see it there, all circled and ready for a Saturday drive to the ratty campus screening room, where they would chat with all the State U film geeks and see a bad print with bad sound. Gretchen, Malcolm, and Susan had done scores of Saturday classics together with the geeks, who brought microwaved popcorn from the dorms. After the film Susan would insist on hitting the campus bookstore and then the antique shop that had been about to go out of business for years. Gretchen had treasures from that shop—the ceramic swan that she hung at the side of her mirror along with her three glass-bead necklaces. The store owner, Mr. Haas, was, as with so many people, clearly energized whenever her mother pushed in, tinkling the little bell above his door. He smelled of Liquid Gold, camphor, and cedar. She must go see that little Mr. Haas. She must let him know she was all right.

On Monday she delivered the magazine article to Sharon and let her left shoulder touch Sharon's right shoulder.

"Pass this along to Chuck," Gretchen said. "You need the points."

It was a sweet moment. They hugged. They'd last kidded each other about needing points only two weeks ago. To Sharon, the old kidding around must have seemed unreal. "Thanks," she said, a little catch in her throat.

"You're welcome."

How do you hang out with Wyman's grief-girl? Gretchen thought. Well, this was how; she was giving a free lesson. It was all pretty simple.

But when Sharon proceeded not to mention the article again; when, in her continued fear, she let more days go by without a word about it or anything else—keeping her distance and smiling at Gretchen and Uri as they passed—there were, after that, only two kind words to choose from when it came to Sharon and the rest. There was *chicken,* and there was *twerp.*

Sometimes in that second week back at school Gretchen went silent. She stopped quipping to Uri, stopped smiling at the others passing by. She declined all hugs and began to be more attuned to her mother's patient and very graceful style of slipping away. One could either resist her or stay tuned. In either case, she was going to slip away.

While she was still close, Gretchen knew she must help by sorting through Susan's mail with Malcolm's permission, sorting through all of the clothes that were good enough to be laundered or sent to the cleaners before being given away. The leisure clothes—the jeans, the turtlenecks—she boxed up to await the return of the good stuff from the cleaners, whereupon she would sort again and decide things again. Meanwhile she threw out all underwear and hose and old sneakers. Then she stopped. It was a first round, enough for now. She was exhausted because she kept finding little things—a piece of sugarless gum in a jeans pocket. She had a basket full of the kind of trinkets that to throw away would have seemed almost to finish Susan off—ticket stubs, a receipt from the turnpike, a lipstick.

At school she managed better. She explained to a puzzled Uri that he'd been a good friend, but she was in this aftershock or something; could she just be on her own for a while?

She gave him the term *aftershock* so he'd have it upon his reentry into ordinary civilian life with Sharon and the others. It was one thing for Uri to have tried to hog her, and worse yet for her to send him back to them miserable. They would enfold him. What did she have in mind? to hog all the pain?

It was a relief to be clear of them, the profoundly death-challenged. She did not blame people now, but knew that they would continue to distract her not just from what she wanted to think about but from how to think at all.

A few evenings later she sat rereading her scene from the *Uncle Vanya* assignment and found that the part was all different. She went straight to Malcolm and pointed. Was she dreaming? Some of this stuff from the play seemed to leap toward her now, as if leaping through time—starlight, billions of years old, just now reaching Earth. In laughing sobs she confessed to Malcolm that she wasn't, in all good faith, going to waltz into her school, twerp-years later, and waste real words on tenth graders.

Malcolm started to laugh. "You get this from your mother." He began fishing in his pocket for a tissue. He blew his sore nose.

She eased down beside him. They no longer left the room when the gale winds swept in, uninvited, through windows. They'd taken to hanging on. The crying was not frightening and even sometimes brought Susan rushing into the room. "You two! Come on now! Come on, buck up."

"Dad, I'm thinking of taking up home schooling. You think Mom would have flipped out at the idea?"

"No," Malcolm said. "Quite frankly, I don't know how you attend regular school right now. Me, I still don't go out on the front porch. You've been nice not to say anything about it."

"Nice? I'm not being nice!"

She knew now. She was wasting her time at regular school—the want of quiet, the impossibility of getting beyond the huddle and hog of it all. She was racing headlong at something having to do with the way mouths speak but rarely say things. Here, in these older words of the play, it seemed quite the opposite. Here someone was wrestling speech to the ground and demanding a blessing.

"So, I can try it?" she said. "I know I can't reinvent life."

"Maybe you can," Malcolm said. "Maybe you have to."

The next day he took her to see the high school principal, whose name was Albert Hart. Al, he liked to be called by the other teachers, but the kids had changed it to All behind his back. All Hart was famous for kindness and popularity. In fact they liked him a lot.

He greeted Malcolm and Gretchen warmly, closing the big door to his carpeted office, leaning against the front of his desk, and listening with large listener eyes. He said Gretchen was a terrific student, always had been; she could take whole weeks off and still stay caught up. He'd assist in whatever way he could. By every report she was doing great.

She didn't wince. She suddenly realized something. All Hart had a big soulful face meant to make the weak feel strong and the strong, weak. He was an Ace bandage.

As soon as he walked to the other side of his desk, she felt that there was more in the room upon which she could put her finger. All Hart was playing out a kind of enjoyment of Malcolm, who was not just Malcolm anymore. She sensed it in the way the principal emitted a small squeak from the swivel part of his chair; *Malcolm Robb, of all people.* She remembered the unlikely senior boy who was expelled last year from school for selling certain magazines, or so the rumor went. That senior had entertained them, she saw that now. He had entertained them by being someone for whom they could as a group think, *Of all people,* and enjoy the surprise. No thought of pity, much less innocence.

When they got back home, Malcolm put on his oldest jeans; he was banging around in the mud room by the time Gretchen got into bed and started reading her textbook, *Six Great Plays of the Modern World.* All that wasted time, she mused, trying to strain through a straw what she should have been chewing on like steak. She read and read and then fell asleep dreaming of herself, the way she used to fasten cards near the spokes of her wheels to get a kind of artificial clatter going. She'd skipped the meditative life. She was going to change that now.

She woke again and read, feeling her bean brain move. She thought of those time-lapse nature films she used to love. They were hilariously true. If she could be filmed right now, she'd look like one of those time-lapse beans breaking open, its ridiculous but true root tunneling down three feet in two seconds flat.

Later Malcolm looked in on her and announced that the mud room door had a worn-out air pump. He was off to the hardware store and would be back in a jiffy, his first solo trip out of the house. She hadn't planned on this—how, to him, he couldn't afford two limp survivors taking to bed at the same time. In his economy, one of them had to be up and about. Home schooling, she was thinking. It meant staying home and getting on with it like this, reading for no other reason than you wanted to feel it work in your head, the way it never does at school. School can't help it; school is clatter's natural home. Smart noises and initiatives hurry to the rooftop lightning rods and then safely, rather stupidly, to ground. It is no one's fault, since surely all real events of the mind happen in private.

She woke later smelling fried tempeh. The fragrance made her sail downstairs for food. She and Malcolm had eaten wheel-meals for weeks without tasting. They didn't have to confess this to each other. Their wet eyes met as they sank into the egg and tempeh sandwiches Malcolm had put together with toast, tomato, and homemade mayonnaise. It was good. He wanted to know what she'd eat for dinner tomorrow and the day after. He blew his nose. Even being hungry again made him cry.

So she was doing the dishes, humming to herself, when she turned around and saw him standing in the doorway after she thought he'd left to do some shopping.

"I'm sorry I frightened you," he said. "Honey, don't cry. I didn't mean to scare you."

But there it was. She was a complete mess again, just like that, blurting out something she still didn't quite know the meaning of: "We're not going to make it. None of us are going to make it."

"Of course we are. I just gave you a scare. That was terrible. Here, come with me. It's only that I have to show you something. Come with me."

He seemed so much to be counting on her that she did manage to stop crying. She walked with an effort to be poised and tall, following him into his study and looking, incredibly, right through the little slat he had raised. Standing on his porch was Oren Abel with one arm above his head. He seemed to be signaling.

She spoke as calmly as possible in order to calm herself. "Well, you aren't imagining it. It's him."

Their old neighbor was making signs almost as a distant figure might hail them from across a large body of water—*Friend, not foe.*

"What does he want?" Malcolm said.

Oren continued—first one arm and then the other, starting low at his waist and ending on the other side. "He's letting us know he's back. If he'd telephoned, we'd have been startled. Or tonight his lights would have startled us, I suppose."

She watched Malcolm go into the hall and opened the unused front door. From the porch he returned the signal, slowly, back and forth above his head. This caused Oren to stop and retreat into his house.

"I think the only thing to do is go right over," Malcolm said. He was headed back into the house and opening the front hall closet. "Do you have a jacket in here?" He was slipping into a jacket of his own. "It's going to be cold over there."

Then he was yanking off moccasins; he was looking for a pair of sneakers in the closet. She stood watching how he put them on— in a rough, determined way, as if he had a tennis tournament ahead of him. She had to trail after him, back up the hall and into the kitchen, where he slammed and locked the back door before he finally slumped into a kitchen chair. "Do we really have to do this? What if I end up throttling him?"

Then he was up again, fast. He was unplugging the coffeepot, tightening the tap. "All right," he finally said, taking a deep breath, "I'm going to get it over with."

"No!" Gretchen said. It was a shriek. It surprised her more than it did Malcolm.

He stopped. "Honey, what? It will be a relief, I think. And you certainly don't have to come."

"No, I want to! I just hate what you just said!"

"What did I say?"

"That you're going to get it over with. I can't stand that expression."

He looked at her. He walked to her and held her. "I've been very angry, that's all. Now I get one glimpse of him and feel ripped up inside."

"Just don't use that expression."

"Okay."

They stood there a long while.

"Ready?" he finally said.

No one was visible on Oren's porch when they got to the steps. She sensed Malcolm balking. Both were looking at the very threshold over which the bull had burst in his rage and headed for them.

"Oren?" Malcolm called. He put a loud call in his voice. "Oren!"

Gretchen eased her hand to his upper arm to make the climb up the steps, and Malcolm in turn made a crook at his elbow, as he'd done when they'd headed out from the choir room to take a front pew at the packed funeral—all of Wyman and half of a Danford high school. She had felt herself age both then and now—facing the poor man who had set it all in motion and knew he had. That's what she'd seen in that wave, she realized.

"He's crazy," Uri had said. "They're saying the pimp guy used to charge him just to watch."

"Oren!" Malcolm called.

He knocked on the frame of the door and then opened it up. Gretchen hung back. Once inside the hall, Malcolm seemed to disappear. Then she heard his low greeting. When she entered herself, she was in accord with the dark and with Oren, seated just to the right, just inside the living room where, on the night she'd baby-sat, she'd made a pallet for Ricky and had sat looking out at Malcolm mowing the lawn. Years and years ago, it seemed to her now.

Oren sat in one of the old wing chairs she liked. He didn't stand. Something mannerly had gone out of him. He had on something old and frayed. Not his usual white shirt and tie. He refused to speak. He gestured, however, at places to sit—the couch for Malcolm, the opposite chair for Gretchen. He'd draped a blanket over his legs, and again she felt that she was accurate: he knew they had needed special preparation; a special meeting that he arranged. And that they would need him to be unfamiliar—a little strange and distant, as if silenced by new thought.

And he was giving her the same thing for herself! He nodded at her, as if to acknowledge her change. The last time he'd seen her she'd been a nagging little put-on in some attempt to impress him, claiming they needed a lawyer for Matt. She'd not even meant it. She'd been improvising, practicing. In those days, she used every minute to try out stuff.

"Well, here we are, Oren," Malcolm said. He collapsed into the couch, exhausted by the anticipation. And she could see that this really was needed—not a getting over with at all. More of a square one for the three of them. She looked with affection at Malcolm's clown feet flopping out in front of him as he sank into a kind of faint of sadness—all that was left in him after the effort of crossing from one fatal side of the street to the other. He could hardly move.

Oren let out his own breath. Gretchen herself felt flattened, her limbs turning to lead, her clearer mind knowing that this was the only place the three of them could be. They were people who had had very little thought of inhabiting the planet without Susan. Gretchen sat in the chair opposite Oren and put her head back. "So," she heard Malcolm breathe.

They all three closed their eyes, letting the awful hour have its way with them. It's a kind of giving in to it, she thought. Where had she read that idea—the bending to keep from breaking? The hour of Susan's death came every afternoon at the same time like this, no matter what, no matter who. All one could do was push deeper inside its rooms and corners. She had known for a week now to be grateful that it would always be the late-afternoon hour when she was more likely to find a retreat for the first shadows triangulating a wall.

When she opened her eyes, she saw that Malcolm, smiling, had been watching her closely. But at some point he'd eased off his shoes, stretched out fully, put a pillow under his head. An empty mug sat on his chest. She must have slept! He moved one finger up and down at her. His eyes were softened as if he, too, had rested and then been served a soundless cup of tea as both men waited for her to wake up.

Oren looked at her and did not smile. Those smiles at school always accompanied loss of nerve. Oren was keeping his gaze keen, motionless. They all took turns for a while—looking at each other rather bravely. She could sense that the two men hadn't spoken, even in whispers, but had been content to sit in the dark and wait as if they wanted her to know something important: that there was nothing they had to say to each other that did not include her.

Oren leaned forward and removed the top from a thermos. Gretchen breathed in the smell and accepted a mug when he filled it for her. Malcolm seemed to sink to another place of rest as he watched this quiet movement and her leaning forward to see what Oren had assembled for them to eat. It was a covered plate of bread beside which were two tubs, one of butter and the other of wild honey. She took her time with a knife and then a spoon. The honey was the kind sold at farm stands around the country; Joe Walsh kept a supply at his bakery in very small containers. Gretchen looked at Oren. She had no idea how her voice would sound. She didn't care. She cleared her throat.

"Do you know what she used to call this?" she said.

No one answered. Oren's eyes danced in tears. One could tell he was so glad to be home, but that it had all depended on them. On how they would accept the idea of him. The very idea.

"She called it allergenic honey," Gretchen said. "You can taste the ragweed in it, she used to say. You can taste brine in it, and paw of bear."

She saw how her father had to sit up, wipe his eyes, grin, cough a few times. His shoulders gave a little stir as if he were interested in having some. She handed him the plate she'd been preparing. An expense of courage had left them ravenous. Oren sighed, and after another wait in which they all received a plate and began slowly chewing, he leaned in and reached for matches. He lit candles that were burned down almost to nubs. This was a little service, he was saying in effect. He finally stood up out of chair as if to make an announcement. But Gretchen saw almost at the moment it was happening that it was an unveiling of sorts. He was standing up in order to let the blanket fall.

16

RAW AWE

OREN HAD APPEARED TO BE WEARING A COTTON SWEATER with a hood. Now that he was standing Malcolm could see the sweater was part of a larger piece, something belted. What? A beat-up old sack dress from a thrift store? Malcolm thought of a priest or monk's alb for a moment, but then his gaze kept stopping at the point where the hem of the thing hit just below Oren's knees.

"They'll kill you!" Malcolm murmured. Below the hem were two white hairy shins, then the hugely exposed men's shoes and brown socks. One knew instantly the man was not going to apologize, either now or in the future. In private or in public.

"I've been killed already," he said. "No one can kill you a second time."

He sat down then but remained upright, his eyes brimming as he stared out above their heads. Malcolm watched Gretchen get up and stand beside the man's chair.

"It was as much me, Oren," she said. "I should have waved!"

"Waved?" Malcolm said. He was confused but clear that his daughter was right: Oren *was* sitting there as if to say, I shot her.

But he felt he must get her out of there. Oren's confession was going right to some absurd sense of her own part. Who on earth should she have waved at? Poor girl, he thought. In the dark he felt around for his shoes.

"I'm having a cleaning woman come tomorrow morning," Oren said, out of nowhere. "She'll help me around the house, you see, and in this way people will start to get used to me." He turned to Malcolm. "Are you leaving?"

Indeed, Malcolm was hurriedly tying his laces and then reaching out for Gretchen's hand. "Why don't we come back another time, Oren? We'll do that soon."

"Freda's told the cleaning woman about me," Oren said.

"I see," Malcolm said. "Gretchen, we have to go, honey."

"Next week I'm hiring roofer friends of Freda's. I've been needing a new roof, but the point is that they'll be warned first and then they'll see me. Soon other people will have begun to hear about me and will have half accepted me in their minds. That's all going to help."

"Oren—" Malcolm said, as he tugged on Gretchen's hand.

"I want a few things generally known, you see, so people have some preparation." He was politely accompanying them into the dark hall and springing to open the front door for them. "It's going to be fine, I think," he said. Then he added, "I hope. I don't have much choice."

Malcolm waited until he had Gretchen out to the porch steps and down them. At the bottom she balked, so he paused with her and turned. "Preparation, Oren?" Malcolm said.

"That's right."

"To what purpose?"

Oren gave a little laugh. "To the purpose of not getting myself killed. She was having me step to the plate and be bold, Malcolm, but I don't think she was suggesting foolhardy." He was closing the door softly on this observation—the one that left the two of them standing there holding hands. After a moment Gretchen looked up at Malcolm. She smiled. "He meant Mom," she explained.

Malcolm was in quite a snit all that evening. In the past he'd hated snits, but Susan's death made him forget that in having one he could feel back among the living, especially in having to listening to Gretchen reason over supper that tomorrow Oren was going to need her over there while a new housekeeper was getting used to him.

"You seem to understand what's going on," he said.

"No. I just feel like helping him."

"You can forget it," he said. "We've smoked our pipe, and that's all we can do. All I want us to do."

"What's that supposed to mean?" Gretchen said. There was something in her voice that he didn't quite recognize. Then again, he did.

"It means no, Gretchen! It means no, I don't want you over there!"

"That's too bad," she said. It was not sarcastic. It was not even defiant. She really meant it was too bad he felt that way.

"You're not going to mind me, are you?" Even to him the terminology sounded laughable.

"It's not a matter of that," she said. "I just gotta to do what a woman's gotta to do. Sorry."

They hadn't played the old John Wayne bit in a long time. John Wayne had been her first, at around age six.

It was a snit, all right—completely one-sided. Gretchen was as calm as a swami, while he rolled and tossed all night, attributing to Oren every sort of underhandedness, none of which computed, as much as he tried to make it.

The next morning he got up, unrested. With coffee he shuffled into his study and lifted his slat to check if Oren's newspaper was still out on the lawn. About three seconds later Oren hobbled out in the alb-dress. Because of a light rain, he was being careful of puddles, his shins flashing as he tiptoed out to grab the paper, to straighten up, to wave at someone, and sprint back inside.

Malcolm told himself over the coffee that he must try to respond rather than react. But later when he heard Gretchen come in, having been over at Oren's all morning, he asked her an irritable-sounding rhetorical question that just came out of him, out of the old Malcolm, flummoxed and feeling excluded—What in God's name is the man up to? or something such as that.

Schooled by her parents in the low standing of angry rhetorical questions, Gretchen didn't pause. She went on up to her room, calling over her shoulder that if he was going to the store any time soon he could pick them up some olive oil.

That evening they ate together, but Gretchen would not discuss Oren. She said she was making up her own mind, and she'd like to take her time.

"Take all the time in the world," Malcolm said. He let healing warmth come into the conversation. He leveled his voice into something as neutral as possible. "What do the roofers think?" It was a reasonable enough question, he thought.

"Think of what?" Gretchen asked.

"Of Oren, of you being over there."

She could scare him when she was like this, her sense of timing so much better than his. She could heap coals of fire by following up his question with enough silence to make it all sound completely beneath him. "I don't know what they think," she finally said, "but I met Freda! Freda Wilks."

"Well, tell me about her."

"She's a nurse Oren met in Danford. The roofers are liberals from some country church Freda Wilks has been going to for years."

He didn't quite see the roundabout way in which she was baiting him. "Country churches aren't usually liberal, sweetheart," he said, smiling.

Gretchen shrugged. "More so than you, it would appear."

But suddenly she was smiling too, and she had such a happy look of expectation on her face, he felt for a moment he would burst into tears. She'd never tortured anyone in her life, and now she came bounding to him and hugging him and then showing him a booklet— her ace.

"What's this?" he said, still hugging her, then holding her out from him, allies.

"A thing with which to barter," she said, opening it up on the table in front of them—a booklet she'd checked out of the college library on his card. It was the Florida Board of Education's brief guidelines for home schooling statewide.

"There aren't any complicated laws in Florida," she said with a kind of pride in her voice. "All we have to do is tell Al Hart I've decided not to return next month and then go register with the school superintendent. I know it'll be work for you to tutor me, but I thought maybe you'd like it."

"This is so I'll have something to do," he mused. "I'm on to you, don't think I'm not."

"You'll help me with English and social studies, Oren algebra."

He looked at her. "Okay," he finally said. He couldn't resist her, her happiness.

"Oh, and Oren wants to do the Shakespeare."

"Wait, *I'm* English, I thought you just said!"

"I tried *Macbeth* in September with Ms. Blanding, but it doesn't count. I couldn't read then."

"Couldn't read?"

"Never mind, I can't explain." She hugged him and sighed. "Oh, I'm so excited."

The phone rang, and she made another bounding motion toward it. He grabbed her arm. "Let it pick up," he warned.

"Right."

They both waited. Listened. It was Beth asking Malcolm to give her a call when he had a chance.

"See," Gretchen continued, "Oren tutors me, and in exchange I go shopping for groceries with him."

"I don't think so," Malcolm said.

She wasn't listening. "See, the way I figure it, I'm still the mur- dered woman's daughter, so what are people going to do, call him names in front of me?"

"Gretchen, read my lips. I forbid you!"

"I figure I still have a few weeks of awe to work with here. I know it's not a lasting emotion, but there's still some left, right? A little raw awe?"

When Malcolm called her back, Beth's news distracted him. It was the starter rumor about where Angela and Cooper had lived and breathed prior to being in Wyman—a rumor recently passed along to Beth through a reliable friend in Danford. For Malcolm it couldn't have been more unexpected.

"I don't know if I'm doing the right thing in passing things along any further," Beth said, "but here goes."

Angela and Cooper were arrested for prostitution in Danford, the rumor had it. Back in December junior high boys were involved, so the charges against everyone were dropped because of certain key families. Beth's source was feeling guilty; there would have been more information on Angela and Cooper from the start if the police weren't feeling compromised. Randall had to know all this, but apparently a Danford police captain was related to Randall—his brother or cousin.

"I've been trying to put myself in your shoes, Malcolm—the hideousness of having to confront Randall and watch him pretend he hasn't been keeping things from you."

"Maybe it doesn't make much difference."

"That's why I almost didn't call you, because it was my first thought. And then—"

"What?"

"Malcolm, like Ted said, Cooper was a bomb waiting to go off, but if he'd been in jail at the time then he couldn't have been in Wyman going off in your front yard."

He felt himself getting sick. Beth's logic was the old carousel he and Gretchen had been on for weeks—if this hadn't happened, then that wouldn't have happened. If Malcolm hadn't gone into town, if he hadn't offered to get her cash for the phone company, if Oren hadn't been so Blue Angel as to have turned his place over—

"I thought and thought about it," Beth said. "I decided I'd want to know if I were you. I'd just want to know."

"We've got Oren back again," Malcolm mused. "Before I go asking Randall questions, there's Oren to ask. How did he meet Angela and Cooper? Was he lined up with boys waiting to crawl into the back of a car? If he'd refrained, wouldn't Susan be alive? There are a thousand links in the chain, Beth. If just one of them had been broken, it would mean she'd be alive. Just one. So which should I obsess on—Oren's or Randall's? I've got some links of my own doing, people assume."

Beth was crying. "I'm sorry, Malcolm."

"It's okay," he said. "It wasn't wrong of you to call. Hey, I probably will speak with Randall."

"I'm sorry, Malcolm."

There was nothing to do but hang up.

Funny. It was Randall who came to him.

Damage control, Malcolm thought. Malcolm hadn't himself been in damage control twenty years for nothing; he could hear it in another man's voice—a phone call asking Malcolm if they could just have a little chat about a few odds and ends.

They met at a diner four miles south of town on the way to Danford. Randall began. "I would have come to you with the prostitution info myself if I'd thought it would have made much difference in your wife's case."

"It's just what my source guessed you'd say," Malcolm said.

"You don't trust me now, I suppose," Randall said.

"No, not as much," Malcolm said.

"So, what questions do you want to ask me? I'm not going to hold anything back."

"Well, let's start with whether it's true that the Danford police had Cooper in their custody before he headed up to Wyman. And is it true that charges weren't pressed because of wealthy parents?"

"Both."

"So, is this what we call graft? Do people actually get to pay cops not to prosecute in order to keep their kids out of court?"

"Malcolm, when you got young boys involved, you yourself might figure you better go easy. Maybe it's better to give them a second chance than let the whole world in on it—at their schools, their churches. You've got a son, you can understand."

"And the police needed the boys' testimony? They couldn't have held Cooper otherwise?"

Randall shook his head. "Be pretty hard to do that, Malcolm. You think about it."

"I have been. I can see the whole thing, even understand letting him go. But they must have had mug shots, right? Here you are with a murderer on your hands, and you all are going around with police drawings of him when up in Danford they must have had mug shots."

"They didn't take any. That police sketch was done down there in Danford after the shooting. The men got together and did it for us. My brother-in-law Eddy was one of them. That composite drawing came out of Eddy's office."

"I suppose I should thank him!"

"No, I'm not saying that. Procedurally there should have been a photograph. You might as well know the worst. They didn't even print the guy."

"Once something's been repressed, Randall, then doesn't it keep going? I mean wasn't it in your best interest not to have him found, since then the whole Danford thing would have come out? You're damn lucky he was dead, right?"

Randall was a study in the obtuse. "What makes you think it's not going to come out? If you know, then it's out." He leaned in. "And you'll be surprised who some of those young boys will turn out to be. They weren't all from Danford. One of the boys was from Wyman."

"There's no secret here, Randall, if you're talking about crazy Oren. Don't tell me *he's* paying you to keep this quiet?"

"I'm talking about a real real innocent boy, Malcolm. And knowing who that is would make a huge difference to a person you and I both know."

Malcolm's lips curled in spite of himself. "Let me guess. A boy of some prominent Webster faculty member?" He laughed. "So you figure I won't squawk too much about you sparing your brother-in-law, since I get to find out you've been sparing Webster College and its public image? Is that it? You see me as an image man, don't you?"

"You're getting warm."

"This is my wife, Randall. What do I care about sparing Webster?"

"I said you were warm. You don't have it hot on center yet."

"Well, hell, are you going to tell me who it is? Are you going to pick now to hold back, for God's sake?"

And so that's when Randall supplied him with the name of the boy—at the point when he had Malcolm sounding just a tad bit more self-righteous, just a drop more, than Malcolm had sounded throughout the entire conversation.

17

MATT'S MONEY

THE FIVE HUNDRED DOLLARS KEPT STUMPING HIM. NEVER mind about Randall for the moment. By that evening Malcolm had had a talk with Oren and found out about Matt giving him that sum, five hundred, for Angela. For a day and a night Malcolm circled around the amount like a buzzard.

It was not just the fact of it, but the way it got passed back and forth in an envelope several days before Matt was saying things like "I'm going to have to pay you back" to Malcolm and Susan. As a puzzle, it kept seeming up to Malcolm to solve, beginning with his towering over Oren and wanting to pound on the man's bowed head before he stepped through the door. After that, it took a while to stop ranting. He would grow calm and then erupt again. "It's hard to stand here and have you tell me you don't have any idea what the money was for! Lord, was the girl pregnant?"

Oren shook his head. "Malcolm, it's only that I've been in an odd position of having no idea what you and Susan learned from Matt about the Danford night, of having no idea what Susan did or didn't tell you. Which is not much, it turns out." He added the last phrase carefully, but Malcolm wanted to sock him.

"Let's just keep to what *you've* known all this time!"

"Okay. The day after the Danford night, I hoped that Matt himself would find a way to tell her what his arrest was for, and that she, in time, would share it all with you."

"In time," Malcolm said. "She didn't have much time, did she, Oren?"

"She didn't know about the money, I know that," Oren said.

Then he recounted for Malcolm how amazed he was to get the money back from her, to be told that Matt found it in the grass. That would have been the morning after Oren's transformation.

"Your transformation doesn't interest me," Malcolm said. He tried to keep the bitterness in check. "Your transformation landed Cooper on my porch. A mental case, an addict with a gun, Oren. I don't care about you just now."

Oren promised to keep himself out of the discussion, but explained that what had happened to him was coloring everything. From the moment Susan knocked on his door, he'd seemed to himself a targeted soul.

"See? Hear what you just said? You weren't targeted, Oren. Susan was!" Malcolm finally sat down. This was not the point—to lambaste a man who was mad, in guise or in actual fact. "For heaven's sake, where were we?"

"You were headed toward the idea that Matt may have been giving me money to give Angela for an abortion."

"No, no," Malcolm said wearily. "I wasn't headed there. Not really."

"Or giving it to her out of some teenager's sense of obligation?"

"No," Malcolm said. "Not even that."

"Good. My strong sense is that Matt is on some other plane. But you know it, don't you?"

Malcolm nodded. "He had that kind of money only because in December we'd put it in his account ourselves. He was supposed to write the fee checks—Well, never mind." Malcolm let his head fall back. But then he got up abruptly to leave. He was feeling renewed

anger at Oren, wearing this odd dress that he'd roped at the waist—
half monk, half housewife. Malcolm couldn't handle Oren's possible
motives of distracting blame away from himself. The man, in his
own fashion, had been doing that his whole life. He was a real pro.

"I'm going home now, Oren," Malcolm said, feeling winded almost. "It's okay," he added softly. "We all have to get through this.
You're helping Gretchen in some way. I see that. I'm going to have to
trust in that, Oren. Do you understand?"

"She's remarkable," Oren said. "Thank you, Malcolm. If you trust
me even a little, I'm grateful."

"Don't be," Malcolm barked. "We'll talk again later."

"Yes."

In circling around the money question alone, Malcolm kept
hearing, *I'm going to have to pay you back.* He remembered how the
two of them had helped Susan fix the birthday dinner with the
money greatly at issue. It was part of the last arrangement the boy
had made with his mother. He'd agree to let her send in all the forms
while he was away at his sudden camp and to let her write the
checks he was supposed to have written against his own account and
sent in long before. *I'm going to have to pay you back.*

That night Malcolm sat in his upstairs room trying to guess if
busy Susan had managed to find the time to get those applications
off between the Sunday-night birthday dinner and the day of her
death. Busy. Remember busy? His former life came rushing back—
the two of them flying around after Matt left on Monday. They'd
both had a ton of deadlines—faxing off this, e-mailing that; who
was going to drop the laundry; did she remember she was about to
let her inspection sticker expire; could she take care of it the same
afternoon she was seeing the dentist? Remember busy?

Finally he found the strength to dig up her dead checkbook to
see if the balance pages indicated that she'd written the six needed
fee checks to be attached to Matt's applications. The figures were all
there in her tight, neat hand. It broke his heart just to see the familiar strokes, to see the last crossed *t*'s of her life, busy to the very last

and now all her silence, the hum of the house without her, the driveway with her parked car he'd not yet been able to look at since Andy returned it, newly inspected.

His mind flared irrationally as he made a quick tabulation of the check amounts, ranging from forty to a hundred dollars each. If Matt had merely written the damn checks himself—which had been the plan, which is why they'd given him the four hundred to deposit in his account, which is why he even had anything in that account, which is why he went over to Oren's with the five hundred, which was why it had all happened.

He returned the checkbook to the top drawer of the tidy desk in her office at the back of the house. Then he had a look around just to see if by any chance she'd enclosed the checks in the proper application envelopes but had not had time to get them mailed off, in which case he'd better do it himself right away.

Then he feared finding them; he feared finding them and rushing out the back of the house with matches and lighter fluid, feared taking Matt's future out to the barbecue pit and torching it.

He repented his anger. That night he lay awake and tried to pick the simplest scenario: at around Christmastime, Matt had somehow stumbled upon Cooper, who at that time was gamely offering kids sex for twenty dollars. Matt was tempted. It was not easy to place him in the back of that seedy car, exactly, but Malcolm followed the steps, innocent or halting, that might have led up to the moment. At seventeen we're often a groin on two legs. So, okay. It got Malcolm a long way in his mind.

And once he had Matt in the car, he could imagine the details quite sadly just because of who Matt was, so very hard on himself. And never a glib sort of kid. The arrest would not have bothered him nearly as much as what he'd done. But, okay, so now he was back home, let's say. During what was left of that night he must have had strong feelings of concern for the girl—her situation, if not herself. Both. Such feelings had probably set in while he was still behind the curtains of the car. That all made sense to Malcolm. The next morning Matt must have gone to the automatic teller in cap and sunglasses and drawn out his college fee money plus another hundred dollars. Everything he had, because the gift would seem symbolic of his future in a way. Matt might have some fanatic's sense of direction, a forcing of his hand, of his courage just to go ahead to a junior college like a lot of other commuter kids—the poor and disadvantaged kids who start low; he'd commute with them from a camp.

Later had he made the connection—between the needy girl he'd wanted to give five hundred dollars to and the girl who ended up at Oren's with a boyfriend capable of shooting someone point-blank? If so, it was terribly Freudian—having one's first female contact only at the expense of one's mother. Matt could be self-imprisoned out in Torreya right now, because apart from pain of loss, there was the inevitability of Malcolm and Gretchen learning of the connection themselves. Not that Matt's torment wouldn't always be of some other more saintly nature entirely—a life in which almost everything sets us up for something. Helping one person had destroyed Matt's family, but if you were Matt, then there must be some point to it.

And if you were Malcolm? What should you do if you were Malcolm? Go find him? Go tell him there was no point to it, none at all? It seemed such a terrible thing for a father, in particular, to do.

But you have to go, Susan was whispering. You have to go and trust that when you get there you'll know what to say.

Oren was not unaware that his position was precarious, but the vertigo kept him bold. Even perceptive. About Gretchen, for example, whose first stages of recovery had left her bouncy and what they called empowered. Such nonsense. Anyone could see the stitches were not holding. It seemed whenever Oren looked out his front door he saw her sitting out there with her Shakespeare, not wanting a tutor so much as his coffee, his company.

For several days Oren emerged from his house to find the same knees pulled to chest each time, nose as swollen as a tulip, a big brave smile.

"Ah, there you are, my dear, there you are!" he would say in tones of cordial surprise before sighing loudly and falling into his rocker in a way that meant surely it was he who needed her, not the other way around.

It was usually twilight when she showed up—her mother's hour, was how he thought of it, although he gave it no name. And Gretchen seemed to be using the ritual of evening in order to look up at the unstoppable bullet, now orbiting the earth but refusing to signal her. One day it would change its mind, send her some message, some meaning in all this. She was waiting.

Two days ago, she had finally piped up: "So did Cooper try to kill Angela too? After he threw her in the car?"

It was what he'd been hoping for—for her to go to the right launching place—the Cape Kennedy of all their woes, the center, the source, the jailer with keys. Gretchen knew there was no easy way of getting characters removed from the third act.

Oren repeated her question by way of reply. "Did he try to kill her too?" he mused. "I don't know who's going to get that story out of her, Gretchen. I wonder if you could. Some day."

All conversation was a bit like the garment he was having Freda make for him to replace this sack dress she'd loaned him. He had bought her cloth but was having her go slowly before she cut into it. Slowly. To make one's point, would one want her to cut it long or short?

"Angela doesn't talk to me yet," he began. "She's with friends of mine. They're getting her professional help, but so far she's not doing well."

One could read Gretchen's emotions by her knees, first relaxing into Indian-style folds for a girl's game of jacks; then moving up to the chest to be hugged. "I guess she thinks it's her fault," Gretchen finally said, nodding her big head of wild high school hair.

"Yes, just like you think it's your fault."

He watched the bony knees come back down. "I'm doing better. It's not like before. Only now Dad's doing worse."

"It's going to come and go, I think."

Her feet had disappeared under the Indian-style bow that, at its most relaxed, provided two armrests. "What makes you think Angela would talk to me?" she said.

"These days I'm not always sure when I'm on the right track."

"That's not true. You've been thinking about this plenty. You sound very sure."

A slow car drove by. Someone craned a head to see who that was up on Oren's porch. Someone ducked and moved on.

"I abandoned her here," Oren began. "Cooper was way more controlling than I realized."

"You should have known," Gretchen said.

"Yes," Oren said. "Right now she's not talking to me for that very reason. It's complicated by the fact that before me, Cooper was her mainstay, one of those men who played the father and the jailer at the same time. In her mind, it feels like her lot, her just deserts, I suppose. People like me have offered her chances in the past. The Coopers were the only types who came through for her, at least in her mind."

He saw Gretchen give the shrug all fifteen-year-olds give when they fear you're going to change your mind and withhold from them what you begin to see is over their heads. She shrugged and tried to stay uninterested so that he would keep going. He got up from his chair and sat beside her on the top step, she in that lotus position, he with his stiffer, older feet on the third riser down. "I'll start with Corey," he said. "My friends Harry and Margaret think Corey may be a key person to Angela's health. But it's tricky. Angela can't admit to being both relieved to be rid of Cooper and yet set further adrift in his being gone."

"Two competing emotions," Gretchen said, nodding.

"That's right. The psychiatrist has ordered regular supervised visits for Angela, starting with Corey."

"Is she catatonic or something?"

"No, no. Severely depressed, he thinks. How does she process at her age a woman's getting killed, Cooper taking himself out, and so forth? But here's what's interesting. Corey talks about you and Malcolm mowing the lawn blindfolded. Did that really happen?"

He saw the girl smile and nod her head.

"The story makes Angela respond," Oren said.

"How?"

"I don't know exactly. Something. The blindfold and Corey's asking over and over when may she ride that lawn mower again and see that guy. She calls Malcolm 'that guy.' Angela is dead behind the eyes except when Corey is there, animated, just being herself. Corey is quite precocious, I hear. Margaret seems to think Corey knows exactly what she's doing for her half-sister."

He was not quite prepared for Gretchen's huge tears welling. But not falling. He looked again, and it was as if she had power to pull them in again. And her quickness; he wasn't prepared for that either, exactly. It was amazing to see, however. She was suddenly saying, matter-of-factly, with no tears at all, "If Dad ever found out I went to see Angela, he'd feel betrayed. But that's just because he thinks it's all his fault."

"The way you do," Oren said in a kind of murmured echo.

"I didn't wave," she said.

It was the saddest girl's confession he'd ever heard. "Ah-ha," he said. Then he dared to give a little laugh. "So it *is* all your fault!" And right away she smiled at him and wiped at her face. When she finally spoke, she stopped his heart: "What are you trying to do, Uncle Oren," she said, "sound like my mother?"

Malcolm spent a night thinking before coming to see Oren again. The second visit was in part to get himself ready to go on to

Torreya and ask his questions there. Oren was merely a stopgap, the man to whom he could turn and try out a few things first. He had been trying them out on Susan. Sometimes she answered, sometimes not.

"Do you think Matt could possibly have known Angela before he got into that car?" They were seated on the porch this time. It was not yet dawn. Malcolm had seen Oren's lights on and trudged over in the dark. He felt friendlier, more in control. "Let's go back to him coming to you with the money," Malcolm said. "It was so odd of you, Oren, to agree to take the money. But I don't have to tell you, I suppose."

Best not to answer, Oren was thinking. Almost every reply could sound so defensive, especially now that Malcolm was having his delayed reaction to a wife's not having told him about Matt's arrest in the first place.

"She didn't know," Oren said. "She asked me to drive to Danford with her, and I was so smitten after that. The rain coming down."

"The rain, Oren? Are we back to you and your rebirth? What guru gave you that—the rain?"

He didn't want to make it obvious that he was coaxing Malcolm out into the open. The man was in such pain he might not ever notice he was being coaxed. "I had two gurus, Malcolm," Oren ventured, "if that's the right word. Susan and Angela. It's an interesting way to think of them, as gurus."

He could see that this caused a cool, cool bubble to Malcolm's brain. "You're not trying to tell me you're still in touch with Angela, are you, Oren? If you are you wouldn't be so crass as to want me to know about it, would you?"

Malcolm seemed finally beyond losing his temper. So Oren pushed forward. "Would you ever consider seeing her?" he said. "She's doing badly in her mind. She thinks of you and Gretchen as so very innocent."

"We don't need her to tell us how innocent we are!"

"But she needs it," Oren said. "And by the way, Gretchen does too. We're all in this, Malcolm."

"We're not in anything! And Gretchen's especially not!" Malcolm was out of his chair, his empty mug sliding from the arm but not breaking, just thudding. "Gretchen's never been so not in anything in her life!" And even before he left the porch Oren could see that the man's head was clearing enough for him to compose a little threatening speech that put metal in his voice. He couldn't keep Gretchen locked up in her room; hell, if she wanted to come visit Oren out of pity, that was her business, but, goddamn it, this was his family, what was left of it. "And you're not in my family, Oren, do you understand that?"

He appeared energized, heading on home, refusing to look back, refusing to acknowledge Oren, who was clearly trying to ensnare the innocent. Less paralyzed now, less desperate for a course of action, he was perhaps thinking, First go talk to Matt, then come back and get Gretchen out of here. It would feel like an honest-to-God plan. First Matt. Then Gretchen.

18

PERMISSION FROM HOME

GRETCHEN PEERED INTO MALCOLM'S OPEN DUFFEL, WHICH held four loose toiletries rolling around for his planned one night away in Torreya—their first away from each other and the house. He assumed it was all set up for her to stay next door with Beth and Ted. She had no intention of doing that, but she knew he detected nothing, since she was the big actor after all—a fact not to be overcome, not to be repressed in herself.

There it was—who she was—sitting on his bed, watching him get ready to go ask Matt a few questions, noting without comment his insanely focused stare and the one mad spiky caterpillar eyebrow headed east and west. She didn't know who to feel more sorry for—him or Matt.

He now knew about the arrest and confessed he was angry at Susan's not telling him that there'd been one.

"She assumed it was some mistake."

"Yes, but I could have been told. Why wasn't I told?"

"Probably because you take things hard when it comes to Matt. I think Mom figured he could be in some group that was handing out leaflets. She was used to protecting him from you overreacting all the time."

He stared at her, dumbfounded. "Leaflets? You mean tracts? You think he was giving Angela a tract?"

"I don't know! Which is harder for you when it comes to Matt? Leaflets or a blow job?"

"Hey!"

She'd caught him off guard with the phrase just ready-made like that. "With you," she continued, "I wouldn't be able to guess which would upset you the most. You don't *like* Matt, so when we do tell you stuff, we lose either way."

"Don't like him?"

"I've always sensed Mom having to make up for you not being close to him." Hell, why stop now? "Mom sticks up for Matt, no matter what. You don't. There was probably lots and lots of stuff she never told you."

She even caught herself thinking, Don't look at your feet, girl, look at him. It was a real scene, and while her lines were not false, it was not what she wanted to be doing with the truth—giving it a performance like this.

An hour later he came to the backyard to sit with her, put his arm around her, pull her toward him, his duffel on the ground. He was ready to be on his way.

"You're right," he said, "you're right, you're right."

She rested her head in the crook of his arm. Once Susan had said to her, girls and their fathers just do better, that's all.

"I have a favor to ask," Malcolm said. "When I get back tomorrow, can you and I talk about leaving here? How can we stay here? You asked that right away, remember?"

"But it comes and goes for me now."

"Then we'll talk about that too." He sighed. "So, you're all set up with Beth for tonight, right?"

"Yep," she said, kissing his cheek. "I'm going over after dinner." It was an outrageous lie. "Beth's feeling guilty," she mused, because it was so easy to lie in a nondestructive way. "She so guilty about having snuck off after the funeral like she did. She's relieved we still want her."

"Sneaked, I think."

"Are you sure, home school teacher?"

Earlier she'd gone next door in order to appear to be confirming an overnight with Beth and Ted, who were just back from the house on Lake Jessup, looking as if the escape hadn't much helped. The very sight of Gretchen made Beth cry. Gretchen had suffered a hug, welcomed them home, and never said one word about staying over. Right now she'd shamed Malcolm too much for him to suspect her. He would never check. Besides, she had better things to worry about.

Touchy things; illegal things. As soon as he left, she was to be driven to Danford by Oren, who didn't have a license to drive that respectable-looking gray Oldsmobile stashed in his garage and who had absolutely no right to take her to see Angela without asking Malcolm's permission. She herself hardly knew how to analyze all her motives—either clear or fuzzy. But, strangely, she knew she was doing the right thing for herself. Nothing else mattered.

"Will you spend the night at the camp or at a motel?" she asked Malcolm.

"Don't know. I'll call Beth and Ted and leave them a number when I have one."

"Leave it on our machine. I'll only need to know in an emergency."

"I shouldn't call them?"

"I just thought the machine would be easier on you."

"It would."

"Good."

Okay, so if he changed his mind and called, so be it. She was nervously free about it all. Dizzy a bit. As if her visit to Angela behind his back was not so much a betrayal. More like a skydive without any instructions. Just jump.

A similar daring on Oren's part made him spooky as he drove—the road ahead first a narrow slither, then wide, careening rapids. They were driving as if with the last people innocent enough to be approaching Niagara in a barrel at just the spot where recently the only other last innocent people had already gone over.

"We best clear the air," Oren had said to her yesterday as they finalized plans. "I can imagine what rumors you've heard about me and Angela. I was thrown for a loop, but not sexually, at least not by her. The sexual feelings were for your mother. I can't defend myself and won't try at this point."

Gretchen fell back on her old sense of timing. Don't strain. Keep it understated. "People are going to think you're gay in this dress. Is that what you want? A distraction?"

"It's what Malcolm thinks, right? But I hope he's wrong."

"You mean you don't know?"

"It's more as if I have no choice. I have to be mindful. I have to help someone. That's all I really know. This marks me; it's part of some process for me—to come out, yes. The gays have given us the best of metaphors."

She herself felt as if she'd been given it too. During all this she'd had such bad moments, remembering how she'd credited Cooper with Chuck's idea of passionate restraint. Cooper had none of it. She'd invented it for him. Her mother was the one who had it. Now Oren and Malcolm. Perhaps Matt. She was seeing it everywhere—here, there, and yonder—as if, like Oren's dress, it was all she had to wear to cover herself, her lack, her emptiness.

"You're lucky," she suddenly said, thinking how for her Oren's dress might take the form of shaving her head.

But while her old neighbor was seriously engaged by the whole of his transformation, what made him truly credible was how light of heart he was. Not that it resulted in happiness or fluff. More as if he was light of heart by drawing breath only in the reality of Susan's death, knowing exactly how many intakes of air he'd had since getting the news. People like this she must guard with her life and learn from—how to glide like Oren, how to let go of the conventional sob, how to swim a dangerous shoreline, some of the waves drowning him, others sailing over his head.

But. He should get his license, she reasoned. This driving without a license was ridiculous. Tomorrow she'd go get one of those study booklets for the written part, followed by the eye exam; later she'd get him set up for the road test. "How did you even register this thing, Uncle Oren? You can't register a car without a license."

"A friend arranged it for me."

"Another one? There's Harry, there's Margaret. You used not to have any!"

"Or enemies either. Now I have those too."

What could you do with him?

"I bet your friend doesn't know you're driving his car without a license?"

"Her car. Freda's loaned this to me. Without really meaning to, I may have lied to her about me having a license. I knew she assumed I did."

"They warned me about you," she said, hearing him laugh that, yes, he could certainly imagine.

She looked out the passenger side and studied the great expanse of horse farms with their white fences and spreading oaks here and there for shade. She could easily make Oren pull over and let her take the wheel. God forbid if they had an accident. If they did, it would be better if the driver at least had a learner's permit.

Soon she put her head back and rested, letting the hum of the car prove itself in its connection to Susan. Being here was like being with Susan's laughing snort. She was no longer getting a clear voice. But still she could well imagine her mother encouraging them, even imagine her stretched out on the backseat of this comically appropriated hearse with all its pristine gray interior and well-maintained chrome. "Be bold, kids!" her mother might say. Susan used to pretend to be just a little bit tight whenever her own bursts of enthusiasm did not quite make sense to her. Driving without a license, say. Her mother was not reckless, but she was extremely interested, she'd once told Gretchen, in those found or absurd moments pulled free of their connection to rules and regulations.

Right now on the floor at her feet was Susan's appropriated Coach bag. Malcolm had given it at Christmas, not even a month ago now. She'd found his card to Susan flattened at the bottom of the bag as she had gone through it last night, seeing if there were any lipsticks she could save and later have the audacity to use. Was it a sign of health that she was able to recycle all that sort of stuff? No rules now, no rules? There would be no other time in her life when the profane would be so sacred and the sacred so profane. Not to be dizzy was not to be alive.

The lipstick color in the fairly new tube she'd found was of a shade that was probably hilariously wrong—too dark, too mature. On Susan it had always turned a heavenly red; on Gretchen a flat prune-bruise blossomed on her lips. It would be the first thing Angela would see.

Unassailable was written among the vocabulary words at the back of Angela's diary, found at Oren's house. That was it: unassailable. Gretchen was scared but unassailable—the oppositions for the moment. She was finding them everywhere.

In her bag she'd brought the diary, as Oren had suggested. Also she'd packed a pair of scissors and a piece of paper—two items that were part of a half-formed plan to get Angela snapped out of it.

It's almost appalling to anticipate seeing someone who feels responsible that you've lost your mother. Not only that; her boyfriend shot her after an argument about Malcolm, and now she's having to face the daughter; and she'd loved and hated the boyfriend, loved a rotten person who wasn't rotten every second. "He screws up everything in my life," she'd said that time. But he was what she'd had. Now she had zilch.

"I think she's glad you're here," Margaret said. "Uncertain of herself, though, which is good. It's an emotion."

Gretchen stood with Margaret Rawlins in a kitchen that had a view of a golf course abutting the Rawlinses' farm property. Angela's room had the same view; when Gretchen went in there a moment ago, Angela had had her chair pulled up to sliding doors as if she were watching the tiny figures out there in their golfing carts, some on the nearest green but most others way off in the distance.

"I'll go get myself a Coke or something," Gretchen had said. "You can think about it, Angela. Just think about it." She'd put the scissors down on the floor beside the beanbag chair. Under the scissors was a folded piece of paper with a typed note inside. It was even signed.

Her heart raced as she stood by Margaret looking at the golfers out there swinging. They took a lot of practice swings. She knew that Angela was reading the note she'd left by the beanbag.

"I feel like I'm going to throw up," she whispered to Margaret. They were waiting to see if Angela would read the note and come out of her room. *Dear Angela,* the note said, *I give full permission for you to cut Gretchen's hair. Big hair is out of style now. Cut it short. Susan Robb.*

"Butterflies?" Margaret suggested.

"I'm scared to death," Gretchen said. "It's the most far-out thing I've ever done."

"You've got to be about the best person I've had the pleasure to meet."

"Not really."

"Really."

This Margaret, this total stranger, reached out and pulled Gretchen right to her, big bosom and all. It was like a family hug, long and sustained and not going away anytime soon, as they waited to see if Gretchen's outrageous note would work or make things worse.

"I can't do her like this," Margaret said, "so I thank you."

Gretchen laughed and did not release the woman. "You like her?"

"Very much."

It was the fat; Gretchen felt mixed in with the woman's goodness. If she herself gained weight like this later in life, she wouldn't fear it because it might mean she'd have it stored up for someone skinny and cold.

"Hey," she heard someone say. "I thought you came here to see me!"

Angela had had a loss of nerve. Loss of nerve was Gretchen's best guess about the girl after an hour or so of being with her, talking to her. Call it depression, but she didn't think so. It was Cooper lifting her off the ground like that right after the shooting, breaking her in half inside the car, its door handle against a knee, a foot turned to three o'clock, and her head under the steering wheel as he drove away.

"My neck is still purple from his hand."

"Let's see," Gretchen said, leaning in, squinting.

"Why I thought I'd ever be able to lose him, I don't know. He wasn't supposed to find out where I was."

It was a good sign, her talking a blue streak, Gretchen supposed. Still. "You didn't call him up?"

"Is that what Oren thinks?"

"No, he thinks Eddy Jenson told him where you were."

"Who's that?"

"It doesn't matter. Was it you?"

"No!"

"Then why did you let him stay?"

"Yeah, I remember you now. You said I should dump him. Remember? Just dump him? You ought to try it some time! You think I didn't have plans? I was going to change everything! Then there he was, the same night. Like he owned me. My deals were his deals; my luck, his luck."

She'd been trying to dump him. No one believed her. Margaret and Harry didn't believe her. She could tell. "They think I called him and told him where I'd be, but I didn't. I don't know how he found me. Somebody tipped him off."

"Who?" Gretchen said. You couldn't just let her get away with stuff. "Not Oren."

"See, you won't believe me either. How should I know? Maybe you did it."

Suddenly Cooper was there at the house, she went on, asking her where she thought she was going without him, huh? Think she could just run off without him?

She'd offered him money, and he'd taken it, but he'd laughed when she'd said, Now that's it, that's it, you have to leave me alone.

"Leave me alone? Fat chance. A big fat Chinaman's chance."

He was out of jail just one afternoon, and he'd found her. Drove straight to her, so it had to be somebody tipping him off. He arrived already shooting up out of the trunk of his car—a flight bag full of stuff. An American Airlines flight bag, because when he went to general delivery at the post office there'd have been his monthly check waiting for him. He blew his whole check on one haul and came straight to her. It's what he'd been doing for six months.

"Did you leave the address somewhere in the apartment? Maybe some neighbor recognized Oren and gave out his name to him?"

"Neighbor?"

"A person living in your same building, Angela!"

"You kill me. You really kill me." She didn't mean to be mean. "Yeah," she finally said, "I guess it was one of my close neighbor friends."

They argued from the minute he walked in, looking all around, rocking on his heels, laughing in a high thin way that was half between being impressed and being ready to wring her neck with her thinking she could run out on him just when her luck turned.

"But then he said that we should go get Corey. That this wasn't going to last, so I better let Corey come to the house if I ever wanted her to believe I was up to any of my promises. So he drove me, and they let me take the kids for a walk to get ice cream. It was stupid what I did, but at that point I just figured what the hell."

"Then what happened?"

"Well, then he was *really* weird. It went through my mind that when we returned the kids to the Sulloways, he'd kill me. He just kept looking at me and saying 'Disloyalty, thy name is slut. People like you have about as much loyalty as a cockroach.' I tried to keep him calm, but he was strung out. Permanently. He kept seeing your dad across the street at his window, or out on his porch, or out getting the mail, looking in our direction.

"I tried to warn him. When I got back from your house that morning, Cooper said he knew then; he knew that guy was somebody I was already doing. So then I said why didn't he just take me back to the Sulloways so I could drop off the kids. I was kind of ready to die. He seemed ready too. We started out to take the kids back, but then he changed his mind. He turned the car around and came on back to the house. He said I wasn't planning on him in my life, so I must have had my own plan on how I was going to get them back and forth to Danford. Why was he even helping me?"

On the afternoon he ripped the phone out of the wall and went crazy, the trunk was full of smack. It would get him confused from time to time after the shooting, those two days they drove around, his hand on her neck all the time, his threat being that if she tried to run, then Corey would be the first person he'd go for. All he'd have to do was go to the Sulloway house, and when she came outside to play in the yard he'd say, Hey, get in, he'd take her to where Angela was.

She stopped. "What? You crying about your mother? Give me a minute and I'll cry about that too."

"Go on," Gretchen said. It was, at the very least, the Angela she remembered.

"The whole time he drove he was furious about having to leave his hand on my throat to keep me from over and over asking if he'd shot Ricky. *No, so shut up!*"

Her sense of death had been powerful as Susan fell forward, having taken Ricky from her, and then Angela feeling herself being dragged away. She saw sky. She knew he was going to kill her. That woman was Gretchen's mother; she must have known it was Gretchen's mother, but two days passed before he overdosed, before she knew if Ricky was alive, so she hadn't been able to think about the woman. Gretchen's mom. Part of her knew, but there was this way she'd been able to close it off. Hide it.

During the actual getaway, he hadn't hit; he only crushed her windpipe in a warm squeeze every time she cried or asked things—was Ricky shot? Could they at least listen to what they were saying on the radio? He started hitting the next day. If you looked at her right ear you could see where later he'd taken the edge of a book and come down hard once. An earring had torn out of its hole. He'd been trying to read to her while they were hiding on the beach, pretending to sunbathe, and him suddenly thinking she'd fallen asleep on him. *No hope for you. No hope for you.*

A hit for having fallen asleep, for being rude; because by late that afternoon it was starting to slip away from him that he'd maybe killed Susan and Ricky. No radio, as if not knowing was the same as not having to know. He'd started bragging how he was going to get them a vacation packet. He was going to fly them to where ancient Romans once lived, and she'd lain there needing a drink of water and had wondered, which country? Which country was he talking about? He kept on and on.

"Hey, try to sleep now," Gretchen finally said. "He must have meant Italy."

"Italy?" The girl was exhausted. "Italy's in Rome, right?"

"Right."

At midnight Gretchen went into the empty kitchen and found chocolate syrup in the Rawlinses' fridge. She stirred it into milk and put it in the microwave. Angela ended up sinking her whole nose into her cup. Her straight Roman nose like Joan Crawford's. "Aquiline," Gretchen said later as she rubbed cream on Angela's nose, almost ruined from that long mad day in the sun with mad Cooper reading aloud. Under the peeling, burned skin sat rosettes of raw pink meat.

"Aquiline? What do I know? Nothing. Is this about getting me out of myself?"

"No, go ahead and sink," Gretchen said softly, "you have to sink, at least I did. So what happened then?"

He dragged her off the beach after dark. He said they needed to find another car. Find a travel agent! He was bonkers. He didn't think about food; didn't trust her in a shiny fluorescent store not to call out; and besides, he'd guessed about the manhunt either way, with people either dead or not dead. Figured there'd be a drawing of him. He'd be talking about their vacation, and then she'd know he was thinking that they could be spotted any moment. She thought then that he was considering killing himself; he wasn't quite crazy enough to keep believing in getting them to Rome, for God's sake.

"I couldn't decide if I was part of the plan. You know. The whole death plan. The one older cop thinks I killed him. Just the way it looked in that motel room. I'm frozen there and he's right in the other bed, me obviously doing nothing about it. The older cop didn't treat me rough, he didn't treat me gentle. He just took me to the patrol car and told me to keep my mouth shut."

"That was our sheriff?"

"I don't know. The jug-eared guy. How come you know him?"

"He was at our house. Because of Mom."

She could tell Angela had to swallow a knife, putting the two things back together again—the two locations of pain, hers and Gretchen's. Hells usually fly apart. Two torments aren't meant to realign. "How come you don't hate me?" she began saying, rocking back and forth, hiding her face again, outraged once again at the impossibility of this, that anyone thought the two should see each other. Naked. "How come you're really here?"

"I told you. It's Oren. The reason he met you was because of my brother. It goes back. We don't think you'd remember Matt getting into your car, but maybe you do."

"What if I did remember him? It doesn't have anything to do with your mother dying, does it?"

"No."

"So what difference can it make? I killed your mother, so what could it matter if I ever met your stupid brother?" She looked up. "No, I just mean I can't see trying to remember which boy it was. There were a dozen and it was all the same kid."

"Were they any of them that tried to talk to you about God?"

"Hey, they all said the same thing. They said, Jesus, Jesus!"

You couldn't blame her for Matt being the last straw.

"Is that all you care about? Your brother?"

"No."

What Angela was really saying was, Where was she going to live, *how* was she going to live? Before, she could stand being nowhere. Now she couldn't. Her mistake had been to bring Ricky and Corey to Oren's for those first two days, but it showed what kind of mettle she had. She'd about pulled it off, and more than in her mind only. It showed she was going to get them under one roof; just doing it for a couple of days had made her feel something. Now she didn't. Now she was going to fall apart.

To calm her down, Gretchen tried to put some more cream on. "Your nose is going to fall off for starters," Gretchen whispered.

"Hey, I'm not joking, I really am."

"No, you're not. Keep talking. Don't you know about the talking cure?"

"No."

"Yes, you do. You never stop."

After a while, Angela began again with the part about Cooper showing up at the house just when she thought she was free. "I was pretty sure I knew how to get him to leave. I was going to let him have all of Oren's account. It was ten thousand. With that you can get rid of anybody, right?"

"Wrong," Gretchen said. "He would have come back. You needed a protection program. Oren was supposed to follow through. He knows that now."

She shook her head. "What difference does it make now? I'm falling apart. I forgot Ricky's birthday last week. The visits from Corey aren't natural. I can tell. Like this visit from you. They're bringing you over just like they're bringing Corey, right? To get me out of myself? Well, I'm not sure it's a good idea to get out of myself. As soon as they think you're okay again and you're not going to kill yourself, then you can be farmed out anywhere. They think, how can it matter to you since you don't have anything in the first place?"

Gretchen saw how easy it was for Angela to get caught between truth and self-pity.

"Oren says you have his house."

"That was a trick."

"Yeah, but what kind?"

Angela looked at her. "Who said that that time? You or Corey?"

"It'll come back to you."

"Cooper laughed his head off at me when I told him I had a house and I was moving and he couldn't screw this up for me, not after all these years of me helping him."

"So you did call him?"

"I didn't say that."

"It sounded like you meant you told him. You just said 'I told him I had a house,' like it was a phone call or something."

"No, I didn't. I didn't say that."

"Sorry."

"Listen, he was at the house, and I told him it was mine and he couldn't screw it up. That's what I said."

"Okay. Forget it. It's not important."

"—that he couldn't screw it up. This was my last chance. But you know what he said? He kept saying no minor can own a house, didn't I know that? So then it felt like the only smart thing I'd managed to do was not tell him about the money." She started crying for the first time. "Oren gave me ten thousand dollars. He really did. It was going to help me change my life."

"So why didn't you just tell him about Cooper?"

"I'd broken the only rule he made. I wasn't supposed to let Cooper in."

"But you could have told him the guy forced his way in. Isn't that what he did?"

Angela fell back on the bed. "You know what? You're like all the girls I ever wanted to be, just like all the ones I've always wanted to punch out, with your mothers and your houses."

Gretchen dug in the Coach bag and handed over the diary. "I'm supposed to give you this from Oren. He thinks it shows what potential you have. You and your list." Gretchen handed over the diary. "Don't worry, I didn't read your private thoughts."

"There aren't any! Cooper said if he ever found a private thought, he'd kill me. That's when he used to say kill me and it didn't mean kill me."

"Then it did."

"Yeah. Just like that. It did."

"Bing."

"Bang."

"Bong."

Several long hours later, every time Gretchen closed her eyes, the room would start to spin.

"You remind me of my friend Desiree," Angela said at one point in a cracked voice, raw from talk. It was getting toward dawn, and they were both drunk with lack of sleep. "She's about the most decent person I know. She's probably dead by now."

"There's ways to find her. They can find people."

"Then what?"

"You feeling sorry for yourself again."

"Yeah, you mind?"

"Angela?"

"What?"

"Maybe you remember the last thing my mother said."

Angela looked up. "I did all the talking. Didn't they tell you?"

Gretchen smiled. It was what she liked. The nerve.

"So you can't remember anything?"

"No. Is that why you're here?"

"If you think that, I'll leave. If you think that, then we're not really friends."

"I didn't mean it. You're my friend. You'll do for now."

"You might not want to remember."

"Why wouldn't I want to remember?"

"So then try. It's supposed to be good for people in shock."

"Am I in shock?"

"It's why we get along, Angela. I don't ever plan to come out of shock."

Angela rolled over, propped herself. "What's the last thing she ever said to you? Tell me the very last words your mother said to you before you went off to public school. Hey, if anyone dead ever sent me off to public school, I'd remember what they said."

"This *is* a trick!" Gretchen said.

"Yeah, but what kind?"

19

WOLF DEN

As soon as he left the highway, Malcolm seemed to sink into a rich stand of white oak and pine. Within a few hundred yards he was having to snake his way in, then shift to low. The sandy private road was underused and minimally maintained, the scrub pushing into the car's open windows.

He stopped once to look up, get a reading on the numerous towering cabbage palms. Some would have to be a hundred years old, judging from the height of their tribal headgear. By Malcolm's own tough standards, this was Country. Rare. Valuable.

In a mile, the road bowed one last time and ended in a graveled clearing containing a battered pickup, sitting in a drop cloth of shade. Beyond the clearing, more moss-slung branches, vines, thickets of scrub. Black-green in there, the way he liked it, all the vegetation soaking up light as into a sponge, emitting nothing. She was to have dragged him here that first weekend of Matt's mystery camp. This was why. Part of the surprise.

He cut the engine and sat listening, as she would have done, to a scolding chorus of crows and mockingbirds. There was nothing else to annoy them except his car rolling into their narthex. Off to his right he began to detect the low wing of a wood-framed construction, painted camouflage brown. It was slow coming into view. An old house for headquarters, as he'd suspected. Soon he was seeing a lone army-green cabin several hundred feet behind the house. Three more cabins began to appear, each one tucked in more deeply than the last. He tried guessing if this George Murray had a couple of acres here or five, ten, or a hundred. All of it disappeared into a loamy black hole with no horizon or flat line to stop it. Bromeliad buds and other air plants and debris from the trees had fallen over everything, as with all untouched places too dense for storm and wind to rearrange. In a downpour one could stand in such woods and get wet from the ground up.

As he got out of the car he could see someone coming toward him from his far left—a tall man picking his way around scrub or else following a twisted path. Swinging hammers and screwdrivers rode low like six-shooters on a tool belt. The man was blond and sunburned. "Malcolm?" he called out.

"I'm early!" Malcolm called. "You warned me Matt doesn't get home from school until around four."

"That was so you would come early, and we could talk!" He was drawing closer—the man not just foster parenting but safe housing. The thought propelled Malcolm over the logs framing the small clearing. He reached out to take the man's hand, telling him no, he'd had no trouble finding the turnoff. Good directions. Thanks.

George Murray had a large mouth and well-kept teeth, except for one unself-conscious big front job that was yellowing and needed a cap. It made him appear to have been isolated in these woods for a while. Malcolm caught a brief glimpse of a thick ponytail when the man bent his head to brush sawdust from his knees. "I had the feeling you and I were going to be the same vintage," the man said. "My son is a year older than yours."

"I didn't know," Malcolm said. "Greg? the boy who drove Matt?"

"No. Robert. You'll meet him later." George stood, hands on hips, gaze moving over Malcolm's face, reading it. "We're both probably a little unsure how to begin. Your wife told me you were worried I was a cult leader."

"Right," Malcolm said. "Forgive me."

"Let's go up to the house. I'll show you around." The man began leading the way, calling over his shoulder as he walked. "This is a small operation, Malcolm. I charge rich people an arm and a leg to send their scary boys here."

"So how is it I can afford you?" Malcolm called.

The other man's appreciative laugh sailed back to him. "You can't! You owe me!"

They were approaching the side of the house, entering a screened-in porch and then an old kitchen. It had the scrubbed look of a place that could gear up to big communal meals. Right now there was the smell of coffee, the smell of a man making do on thin sandwiches for his lunch. They had the place to themselves, he explained. His wife was gone for the week, and even with her here it was quiet until summers or breaks—a part-time secretary, a few weekend campers, several "big brothers" like Matt and Greg.

Malcolm was out of energy now that he was seated. He was relieved to hear the other man start in.

"Matt wrote to me several years ago," George began, leaning a little from the other side of the large, scarred table. "He also enclosed a check! Was that something he was doing quite a bit of?"

"It started when he was twelve," Malcolm said.

"What did you make of it?"

"I was at my worst whenever he went underground. Announcing this camp made it seem like that was happening again. He hadn't done his college application forms, that sort of thing."

"And your wife?"

"Susan was—"

"Malcolm, she was lovely. I liked her. Linda too. My wife met her." The dark kitchen grew bright as clouds uncovered a weak winter sun. "I guess it was late December that Matt called and asked for a job interview, which I arranged for in Danford. We'd been corresponding for a few years, me writing back to thank him for his checks. Maybe I have been a kind of mentor to him." George paused, then grinned. "Hey," he said, "sue me!"

The challenge was so disarming and so unexpected that Malcolm laughed out loud.

"I know it must look to you as if Matt wants to stay on here with me where it's safe."

Malcolm considered this—its accuracy, its frankness. "Well," he said, "we could all use safe at the moment. Mind if Gretchen and I move in?"

They heard a scratch on the other side of the kitchen door and turned to see a large, ancient dog with bloodshot eyes creeping forward. Malcolm reached out to offer a headrub. "Listen," he said, "looks like you're doing something real here, and I'm very relieved, very grateful. She knew you were up to something good. Eager for me to see it and all that." He began to laugh. "By the way, what good *are* you up to?"

As the old dog began to collapse, George reached in with a gentle hand and suggested to him that he not fall unconscious on Malcolm's feet. "You guys want a snack?" he said, as he stood up and walked to the fridge to stare inside. He began rummaging. At the sink he washed a couple of apples and then handed them to Malcolm with a knife out of his own pocket. "It's the only knife around," he explained, "I shouldn't even have it. Not in the insurance policy." George stared at Malcolm, who was slightly openmouthed, a blank. "Yes, your wife didn't know either. This is a psychiatric camp I'm running."

Malcolm shook his head slowly. "I didn't know," he said. He felt sad again, just the not knowing. "I'd like to hear," he said, careful not to slice a finger as he came down with the knife.

"About which? The biters, scratchers, kickers, twitchers, ranters, or ravers?" George was pouring them cold soda into glasses. "It's fairly simple. You have to be under thirteen to qualify, and my betters have to have given up on you." He raised a glass in salute. "This camp is my bit for the halt and the maimed."

"The what?"

George reached in for a half an apple from the table. "Biblical, Malcolm. It's the way of your son." He made a firm forward motion with one hand to illustrate. "Straight into something purer. He wants to work with the really poor. This is a little too tame for him, this place. Come on, I'll show you where he stays."

"He doesn't stay here?"

"In this lap of luxury? You kidding?"

The undergrowth was less thick in the older part of the camp. They were soon passing through a meeting area—stones to hold a bonfire and a few logs for seating. The cabin on the other side had a sign Malcolm could read—"Wolf Den"—a burned-wood board nailed to the low lintel. There was a screen door and then a panel door, unlocked. Beside a neatly blanketed cot, an upturned open crate held a snapshot of Matt standing next to what looked like a child with a receding hairline. Malcolm stared at the familiar-looking prominent forehead; there, too, were the soft and vaguely bulging eyes, the full slack mouth of love.

"People credit me for stopping my life and building this camp just for Robert," George said, taking the photograph from Malcolm. "I do enjoy him a lot more out here, the reason being that I'm so different. I hope I am." He was looking at his watch. "You'll win Robert over by meeting his bus at the highway in a couple of hours. Everything with Robert is at least an eight. Having his bus met is a ten."

Malcolm looked around him, then sank slowly onto his son's simple cot. The cabin was swept clean, and between the open studs were a few watercolors, framed and matted.

"One of our boys is quite a painter," George explained.

Malcolm felt something of Gretchen's raw awe descending.

"I promised Matt private quarters," George continued, "not that he even asked. Next thing I knew, he was granting Robert permission to bunk with him. That probably doesn't surprise you."

"No," Malcolm said. "Can you tell me about these campers, a few details? You don't have to name names. I'm trying to get the picture a bit better."

George sat down. "Let's see. On the nonviolent end? There's A. He's eleven. Last summer he broke into the mainframe of a small bank. But that's just sensational. A has multiple social problems. Moving a fraction away from him, there's B. Small animals aren't safe around him. C drinks. That's actually very common in border-lines, but C goes into rages. D is the oldest. He's twelve and a half. He has homicidal fantasies, the most recent of which involves kidnapping a toddler from a playground, raping him, killing him, and then reading about it in the newspaper."

The ancient dog had followed them. He stood outside the screen and, trained, did not beg to come in.

"Full camp is not so hairy. But those are our four special school weekenders right now. They get here on Friday afternoons. It's part of an experiment—giving the family seventy-two hours to, you know, regroup, visit shrinks. See, I'm the one you ship your boy to right before you have to commit him."

George sat down opposite Malcolm on Robert's cot—the one that copied Matt's in its matching blankets and crate stand devoted to a photograph of what must be the mother.

"Did I mention that our painter comes all the way from Boston? Every weekend, fall, winter, and spring. I'm told he's from the Cabot line, just so you know what your boy's stepped into. Some day all this could be his!"

George stood up. In a soundless push he eased himself into an upper bunk in order to stretch out. The bunk was too short; he let his feet rest on a bottom rod.

Malcolm continued to study the photograph, then took in Matt's neatly folded blanket again. The only lush items in the square room were the watercolors. A framed black-and-white postcard hung over Matt's cot—Ansel Adams's shot of Half Dome in the Rockies. A million years ago they'd camped for a week at the bottom of Half Dome. He took a moment to examine the books stashed inside the upended crate. There sat Matt's huge Bible, with the many tasseled markers Malcolm had always hated. Really hated.

"You say it looks as if I'm up to some good," George mused, arms behind his head. "I don't always feel that. One day I believe, the next day I don't."

"You believe in Matt," Malcolm said. "Maybe all I need to know, if you can tell me, is how he's handling what's happened to him?"

"You mean his mother's death?"

"And his accidental connection to it. Someone might have found the time to tell me." He looked into the upper bunk. "Everyone had their reasons for not telling me," he said. "I'm not sure what Susan's reasons were. Did she confide in you? I'm still half praying Matt was in his tract phase—"

"What? You mean religious tracts?"

"Yes! He might have been handing out someone's tracts! If that was the reason he was in her car—"

"Whose car?"

"Angela and Cooper's!"

"And so what about these tracts? You think he was proselytizing?"

"I don't know. Maybe it was for sex. Either way it's got to be hard on him—just his knowing Angela, getting arrested with her, Susan's having to get our old neighborhood lawyer involved—all of that started with Matt. It's how he must see it. I would if I were seventeen. He came rushing back here, George. What else can I think? He must have confided in you, in someone."

"Have you asked him?"

"I've known for only two days. You can give me an approach maybe. I don't think he trusts me. It's you he trusts. He trusted Susan!"

They were quiet a long time. When Malcolm looked into the upper bunk again, he saw that George seemed to be getting up to leave Malcolm alone, but instead he moved to Robert's cot again, the one closest to Malcolm. "First thing you need to know? Matt hasn't told me a thing—"

Malcolm closed his eyes. "Then that's bad. He really is going to need a shrink."

"—and as for his rushing back here—some of that was just him. His work is here, Malcolm. Life is here—Susan's death may not be the important thing in his theology."

"And you understand that?"

"No, I didn't say that."

"Then what are you saying? It's outrageous, what you're saying."

"Maybe you're right." George got up. He went to the open door of the cabin and looked out. "I know the fiction too: we must understand our children at all times. Let me tell you something, when Matt got back on Monday, he went straight to work. It doesn't mean he wasn't sad about his mother. Mind you, I didn't know what to make of it quite. I have to tell you, I was moved, however. Or else I was shaken. Maybe it was my ego, in seeing someone so young know where he's supposed to be."

George came back to the cot but kept a kind of polite distance. "That doesn't help, does it? Malcolm, I don't know a thing about Matt and Angela. I'm really sorry." He sat down. He hesitated.

"What?" Malcolm said. "Don't spare me."

"Okay. It's just a couple of things. I realize how I sounded just then. Asking you if you've questioned him about Angela. Let me qualify. I'd try to be prepared for whatever reasons he's had for not telling you. He's so—"

"—pure."

"Here's some context. I employ this young Mercer College lifeguard when we're in full session. Hamilton. He's very sincere and out with his religious feelings. Matt can look as if he wants the earth to swallow him up whenever Hamilton starts in."

"That's what I mean by underground," Malcolm said.

"I think you're wrong. I think his sense of the unspoken truths are so strong that he's really quite mature. He's been where he is for a long time, I think."

"He's the real thing, you mean? It's what Susan thought."

"But I'm not sure your wife understood him better than you."

"She was much calmer at least."

"Thereby leaving you with all the worry, all the reality?"

"No."

"Sounds like it to me. Somewhat. As you said, she might have confided in you about the arrest so you could both find out what it was about."

He suddenly felt so defensive, so protective of her. "What can I tell you? I had a bad track record when it came to Matt's fervor. She may have been dreading us finding out what group he'd joined. And at the same time shielding him from me, you see."

"Mothers do that. But it hardly makes you a terrible father."

"I didn't say it did."

"You imply that she, on the other hand, was perfect."

"Lay off, will you?"

"Okay," George said. He smiled. "We're not sure you can afford me, right?"

"Right," Malcolm said.

"I was pushing. Why don't you rest? Stay here and rest for a while."

An hour later when Malcolm finally located steady hammering sounds, he found George standing on the bare ground between open studs. It was a twelve-by-twelve unit, its windows and one door framed out. George motioned to Malcolm to give him a hand lifting a section of subflooring into place.

The fit was right. Soon the two men were climbing on top to begin working at opposite ends. Malcolm knelt beside a heavy soup can full of nails. They both got their hammers going almost immediately, first in unison, then counterpoints and oddly arrhythmic beats as one or the other came to the last mean licks to the nail head. Everything went out of Malcolm's mind for a time; a brief respite. The flooring sent up its smells of wood chips and glue. That canopy of branches and moss let light filter through only in bright, blinding patches, the remote rural air cleaned of everything but an acrid vapor from the ground.

In an hour they had the last of five sections in place. Malcolm turned to see George sitting with his long legs up like clothespins, his back against a stud. He was panting, grinning. "Getting old," he said. Malcolm threw down his hammer and found a place to sit more or less in the same position. Both took a moment to stretch the kinks from stiff spines.

"You're one of the last people Susan talked to," Malcolm said. "Sometime I'd like to know what she said. Not right now."

"She gave us hugs, Malcolm. I'm sorry, but that was about it. Said she had to bring you right back here to see what kind of neat place we were running. I gave her a huge benefit of the doubt." He began to laugh. "Frankly, I wasn't sure if you two deserved me. Matt did. His parents I wasn't so clear about."

George closed his eyes, breathed deeply. "All I'm saying, Malcolm, is that she was nervous like you. Equally worried that I was the religious leader your son had finally attached himself to."

Beyond the openly studded walls, they watched a lone squirrel hop close to a pile of plywood panels. "You are," Malcolm said. The squirrel stopped, moved closer, stopped. Finally it made its tail into a bristling flag. "I need to talk about something else," Malcolm said, continuing to stare. "Now that she's gone, things eat at me, make me weep."

He felt something soft hit his legs. It was a sweatshirt. "Ball that up behind your head and relax," George said. "We'll have a little session." He began looking with pleasure at the clean, raw structure all around them. "I know you're good for it. You guys get coverage."

Malcolm and Susan had discussed the issue many times, up to a certain point—what it was that made Matt soulful and literal where they were not. Later she was reluctant to talk things over, afraid to be disappointed in how Malcolm would respond. Once she'd tried to tell him that she was getting a glimpse of Matt, and Malcolm had agreed to listen carefully—her earliest encounter with It, whatever It was.

Well, it had been Matt as a fourth-grader, coming to her in an awkward confession. He had seemed to be trying to tell her of some insight he was starting to have, but then he'd held it back and not finished. Some tale of a school stoning.

She'd gone to his teacher with the half-formed story about some other child in the class—some repellent and fetid boy who the other children were isolating, and was she right to gather that Matt was trying to help him and was then unable to explain because of some reticence, some sense that his difference was not to be told for fear of praise coming down on his head?

The teacher had known immediately. It was the Croft child, she explained, who was mildly disturbed. Arnold Croft. He was antisocial at best; he made loud, moist heaves of air, constantly rubbed the lower portion of his face with his tongue or the wet backs of his hands. Even her young class perceived it as a compulsive behavior. The sight of red skin, but mostly the knowledge of its cause, had made her fourth-graders pull back and begin to complain of an odor of old spittle and mucus. The teacher admitted to Susan that the anticipation of Arnold began to be as bad as the actuality. She had to fight her own revulsion. He was the most unlovable of creatures she'd ever tried to be responsive to. Well, she wasn't. Couldn't be. Not as she was with the others.

After a first few weeks in her classroom, the children had seen that only the teacher was willing to sit next to Arnold in the Mars reading group. A scramble would take place each day for any seat that was not the one vacant on Arnold's left. Musical chairs; there was always a loser—a resigned and eye-rolling daily loser, a good sport, who would then sit down beside Arnold and lean away, comically, with the children starting to giggle. One day the loser was a pale and emotional girl, who became hysterical when she was the one left standing without a proper chair and was asked to please take her seat next to Arnold.

No! she would not!

The Mars reading circle had been stilled for a moment. The

other two groups—the Jupiter and Venus groups—had been at their desks doing workbook exercises. They now looked up, entranced to see what would happen.

No! She would not. It would make her sick! She was going down to the principal's office!

The crying girl had actually left the room, and there followed a new and mature silence, as if a blanket of mortal shame began to cover them, smother them. They all sat looking at Arnold. He was not dumb; he knew exactly what had happened. His predicament made it impossible for him to resist bringing that lolling tongue openly to his chin—now much too flagrantly. Previously a remnant of willpower had allowed him to commit this act in secret. Furtive executions of the rubbing seemed to be half the pleasure or comfort or whatever name one gives to the satisfaction these things yield. Now, under great stress of the moment, he could not be secret. Everyone seemed to sense this: That now he could not.

A group protest had risen—a mob shriek. The teacher tried to silence it, but saw that a lot of pent-up fury was being released. The one girl, now out of the room of her own free will, invited mutiny. She'd run from the teacher, not just Arnold.

"Quiet, quiet," the teacher had demanded as the initial sound of outrage began to shift to something like joy or fun. She'd sat one more second, and was just about to lead Arnold out of the room. Then suddenly there was Matt. Evidently he'd come flying out of his seat at the back of the room, running into the Mars circle to fill the empty chair beside Arnold. She didn't really see it all happening. Only a fluttery presence and a kind of silence falling over the group again. Then he was seated. They all saw that he did not have his own copy of the blue reader assigned to this group, so was moving his chair close to Arnold's—shoulders touching. Something was whispered between the two boys; Matt looked up, smiled, and asked the teacher who was supposed to start. She named a child, and the reading session simply began.

The teacher had explained to Susan that she hadn't thought it out whether or not she should mention this strange moment to Matt's parents. Maybe she was waiting to see where it would lead, and so far it had not led to anything extraordinary. Matt did not try to befriend Arnold. The teacher observed both boys in their regular spheres out on the playground. It was only as if Matt had seen what needed to be done in that one moment and simply done it. There were tears in the teacher's eyes. She was experienced. Twenty years of grade school teaching. She had felt she'd witnessed something extraordinary.

"I listened and then waited before I commented," Malcolm said, lifting his head and looking at George.

"And?"

"She was moved by her own story. It brought out something hard in me. I asked her if this meant the teacher was permanently shifting Matt to the Mars group." Malcolm began to laugh. "I meant it to be funny. It wasn't. Then I tried to be serious. I wanted to know what it meant that he hadn't befriended Arnold. I mean, our son had no friends. It was time to face that and not be so moved by some teacher's religious experience. I guess she saw me getting angry. There was this 'Oh' in her look. She didn't say anything. It was as if she said, 'Oh, you're going to be that way. We really can't get anywhere with this. I'll go with it myself.' And you know what? That's what I wanted."

"I see. What happened?"

"Perversely, I did nothing else about the situation. I didn't ask a second time if we could discuss it. I guessed I began to like the way my disengagement created division of labor. And besides, we kept getting spared. Matt's religiosity, or whatever one wanted to call it, would seem to grow less visible. Once in a while it would surface, but he was like one of those savanna rivers that go underground and then emerge again miles later. You know about those?"

"Sure do. Some of them go under and stay under, don't they?" George said. "People go off the deep end, to use the common expression. It's not that easy to call, is it?"

"It's impossible," Malcolm said.

"But it is easier to make her eternally the better parent, Malcolm—to remember her as a better, more accepting person than you."

"She was! Easier than what, by the way?"

"Than forgiving her."

"For what?"

"For leaving you with all this. You needed her around to help you accept it, Malcolm. Matt doesn't need a shrink, but he's not ever going to be easy to understand."

"My God, he really is going? Off somewhere? Somewhere impossible!"

"Maybe. I'd be wrong to dismiss your fears. You're right to have them. He's not anything like us, I don't think. You needed Susan to help you accept that. Now she's gone. You have to do it all by yourself. It would be as if I had to accept Robert all by myself. Very hard. Very hard to do."

All Malcolm could think was how true this all was, but how, finally, he was actually holding on to a Matt who couldn't exit, who couldn't just evolve into a happy freshman in order to oblige his father—become some son more like Johnny, only nicer.

"This business of his not having friends," George said. "I wouldn't dare say something so cavalier as I'm about to say if I didn't know Matt better, if I didn't see what a basically decent and put-together person *you* are."

"You're going to be cavalier? I could use a dose of that."

"Well, I was just going to venture to ask you, you know, man to man, if you didn't think friendship, in the long run, isn't a bit overrated. Take this with a grain of salt, Malcolm, because you see what a consummate loner I am—" He motioned to the trees. "I'm not saying my isolation has the same source as what you're seeing in this unusual person you've raised. Nicely, I'd like to add. I'm not saying my thing is the same as his at all. But I'd just like to know from you. What *is* friendship? I mean, I know it in some ideal way and all that. Rumi's conversations with Shams, if you know that one. A platonic

David singing to Jonathan. Stan playing to Oliver! Once you've found work in life, I mean real work, your important bit, as it were, then friendship—"

"You're suggesting that Matt has saved himself a lot of time?" Malcolm offered, half whimsically.

"Exactly. Friendship is shallow in cultures such as ours. At the adolescent level, it revolves around matters of class, and never ideas. Adulthood is no different, is it? for Americans, it's not. It's why our lover and mate is so weighed down as a concept, and this fact has hardly gone unnoticed. I just want to suggest that in Matt's case there *will* be friends, Malcolm, but not casual ones." George grinned. "He's not afriad to check out the hermits, if I may be presumptive and suggest myself as his friend."

Malcolm nodded.

"Or put it this way—friendship is just not interesting to him. He's above it, and I mean that in the best sense. What engages him are people for whom the casual is not even in the offing, short of a miracle. My boys, for example. Don't think I've given up on psychiatry, Malcolm, but I do work in awe about forty percent of the time. Matt can't work any other way. I think he knew that in grammar school. All that time ago! He's not where he is through a recent leap to cultist ideas."

Malcolm had begun to cry behind one large hand, his throat as big as a python. He finally said, "You actually *like* him."

"Ah," George said, as if understanding something for the first time. "Maybe that's all you've ever needed to hear on his behalf, Malcolm. Ironically, he's very secure in his likability. Knows that his love is returned, if not in ways you can easily see as a parent. Too bad it's never occurred to him to tell you."

"I've always felt sorry for him, you know." Malcolm shook his head with the shame he felt.

"Yeah," George said, "and you're forgiven that too. Your compassion."

*   *   *

Malcolm wasn't sure what the bus tooted at. He stood up from where he was sitting alone on a stump and waved as the boys alighted—first Robert and then Matt—not seeming to notice him yet. Robert began dancing his way, a lunch box crashing and the boys having to pause to pick up the few scattered objects. A lively orange rolled from one side of the highway to the other as the bus slowly pulled away, tooting again.

Malcolm saw Matt raise a fallen thermos and give it a shake to check if it was broken. Robert, in rapt attention, awaited a verdict. At fifty feet, one could hear the low deep tones of Matt's voice. "It's fine." Then they both headed toward him, his misgivings half vanishing. He asked not to begin tightening up in that worried expression of his. Lift that look from my face, he prayed angrily, get that sound out of my voice.

"Hi, Dad," Matt called.

"Hi, Dad!" Robert called and resumed his dance toward Malcolm.

"Hello," Malcolm said. As the rubbery boy got closer, he added, "Is that for me?" He was being given the orange. One could start with that. "Weren't you hungry enough to eat this at lunchtime?"

"I didn't! I didn't eat it!"

"I see that. Thank you."

"Wait, give Matt some, give Matt some!"

Matt had caught up to them, and as he drew close Malcolm heard Susan, close and intimate, one last time. *Where will he go?* She, too, was a little bit frantic. *How will he even find the poor? In what way?*

"Took me a long time to get myself here," Malcolm murmured as they hugged. Malcolm grabbed and hung on for a longish time. He did it for her, for himself. It was all they had of the boy at the moment.

Then they were being knocked down as Robert lunged for his place. The three became a rough tangle of arms and heads, a large fattish boy gaining deft control over the moment. Robert took the orange away from Malcolm and waved it above his head. "Give some to George!" he said, slightly pigeon-toed as he lopped away, suddenly remembering who it was he adored the most, who it was preparing a place for boys having nowhere else to go. At least for now. *Not just where will he go; I want to know that when he gets there, can there at least be electricity? Is that too much to ask?* Malcolm began to laugh. *Can there at least be e-mail?*

"What?" Matt said, smiling, glad to see his father laughing. "What's funny?"

"I don't know," Malcolm said. He threw his arm around level shoulders as they began to retrace steps back to camp. "I don't know, I was just wondering if you'll just call once in a while."

"Call?"

"I mean when you get really out there."

Matt waited, as if wanting to think fully about what Malcolm was asking. "Oh," the boy said, getting it. "You mean when I'm way, way out there?"

"Yes! Am I going to have to get a shortwave radio?"

Matt smiled. He was deliberately taking a long time to reply, more of Gretchen's timing than Malcolm realized. "I don't know," he finally said. "You might. But I could end up in Danford, you know. I could end up very close."

"I picture you very far."

"You do?" He stopped and looked at Malcolm. He was taking this as a compliment. As if he needed a small bit of recognition that he was the type, the extremely rare and uncalled-for type.

"Yes, very far," Malcolm repeated. "I'll need to have something, you know. A satellite dish?" He was smiling and yet growing serious of face, honest. He made the boy look at him again. "Something, Matt," he repeated.

"I know," the boy finally said. "I know."

20

TAKE NO PURSE

A FEW DAYS LATER OREN SIGNALED FROM HIS PORCH, AND Gretchen went over in the morning, not at her usual afternoon time, to learn from a young social worker that Angela was missing. Harry and Margaret were out looking for her, rather futilely, this Sara Johnson said, briefcase still on her shoulder. Angela had done this her whole life, she said—just walked to the nearest highway and put out her thumb as if it were nothing.

But it couldn't be nothing, Gretchen reasoned; Angela had to be testing them. "We've gotten to know a little bit about her hopes and dreams," Oren explained, after he offered tea and coffee.

"Maybe," Ms. Johnson said. The briefcase finally came off, and the young woman sat down. Gretchen saw immediately that she was a sweet person, hanging on to a Georgia drawl and coming equipped with a whole set of assessment skills that were neither admirable nor indictable, exactly; they were statistical. "Maybe," she repeated, "but these girls sometimes bolt just to keep their street smarts from growing rusty."

She wanted them to call her Sara, she said. She had pert, intelligent eyes that took notes for her, her glance flashing into all corners of Oren's dark living room. "And these girls do have resources. You have to admit that in Angela's case her resources are considerable. She's a survivor."

Oren tried warming up this Sara by asking her a few tactful questions about herself. Was she a long way from home, did she miss her folks? Gretchen, taking up Oren's lead, asked about graduate school. Soon Sara was telling them all about her master's and that she was going on to her Ph.D. as soon as she had a little more experience. She'd had to work hard to be where she was today, the first member of her family to get off the farm. The briefcase was a present. For when she got her fellowship.

"Handsome," Oren said.

She studied rough hands, shifted in her chair, then smiled again, this time at how quickly they were on to her. So, okay, she was quite exasperated with her clients and pretty tired of runaways like Angela. "I used to think I was going to like this line of work, every case so different and everyone having a unique story." She eyed Oren's legs and smiled.

"What happened?" Oren said. He leaned in to pass a plate of sliced bread around.

"The sheer numbers are getting me," the young woman said, giving an unconscious tug to the end of her skirt, the way people touch their faces on a spot where a friend they're talking to has a troubling, clinging food particle. Oren refused to respond. His big knees, shiny as bowling balls, did not move.

"And I'm judgmental, it turns out," Sara continued forthrightly, with both a certain confidence and an apology. "The hardest part of being a caseworker turns out to be me wondering why these kids can't settle down when something good happens to them." She crossed her legs at the ankle. Oren's men's shoes and socks stayed flat on the floor, a foot apart. "Objectively, I see why they can't," Sara said.

"Tell us," Oren suggested, sitting back in his chair, folding his hands in his lap. The new alb Freda had made for him was a lush subdued brown, and it had pockets, a hood, and a gold drapery rope gathering the fabric into official-looking folds that fell in plumb lines. Short was a matter of penance—a matter that this Sara, from Georgia, did not know a thing about. But she was dealing fairly well with the mystery, nevertheless. One could see her mind at work: The man was in some kind of group? Were those roofers up there his followers? Gretchen saw Sara glance at the ceiling. She could do all this and keep right on talking. "The way I see it, a life that has been pretty much all adversity negates hope."

"Surely not," Oren said.

Sara leaned forward with the urgency of her idea, and all nervousness fell away: "My theory is that when it's been all adversity, then new experience must be fairly useless. Even wasted. You see what I mean?"

"No!"

"See, they don't know about variety. If everything is rocky all the time, there's no stability to long for, to believe is going to come round again. It never has before; why should they expect it? *We* have a context. That's all I mean. We have the patience to wait for change. See?"

"It's very sad," Oren agreed. He proceeded cautiously. "But Angela can imagine stability, I've found."

The young woman smiled kindly. "You think so? I wish you were right."

In her mind Gretchen took the next step in Sara's philosophical reasoning: without variety, with only adversity, then—

"Does Corey know she's gone?" Oren asked. "Corey and Ricky are what will make her turn up."

Sara had begun to look around her. It wasn't like a monastery. Oren's house was full of antiques that she'd already commented on with admiration; she didn't get to see older homes like this on a normal day. "Corey and Ricky?" she mused, gazing almost with affection now at Oren's legs coming up from the carpet. Stovepipes. She had stopped caring one way or the other.

"Corey and Ricky are an interesting twist." Then Sara added

hopefully, "You could be right." She turned to Gretchen and gave her a little wink. It was a complex gesture for which Gretchen was grateful. The wink said, Good luck, who knows, who cares, he'd be my friend too, I know what's happened to your mother, if you ever need me, I wish I could stay, good-bye, keep the faith.

This seemed to be part of life's secret—that wink. It meant the attempt to know what time one is in from moment to moment and to respond as fully as possible to being in it and no other. For now Gretchen's time was partly the secrecy of her knowledge of Angela and their shared hours at the Rawlinses'. She didn't think it fair to test Malcolm with it; didn't think it right to force a look of relief on his face at the news that Angela was now missing. After all, he had his own secrecy about what he'd learned from Matt about Angela and the arrest; he wasn't sharing that at the moment. And it didn't matter. Each thing in its place. From Oren she learned the Zen of it. On their first joint trip to the grocery store the day after Sara's visit, someone rolled a grapefruit at them as they were rounding into the dry cereal aisle, and all Oren said was, "Dear Lord," as he jumped to keep from tripping.

He reached down and picked up the heavy fruit and put it carefully into the cart. "I think we've been spotted," he said.

"Should we leave?" she whispered.

"No, no. Think about Susan."

"How?"

"She's a thought, Gretchen, a perspective. Keep your eye on the ball."

A package of frozen broccoli came sailing over the tops of the cereal boxes. "We can use that!" Oren said, pretending to read the item off his list. The miracle for Gretchen was that the toss did not send the cereals crashing to the floor. Oren took over the cart and began pushing it slowly but firmly around the U-turn into canned goods—the beets and green beans near to hand but the pasta sauces, their goal, a million miles farther down. "Here we could get hurt," she whispered, and the observation caused Oren to find the safest possible central path for the cart, his head high, shoulders back, heel to toe. Soon they were passing the list between them and pulling things from the shelves in an unhurried but nondawdling fashion.

"If we make it to the end," Oren whispered, "I say we call it a day."

"Roger," Gretchen said.

She looked up to see swimming before her one of her last-year teachers, now retired and calmly reading the label on a tomato sauce can. Old Mr. Clayton. He lowered the heavy can slowly and gave Gretchen and Oren an examination head to toe from over the tops of his famous half-moon spectacles. He should judge, Gretchen thought; him and his statement bow ties and fancy socks. But when she looked again she saw something in Mr. Clayton that suggested concern, maybe even a considerable sense of it.

"Gretchen," Mr. Clayton said, nodding. "Oren. Good to see you both."

"Yes!" Oren said. "Good to see you too!"

She could have hugged the man. Or perhaps he was blind? Nearsighted? Not interested enough to have Oren's outfit register on him? Not a leg man?

She was beginning to feel her heart pound at her own disloyalty. Her inability to look bravely at Oren, who was such a sight after all. Under the fluorescents, he took getting used to all over again, even for her.

At the checkout counter, all their items were rung up and bagged by the manager's son and a boy who'd graduated from her high school several years ago, who kept his eyes on his work and talked at the food as it passed under his pale fingers—"Three cans of Classico, mushrooms, celery . . ."

"Hi Gretchen," someone yelled. This time when she looked she saw Sharon's younger brother with a gang of other eighth-grader hecklers, whose final prank had been tossing three packages of pantyhose into Oren's basket. Now they were finally leaving the store and making a run for bicycles. She saw the backs of T-shirts and feet in huge sneakers pumping away.

The store manager had acted as a bouncer, first calling to them to leave, then holding the door and shouting something authoritative before coming to the counter to help bag. The people and carts gathering behind Gretchen and Oren were as silent as an unemployment line. It was upsetting to have the manager appear red-faced, apoplectic. Everyone stared at Oren's selection of food gliding on the automated countertop. Gretchen observed that to keep his eye on the ball, Oren lingered a few paces behind her and spent time in the tabloid rack picking out a single candy bar for himself and then a second one for her.

The manager, not appreciating this twosome, this clientele from Everett Street, walked them out to the Olds. He didn't say a word as he waited for Oren to open the trunk. That was the thing that got Gretchen the most. He was there to fend off further incident, which maybe she could understand if he'd used the opportunity to say how sorry he was about her mother or something simple like that.

"Perspective," Oren repeated, sensing her emotions rising once she was behind the wheel and backing out.

The situation was a bit more legal than the other day; he was letting her drive. Technically she was supposed to be in the company of an adult who also had a license. They tried small talk about just when he would get himself to the motor vehicle office. Then Oren snapped his fingers; he'd forgotten to put diet soda on the list.

"For Angela? You really do think she'll turn up?"

If he was worried, he didn't let on. But how could he not be, of course—natural worry for a girl with nothing but a restraining order and a beat-up diary of words. Was she right now at the beach, working the concession stands? Gretchen knew that's what he was thinking. From Sara they'd learned that the beach was where lots of runaways went; the bathrooms there had showers, and people, generally speaking, seemed more like you.

"How do you mean?" Oren had asked.

"More, you know—at large."

Gretchen could point the car toward the Atlantic or toward the Gulf. "An hour away in either direction," she observed, "beaches, a ton of them."

"No," Oren finally said, after seeming to give it some thought. "Let's go home. We've put enough strain on Malcolm, going out on this first jaunt. We have to break him in, you know, dear man."

That night Gretchen knew she would have upset Malcolm greatly had she not been such a good actor, hiding her worry about Angela. Innocent Malcolm came to her with a packet of photographs he said that Susan was planning on showing her. Days before her death she'd suggested telling Gretchen that their real wedding had taken place in a Nebraska jailhouse. The wedding shots in the family album were fakes, staged later in front of a university chapel to spare the already hurt feelings of their parents.

Gretchen stared at the secret photos and gave out the expected appreciative, affectionate laugh. But in some real way they made her more aware of Angela's life by contrast. Privately she was thinking how runaways got arrested all the time with absolutely nothing sweet ever coming of it. Her parents looked adorable. They were big blonds with good teeth. They were nabbed once in their lives and ended up married, for God's sake.

"Maybe this wasn't a good time to show you these," Malcolm said, sensing that she was sad. He could only assume she wasn't ready because of Susan's death.

She patted the hand that rested on her shoulder as he stood behind her looking at the spread of a dozen or so faded color shots of him and his bride, flanked by a sheriff and deputy who could have passed for Andy Griffith and Barney Fife. He pointed out to her how he'd made sure the deputy's wife included the bars of the cell where he and Susan had spent the afternoon. And that funny-looking cake was really homemade banana bread.

"See that mug?" He was pointing to himself. "I knew how lucky I was. I was an idiot, but you can see some wisdom in my face. See those old guys so jealous of me?" He bent in close. "Lord, look at them! They're younger than I am now!"

She continued patting the hand, the same hand going around her mother's little waist. In all the other shots, a young girl is laughing, kidding around, shoving banana bread into Malcolm's mouth, holding up handcuffed wrists, wrapping hands around the bars and making a scare-face, as if she's never going to get out.

Gretchen closed her eyes, opened them again. Perspective, Oren would have said. There, in the one group photograph, was her mother's straightforward look into the camera and beyond. She was not kidding around in this shot. She was looking to a point where she seemed to see Gretchen out there in the future, along with herself, Malcolm, and Matt—a life replete with the richest possible meanings. In this dream for themselves, her parents had not failed. But the youthful kidding around of all the other shots almost appalled Gretchen, and for the first time in several days of elation and purpose with Oren she sensed that general sadness was what had to win out if she were to be better attuned to the world.

The next morning Angela was in the front yard, sitting in the spot where Susan had fallen. Gretchen stayed indoors, watching how Malcolm's first impulse was to get her away from that spot, how he shoved hands in his pockets to keep from grabbing the girl and dragging her by the scruff of her neck, almost the thing Angela expected from life, provoked from life. It gave Malcolm something important to see for himself, Gretchen realized, to be the first to encounter the girl whose whereabouts he did not even know were in question.

She sat crying rather pitifully and repeating that it had all been her fault, while Gretchen waited, heart in hand, having no idea what Malcolm would do. In this area, Gretchen and Oren's minds were already made up, while for Malcolm there was a ten thousand feet of mountain to overcome.

* * *

He spoke kindly to her, but his motives were not pure. Plain and simple, he could not help thinking that maybe now he'd find out what had happened. Who had he been kidding? He really wanted to know, and now he would.

"I sent Cooper out of his mind that afternoon he came over here," she began. Perhaps she wanted to show her hand—her power to dole out information when it suited her. Malcolm wouldn't put it past her. "I sent him right out of his mind," she repeated.

The two of them had not seen each other since that afternoon. He'd reconstructed every frame of the day by then—the way it had begun so very early in the morning. He'd stood out on the porch with a cup of coffee after a night in the hospital with Lloyd Reniere. Angela had come flying over to say she'd call the cops if he kept spying. Now, convincingly remorseful, she was confessing that hours later she inflamed Cooper about Malcolm's happenstance loan of money; made innuendos, made Cooper jealous.

She was shivery and underdressed. She was a child, and it doused him. "A hard lesson for you," he managed to say, no longer sure she was being cagey. He felt pity when she asked him if he would please not contact the social worker or Oren or the Rawlinses right that minute. She'd be grateful to him, not that she deserved it.

"You telephoned Cooper, didn't you?" he said. "Before you even moved into Oren's, it was you who let him know how to find you. Oren thinks it was Eddy Jensen!"

"But he took care of me before," she said in a burst of tearful rage. Then she stopped crying. "Some, I mean. When he wasn't trashed. He built me up and everything." She began to laugh. "Then he'd tell me I was whale piss, so I had to, you know . . . sort it out." She looked around her, looked bravely at the spot. "Yeah, I called him. I didn't know I was even doing it until he picked up."

It went a long way, her telling him one big truth like this. But she balked when he accused her of only pretending not to remember

Matt. Just as she'd denied remembering him to both Oren and Gretchen, she denied it to him. All those boys ran together, she said, insisting that the one she was arrested with didn't fit the description. And anyway, she added, why was he still blaming Matt?

"I'm not blaming him," Malcolm said.

"Oh yeah? So why isn't he here? Why did he run from you?"

He looked her straight in the eye. "I figure he ran from you." It was mean. But for a second he had a sense that direct questioning was about to work. The girl's mouth came open and then closed.

Gretchen was there in her nightgown. He turned and watched her come down the steps. She looked like her mother, which wasn't fair. The illusion killed him. It's what would have happened if there'd been no gun—Susan taking her inside the house to fix some milk.

Warm milk was Angela's request for the sake of her ulcer, which later Malcolm was surprised to learn was real, verified by Harry and Margaret's own doctor. That first day he was sure the ulcer was made up. She was a doubled-over caricature, a groaning heap sitting at the table trying to sip on milk. Gretchen took her to the spare bedroom that Malcolm had just moved out of while Malcolm yelled loudly up the stairwell that the Rawlinses had to know she was all right! Oren too! And the social worker!

He made good on his threat, but it kept him on the phone for a few hours.

"We can try and place her, Mr. Robb," Sara Johnson explained. "But it's hard when they get this old."

"Old?"

"Yes. That's the word. I can place her probably by tonight, and then we can hope she doesn't run. It's her pattern, though. We could lock her up, but that's fuzzy. She's not criminal, having been detained once for giving hand jobs to boys."

"Please," Malcolm groaned.

But Sara Johnson had a flat tone that startled him. She was on the edge of being short with him. "Her crime is falling in with an older man, an addict who exploited her. When girls are this close to being eighteen—"

"She's not close."

"—best thing is to support them wherever they land, hope that it's them who find a spot they can feel at home in long enough to mature, to get somewhere."

"Are we safe? She's in my house!"

"You going to call up the Rawlinses? I think that would be a good idea. They had her two weeks, you know."

He did *not* know.

"Well, I'll tell you something, Mr. Robb." He heard her laying it on thick now; it was a way of indicting him without anyone being able to accuse her of it. "You just have a talk with them, and maybe they'll reassure you that she's not really likely to stick around much beyond what you can take anyway."

Hurt, he almost didn't call the Rawlinses. But in a few moments he was dialing.

"Thank God," Harry Rawlins said.

Margaret laughed in relief. One could hear the concern, the regret, the feeling that this was somehow their fault. Malcolm began reassuring them, much to his surprise.

"I think she's quite remarkable," Margaret ended up saying. "I'll be frank. She's what they call borderline in some of the psychology literature. I can give you a whole book to read if you want it. Many are funny, bright, indomitable. But little can be done for borderlines. I was preparing myself for an interesting ride. Not that I'm saying it would work." There was a pause. She added, "Well, it didn't work, did it? Not with us."

That first day, Gretchen sat on the spare bed chatting, playing the part of fellow teen. It was quite a sight—Gretchen reading aloud, shuffling cards, showing a movie, getting a facial, getting another clip from Angela's quick scissors. It was the first he knew that they'd been together at the Rawlinses, much less become so close as to be trimming hair. Angela, that quite obviously crafty girl, was going slow on the hair, he pointed out to Gretchen when they were finally alone. Only another inch from the last time? He wouldn't put it past her to win trust and then lop laughing Gretchen off above the ears.

"I don't care," Gretchen said.

He lay awake all night, listening. Was he crazy? When he finally slept, it was toward dawn. He woke up hearing more laughter and went up to find Oren had come over—the three of them up there. Later Gretchen told Malcolm that she'd prepped Angela about the alb-dress. No, they hadn't been laughing about that, Gretchen told him, when she came down to make sandwiches for an ongoing session.

"Well, you sound like a Shriner convention up there," Malcolm said, suddenly feeling a rush of jealousy, the outsider. "Tell me, what's so funny?"

"Oren! He's so glad she'll finally talk to him. He's trying to convince her. His method is hilarious. In that alb-dress he can say almost anything, and it's a scream."

"Convince her of what?"

"Of purchase. He really did give her his house so she'd have that much toward her goal."

"And what did you just call it?"

"Purchase. She thinks he's crazy, which he is, of course."

And even as she searched for the right words to explain Oren's hilarity, Malcolm saw the further deepening in Gretchen—a unmistakable sense of her protectiveness, her agreement with Oren and with herself to help this girl; Malcolm could like it or lump it.

"She's going to need to see Corey and Ricky once in a while," Gretchen said that same evening. By now it was a given to Gretchen that this was Angela's chosen safe house. "I'm going to see what I can do about visits, Dad."

"No, you're not."

The next day he was in his car, driving aimlessly on back streets, talking himself out of Angela staying a day longer than was absolutely necessary. How could he risk it? By God, enough had happened to them; no one was even mentioning the fact that this had been (was now!) a sexually active fifteen-year-old.

He woke up, in effect, put on his brakes; a woman was flagging him down. She wasn't someone he knew, and so he stopped. She came to his window to explain. No, she didn't know him either, she was being friendly, was new to the area, saw his car going by slowly. Wasn't there something here he could take off her hands? She and her husband had found all this stuff the former owners left in the attic and in the garage. "At first I was mad, now it looks like I'll meet people. What do you need? It's all free."

Her cluttered yard looked like that of a house whose roof had come off in a hurricane.

"Is that a child's car seat?" Malcolm found himself saying. In all the mess, the car seat jumped out at him. It sat alone in a patch of shade. Malcolm was still behind the wheel.

He didn't remember thanking her for the seat; he remembered getting out and being handed the thing and then hurting his back as he struggled to secure it correctly. The woman showed him the knack of it. For his baby or grand-baby? she asked.

He wasn't sure if he answered. He'd stumbled on the one person who wouldn't wonder in some small town way what in God's name he wanted with it. So the blessing of anonymity was part of the experience. But also he remembered pulling away, knowing he was going to drive on to the Sulloways' and start with them, see how they felt about a visiting arrangement before he started up something with the caseworker. He turned to look. The seat touched him with its simple lack of reproach, its serviceability, its mute, awkward, space-age shape.

And when he got back home after talking to Ed and Enid about visitations, he saw he was being outrageously set up in a whole other area. The dining room table! Car keys still in hand, Malcolm stood looking at a spread of news articles the two girls were putting into a common notebook.

"Current events," Gretchen explained.

"Hmm," Malcolm said. He was as poker face as the moment demanded.

"The war in Bosnia," Angela said. Her script from Gretchen was to play it business as usual; act like she'd been doing this forever.

"Relocation of various groups," Gretchen said. Neither girl looked up from her work.

"Timely," Malcolm said.

"You're supposed to review this with us in a few weeks," Angela said, a seasoned current events girl in one afternoon. She was already improvising.

"That's right," Gretchen said.

"Looks like you don't need me, exactly," Malcolm said.

"Sure we do, Dad!" Gretchen said.

What touched him was that the word "Dad" rattled Angela a bit. She suddenly didn't know where to put her eyes; clearly, she had no idea what to call him.

Mr. Mom was what she hit upon for Oren's role in Corey and Ricky's Monday visits. Malcolm was Mrs. Mom, interestingly enough. Gretchen was Gretchen when she wasn't an angry epithet—Pie Face, Egghead, Miss Superiority. Gretchen gave it right back. Within a week the girls were producing very loud laughs with odd tails attached at the ends. The odd sound was something laughed at in death, in their having walked through it, in a shared early visit to low celebrity—each because of the other. They knew that the teenagers in town would view them as grotesques to have ended up under the same roof, friends. That made them laugh the most.

Awe-inspiring, if you were Malcolm. Worrisome, too, of course. Was Gretchen in over her head? Whenever she sensed his worry, she gave him piercing looks. Worry—that had been the thing with Matt, she seemed to warn him; he was not to transfer it to her.

At bottom they were allies. From the first Monday they asked Oren to help them with the experiment. Routine was both difficult and necessary for Angela and the two little guys. Mostly there was peaceful play and interaction. One Monday, the third visit, there was war. After an hour Corey cursed them all and refused to come downstairs. Ricky sobbed for Enid Sulloway, his "mama," which contributed to a larger jealousy problem for Angela. Then Corey, not to be outdone by Ricky, threw a fit over the color of a balloon. She later hid and didn't make a sound until she guessed that they were about to call in help, that they were at the end of some rope or other.

And Corey's mouth! She let them have it, once she got used to them and could get them alone. One visit, just when they thought they were about to do nothing more advanced than get out the Monopoly set for a rainy afternoon, Corey announced offhand while Angela was in the kitchen that her sister used to steal when she lived with Cooper.

Used to steal? So far there was no evidence of Angela stealing, or Cooper either, for that matter. This could be something she'd seen or overheard. It could be a warning, or simple jealousy about Angela getting to stay with them. Corey was not old enough to understand that much of life's luck was by default.

Meanwhile, jealousy, devotion, telling tales—all of it seemed to be grist for Gretchen's mill, as far as Malcolm could see. She was swimming upstream beautifully in what she'd arranged. Indeed, he must not worry; he saw that. Gretchen was seized, inspired, driven like a madwoman with a vision that could come to her at any time and send her flying to her desk or her bed, piled with pages from a legal pad. She would only explain that she was having all kind of ideas about what was happening to them. A meteor shower.

The energy of her new direction, the matching quiet of Angela sitting with a book—it could sometimes fool Malcolm. That and Oren, who stopped in every day, not wanting to sort it all out, just wanting to urge on Malcolm the little bit of free wonder he was entitled to. Oren began what he called "a conversation" about money. He introduced it in fits and starts, and it was a while before Malcolm realized the cockeyed drift.

"I've never understood work," Oren might muse. "I'm sure this was a bad thing in me, given the ease with which I can be slothful. I've followed daytime soaps, Malcolm. Perfectly happy at it. But you're different. You've proved yourself. You don't have to work at a paid job any more."

Malcolm didn't feel free to speak of the blank he experienced daily about all that. He knew he'd been out there doing something called work, but it was all lumped together now. It was a fist of time, a callus, an old bunion he barely noticed. He wanted no one to pick up on it. It was guilt-making to him that he couldn't remember most of it.

"I have the money to get all these kids through college," Oren might say.

"Yes," Malcolm might answer. "There's always college."

"I'll back them, in effect. And you don't need much, do you? Ocean cruises or vacations to the Bahamas every other month? Women?"

"I hardly need air," Malcolm once confessed.

"You make a terrific parent. Not me. I see that now. I make a good backer." Repeated a few times, this became part of the cautious terminology they needed. They were the backers, the three of them.

None gave him or herself credit for charitable thoughts. That stood almost in opposition to what they felt. In Gretchen's case there was just a powerful connection to Malcolm, Oren, and Angela—people who would never get over it. A strong spirit had gone at them roughly, she wrote. They were a matched set of old cooking pans, scoured to a new surface. She wore the key to this idea around her neck and kept a locked box of urgent writing in a hidden place.

For Malcolm and Oren there were the two little guys—Corey and Ricky—doing their wicked parts, lodging themselves in the imagination from one experimental Monday to the next. Suddenly, the Mondays were especially anchoring to the two men, kicking them into Tuesdays—a fresh start-up of reading, of attempting to follow the high school curriculum and chaperon the two older girls in their strangely connected convalescence.

From Tuesday through the next Monday visit they had a dozen ups and downs just with Angela alone.

"Okay, I can't find my money."

"Not again!"

For days running she accused Gretchen of having taken something of hers, something different each day—a piece of jewelry, a magazine, ten dollars she claimed was loose in her purse and was no longer there. These were excruciating moments in which Malcolm wanted to throw in the towel. While the fits were happening he'd be full of patience, following Gretchen's lead, her instinct for calm. He could see understanding despite the angry glint in her eye as she began, each time, to turn the house upside down. The missing items were always found, always in some logical place Angela claimed to have looked—the sideboard in the dining room, the work hutch in the mud room, the little table in the entry hall that used to be Susan's putting-down spot. No one mentioned this, Angela's habit of cluttering the very place Susan used almost exclusively for her school bag and packages.

He was patient until nighttime. Then, alone in the room he briefly shared with Susan, the addition they puttered in for donkey's years and then finished just last year, the one to which he had been allowed to return through some mystical interventions from her— there, alone in that room, Malcolm lost patience with Angela over and over. Or was it hope? He could apply understanding upon understanding when it came to her deprivations. Family life was both hard and necessary for her. They were doing the right thing in providing it for her. No, insisting upon it. Team effort was a house rule. If she didn't like it she could leave.

Monday would roll around as a kind of holiday, a marker. They'd made it. Ricky, at not quite four, finally read his first words on one of these visits. They'd been coaxing him, partly because of the phenomenal older sister Corey, who they had read to them from *The Yearling* as a way to include her, unofficially, in the Robb home schooling. One Monday Ricky came into the kitchen carrying a stinking load in his diaper, a bottle in one hand, *Goodnight Moon* in the other. It was Oren who picked him up, let him read, Oren thinking that Ricky must be reciting the pages by heart.

No, Angela said, probably not; Corey read at about four; they should test him. So Oren printed out a short word not in the book. He began phoneticizing it a little bit to clue the child in, but was told by Angela to stop cheating.

"Frog!" Ricky yelled.

They all went crazy, including Angela, whose capacity for showing happiness she often withheld as is the wont of people needing more power. That day they had a tremendous breakthrough, not just for Ricky but clearly for Angela. It was she who added a word to frog, with Ricky already sounding it out by himself. "Legs!" he shouted.

The roar of cheers at "frog legs!" caused Corey to leave the room and go hide.

Malcolm put his word at the front of the phrase, thinking, Holy moly.

"Eat frog legs!" Ricky yelled. Angela began kissing his neck.

Gretchen took her turn next.

"Never eat frog legs!" Ricky yelled.

"So now we know," Oren said.

"You were this young too, weren't you, Angela!" Gretchen said, her arm around the girl's shoulders, everyone having begun to sense that Angela was still as young as the little guys in many respects.

"You'd have to ask good old Rayleen," she said. An expression passed over her face that was suddenly pure fury. It froze Malcolm's heart. It looked incurable.

They came to know the mother's contemptible voice. Angela began to imitate it. In that voice she began to make fun of herself. And them. Then she began to go into an imitation of Cooper's hyena laugh, the one Malcolm heard only the one time when she stormed across Everett, and Cooper came out in his underwear and boots to mock them both. Suddenly she asked, What was the point in her studying? Flushed, she would go off to her room to turn on the radio full blast. Gretchen's ability to study—with earplugs—was becoming a huge source of resentment. Angela considered Gretchen, alternately, a role model and a tormenter. They began to be unsure how to pass on to her the mystery of Gretchen's self-discipline, its art felt unteachable—learning its own reward, and all those other bromides that were so true.

But sometimes—wa-la! She would sink into her history textbook and do well for a chapter. Routinely she wrote out the study questions, and either Malcolm or Oren corrected her grammar and spelling errors. Some answers were long and surprisingly well considered; others sarcastic and aimed at her readers—"Who cares?" "How should I know?" "You tell me, Mrs. Mom."

Gretchen reasoned that Angela too often let her fears creep into her study time. "I should just get a job," Angela screamed at the walls on several occasions. Almost every night they went through a set of doubts, balanced as doubts were by the backers' sense of her promise. Yes, she happened to be the throwaway that fate sent them, and it was okay to admit it; they got lucky; deep down she knew something about self-motivation long before they came into the picture. There was hope.

This was the first of two different types of family conferences they held regularly—the one that excluded Angela, the one that had to go on almost in silence, in eye contact, in quick huddles before she came in and caught them. But they were full of praise, that was the thing. Her intelligence was apparent and made her exciting. All of them concurred that one day, if she had the patience, she might come into her own, find a way to affirm herself. It was jargon, but it was all they had. They believed there was a truth to it.

One Monday morning they met in the kitchen to sort out the routine of the visiting day—Malcolm about to leave to collect the little guys, Gretchen to the shopping, Oren to the cooking, Angela to her preparations. Monday was her chore-free day. But first a bit of inexplicable pouting over breakfast and then a great moment of fun, so typical of Angela. She entertained them with a story-incident linked to Malcolm's getting Ricky's child seat at the yard sale of other people's things—the time when she was living with Desiree and Trudy. "Old Trudy decided to sell a ton of items left in the attic by the previous tenants. To surprise Desiree, she kept it a secret. I decided it was okay. Desey came home and found stuff spread out on sheets. You should have seen her face."

Oren, Malcolm, and Gretchen waited for the end of the story. "What happened?"

Angela's mouth became dark. "They got busted."

"Who busted them?" Gretchen said.

"The neighbors, stupid. We were minors. How should I know who busted us?"

"So you all got busted, you mean? All three of you?"

She'd been smiling as she told of Trudy's little tags tied to every-thing, her need to be connected to people in the sixplex where they were trying to look like normal girls. Now Angela's mouth was dark. She looked at Gretchen and shrugged, trying not to reveal that she'd begun to feel depressed or a bit uncomfortable with the details. She could often snap out of it and get her last word in. "Boy," she said, "that Trudy kept old Desiree in blue balls the whole year." She picked up her coffee and left them looking at each other.

It was not the first time she'd gotten depressed as soon as her entertaining story-moment was over. Gretchen called it perfor-mance letdown. Malcolm and Oren thought they detected and understood completely the mild psychoses involved. She feared her strong personality and daring would not be enough, could not ever be enough, to win a place in a tightly knit family. Hell, she was an addition, she once said to them; she could never catch up, be vener-ated. It was funny and heartbreaking, her occasional use of college words from her old vocab list.

She was not articulate enough, however, to explain her situation in truly advanced terms—that she had no history, that she was like a long-term victim of amnesia who wakes up in arrears. To her it was Malcolm, Oren, and Gretchen who were in arrears—with their time, love, and attention. They would never be able to give her enough. She could be galled just by the accoutrements of a normal girl—books given to Gretchen years ago, say, and how they sat in shelves painted as part of a Girl Scout badge. The backers were always finding her with her nose in the family photos. She seemed to get a hooting kick out of the Robbs—Malcolm's bell-bottoms and headbands; his seventies muttonchops. Gretchen didn't let her see the bouncy jail-scene beginning of it all. The chubby babies in antique wooden high chairs were enough to deflate her. Birthday parties. Grandparents. Invariably she ended up grim. She was not in the album. Or anyone's.

Maybe she missed Cooper. Hey.

Gretchen started an album for Angela and just herself, Malcolm, and Oren. She called it "post everything." She presented the album one time at the second type of family conference they held—the type that included Angela, and why not? It was the whole point—to include her in as much family as possible. When Angela made fun of the album as an idea, Gretchen let her have it. "We're in exactly the same place, me and Dad and Oren. We're all starting from square one, you twerp. You fit into our family like no one else would. No one! Can't you see that?"

"Right now all I see is your fat face."

"Check out the world, Angela! Most of the people of the world do nothing but start over. All the time. Check out Bosnia. Check out Rwanda."

"Check out this!"

So it was a bit of a madhouse, and that was before one considered Oren's situation.

Malcolm chose not to most of the time; Oren was connected to Susan in a way that ruffled him irrationally. For Malcolm it was better to focus on the youngsters rather than his old neighbor, who he accepted more or less unconditionally as a part of their lives for good. In light of the town's confusion, Malcolm enjoyed watching Oren flapping back and forth between the two houses. Sometimes there was a parked car full of teenagers awaiting the occasion.

Oren took his evening meals with them; he tutored Gretchen and Angela openly on his front porch. When he spoke, he was wry and hopeful; he said he was willing to wait on Wyman coming to him, that what he wanted to be generally known was, in fact, starting to be generally known. The gift of graceful change was to behave as if nothing had changed.

The thing about Oren was that once you'd seen the exposed shins of a man doing little more than going against a dress code, the result, at least for Malcolm, was a bit like discovering a human emotion not previously charted. Oren didn't need protecting exactly, but the vulnerability was there, and thus Gretchen told Malcolm privately that without knowing it, he might well be willing to die for Oren—the freedom of the man.

Oren certainly had more authority than he'd ever had in all the years Malcolm had known him—he had been a terrible wastrel. In this area Oren couldn't possibly be unaware. The alb-housedress seemed to keep his language more terse, more pointed than what used to be within the man's grasp. He was focused, Malcolm observed, as if he might be in a constant state of meditation. No, no, no, Oren insisted. Not a bit. He was doing nothing more than his part.

To take the next step, Oren began intercepting the postman and going through the mail for both households, sorting out all Malcolm's bills and paying them. It gave Malcolm and Gretchen the oddest feeling, more as if they were both doing something for Oren that was fairly basic, given the fact that life had turned them all on their heads like this. Oren spoke only about other matters—how for example he'd decided to throw himself into the renovation of Angela's house. The odds were not high of them getting her through the next few years of anger and frustration, he reasoned, but she could so easily become a waif project if he wasn't careful.

"See, in taking charge, Malcolm, you and Gretchen aren't doing that. It's a credit to you. Me, I'd make her into my project. It comes with the boldness thing, at my late age. I can't change it."

It was due to this danger, this scruple, if you will, that he had turned to the house. It kept him honest, he said. Malcolm went over from time to time to observe what this honesty might mean. He sometimes felt he was on the brink of grasping something profound in what Oren experienced as a constant. Gretchen said she thought of a mind sent into a desert, something polished smooth from a blasting of sand. They'd learn from a workman that there was a waiting list of people from Freda's church who wanted to be there to replaster a few walls, plan the new moldings.

Or to ogle him? To turn Oren into a project?

Or to be around a desert-swept mind? They couldn't quite decide. They found Oren and the workers sometimes sitting around talking, and there was a feeling in the kitchen as if the man was trying to learn, in his grief, just what it was that people were made of and not the other way around.

And the younger you were, the easier the alb-housedress. Ricky and Corey didn't notice Oren's clothes. As for her own group, Gretchen was convinced that notions of gender were expanding as fast and as visibly as the universe. "Zoom!" she once said, making a rocket motion with her hand in a private talk with Malcolm. "Go to the Web, Dad. You can be a sky diver. No one knows! A buyer for a department store, a stockbroker. Someone will ask your gender, and suddenly you'll flame them for being beside the point. You'll say all kinds of stuff—that you're fifteen, thirty-five, eighty-five. I have the most fun as eighty-five."

Malcolm didn't dare ask what she might mean by fun.

"Then one day major difference just breaks down altogether, and you'll announce you're a woman. It won't even blow you away. You'll say you're a paraplegic belly dancer. You'll just feel, you know, fab."

He finally had to stop her. "This isn't the topic! I don't think Oren's dress is about the breakdown of gender. I happen to think Oren is very male. Conventionally male."

"Then, for God's sake, what's your problem!"

"That he wants to be a monk wearing a dress, and it's just really disturbing to people. Just the look of it."

"But not to you."

"No! Not any more. But it still doesn't answer the question of why he does it!"

"It keeps him, you know, mindful—"

"Mindful," Malcolm repeated, knowing almost what his daughter meant at all times now, but never quite how she would put it. Ever.

"—that he killed my mother," she said, hugging him, reassuring him, then leaving him to go to her work.

21

ANGELA'S CONFESSION

COREY CALLED HIM "MR. HUNKY" FINALLY. BUT BY THE TIME she up and said it, he didn't hear it in a warning way. He missed the signs of it.

"I know lots of ways to get you in big trouble, Mr. Hunky," she said. This morning as they left her kindergarten building Malcolm almost lost her to traffic at a busy intersection where she knew to stop and wait for him to catch up and grab her hand. She was silent until she was sure he was finished scolding her. Then she made her announcement, something she'd been thinking about since last week apparently—the ways to get him in big trouble.

"Aren't you going to spank me for almost running into the street?" she nagged on the walk back to Malcolm's car, where a sympathetic teacher's aide sat with Ricky in his safety seat. The aide had volunteered as Malcolm began to make his mad dash to the corner.

"Spanking is not considered good form," Malcolm finally said. It was the advanced way he'd learned to speak to the child in order to get anywhere with her. Also he wanted to put her threat to some good use, if possible. Was this very bad behavior or chronic insecurity? Clearly it was some of both.

Still, it was through Corey rather than through Angela that he understood his part in the waif project as it continued now in some murky way all on its own. It was not exactly fair that he understood through the younger girl—not fair to Angela that Corey had showered him in admiration from the moment he drove the big sit-down mower into Oren's yard. Not fair, but he thrived on it.

"Everyone's too afraid to spank me," she mused, leading him on.

"That could well be true," Malcolm said. "But no one is too afraid to love you, so why don't you consider that instead? It's the more interesting problematic."

One had to confuse her a little. Whenever they tried to say things in five-year-old terms, it backfired. Simplifications were like lies to this child.

"But you're going to keep Angela, aren't you? You love her, not me."

Corey knew this wasn't true. She had a very precocious and even gleeful sense of how difficult Angela was to love. Corey sighed, as if made sad by this hard fact about her sister. She smoothed out a new pink skirt and a long fuchsia sash. Would Gretchen like this outfit? she asked. Did he like it?

She was in heaven, sitting beside him up front, buckled in and allowed a private conversation, since Ricky always obliged her by falling asleep for these Monday trips to Wyman. She liked folding her hands daintily in her lap while she kept things interesting. "I make it hard for the Sulloways," she mused.

"Do you now?"

"Soon they're going to beg you to take me."

It was usually around noon when they got their Mondays rolling. Today Gretchen waited as Malcolm was pulling in. She waited in that lull of time it took for doors to open and for Malcolm to undo the complicated harness on Ricky's seat. Corey got out of the car and faced the porch to let her see she was still in her dressing-up phase, more elaborately worked out today—the new pink skirt and the long fuchsia sash.

"Pretty snazzy," Gretchen called and started down the steps. There followed a considerable amount of high-pitched screaming when Corey discovered grease on the sash. The lock of the door had been biting it for the whole drive. She cried loudly for Malcolm, her love, to come see the damage. Malcolm passed Ricky to Gretchen. Dear oh dear, Malcolm said.

Corey mounted the steps. Inside she gave Oren a ritual hug, explaining to him what Malcolm just told her—that there was a secret stain remover he'd kept under his sink for donkey's years. Corey never heard of donkey's years, and Oren had to admit he didn't have any idea where that phrase originated; perhaps donkeys lived a long time.

"Where's Angela?" Corey wanted to know, but not really. She entered the house with authority, her turn to be queen for the day, to rule the roost.

There was no sign of Angela. From week to week they'd detected various delay tactics whose causes might range from her liking to make entrances, to feeling jealous, bored, angry at the isolation the family put up with. Rumor had it that Malcolm was fired as admissions director at the college; that he, Matt, and Oren were all three involved with her; that Gretchen's home schooling was understandable in the light of what must be her embarrassment and sense of scandal. If her friends were certain that she should be embarrassed, then Malcolm saw all the more clearly how badly the present household arrangement was probably going down at the moment. To have to hear that Angela was one of the Robbs' own now was to have one's nose rubbed in it.

He had nights in which he woke up wondering if it was Matt's nose they might be rubbing in the arrangement. They'd tried to keep him abreast of the program. He was, as always, difficult to read.

"What's happening is likely be a little mystical to him," George offered in one of their weekly updates. "It is to me."

"Up close the mystical comes equipped with a three-ring circus, doesn't it, George? I don't have to tell you, do I?"

"No," George said. "And it took me a while not to be stunned by where I ended up."

"I'm at least a little less so than before."

"Interesting."

"Why is that?"

"Oh, that's much too personal a thing," George said. "Only you can figure that one out."

The unconventionality of their lives both saved and tweaked Angela, the backers knew that much. She commented on how great it was that she'd finally found a crazy family; who else would have her? The flip side of this idea might soon start to eat at her, the backers feared. She would want them to have friends, and they didn't at the moment. Angela goaded Gretchen into arguments about such things, accused Gretchen of having friends but just not wanting to introduce them to *her*.

Gretchen explained that, hey, she was not in school, the neighbors were in hiding, the gang was in college, thank goodness. Besides, for her there was this intensity now. She used to hang out but now didn't. She wouldn't apologize if she was different from what most people wanted and liked. Her life changed.

For a moment they thought Angela got it. Then she sulked and left them with, "Yeah, it's because of me that your life changed. If you were normal, I wouldn't get to be in it."

"That's not an original idea, Angela!" Gretchen yelled at her retreating back. "It's really not!" She looked at Malcolm, dropped her shoulders, and then followed Angela upstairs. In a few moments he heard them laughing. Someone was getting pounded with a pillow. Someone was being dragged into the shower fully clothed. Breakage. Negotiations on who had to clean it up.

Camp, he thought.

* * *

Corey stood watching them use the kerosene rag on her fuchsia sash. They were chatting when Angela came in and gave them a look as if to say she'd caught them again. It was hard for Angela to know who was the real culprit; it was so clear that most of the affection came one-way from Corey. Malcolm and Oren's cool was what attracted the child. They never gushed over her; they treated her in an adult fashion that had always been Angela's winning method. Malcolm and Oren really were adults; she couldn't compete with their subtleties, the kind fatherliness of their deep voices and graying hair. "Grease monkey," Oren had been saying to Corey. Now there was another expression, in addition to "donkey's years," he didn't know the origin of. Where did that one come from—grease monkey? He looked up and winked at Angela by way of including her in this. Did Angela know?

She groaned, then whispered an obscenity.

"Hi, Angela," Corey said. "What's the matter? You all mad again?"

"No." In fact, she suddenly brightened. "How you doing, kiddo? Come here and give me a kiss."

This was what the time was for, of course—for Angela to be Miss Mom. They started the visits by trying to have a little lunch. Today Oren made a complicated tuna salad with tofu dressing. According to the doctor, his blood pressure was high, so was his cholesterol. He happened to like how the tofu tasted, but for the little guys he put out what the older girls called medium-disgusting food—potato chips, processed cheese, white bread, mayonnaise, lunch meat. Backers tried to tempt players with healthy fare—raw vegetables, hard-boiled eggs, fresh fruit salad, and the tuna salad. When Angela was in a good mood, she was completely in accord with their efforts to eat right. When she wasn't, she stared.

"What's the matter?"

"Nothing."

Week to week Corey and Ricky proved to be hopelessly bad eaters. In Angela's opinion, this was evidence that the Sulloways didn't know what the hell they were doing. Today, Corey frowned and took a small bite from a cheese slice, wafer thin. For Ricky, only milk. "I want my bottle," he said plainly, and Angela got up to get it out of the fridge. He was walking and talking (not to mention reading), but not yet weaned or out of diapers. Evidence, Angela muttered, reminding them again of Enid's downfalls.

"What's the matter, Angela?" Corey said. "You seem real bummed."

"Am not."

"Are too."

Demonstrated baiting. And it was finally as if the older sibling was helpless to resist it, as if she was in need of little more than a tug to come unglued. Later they conferred that the episode was probably triggered by the story she'd told, about girls holding a yard sale as if they were legitimate. Their getting busted had thrown Angela into Cooper's protection for the next eighteen months, which had ended in the death of the woman whose house this used to be, whose son she secretly did remember.

She slumped to the middle of the kitchen floor. Oren and Gretchen were right there at her side within seconds. They were witness this time to a family member's going down, in slow motion, the way Susan had. Angela collapsed forward, her head hidden under her arms. It was a soldier's tuck for incoming mortar. Her words were incoherent, but there were words, coming up at them from under those arms, muffled phrases, somehow amplified.

"You're okay, Angela," Oren said, "you're okay."

Corey stopped chewing. She gave Malcolm a look of something close to terror.

"How can you not hate me?" Angela was saying.

The question was clearly general, but Corey couldn't grasp this. "I don't hate you," she wailed. Malcolm saw the child's face start to quiver. On the other side of him Ricky's mouth came open and caught. When the boy finally found his breath he gave out a bellow of such desperation it went straight into Malcolm's empty well of spent sorrow. He grabbed the baby and hung on for dear life.

"It's okay," Oren was saying over the humped back, motioning with his hand that someone better take the little guys into another part of the house. Malcolm and Gretchen flew into action like harried staff having to divide the wounded into groups of critical and less critical. The one took off with Ricky and the other with Corey. "What's wrong?" Corey wailed, Ricky continuing to drown her out as they all headed for the living room.

Oren kept beside Angela. "You're having a delayed reaction." Malcolm and Gretchen reentered to hear this explanation. "It's normal," Oren was saying. "You'll be all right." They all exchanged looks.

"When's their delayed reaction?" Malcolm heard from under Angela's arms. "They'll have to hate me *some* day."

"You mean me and Dad?" Gretchen said, taking Oren's place on the floor. "Why? What more can happen?"

"A lot."

Oren reached out, and Malcolm pulled him up. Oren indicated with his hands that he was going to go for a walk with the little guys; they were already starting to trail into the foyer.

"You can tell us stuff now, Angela," Gretchen was saying. "We know there's stuff. We all have it, you know."

Angela sat up. "Matt's not here because of me," she whispered. Her face looked old and battered; hard to love. Malcolm felt an ache in his hands; he'd given up on this kind of information; did not really wish it now. He drew a breath and eased himself into a kitchen chair out of the girl's sight line. He put his head down quietly on the table. He waited, hollow as a drum. He would miss Matt all his life despite his full acceptance of whatever path the boy took. When was Malcolm going to just let himself feel that, grieve that? Perhaps he couldn't because there was still Susan to miss. How many disappearing people can a man reasonably mourn in a year, or a life?"

"I stole from him that time," he heard. It was a strangled voice, full of self-pity. "He opened the door of the car and got in. I recognized him. He was the one! I figured he was going to beat me up, that he'd been all over looking for me. I had my hand in the paper bag Cooper kept in the car in case some psycho started up something with me. I almost shot him."

This last information was what was hardest on her, a kind of waking fantasy. Malcolm closed his eyes, his own replay starting up. It was that dream of Susan floating down the steps again, pulling away to reach out to Ricky, of his utterly stupid act of letting go. The both of them—wife and son. They would keep on slipping from him. He was homesick, he realized. When had he waked up to this new crop, as if all along he'd been some bigamist with a second family he'd forgotten about? He was homesick with this bigger bunch.

"But you didn't!" Gretchen was saying. "Angela, you didn't shoot anybody!"

Malcolm couldn't move; his arm clamped down on nothing. Gretchen, as calm as toast, was rubbing Angela's back. "He wasn't angry when he got into the car, was he?" she said.

"No!"

"So what happened? It's okay now."

"He gave me a tea. He said he'd seen me order it. In the diner. And he knew I took his wallet." Angela was sobbing, brokenhearted. There was more, apparently. "He was saying he wanted to get me some help, that I had to get away from that guy. He'd been watching us in the diner. He didn't like what he saw."

She was homesick too, Malcolm thought.

"So he wasn't there to get his wallet back?"

Angela shook her head. "Both doors came open. Somebody filming us. I yelled at him again. I went nuts. I thought he was part of some setup." It was as far as she could go. "You don't know me, you don't know me," she sobbed as if she was being hit.

"I know you pretty good."

"It's because of me Desiree and Trudy got busted that time."

"No. Come on. Shhh."

"They'd have been fine if it wasn't for me knowing Cooper. One day he just started making phone calls, is what I figured out later. He reported them so he could be the one with the place for me to go. He had a clear shot. I just gave in. *Tramp.*" The last word was from Rayleen.

Gretchen held the girl. She looked at Malcolm, shaking her head at him as if now they knew. It was Matt disappearing, it was Desiree, it was Trudy, it was Cooper, it was Susan. It was the stupid story of her stupid life; check out the world.

When they all got back from taking the little guys home, the backers sat on the front porch late into the night. Angela's story was finally coming together: Matt had been a total stranger to her. She'd picked him out in a diner. Not even that. She and Cooper, arguing, were getting some sandwiches before their car gig, and they happened to be in a booth across from Matt. He'd gotten out his wallet to leave a tip. Cooper accidentally distracted him, and Angela palmed it. Matt realized right away what she'd done. He had the strangest expression on his face, she'd told them.

"So," Gretchen reasoned with a whisper, "here Angela's been, studying that face in a family album all these weeks.

"I'm going up to get her," she added. "She knows we're down here talking about it. I have to go get her, okay?"

So it was a foursome that continued out on the front porch, the girls in their nightgowns, Oren in his alb-dress. Malcolm excused himself for one moment, went into the house, brought back the big can of cashews.

"They're not a project," he said aloud to himself, out in the kitchen. "They don't need me here all day like this. It's time, right? I have to go back to work. I can tend bar, if I want." He laughed. "I can be a waitress."

Matt must have wandered around later that night and recognized Cooper in front of Wendy's, Angela was saying on the porch. He must have followed one of the junior high boys to the car and figured out what was going on. He was lucky, because if Cooper had caught him in there without paying, he would have broken his head open, not to mention her putting her hand in the bag until she decided he wasn't some psycho, him and his hot tea. And him wanting to know if she needed more money. Naturally she had assumed it was a come-on. Then just a mean joke, since Matt seemed to be part of the sting operation.

So the next day she hadn't made the connection with Oren at all? Malcolm asked.

No. To her Oren was just a rich parent's lawyer trying to pay her off. She was sick that day. She was throwing up. She was completely on her own, with no Cooper. But it had felt so great, to think she could just spring herself. Somehow.

"And you did," Oren said, quietly interrupting for the first time. "Stepped right up to the plate! It was bold."

"But then I called him," Angela said softly. Malcolm feared she'd break down again, but she didn't. She repeated the statement instead— repeated it loudly, as if to keep on facing the music. "I called him, Oren!"

"Yes," Oren said, "I know."

Each grew quiet, and Malcolm, alone, spun on the question of what must have gone through Matt's mind when he realized she was moving into Oren's—that he'd set this in motion. Well, no, it had been she who had. He would have seen her at Oren's and figured Oren was doing something right for a change. And after his mother's death, his having had his wallet stolen wouldn't be something he could talk about. If he hadn't revealed a stolen wallet at the time of his arrest, why would he reveal it later? It had never mattered to him except as an indication that she needed more.

"You want to know when *I* made the connection?" Angela said.

"I do," Malcolm said.

"When you got me the cash out of the machine that day. You just up and said you could get me some money. It's what he'd said, and I saw the resemblance in your faces."

Malcolm felt stunned. It was so ludicrous. He was an adult helping a child with two crying babes in a phone booth. He was nothing like his son. He sighed. "Matt looks like his mother," he explained.

They sat for a long time in the dark of their deeds—one's goodnesses never feeling like much of anything at all. Susan would have said so too. At most she would describe her float down the stairs as an involuntary impulse, forcing open Malcolm's arm and going down the steps to take that baby from a girl who was yelling and looked like she didn't even know she was holding anything at the time. And Susan. Cooper had shot the wife of the man who had been— Suddenly he had a horrible realization. Oren's daily wave at him! Gretchen saying she should have waved! "Wait a minute!" He stood up. "It was me looking through that slat. That's right! You could see me. Gretchen, you could see me that day you were over there talking—you said you should have waved!"

"What?" Gretchen said. "What are you talking about?"

"You could see me!"

"When?"

"Angela! That was what set him off, wasn't it? Not me in the yard or porch but at the window. My habit of looking out from there. I've been doing that for years!"

"I don't know what you're talking about," Angela said. "I never once saw you."

"Dear God," Malcolm whispered. "I did kill her."

Tears welled up in Gretchen's eyes. "Dad, for heaven's sakes."

Malcolm watched Oren's arm, then two clever arms, reaching out and grabbing at Angela and Gretchen. "Is there any cake left?" Oren said. "Let's get cake for everyone. Come on. You girls can zap the ice cream. I always melt it."

"It's because you don't zap," Angela explained, whining. "You fucking nuke it."

"I know. Come on!"

"I'll stay with Dad," Gretchen said.

And she does. Sits with him, just letting him have the moment. She knows Susan's six last words by now. Nothing sensational, of course. Susan was just being practical. Sometimes Gretchen says the words, *does* them. *Here, honey, let me take him.*

She shakes herself not to think of them now. They can get her bad. "So!" she says, forcibly lifting her voice and spirits as they sit in the dark. "Oren walked into town this afternoon and got the little guys Dreamsicles, right? I wonder how it was for him out in the open?"

She means the alb-dress, of course. He'd sailed out on his own and come back alive.

But Malcolm can't answer, overcome by a memory of her coming into the kitchen and checking on the cheese she'd left in the grater, her nose touching his hand. His and Gretchen's tears are welling up yet again. Lord, they don't know a day when this hasn't happened; anything at all can cause it. Strong tea, he thinks. He can see the tag hanging down, the plastic lid secured on the take-out cup of hot water, the sugar packets inside his son's only shirt pocket.

And Gretchen too is thinking about those hours after Susan got a call from Danford, and the two of them went running in the rain across Everett Street to Oren's. Gretchen had even jumped a few puddles like a kid glad to be called out at night, then to get to see Oren all flummoxed, to see him fall in love.

God, she'd been so easy to love.

"Desiree and Trudy," she muses aloud to Angela, as she and Oren come out with the plates of cake and ice cream. You have to keep in the moment, keep in control. "We can help you find them, you know."

"In the cemetery," Angela says.

"Both of them? Come on, don't be sappy."

Angela begins laughing.

"What?" Malcolm says, suddenly looking worried for the girl. Her laughter *is* kind of scary, Gretchen thinks; but they are getting used to it—so loaded with life and death.

"See, it wasn't Trudy's stuff to sell," Angela says. "Trudy thought it was left in the attic above our complex, but that was common storage up there, we found out. The hard way. What she'd done was haul people's personal belongings out in the yard. Everyone went crazy."

For the backers there is a shared gasp, a shared vision of the girl's awful mistake. "Lord," Malcolm says, "what happened? Did people start noticing right away?"

"Sure! They didn't like us in the first place, so that was all they needed. One man walked to the cash box and pulled Trudy up by her front. I had to pound him. He was blubbering about that set of golf clubs given to him by his dead father. Someone from across the street was ready to buy it off Trudy."

Malcolm is laughing, his head held between his hands. "Honestly, Angela," he says. Oren is starting to get it, his eyes watering over, his mouth stretching wide and soundless.

Gretchen sees their efforts to stop, but they are caught between restraint and hysteria. Angela, now center stage, starts up an imitation of a woman holding a whole bowl of faded plastic fruit, claiming that this is *hers*, goddammit, and she'd really like some kind of *explanation* here.

Angela's got it down—the voice, the sputters of outrage. She does a half-dozen different voices before she lets the backers have a rest. And her items make Gretchen jealous—good material, old, borrowed, and blue. A box of 45s, stamp collections, *Playboy*s, ice skates, fondue forks.

When they are all calmed down again, Oren, still laughing a little, gets up to go home. Malcolm says good night, and if they want to sit out here a while longer, be sure to lock up and get the lights.

No, Angela says. She's tired. She's coming in too.

So Gretchen is left blessedly alone. After a time she gives into something she's been trying to train herself not to do, now that all these weeks have gone by. She lets it happen, herself being lifted up to her blimp's view of the neighborhood, a quiet big eye on the street of her parents' long-ago choices, and she does not now push away the horrible image of Susan, refusing to be diverted from her confident stroll home.

Already she has emerged from the old campus quad. Gretchen hangs waiting, seeing again into Oren's house without its roof. In her earlier replays, Cooper has always been pointing an angry finger at Angela, reading her the riot act for flirting with that venetian-blind creep over there.

Suddenly Cooper is not visible to Gretchen. And Angela is in the other roofless house—the creep's house. Sweet creep, Gretchen thinks, starting to cry.

She sees Angela in the spare room, safe, as Susan turns onto Everett Street for the last stretch of her walk. A bullet of sun is shooting her from behind in its downward sink. Her lithe black silhouette keeps on coming toward the window lights twinkling back at her, greeting her like early evening stars. And this time Gretchen smiles, happy for her mother; happy at what she will find when she gets home. It is a fantasy, but Gretchen goes ahead. She watches a female actor take the part of Susan, an actor coming on the porch and entering the house, late on a Monday visit; she dumps her things on the little hall table and calls out.

Silence for a moment before they all come running—old and new—to greet her. The man who plays Oren will have to wear some kind of clerical garb, because the alb-dress just won't get at it quite; it's too one-thing to people. And Matt—how to convey both the presence and absence of him.

Also this final bit of the homecoming is sentimental, but less so if Gretchen can get all the jokes and the razory edges in. The script has gotten better just this week. She'll need more than a good actress for Susan—someone who can do darkly charmed. In the play, this character has been away for a while. Many complicated things have happened to her family that she will have to grasp. The complications are quite beyond the dividing tendencies of speech. The actress will have to perform the whole, and Gretchen imagines spending a long time rehearsing her in how it can best be nuanced. If she can do passionate restraint most of the time, Gretchen explains, then at the end it will be okay to throw it all out.

Is Gretchen sure? the woman asks, a bit uncertain.

She tries it again, but is still too subdued.

Why not scream it, Gretchen suggests from the darkened theater. She stands to shout at the woman, give her courage. It's fine to take a chance now, Gretchen calls. Go on and be bold, why don't you! Try floored! Try astonished! Try falling apart!